Katie Fforde lives in Gloucestershire with her husband and some of her three children. Recently her old hobbies of ironing and housework have given way to singing, Flamenco dancing and husky racing. She claims this keeps her fit. *Going Dutch* is her thirteenth novel.

Praise for *Katie Fforde*

'...mother-daughter bond the women develop is ...earing and the heartache caused by a failed long marriage is touchingly conveyed' *Sunday Telegraph*

'A fairytale-like, gently witty read . . . Heart-warming – made for sunny days in the park' *Cosmopolitan*

'Acute and funny observations of the social scene' *The Times*

'A heart-warming tale of female friendship, fizzing with Fforde's distinctive brand of humour' *Sunday Express*

'Delicious – gorgeous humour and the lightest of touches' *Sunday Times*

'A witty and generous romance . . . Katie Fforde is on sparkling form . . . Jilly Cooper for the grown-ups' *Independent*

Further praise for *Katie Fforde*

'Fforde's light touch succeeds in making this a sweet and breezy read – the ideal accompaniment to a long summer's evening'
Daily Mail

'Old-fashioned romance of the best sort . . . funny, comforting'
Elle

'The romance fizzes along with good humour and is a good, fat, summery read'
Sunday Mirror

'Joanna Trollope crossed with Tom Sharpe'
Mail on Sunday

'A spirited summer read that's got to be Fforde's best yet'
Woman & Home

'Can be scoffed at one sitting . . . Tasty'
Cosmopolitan

'Perfect holiday reading. Pack it with the swimsuit and suntan lotion'
Irish Independent

'Fforde is blessed with a lightness of touch, careful observation and a sure sense of the funny side of life'
Ideal Home

Katie Fforde

Going Dutch

arrow books

Published by Arrow Books 2008

2 4 6 8 10 9 7 5 3 1

Copyright © Katie Fforde Ltd 2007

Katie Fforde has asserted her right under the Copyright, Designs
and Patents Act 1988 to be identified as the author of this work

Lines from 'Hit the Road Jack' – the author and publishers have made all
reasonable efforts to contact copyright holders for permission, and apologise for
any omissions or errors in the form of credit given. Corrections may be made in
future printings

First published in Great Britain in 2007 by
Century
Random House, 20 Vauxhall Bridge Road,
London SW1V 2SA

www.rbooks.co.uk

Addresses for companies within The Random House Group Limited can be
found at: www.randomhouse.co.uk/offices.htm

The Random House Group Limited Reg. No. 954009

A CIP catalogue record for this book
is available from the British Library

ISBN 9780099547723

The Random House Group Limited supports The Forest
Stewardship Council (FSC), the leading international forest
certification organisation. All our titles that are printed on
Greenpeace approved FSC certified paper carry the FSC logo.
Our paper procurement policy can be found at:
www.rbooks.co.uk/environment

Typeset by SX Composing DTP, Rayleigh, Essex
Printed in the UK by CPI Bookmarque, Croydon, CR0 4TD

To Desmond, without whom this book
really would not have been possible.
With love, as ever.

Acknowledgements

To the DBA, the Barge Association, for the rally and other barge related events, including a kind man called Alan, who thought of the title for me.

To Jonathan Early for the gilding which really was magical; to B J Wood & Son, who are an extraordinary boatyard; to Harriet Jones for many things, including her pink engine, and not forgetting our own dear *Accacia*, who is the star of the show, in my eyes, anyway.

To the wonderful team at Random House including Kate Elton and Georgina Hawtrey-Woore, the art department, the sales force who are as inspired as they are outrageous, and the wonderful Charlotte Bush who has brilliant ideas and an excellent taste in hotels. None of it would be possible or anything like as much fun without any of you.

To dear Richenda Todd who stops me embarrassing myself so tactfully and so frequently.

To Sara Fisher and everyone else at A M Heath, including Sarah Molloy who is still my friend!

It is a privilege to work with such talented, diligent people.

Chapter One

Dora put down her bags and looked at the woman who was waving to her from across the water. As instructed, she had taken a taxi from the station that serviced the pretty Thames-side town and had been deposited at the gates of the moorings. Then she had telephoned to announce her arrival. Her new landlady was going to meet her and let her in.

She did recognise her, of course, but her best friend's mother had changed a bit since she'd last seen her. Now she was wearing a long overshirt and a pair of baggy jeans. Before, she had worn the sort of County women's clothes Dora's mother wore: skirts, silk shirts, or possibly a shaped T-shirt, with a cashmere cardigan round the shoulders. Her hair, which used to look coiffed in a hairdresser-once-a-week way, was now rather wild. She was smiling warmly, however, and Dora felt that going to her for refuge may not have been such a bad idea after all.

'How did you manage this lot on the train?' asked Mrs Edwards when she had crossed the bridge and reached Dora. She picked up a selection of 'bags for life' that bulged with woolly jumpers. 'And why do you need all these jumpers? It's May!'

'My mother said it's always cold on boats,' Dora explained apologetically. 'And people were very helpful,' she went on, remembering how their kindness had nearly made her break down and cry. She was so brittle, the smallest thing was likely to set her off.

'I do really think that on the whole mankind is nicer than it gets credit for,' said Mrs Edwards, politely ignoring the remark about the cold and boats. 'Now, follow me.'

Dora heaved her rucksack on to her back and followed her along the path to a tall steel gate. Mrs Edwards leant forwards against a metal plate. The door beeped and she pushed it open.

'I keep the fob in my bra,' she explained. 'I've usually got my hands full. I'll give you one, then you can come and go as you want.' She sent Dora a glance. 'OK?'

Dora nodded and followed Mrs Edwards down the walkway to the pontoons. Tied up against each one was a barge of some kind. Although she longed to look at them, Dora was grateful that Mrs Edwards didn't stop – her rucksack was so heavy. They had passed about four barges, each different from the other, before Mrs Edwards halted next to a huge vessel painted dark green.

'This is *The Three Sisters*. It was originally called that in Dutch, but no one could say it, so Michael, who owns it, translated it. It's a common name for Dutch barges.'

Mrs Edwards swung the bags over the side of the barge and then followed them, her legs going over in a surprisingly nimble way. Dora thought her own mother would have made much more of a meal of it, but reflected that her mother had always made a meal of everything, which in part explained why she was here.

Mrs Edwards turned to give Dora a hand. 'You give me that lot, then if you put your foot there, you can get on board quite easily. A bit of practice and you'll be leaping on and off like a young lamb.'

'I'm not sure about that,' said Dora, clambering aboard awkwardly. She followed Mrs Edwards up the metal step and through a door.

'This is the wheelhouse, obviously,' said Mrs Edwards,

2

indicating the huge wheel. 'But also the conservatory.' Amongst a row of flowerpots containing tomato plants and geraniums Dora also spotted pots of basil and parsley. 'All these would have to be moved if we ever went anywhere, which, thank goodness, we're not doing.'

'You get a good view from here,' said Dora, looking around her. 'And, presumably, lots of sun.'

'It's a lovely place to sit, I must say. There aren't usually so many barges here, but there are lots of visitors, because of the rally. It starts tomorrow.'

'Oh, have I come at a bad time?'

'Not at all! It'll be nice to have some moral support.'

'Isn't the rally fun, then?' asked Dora. She wasn't sure what a rally involved but she decided just to go along with anything Jo – Mrs Edwards – suggested. She didn't feel up to any decision-making herself quite yet.

'In a way.' Mrs Edwards was more cautious. 'But on Sunday there's a parade of boats, which means you have to let anyone who wants to, come and look all over your boat.' She looked concerned. 'I find the idea of strangers tramping about my home completely hideous! I'll have to have a massive tidy-up.'

Dora now dimly remembered that her friend Karen's mother had always had a more laissez-faire attitude to tidiness than her own mother. She'd been very relaxed about them making a mess in the kitchen, experimenting with recipes for toffee, fudge and, later, pancakes. 'Well, of course, I'll help you.'

'Let's not think about it now. Let's go down and have a glass of wine. I know it's only five-thirty, but as far as I'm concerned, the sun's over the yardarm,' said Mrs Edwards.

'What does that mean?'

'I'm not quite sure, but I do know it means you can have a drink. I think when you've had a long journey and not a

3

very brilliant time recently, you deserve one. And I have to keep you company.' She smiled and Dora thought what a nice-looking woman she was. Middle-aged, of course, but quite attractive.

She returned the smile and followed her landlady down a flight of wooden stairs.

When Dora's best friend Karen had called, all the way from Canada, and said, 'Go and stay with Mum on her barge,' Dora had been diffident.

'She won't want me inviting myself to stay. She's had a ghastly time herself!'

'I'll tell her. She must know what's happened anyway, she was invited to the wedding. But she'd love having you. She needs the company. Whatever she says, she must be lonely, and you might be able to stop her getting too eccentric.'

Dora wasn't nearly as bossy as Karen and had no intention of trying to put Mrs Edwards back on the path of conventionality, but as she really needed somewhere to go, she eventually agreed. 'Being a social pariah, I don't have much choice,' she'd said.

'You're not a social pariah! You fell out of love with a man who really was quite boring and then changed your mind about getting married. People do it all the time. It's no big deal.'

Dora had spluttered her disbelief. 'Yes it is! We'd been planning this wedding for about five years.'

'Not since you were seventeen, for goodness' sake! You only met John when you were seventeen.'

'It seems like it. I definitely caught my mother with a bride's magazine very shortly after she and Dad met John's parents.'

Karen had sighed.

'And there isn't a soul in the village who isn't best

friends with, or related to, either John or me!' Dora shuddered at the thought of all those disapproving looks and forthright comments she had left behind. 'And as they all say I've broken John's heart, and perhaps I have, that leaves me as Norman No-Mates.'

'Norma No-Mates,' Karen had said.

'Whatever!'

'You go to Mum. You can keep an eye on her and she'll look after you. She loves looking after people.'

'She may be relishing her freedom,' Dora had pointed out.

'Freedom is something you choose to have. Mum was dumped for a younger woman. She'll be feeling awful.' Karen's indignation was audible over thousands of miles of airwaves. 'I know Dad wouldn't have left her if I'd been around. He just waited until I was out of the way. Bastard!'

Dora had tutted. 'Karen! That's no way to talk about your father!'

'But Dora, how would you feel about your dad if he'd left your mother after nearly thirty years?'

Dora had considered. 'Yes, OK, I see what you mean.'

Now, she looked around her while Karen's mother found glasses and a bottle of wine. They'd dumped her various bags in the cabin which was to be Dora's 'for as long as she needed it'. The saloon was much larger than she'd expected, with a sitting area down one end, a kitchen – or should that be galley? she wondered – and eating area down the other. The walls were painted white and the ceiling was panelled wood. There was some sort of stove in one corner, and a banquette and chairs nearby. It was very cosy, but not, now she thought about it, terribly tidy.

'There's a packet of crisps in that cupboard,' said Mrs Edwards. 'Get it out, would you? There's a bowl in there somewhere, too.'

'Would you like me to use the china bowl or the wooden one, Mrs Edwards?'

Mrs Edwards regarded Dora with a horrified expression. 'Oh, call me Jo, please! No one calls me Mrs Edwards these days. I'd assume that my mother-in-law had risen from the grave and appeared at my shoulder.'

Dora felt embarrassed. 'Have you gone back to your maiden name, then? I wouldn't blame you—'

'Oh no, or at least, I suppose I might, it's just that everyone calls me Jo. You must too.'

'OK, Jo. Which bowl?' Dora lost her shyness now she was using Jo's first name. It put them on a more equal footing.

Jo pointed to the wooden one, handed Dora a glass and sat down on the banquette, finding space for her own glass among the piles of papers, recipe books and a make-up bag. 'Put the crisps down somewhere while I think what we're going to have for supper. Tomorrow there's a gala dinner. I've bought you a ticket.'

'You must let me pay you back for it,' said Dora, sitting down opposite her new landlady. 'You needn't worry that I'm going to sponge off you. I'm going to pay my way.'

'I'll accept a small rent,' said Jo, 'because one must be sensible about these things, but not until you've got a job.'

'I've got savings,' protested Dora. 'It was meant for the honeymoon.' Then she realised she'd said a trigger word for an explosion of tears. She'd liked her job and had hated leaving it when she had to escape the village.

Possibly sensing Dora's potential wobble, Jo said quickly, 'We'll sort everything like that out later. Just drink your wine and relax for a moment. We could go out for fish and chips,' she added.

Dora sniffed valiantly. 'That would suit me.'

'When I think of all the proper meals I made for my husband, when really, I'd've been perfectly happy eating scrambled eggs and salad most of the time, it makes me realise what an utter waste of time marriage can be. You were very sensible not going through with your wedding.'

Dora took a sip of wine to see off the tears that still threatened. 'You should have heard my mother on the subject. I could have been a scarlet woman abandoning my six starving children to become a Madam in a brothel, the way she went on.'

Jo sighed. 'It would have been extremely hard work arranging the wedding, and cancelling it all would have been worse.'

'I did offer to do it all, but she just took over.'

Dora's mother didn't trust Dora to do anything as grown up as organise a wedding, although she felt she was perfectly grown up enough to get married, even if Dora was only twenty-two.

'She's a very efficient woman.'

'Mm,' Dora muttered into her glass.

'But it would have been quite wrong of you to have gone through with it if you didn't feel it was right, just to save face.'

'That's what I think, but Mum didn't agree. She said she could never hold her head up in the village again, and wouldn't even let me send the wedding presents back! She was so furious she just wanted me out of her sight and to do it herself.'

'If Karen had been here, you could have gone to her,' said Jo, 'but as she's not, she was quite right to suggest you came to me.'

'I'm sure.' Dora sipped again. Somehow she did feel better just being here with Jo.

'We're both running away, really,' said Jo, thoughtfully.

7

'I'm running away from the wreckage of a marriage and you're running away from a wedding.'

'Was it awful when your husband left you? Sorry!' said Dora. 'That sounds so stupid. Of course it was! I'm just thinking how John must have felt.'

'He couldn't have felt quite the same as I did,' said Jo. 'I mean, he's in his twenties and has got all his life before him. He's bound to find someone else. I'm fifty, no one is going to want me.'

'Oh, I'm sure that's not true . . .'

Jo laughed. 'It's OK! I wouldn't have anyone else, not now. Years and years of my life I dedicated to my husband and child – did I get a long-service medal? No I did not. I got dumped for a younger woman. Such a cliché! He might have had the decency to leave me for a less humiliating reason. But no.' She frowned. 'He had the nerve to say, "If you met her, you'd understand. She's just like you were when you were young." '

Dora took this in. 'Oh my God!'

'It was as if he'd used me all up and needed a new one of me.'

'I'd have murdered him!' Dora was suitably indignant.

'I would have done if I'd had a weapon handy at the time, but fortunately the moment passed.' Jo chuckled. 'Actually, although I'm still livid when I think about it, I've had quite a lot of fun since I moved on to the barge. It was great being able to start afresh.'

'I know Karen thought you'd want to stay in the house, where all your friends were.'

'The trouble is, I didn't have a role any more. Philip wanted the house and the Floosie – that's what me and Karen call her – seemed happy with the idea.'

'I'm not surprised! It's a lovely house. I have so many happy memories of being there.' Dora thought back to those early experiments with make-up and weird hair-styles, and the little plays she and Karen used to put on. 'Do you remember the soap opera we made with the video camera?'

'*Pitrevie Drive*? Of course! The tapes are still up in the attic. You two were hysterical.'

'It was fun. I do miss Karen.'

'So do I, but I keep reminding myself that she hasn't gone for ever, only for a couple of years.'

'I bet she wanted to come home when your husband left you!'

'Of course. I had to tell her I'd never speak to her again if she did, though. I couldn't have her career messed up as well as my life.'

'You're very strong. I'm sure Mum would have gone to pieces.'

Jo sipped her wine. 'I had my moments, but now I'm a strong, independent woman, with no intention of ever having any sort of relationship again.' She regarded Dora. 'I wouldn't want *you* never to have another relationship, but you will soon find that having a boyfriend isn't everything.'

Dora laughed wryly. 'Oh, I know that. I had one for years and years! It certainly wasn't everything.'

Jo chuckled and picked up some crisps.

'But why couldn't you have stayed in the house? People would have rallied round, been nice to you, wouldn't they?' Dora thought about the lovely Georgian home with the garden that Jo had made so beautiful. Moving on to a barge must have felt a bit of a come-down – or a downsize at the very least.

Jo was eager to reassure her. 'Oh yes, everyone was very supportive while I was still there. They kept asking me out to girly lunches, found spare men for me, but I couldn't bear the pity. When I moved here, no one knew anything about my previous life and I felt I could start being someone different.' She frowned. 'Actually, not someone different, I mean the person I was all the time, when I was pretending to be a good woman who ran jumble sales and sat on committees.'

'Didn't you like all that then?' Dora's mother loved nothing more than sitting at the head of a table of people with a glass of water and a clipboard.

'Some of the time,' acknowledged Jo. 'Lots of it was pretty boring.' She sighed. 'I'm not on any committees now. It's bliss!' Then she bit her lip. 'Except I've got to help decorate the tables for the gala dinner tomorrow. I still haven't quite got the knack of not volunteering.'

'And we've got to tidy up for the boat parade thing?'

'Yes.'

'I'm quite good at tidying. My mother forced me into being a tidy person.'

'Huh! She had more luck than my mother did then! She tried to force me into being tidy too, but she never managed it. It's why I never told Karen to tidy her bedroom.'

Dora was utterly incredulous. 'What, never?'

'Well, no, because there was never a moment when her room was worse than mine.' She sighed again. 'I think it may have been one of the reasons Philip left me, although he never said.'

'You would like me to help? You wouldn't think I was being bossy?'

Jo put a hand on her knee and laughed. 'With a daughter like mine, no one even comes close in the bossy stakes. And anyway, I'm grateful for all the help I can get.'

Dora was almost as fond of Karen as Jo was but entirely agreed with the first statement. 'Shall we put some music

10

on? I've got a CD that always gives me energy. It's quite old, of course. One of Dad's, but I love it.'

Jo got up, laughing. 'That'll suit me fine, then. The CD player's over there.'

The heavy rock music did get Jo into the mood for cleaning. She'd meant to do it all before Dora came, of course, but after she'd done the bathroom and Dora's bedroom, there'd been no time for the saloon and kitchen.

Dora had purloined the Hoover and was putting her back into the floor. Jo was trying to clear the table, a much less satisfying task as it required decisions. Jo hated making decisions. Unaware that she was doing it, she put her hand in her pocket and found a piece of ribbon. It had come off a bale of tea towels she had bought for Dora's benefit. She squared off a pile of papers and magazines and tied the ribbon round it. Then she put it next to the bowl of fruit. She considered. Not quite an artistic statement, but it did make it look as if the papers needed to be there.

Living on her own had allowed her to become even more untidy than she had been before. When she was married, to a tidy man, she'd been forced to clean and tidy at boringly regular intervals. Now she was free of that she'd let things slide rather. She filled the dishwasher with her usual lightning speed. The rock music made her want to dance and she did wiggle about a bit as she wiped the surfaces in the kitchen, but really letting rip might have made Dora worry that she was now living with a lunatic. Worse, she might report back to Karen that her mother had finally lost it.

She wiped a cloth wrung out in a bleach solution round the portholes, where condensation, and then black mould, tended to gather. It wasn't her barge, she only rented it, but it was her home. When Michael, an old university friend of

Philip's, had offered it as a place she might go to, she'd been thrilled.

Philip had been totally against the idea. 'You could never live on a boat!' he had said. 'It's a ridiculous idea! Why not rent a flat or a house somewhere instead?'

Any idea that living on a barge might not be a good idea had evaporated at his words. Living in a cut-down, lesser version of what she was used to would be humiliating. Finding a completely different solution seemed a much better idea. 'Because I want to live on a barge,' she'd said firmly, 'and there's nothing you can do to stop me!'

There had been a side to Philip that was quite controlling, and the realisation that he'd forfeited his right to tell his wife what he felt was best for her had caused him to fall silent for a moment. 'Well, don't come running to me if it all goes wrong!' he had said eventually.

'Philip, you have left me for a younger woman. If I need anything from you at any time, I will ask for it!' She had taken a breath. 'For nearly thirty years I looked after you and Karen, I gave up my career, I kept up the house and garden, I did my bit for the community and I entertained your boring business friends for dinner. You owe me!'

'You are a wonderful cook,' he'd said, trying to placate the woman who had become much stronger than she had been during their marriage.

'I know! But I'm no longer *your* wonderful cook!'

'Oh, Jo, I do feel bad! You know I do—'

'Well, how do you think I feel! I'll tell you: discarded. Like a bit of old carpet that did sterling service for years and then is dragged off to the local tip! That's how I feel. And if I want to live on a barge, I will.'

Michael had been very pleased to think his barge might have a tenant. She had met him and he had shown her round.

12

'I'm going to be out of the country for at least a year, and boats don't like being left with no one to look after them. You'll be doing me a favour.'

'It was very kind of you to think of me,' Jo had said.

'Well, I wouldn't have thought of you if Philip hadn't emailed me and told me what had happened.'

'He did that? How odd! I didn't think you saw each other often enough for that.'

'Oh, we haven't met for years, but we've got each other's email addresses, and he sent one to everyone in his "old friends" file in his address book.'

'He didn't!'

Michael had nodded. 'I don't think he's proud of it, Jo. He just felt he had to tell everyone.'

Jo had sighed, trying not to feel betrayed all over again. 'Oh well, it's worked out to my advantage. It's a beautiful barge, and I'm going to love living here.' Especially when she discovered she'd still be able to email Karen and use her mobile, from certain parts of the barge anyway.

'It's a good community,' Michael had said. 'People from all walks of life live here. Some most of the time, some just for weekends, but they're a good bunch. They'll rally round if necessary.'

Jo had started to say that it wouldn't be necessary, but then realised there was a lot to learn about boat life and she probably would need to call on people for help from time to time, so didn't.

Three weeks later, she'd moved on to the barge. Philip had brought her things, guilt making him extremely helpful. After a few teething problems, when she had needed help to make the pump-out function, she had taken to it like the proverbial duck to water.

'As long as I don't have to go anywhere,' she had said to

13

Michael on the phone when he'd rung up to check that she'd settled in. 'I'll be absolutely fine!'

And now she had Dora. If Dora's situation hadn't been desperate, she would have suspected her daughter Karen of planting Dora. While she hadn't really been lonely, she was programmed to look after people. Having a broken-hearted surrogate daughter was just what she needed.

Soon, she'd have to think about earning a living. Philip had given her quite a large amount of money and she looked on this as a redundancy payment. She'd had no qualms about accepting it. Eventually, when they got divorced, she'd probably be entitled to at least some of the value of the house, but until then, she wanted to keep as much of her lump sum intact as she could. And although having Dora would give her life more focus, she needed something else to do. Since she'd arrived on the barge she'd spent her spare time redoing the paintwork in the original boatman's cabin, which was her bedroom. This was a painstaking activity she mostly did when there was something good on the radio. It involved much sanding down and filling and she had only got to the painting stage quite recently. She looked on it as payback for being given somewhere to live at quite a low rent. But eventually, she knew, she'd have to get a job.

The trouble was, at fifty, she was virtually unemployable. She hadn't been tempted to go to university and had done a secretarial course instead. Then she'd had office jobs. But those skills were no use to her now. Even if she went on a computer course, no one would take her on without recent office experience and her most recent office experience, if you discounted all the voluntary work she had done over the years, had been working for a management consultancy in London over twenty-five years ago. She had had to beg for an electric typewriter.

14

She'd had a computer for several years now, and had used it to write minutes, create notices and, more latterly, to shop over the Internet. But she couldn't do spreadsheets, or use accountancy packages, or any of the things a modern office would require.

'And even if I could,' she had said to Karen, 'no one would take me on at my age.'

Her daughter had tutted but acknowledged the truth of this.

So she'd have to create her own job and work for herself, but for now she had Dora to look after. And they both had a rally to take part in.

'I'm shattered,' she called to Dora, who was scrubbing the grout round the kitchen tiles with a toothbrush. 'Are you hungry yet?'

'Mm. Definitely. Do you want me to go for the fish and chips?'

'We'll go together and I'll show you where the shops are. You deserve a reward. I truly am grateful for your help, especially on your first night here.'

As they passed the shower block Jo suddenly stopped. 'Oh, Dora, I'm so sorry, I've got a letter for you. Seeing where we pick up our post reminded me.' She burrowed about in her handbag and gave the envelope to Dora.

'That's Dad's handwriting,' she said.

'You don't have to open it now,' said Jo after a moment, when she saw the look on Dora's face. 'You can do it another time. Let's go. I can almost smell the vinegar.'

They ate most of their supper on the way home. 'After all, we don't want to make more clearing up,' said Dora, who was, Jo realised, a girl after her own heart.

Chapter Two

❧❧❧

'I should warn you, I doubt if there'll be anyone remotely interesting to you,' said Jo to Dora as they made their way along the pontoon. They had watched the boat-handling competition that afternoon and were now on their way to the dinner. It was a warm evening; lights from the barges twinkled on the water. 'There are some young people who live on a barge at the end but they're away this weekend. I expect it'll all be old duffers. Possibly in blazers and white trousers. Cravats, even.'

Dora laughed. 'I don't mind. I'm definitely not looking for a boyfriend.'

'I know that but it would be nice if there was someone under fifty for you to talk to. I don't want you to be bored out of your skull. Karen would have gone on for hours if I'd dragged her to anything she didn't enjoy.'

'I probably would have done before, but now I just want to chat about the weather to people old enough to be my grandparents. Will you know many of the old duffers?'

Jo chuckled. 'I don't think I actually know anyone of that description. I'll know the locals, but there are lots of visiting boats, and people who haven't got barges but want them. They're doing research. Tilly, from *Appalachia* – that's the boat with the wooden decks and the tubs of flowers near ours – she's going to be there. She's great fun. You'll like her. Her engine is painted pink.'

'Wow!'

'Then there's the couple from *Blackberry*. They're lovely. Quite elderly, and they're not here all the time, but so kind. Doug sorted me out when I had to get gas for the first time.'

'I'm never going to remember everyone's names.'

'Don't worry about it. I won't introduce you all that much anyway, because I'm hopeless at remembering names too. I'll just say that you're Dora.'

'And what else?' Dora stopped and grabbed Jo's arm, suddenly aware that she needed to have some sort of cover story.

Startled by her urgency, Jo turned to her. 'What do you mean?'

'Well, you'll have to say why I'm here, won't you?'

Jo shook her head as she realised what Dora was talking about. 'Not at all. I'll just say you want to try living near London for a while and are staying with me because it's cheap.'

'Well, that's true. It's been free, so far.'

Jo waved her hands in a dismissive gesture. 'You only arrived yesterday, and when you've got a job you can pay me rent. Now, do you think I look all right?'

Dora thought it would have been better if Jo had asked this when they were still on the barge and she could have made any necessary alterations, but for some reason she hadn't. Thus there was no point in suggesting powder, or pointing out that her trousers had paint on them. 'You look fine.'

'You don't think this top is a bit bright?' Jo pulled at it.

Dora considered and lied. 'Um. Not really.'

'That means you do.' Jo let out a frustrated sigh. 'I deliberately left all my tasteful clothes behind. I wanted a new start.' They set off walking again.

'Right.'

'And I didn't want to be invisible.'

17

'Why on earth should you be invisible?' Dora asked in surprise.

'Women of my age are, you know. It's a well-known phenomenon.'

Dora cleared her throat. 'Well, you won't be, not in that top.'

Jo put a hand to her neckline, which was quite low. 'It's too revealing and too sparkly, isn't it?'

'Not really. I mean, it's quite sparkly, but they're very discreet sequins and bugle beads.'

'What about the revealing bit?'

'It's perfectly respectable. Even my mother would wear something that low.'

Jo laughed in relief. 'Karen wouldn't be seen dead with me in a top like this.'

'I will.' Dora tried to be reassuring.

Now the path was wider and they could walk side by side, Jo took Dora's arm in a friendly fashion. 'When Philip left me I bought a lot of very bright clothes, so people wouldn't just look past me. Not purple, of course.'

'Why not purple?' Dora was mystified.

'Because of the poem about growing old and wearing purple.'

'I see,' said Dora, not seeing, but deciding it was easier to humour Jo – she was so different from her mother.

'I don't want another relationship, heaven forbid, but I don't want people not to notice if I come into a room. That would be just too lowering.'

'I'm sure they don't. I mean, I'm sure they do notice.'

Jo laughed. 'Wearing this top, they're bound to.'

Although she didn't say so to Dora, Jo's fear of becoming invisible was partly fear of the menopause. This Sword of Damocles had already descended on many of her friends, some of them younger than her. It couldn't be long now,

18

she knew, and she was not looking forward to it. She didn't want to become non-sexual and feared that fate was inevitable – particularly now she was single.

She and Philip had had sex much less frequently over the last couple of years. She had missed it to begin with, but later had felt that sitting in bed together with their books was companionable and, if not a substitute for physical contact, a pleasant thing in itself.

Now she realised it was because Philip no longer fancied her and had another, younger body on offer, and not because he was getting older that he had stopped reaching for her, telling her she was a pretty girl. The Floosie was in her late twenties. She wouldn't be happy to read a book instead of making love. If there was more to Philip's reluctance to have sex than Jo's shortcomings, he would have to get his act together.

Now, she regretted her scarlet top. Should the menopause choose to arrive during the dinner with a proverbial hot flush, she'd look like a chilli pepper. And whatever Dora said about her mother, she was not convinced it didn't show too much cleavage.

Dora was wondering if she would be asked questions likely to set her off crying again. She decided that Jo was right, all she need say was that she was looking for a change of scene and might get a job in London proper. She'd try and give the impression that she was an ambitious single girl, looking for adventure. Considering how lacking in adventure her life had been up to now, maybe she should look for adventure for real. Although it had felt quite brave before she arrived, going to live with her best friend's mother probably didn't count.

Their arrival at the pub put a stop to their separate thoughts, and they made their way to the top room, which had been set aside for the dinner. They had been there earlier, arranging tables and decorating them, but they hadn't had anything to do with the seating plan and so had no idea where they would be sitting.

They were among the first arrivals. Lots of people were in large groups and Dora, and she thought possibly Jo too, felt rather shy. But someone soon recognised Jo and drew them both into their group. Jo introduced Dora and no one said, 'Who's the little runaway, then?' or anything like that. Logically, Dora realised, this was a highly unlikely scenario, but the previous week at home had been so full of people who felt free to comment on her lack of 'ideas of decent behaviour', as they called it, she was programmed to expect such remarks.

People started looking for their names, and Dora frantically hoped she would be next to, or very near, Jo. But she wasn't. The kind soul who had arranged where everyone was to sit had put her over the other side of their table. There was a young man already sitting down, staring into his pint as if settling in for a boring evening.

Dora read her name from a little way away and hesitated before going to sit next to him. He had curly hair and slanting eyes. He looked up as she approached, saw her and smiled. He had a wicked twinkle. Whoever had done the seating plan must have thought she was doing Dora a favour, but she wasn't grateful. She didn't feel remotely sociable, and while she would have managed to make small talk with a kindly ex-naval officer or his wife, she didn't want this admittedly attractive young man who might flirt with her out of habit.

She looked across at Jo, thinking perhaps she could make some excuse to go and join her, but Jo was sitting next to a pleasant-looking pair of about her own age. She seemed set for a convivial evening.

'Hi, I'm Tom,' said the young man, taking her hand and

shaking it, although she hadn't offered it. He looked directly at her as he said hello. The slanting eyes were dark brown.

'Dora,' she replied, sitting down beside him.

'Unusual. I haven't met a Dora before.'

'It's in Dickens, *David Copperfield*, although she was a bit of a wimp.'

'Are you a bit of a wimp?' he asked.

Surprised, Dora laughed. 'Yes, since you ask.'

'Well, you don't look too bad on it. I always think of wimp rhyming with limp, which is like damp. You don't seem damp.'

'If I fell in, I would be.'

Tom laughed. 'So would anyone. Do you live on a barge, then? Or are you just a visitor?'

'Um – I live on a barge.'

'You don't sound too sure.'

'I only moved on yesterday but I'm here for a while.'

'Which barge?'

'*The Three Sisters*.'

'Oh. The Klipper.'

'What?'

'It's a Klipper. It's a sort of barge. You haven't been here long, have you?'

'No. I said.' Dora fiddled with her cutlery, embarrassed by her lack of knowledge.

'So, are you interested in barges?'

She regarded him. 'I don't know! I've hardly had a chance to find out what a barge is!'

'It's a bloody great boat,' said Tom solemnly.

Now Dora laughed. 'I did pick up that much.'

'So, if you're not a barge fanatic, why are you here?'

'I'm staying with my best friend's mother. I fancied living nearer London and she offered me a room. It's quite cheap.' It would be quite cheap, she knew that, and was satisfied by how all this came out. It didn't sound like she was running away at all.

'Right. So who owns *The Three Sisters*?'

'Well, Jo – that's who I'm staying with – rents it, so I don't know. Jo's over there.'

'She looks nice.'

'She is.' She paused. 'So why are you here?'

'I work in a boatyard but I'm always trying to pick up work as a deckhand. I spend a lot of time around boats but not enough time at sea.'

'Fair enough.'

'Can I get you a drink? I think there's going to be wine with dinner, but as there's no sign of any food, you might need something before then.'

Dora considered. She had been thirsty when Jo had bought her a drink and had asked for a Henry. Now she felt something stronger than orange juice and soda might be a good idea. 'A glass of red wine would be great.'

Tom looped his leg out from behind the chair in an athletic way. 'House red?'

'Fine.'

Jo caught her attention while he was gone and leant low across the table. 'Are you all right? I mean, he seems quite cute from over here, but if you're not happy, I could swap.'

Hoping fervently that this stage whisper was not as audible as it seemed, Dora said, 'I'm fine. He's fun. No probs.'

'That's OK then.' Jo settled back in her seat and then leant forward again. 'Did I warn you? There's going to be a quiz.'

'Oh. That's all right. I won't know anything. I'll just sit and watch.'

22

Jo smiled. 'I only know questions about gardening and cooking and I bet there won't be any.'

They both sat back down and Dora rearranged her knives and forks again.

'So, you'll be looking for a job, then?' asked Tom, when he had returned with the drinks.

'Yes, I suppose so. I mean, I will be on Monday. I did think I'd leave myself the weekend to settle in.'

He ignored her gentle sarcasm. 'What do you do?'

This was a question Dora hated. 'Office work. Nothing very exciting.'

'What sort of place did you work in before?'

'An estate agent's. It was fun.' Tom was probably too young to have had a bad estate agent experience, but Dora was so bored with people telling her how dreadful they were as a breed, she used defensive tactics automatically.

'Was it very high-tech?'

'Moderately. I don't know really. I'd worked there since I left college.'

'Didn't you go to uni?'

Dora shook her head. 'No. I did a secretarial course. What about you?' So far, all the questions had been one way and Tom hadn't had to justify his existence at all.

'I went to college too. Falmouth. I'm a boat-builder. Apprentice, really. I do other odd jobs to make extra money.'

'That sounds interesting.'

'Does it, if you're not really interested in boats?'

'Who says I'm not interested in boats?'

'You're just on one for a cheap place to stay.' He grinned. 'Do you live on a boat?'

'Yes, actually. But not a barge.'

'Oh, do you have to, in your job?'

'No, but as you say, it's cheap. The yard where me and

23

my mates do a lot of work lets us have a mooring if we don't mind moving about when they've got work on. I'm not there at the moment. No room. I'm near here for the time being. It's handy, being able to move your home.'

'I suppose.'

'Does that sound very strange to you?'

'Yes. I mean, I come from a small village, where everyone lives in houses.'

'This is like a village too, only people live on boats or barges. I've just moved villages for a while.'

As Dora was fleeing from the cosiness of village life she didn't want to talk about them all night. She changed the subject. 'What's the difference between boats and barges, technically?'

Tom took a sip from his pint. 'They say a barge can carry a boat, but a boat couldn't carry a barge. It's quite an involved question, really, and I don't suppose you're all that interested.' He glanced at her and smiled. He did have a rather nice smile, boyish and charming at the same time.

Dora felt she could have feigned interest for a little while, but not for long. However, if they talked about boats and barges it would mean he wouldn't ask probing questions. She fell silent as she considered.

'Look,' he said, possibly getting tired of waiting for an answer. 'People are standing up. Food is arriving. Things are kicking off.'

Jo watched Dora from across the table. She seemed happy. The gorgeous young man at her side was apparently keeping her amused and her him likewise. She was such a pretty girl, it would have seemed a shame for her to have married someone she'd known for ever. Jo had got married young herself, and now it felt like a waste of her looks and gaiety to have thrown it away on the first

24

man to ask her. After all, you couldn't sow your wild oats after you were married, not in her book.

She and Philip had been part of a social set that used to do things together – trips to pubs, the cinema, parties. Then they had got married and real life began.

Michael, the owner of the barge, had been part of that early group. He too had got married relatively young, and Jo had thought they had lost touch with him. But apparently Philip had not and knew that he had been widowed and was now living with a very glamorous woman in the South of France.

Jo didn't resent Michael for living with a younger woman. In theory, she didn't resent anyone for following his or her heart, she just resented Philip for doing it, when he was married to her.

Once, many, many years ago, she had fallen in love with another man. She hadn't felt that intrinsically Philip's happiness was more important than hers, but there was Karen to think of, her parents, the in-laws, and a whole slew of other people who would have been desperately upset if she'd run off with someone else. So she hadn't done anything about it.

She had gone on thinking about the man for years, but, eventually, he had faded from her memory and now she couldn't even conjure up what he looked like.

So when Philip had allowed himself to get involved with the Floosie (who was probably a perfectly nice girl, who just had a taste for older men), the betrayal had been doubly hurtful, because she hadn't betrayed him when she had so much wanted to.

Now, she turned her attention to the woman who was talking to her. One of the things she had noticed since moving on to a barge was that having something major in common already was a great aid to conversation.

'You must come and see ours,' the woman – Miranda, Jo thought – was saying. 'We've done a lot to it.'

'*The Three Sisters* is quite basic,' said Jo apologetically, although she had redecorated the boatman's cabin for her own sake, and the bathroom in Dora's honour, 'but as it's not mine, there's not a lot I can do about it.'

'Will you go cruising with her?' Miranda asked, tucking into her food.

'Oh no, I couldn't do that. I'd be far too nervous, not to mention seasick.'

'I get a little nervous when we first set off, then I get into it. Lots of us women feel the same. We don't live on ours, of course, but we spend as much time as possible on it.'

'Like a weekend cottage?'

Miranda nodded. 'Only now Bill's retired, we spend weeks on it too, when I can get away.'

'So, what do you do?' said Jo, more interested than this run-of-the-mill question sounded.

'I'm part-owner of a little antique shop. I don't have to actually be there often, as people who have things for sale take turns, but I buy stuff for it. Lillian – that's my partner – says it's no good us just providing a venue for other dealers. We have to sell for ourselves.'

'That sounds fun.'

'Oh, it is. I love it. We don't make much money, but it keeps me out of trouble.' Miranda paused. 'And what do you do? Or are you retired too?'

Jo hadn't anticipated this question. Unlike Dora, who had prepared an answer, she was put on the spot. 'I don't think I'm retired, I think I'm between careers.'

'Are you? What bliss! Much as I love what I do, how wonderful to have a chance to start again. Don't you think?'

Miranda's enthusiasm was startling and Jo had to think

for a moment before answering. 'Yes, I suppose it is.'

Miranda made a gesture. 'Sorry, you probably don't feel like that at all, but I always want to apply for every job I ever see. And I know they're not going to take me on as a stable girl at my age, even if I did know anything about horses.'

'Have some more wine,' said Jo. She was enjoying herself.

'So, what do you do for fun?' Tom asked Dora when they returned to their table, their plates piled high.

'Um – what do you mean?' Dora knew perfectly well what Tom meant but she needed time to think something up. She and John had exercised his mother's dogs and gone to the supermarket for fun. She didn't think that Tom would be impressed.

'You know, hobbies, stuff like that. Did you have a gap year?'

'No. You?'

'No. I'm going travelling when I've saved enough money.'

'I was going to do that too. When I got the job in the estate agent's, I thought it was just for the summer but somehow I just stayed.' John hadn't wanted to go travelling, and she'd loved him, so she'd stayed at home to be with him. Now she'd have to think of a reason for staying that didn't involve John.

'Oh? Why? Was it so fascinating?'

'Strangely, yes. I love houses.'

'And I love boats.'

She laughed. 'It's a good thing we're not planning to get together then!' She stopped abruptly, aware that she'd brought up the very subject she most hoped to avoid.

Tom seemed quite calm about it, however. 'Oh, I don't

know. I was planning to ask you out for a drink, actually.'

'Were you?'

'I'll let you know if I intend to go through with it,' he said gravely.

'Give me plenty of warning, so I can think up an excuse if I don't want to.' She was suddenly more relaxed. She hadn't sworn off men for ever, she just didn't want a commitment. Tom didn't look like he would want to settle down with a mortgage, a Labrador and a semi, like John did. He was going travelling. That made him safe. She also liked his curly hair. John had floppy hair. Her mother thought he looked like Hugh Grant, and he did in a way. He wore the same sort of clothes. Tom was wearing jeans and a T-shirt with a subversive message on it.

'Here, let me top you up,' said Tom with a lopsided grin.

'OK,' said Dora.

'Which is the longest river in the British Isles, including Ireland?' asked the quizmaster later that evening.

To Dora's relief, the couple next to them had teamed up with her and Tom, so Tom wouldn't be answering the questions all on his own.

'The Thames,' said the male half of the couple confidently. He was called Derek.

'No! The Severn, surely!' said Sheila, his wife.

The argument about which of the two it was went on between them and Tom until Dora felt compelled to speak up. 'He said including Ireland. In which case, it's the Shannon.'

'Are you sure?' Three astonished faces regarded her.

She nodded. 'Oh yes. I don't know much, but what I know, I know.'

'But surely—' began Derek.

'Write it down,' said Tom. 'We haven't time to argue any more. Here's the next question.'

Dora's contribution was valued. Because of John's fondness for quizzes, she'd watched a lot of them on television. It gave her an eclectic, if not frightfully useful, range of information. It was acknowledged that it was thanks to her that their team won.

'That was brilliant!' said Tom, kissing her hard on the cheek.

'Yes!' said the others, kissing her too. 'Now go up and choose a prize for us. Something to drink, if possible.'

Dora came back with a bottle of rum.

Derek and Sheila were so pleased to have won. 'The people on *Cinderella* always win the quiz. Look at them now, pig sick! Now, let's go back to *Avocet* and make rum punches.'

'Good idea,' said Tom. 'Have you got any limes?'

'I'm afraid I can't come,' said Dora. 'I'm with Jo. The woman over there in the red top?'

'Oh yes,' said Derek. 'Very attractive. Well, invite her, too.'

His wife shot him a discerning look. 'She looks as if she's tied up with her team. They came third, I think.'

'I'd better go and join her,' said Dora.

Tom leapt out of his seat to follow her. 'Don't rush off! Come and have one rum punch, and then I'll see you home. I'd like to talk to you a bit more.'

'Look, really, I'm not looking for any sort of relationship just now.'

Tom grinned. 'Nor am I! I want to know if you'd like to work for a boatyard.'

Feeling stupid for rushing in with that statement, Dora hoped he wouldn't notice her heightened colour. 'What?'

'Don't look so horrified, I only meant in the office. But it's local, and you might enjoy it.'

Pleased that he hadn't connected her blush with her use of the 'R' word, she went on more happily, 'Surely you can't offer me a job?'

'No, but I can get you to apply for it. Now, let's tell Jo you're coming home separately.'

'Dora was brilliant in the quiz,' said Tom as they joined Jo's group. 'I'm Tom, by the way.' He shook Jo's hand in much the same way he'd shaken Dora's. 'We're going to *Avocet* to drink our prize. I'll bring her home safely. Has she got a curfew?'

At first, Jo didn't understand quite what he meant, and then found the notion hilarious. 'No she hasn't! She's an adult, she can do what she wants. Just don't let her fall in on the way back. Where is *Avocet*? Is it in the marina, or outside?'

'Outside,' said Tom, 'with the other visiting boats.'

'You'll need a fob, then,' said Jo. 'Here's the spare, I meant to give it to you earlier,' she added as she reached into her bra.

'She's great!' said Tom as he escorted Dora down the stairs. 'And you've only lived with her for one day?'

'I knew her when I was growing up though,' said Dora. 'But you're right. She's great.'

After drinking their prize on *Avocet*, Tom had wanted her to go back to the boat where he lived to carry on drinking, but Dora had been very firm about saying no. Much as she had (surprisingly) enjoyed herself this evening, it was quite late, and lovely as Jo undoubtedly was, she might not appreciate Dora having the hangover from hell the next day, especially when the cleaning process would be continued. Jo was very anxious about the boat parade.

Anyway, Dora couldn't cook with a hangover, and she had promised to make chocolate brownies to infuse the barge with a nice smell, and to bribe the visitors with. Jo had bought lots of beers and wine.

'I know it's silly,' she had said, 'but I can't have people crossing my threshold without offering them something to eat or drink. Hospitality is my besetting sin.' She had paused for a moment. 'Well, one of them.'

'What are the others?' Dora had asked.

'Buying clothes from catalogues and not sending them back if they don't fit.'

'What did you do instead?'

'I gave them to the charity shop. But that was when I was a kept woman. I'm going to be far more practical now.'

So, being practical also, Dora said goodnight to Tom.

Chapter Three

'Do you want a cup of tea and some toast?' Jo spoke quietly but urgently through a crack in the door to Dora's cabin. 'It's nearly ten o'clock. The boat parade starts at eleven.'

Dora opened a reluctant, then a guilt-stricken eye. 'Oh my God, I'm so sorry.'

'So, tea and toast?'

'No, no. I'll get up. I'll have a shower and I'll go back on cleaning duty.'

'We're pretty tidy now. As tidy as we're ever going to be, anyway. I'll have tea ready for when you're out of the shower.' Jo closed the door quietly behind her and wondered if Dora was likely to go back to sleep. It was with some relief that she heard her go to the bathroom a few moments later.

Jo had enjoyed her evening very much and yet she hadn't slept well. It was partly having Dora, she knew. Although she had protested so firmly that her lodger was an adult, she hadn't really settled until she'd heard Dora come in. And then there was Miranda who'd made her laugh so much and who'd wanted a job as a stable girl. She'd been so envious of Jo having a chance to start a new career and had given Jo a lot to think about. Up until then, she'd thought of herself as the injured party, battling valiantly to make a new life for herself. Now she had more or less done that, a new career was what she needed and wanted, she realised.

She'd lain awake much of the night thinking of what she could do. Being a stable girl was not an option for her, either. But she did have skills. She was quite a good gardener, although probably didn't fancy doing it all year round. She could cook up a storm if required and used to produce the most wonderfully creative birthday cakes: sculptures from butter icing, a very particular art. Remembering her ingenuity made her smile, but then she allowed herself a moment of bitterness for the number of dinners she'd cooked for her ex-husband's boring clients. That led her thoughts to the issue of whether he was an ex-husband if they weren't actually divorced yet. Yes, definitely, she decided. He was no longer her husband, he was the husband of the Floosie, even if they weren't married.

She could always cook in a pub or something. That might be fun. She could be a barmaid and wear the sparkly red top that had gone down so well with her fellow guests. Then she remembered that barmaids needed to be younger too. And maybe, if she was stuck in the kitchen all the time, she wouldn't enjoy working in a pub. Or a café? A nice, genteel café where they served teacakes and scones? Her mind had drifted back to her childhood. The Lavender Tearooms. They'd served wonderful things: jewel biscuits, jap cakes, macaroons, German biscuits, Dundee cake, Battenberg cakes, all sorts and all made on the premises. Yes, that idea definitely appealed. She wasn't sure that such establishments still existed, except possibly in Richmond, famous for its Maids of Honour confections and several miles away, but it was a good start.

Eventually she'd gone to sleep thinking about her garden, and wondering which of the roses were out. Would the Floosie learn to love her Paul's Himalayan

Musk rambling up the copper beech, with pale pink and tiny blooms, as much as she had?

'So sorry!' Dora appeared smelling of shower gel, her hair wet and curly. She picked up a slice of toast and put it into her mouth whole. 'You should have woken me earlier,' she mumbled.

Jo smiled. 'You need your sleep. I know you were in late.' She felt a pang of envy for youth, which allowed you to sleep as long as you needed to.

'Oh, did I wake you?'

Jo hurried to reassure her. 'Oh no, not at all. I just happened to be awake when you got in, that's all. More toast? You might as well, I've made it already.'

Obligingly Dora took it.

'Did you have a nice time last night? It was better than I expected, I must admit,' said Jo.

'Definitely. The quiz was really fun!'

'Quizzes are always better when you win them, though we liked it too. What's *Avocet* like?'

'Very sleek. Nice, but not quite enough like a boat for me.' Dora frowned. 'It's strange but I had had nothing to do with boats before a couple of days ago and now I think I could get to really like them.'

'They do grow on you. *The Three Sisters* feels like home now.' Jo wiped at the couple of crumbs that had fallen from Dora's toast. 'Now, can I be rude and ask if you left the bathroom tidy?'

Dora nodded, chewing the other slice of toast. 'Spick and span. I even wiped out the washbasin with my towel.' She swallowed. 'I've got another if using the washing machine is difficult.'

'It's not, and I've got loads of towels too. I'd just bought a new lot when Philip . . . Philip did what he did, and I couldn't bear to leave them. I love towels.' The thought that

34

perhaps she should work in a towel shop or a major department store flitted in and out of her mind like an itinerant butterfly.

'OK, well, I'll wash up. Then what would you like me to do?' Dora asked as she got up from the table.

'Make the brownies?'

Dora had obviously forgotten about the brownies. 'Oh yes. I'll put the oven on now. Where's the chocolate? And nuts? They won't be ready if anyone turns up at eleven. It is eleven, isn't it?'

Jo nodded. 'But apparently if you close the door to your boat no one can come on. It's to give you a chance to see other people's boats.'

'But you won't want to do that immediately, will you?' Dora appeared disappointed.

'Oh no,' Jo assured her. 'We've worked this hard, we're going to open for business.' Her eyes widened in horror. 'Oh my God! Look at those cobwebs! How can I have missed them?'

'I expect they came in the night,' said Dora, ripping open packets of chocolate and throwing them into a heatproof bowl.

'You're very quick with those brownies. You've obviously made them before.'

'Oh yes. I used to make them for John all the time. When he gets another girlfriend I must give her the recipe.'

'Will you know if he gets another girlfriend?'

'Of course. Everyone will tell me, don't worry.' Dora realised this was the first time in weeks she'd been able to mention John's name without wanting to burst into tears. Maybe I've finally turned a corner, she thought with relief. A night out with people who didn't know her or her history, and with whom she could just be herself, had been wonderfully settling.

Jo had dealt with the cobwebs, catching them in a bit of kitchen towel, but had found a patch of mildew she hadn't noticed before, and was scrubbing at it with an old toothbrush when the first guests came.

'Hello! Anybody aboard?'

Jo rushed up to the wheelhouse to usher the couple in. She recognised them from the previous night but had no clue what their names were. 'Hello!' she said warmly. 'How lovely to see you!'

They were a couple a bit younger and quite a lot thinner than she was. Sadly, not only could Jo not remember their names, she couldn't remember if she'd liked them. Being younger and thinner was only forgivable in nice people.

They were certainly friendly. 'Hello, Jo. All right after last night?'

What had happened last night that she might not be all right? Maybe they were just asking if she had a hangover. She smiled gaily, hoping she hadn't appeared drunk. 'Absolutely fine. You?'

The woman grimaced. 'Bit fragile. But you didn't have brandy after the coffee, did you?'

'No. I'm sorry, I can't remember, which is your barge?'

'We haven't got one. We're thinking of buying one though, so we're doing our research,' said the man. 'Can I look at the engine?'

Jo indicated the square of metal that covered the engine compartment. She hadn't penetrated this space yet, having decided against it when she saw she had to step sideways down a vertical ladder to reach it. She had no idea if the engine room was like an operating theatre or a midden and she didn't much care. She'd abnegated all responsibility in that area. 'Help yourself.'

The man swung back the heavy cover and looked down the abyss. 'Hm. Got a boiler suit I can put on?'

Jo rummaged in the lockers under the seats that were built in round the table and produced one. It was Michael's. She had stuffed all signs of him into the locker when she had first arrived and was feeling particularly anti-men.

Jo turned to his wife. 'You don't want to see the engine room, do you?' The woman was wearing white trousers and a blue-and-white-striped Breton top. She shook her head. 'I want to see the cabin, where they would have lived in the old days.'

'That's where I live now,' said Jo, trying not to resent the woman for looking good in a top that should have put pounds on her.

But her little cabin was a picture, she decided. It had looked neglected and unloved when she had first moved on to the barge because Michael had always slept in the cabin Dora now had. But Jo had fallen in love with this little space and she'd made it her project. The redecorating had helped rid her of the sense of worthlessness Philip's desertion had left her with.

Now, she lifted the wooden shelf that disguised the double doors as panelling, and ushered her guest down the three steep steps to the cabin. She felt proud and a little protective of her efforts. It had a thick, deep red carpet that instantly made it feel cosy and yet because of the white-painted tongue-and-groove boarding of the walls and ceiling and four large portholes, light danced over all the surfaces, making it a little sunlit haven.

There was a double bunk, that could be taken apart to make a table, but Jo had got so fed up with sleeping on a ridge that she had bought a four-foot mattress. She wouldn't need to convert the bed to a dining table when she had the whole of the rest of the barge to dine in. The bed was covered with a patchwork bedspread she had brought from home, because it had been made by her mother and was, therefore, hers.

Behind the panelling were lots of little cupboards and storage spaces that were fine for the separate, non-iron clothes that Jo lived in these days. There was even a tiny en-suite bathroom behind one door. The whole space became a shower unit, although Jo had never investigated how this worked as, owing to lack of headroom, you had to sit on the loo while you washed. She did use the washbasin and loo and had now put a little vase of flowers on the shelf. There was another vase of flowers in the bedroom part and all her clothes were stuffed away in the cupboards.

'All it needs is a little stove,' she said to Mrs Stripy-Top, 'and it would be perfect.'

'Where would you put a stove?' the woman asked, more appalled than curious.

'I think it must have gone where this plate on the ceiling is.' Jo frowned. 'I'm not sure it's called a ceiling. Boats are strange places.'

Mrs Stripy-Top laughed, and Jo decided to forgive her for being younger and thinner. After all, she did have smoker's lines round her mouth – she wasn't perfect.

'So, are you looking forward to having a barge?' Jo asked.

'I think so. I love your little curtains for the portholes. Two sets of curtain track! So diddy!'

'I know. I'm not a net-curtain person, generally, but when I saw the two sets I just had to have some.' Michael hadn't bothered with them because he used one of the other cabins. 'There's a shower you can stand up in down the other end, too.'

'I'd love to see.'

Jo decided to make a confession. 'I'm terribly sorry, I've completely forgotten your name.'

38

'Terri – and my husband's Donald.'

Did she look hurt that Jo hadn't remembered? Jo didn't think so. 'Terri, such a pretty name, how could I have forgotten. Come and see the rest of it. Dora, my lodger, barge-mate or whatever you call it, is making brownies. I wonder if they're cooked?' If she got a job in a tearoom, she'd have to ask Dora for the recipe.

The smell of chocolate wafted out of the saloon in a satisfying way, and it looked immaculate, to Jo's eyes anyway.

'Well, this is the saloon, where everything happens,' she announced.

'It's very – cosy,' said Terri, obviously unable to think of anything else to say.

Jo couldn't think of anything either. 'Dora,' she said, brisker than she meant to be. 'Those brownies smell heavenly. Are they ready yet?'

'I'm afraid not.' Dora was apologetic. 'About another fifteen minutes I think.'

Feeling despair creeping over her, Jo said, 'I'll show Terri the bathroom. I wonder if Donald's OK in the engine room?' If he wasn't, how, she wondered, would they get him out up the vertical ladder?

The bathroom passed muster. Dora had hidden her wet towel and the towels that were left were neatly folded over the rail. The loo seat was down and there were no traces of toothpaste on the taps. There were definitely advantages to living a man-free life, reflected Jo as Terri exclaimed at finding a bathroom big enough to have a washing machine in it. Philip could never brush his teeth without spitting on the taps.

'And what's in here?' asked Terri, pushing open a cabin door before Jo's shriek of horror reached her.

'Don't go in there—'

Going in there was not an option. This tiny single cabin was the glory hole, where everything that hadn't got a home was put, where anything anyone had got bored with was stuffed, where the bag of rubbish Jo had mysteriously lost now presented itself.

'I only rent this boat,' said Jo, having pulled the door shut with the nearest thing to a slam she could manage, given that a heap of old clothes had got in the way. 'Michael, who owns it, told me not to go in here.'

'Oh,' said Terri. 'Like the room in "Bluebeard". He hasn't been married lots of times, has he?'

Jo laughed and relaxed a little. 'Only about one and a half times, so that's all right.' She was about to add, 'How about you?' out of habit, but managed to stop herself in time. 'Let's see if the brownies are cooked. I could do with a chocolate fix.'

The brownies were out of the oven, but hadn't had time to set. Jo didn't care, and insisted on serving them while they were still bendy. Donald had emerged from the engine room and proceeded to talk to Jo long and incomprehensibly about it. Her eyes glazed, she smiled and nodded and nibbled brownie-crumbs. Eventually voices from the wheelhouse brought her relief. 'I'd better let those people on board,' she said, and flew up the stairs again.

'My husband helped himself to the engine room,' said a very young woman in a tight miniskirt and high-heeled shoes. 'Didn't fancy it myself.' She looked shy and uncomfortable, as if she'd rather be anywhere but on a barge.

'Come down and have a brownie,' said Jo, spotting the reluctant partner of a barge fanatic. 'They're a bit soft still, but taste delicious.'

'Tell me they've all gone,' said Jo some time later, with her eyes shut. 'Tell me I don't have to answer any more

40

questions, or apologise any more for the state of the little cabin.'

'They've all gone,' said Dora, 'and now it's our turn to go and snoop around everyone else's boats. But you don't have to,' she added, regarding Jo's supine, possibly sleeping, form. 'We could just stay here.'

'You wouldn't fancy going on your own?'

'No.' Although she'd be disappointed to miss looking at all the other barges, Dora did not fancy inviting herself on board them, even if it was what everyone else was doing.

Jo opened an eye. 'No, I want to get my own back,' she said. 'I'll just put another layer of slap on.'

'I should straighten my hair, really.' Dora ran her hand over the curls that were usually ironed into obedience.

'I like it curly,' said Jo. 'It makes you look delightfully dishevelled. Bed hair,' she added. 'Isn't that what's it's called?'

'I don't know, but it sounds good.'

Dora hoped that Jo wouldn't take too long putting on her make-up, and she didn't. She reappeared from the bathroom a few minutes later and said, 'Let the competition beware. Now I'm going to open strange doors and run my finger over the surfaces looking for dust! Kim and Aggie have nothing on me!'

'No one did that, did they?' Dora was horrified.

'Well, no,' Jo conceded, 'at least, only metaphorically.'

'Come on,' said Dora, not up to being metaphorical just then. 'Where shall we start?'

'Let's find Bill and Miranda,' said Jo. 'We know them, it won't be so shy-making.'

The *Hepplewhite* was a replica Dutch barge that Bill and Miranda had had built a couple of years ago. Jo remembered being told all this, and shared the information with

41

Dora as they searched among the flotilla of visiting boats that were moored on a section of the river.

'Oh, there it is,' said Dora. 'They've got it written in big letters on that thing at the back.'

'It's a stern, Dora,' said Jo. 'I know very little about boats and what you call things on them, but I do know that much.'

'I'll try and remember,' said Dora, penitent.

'I'm so glad it's you,' said Miranda, when she saw them both. 'I'm not quite ready. I went on a bit of an antique hunt yesterday and I haven't found spaces for everything yet.'

'Hello, Jo,' said Bill. 'And you must be Dora. Welcome aboard.'

There was a huge rectangular table in the middle of the saloon and it was covered with boxes and carrier bags.

'See what I mean?' said Miranda, who had ushered them down. 'This table takes apart completely and all the bits stow away, and the saloon looks much better when it's down, but there's all this stuff.'

'Well, you bought it,' said Bill good-humouredly.

'I got such a good deal, I had to have it. But that was the trouble, I had to have all of it and some of it is rubbish, really. Look at this mirror.' She picked up a little mirror with a very elaborate gold frame.

'But it's adorable!' said Jo.

'It's terribly damaged,' said Bill. 'It's not worth trying to restore. You might as well just chuck it.'

'Oh, you can't!' said Jo, taking it from Miranda. 'It could be so pretty!'

'But it is very tatty. Look, that cherub has lost a foot, you can't see what sort of flowers those were, and about eighty per cent of the curlicues are missing.' Miranda, whilst obviously agreeing that the mirror could be pretty, felt obliged to point out its many flaws.

'I'm sure something could be done with it,' said Jo, still hanging on to it. 'What's the frame made of?'

'Carved wood, decorated with gold leaf,' said Miranda. 'Very tricky to restore.'

'And you don't know anyone who could repair it?'

'It wouldn't be worth trying to track someone down, and it's a rare craft,' said Bill.

'Then could I have a go?' asked Jo, reluctant to put the mirror down. 'It would be such fun and it's so sad to think of it just being chucked away, or given to a car-boot sale or something.'

'Have you ever done anything like that?' asked Bill. 'It's not easy.'

'I've never done anything precisely like this, but I used to enjoy restoring things. I had a book with techniques in it, like French polishing, lacquering, things like that. I'm stubborn really. I don't like to be defeated.'

'But do you really want to spend all that time? It would take ages.' Bill picked up a box, obviously intending to put it somewhere else, and then put it back, defeated.

'You used to make wonderful sugar flowers and things,' said Dora. 'Do you remember that cake you made for Mum's fortieth? It was covered with flowers and butterflies.'

'I'd been on a course,' said Jo. 'I used to go on a lot of courses.' She sighed, allowing nostalgia to make her sad for a moment.

'Are you really interested in that old mirror?' Miranda seemed to sense the dip in Jo's mood.

'Oh yes.' Jo brightened up. 'I love the old glass – it's really flattering.'

'Then why don't you see what you can do? If it turns out well, I can put it in the shop and you can have the money. If you don't want to keep it,' said Miranda.

'I can't really keep too much while I'm on *The Three Sisters*,' said Jo. 'And I don't even know if I can do it.' She couldn't decide if she wanted the challenge or felt daunted by it.

'Have a go,' said Miranda encouragingly. 'And I have quite a lot of other bits and pieces that need restoring if it turns out you have a knack for it.'

'Oh wow!' said Dora, finding a little dish with a recumbent nymph, currently without a head, along the edge. 'How would you repair her?'

'Mm. Not sure,' mused Jo. 'I'd probably try to find another head of about the right size, to give me the basis, and then just fiddle and carve until she looked right.'

'Tell you what,' said Miranda briskly. 'I'll put together all the things most in need of restoration and you can see what you can do with them. I must say,' she went on, 'I'll be thrilled if you do find you have a talent for it. Those small items are very collectable.'

'I'll give it a go, and if I can't, well, you're no worse off.'

'And now are you two going to look at my barge, or not?' asked Bill, sounding a little pathetic.

'Oh yes,' said Dora. 'I'm looking forward to it.'

'As long as I don't have to look at the engine,' said Jo. 'I don't do engines.'

Chapter Four

❧

'They're all so different!' said Dora to Jo later as they walked along the jetty to where the next ladder down to the barges was. 'Imagine, a full-length bath with a separate shower in a boat!'

'Some of these Thames barges are massive,' said Jo, 'more like loft conversions than boats, really. They offer a huge amount of living space.'

'And those heavenly wood floors in that last one!'

'Wood floors are nice,' agreed Jo, 'but they gather dust terribly. Carpet keeps it to itself until you hoover it. Wood floors need forever dusting. I've got them at home. I mean, I had them at my old house. Talk about dust bunnies – dust Shetland ponies, rather.'

The image made Dora smile. 'That sounds rather sweet! It makes me feel cruel for sweeping them up. Oh my goodness, will they let us on this one? It looks fabulous!' She wasn't sure if Jo had referred to her old house as home from habit, or if it went deeper. She didn't want her to be sad, not just now.

Jo didn't seem sad and negotiated the various rails and ropes that needed stepping over with efficiency. Dora, not so familiar with such obstacles, took a little longer to land on the deck of the *Hildegarde*.

A young woman was there to receive them. She smiled with professional charm. 'Hi there, welcome to *Hildegarde*.

She's a luxe motor, thirty metres long, with a beam of five metres.'

'Oh, right. Nice,' said Jo and Dora, more or less together.

'I'm Carole. The owner's unable to be here right now, so I'm showing people round.'

'Is it for sale, then?' asked Jo.

'Oh no. I'm just showing it off for Marcus because he couldn't be here.'

I wonder, thought Jo. Marcus wasn't all that common a name.

'I used to know a Marcus,' she said, 'years ago, when Philip and I first got together. Probably not the same one though,' she added, noting how old Carole was and doing the sums.

'Let me show you round the deck first.' Carole led the way.

'Lovely,' muttered Dora, trying to work out how this woman fitted into the barge-owner's life. Was she a wife or just a girlfriend? Or even just a friend? She was slim, elegant and wore fabulous silk trousers with a matching camisole top. She was tanned, well made up with really good hair. Although Dora had no intention of becoming a hairdresser – far too skilled, in her opinion – she did fancy herself as someone who could tell when their hairstyle suited them. Carole was an example of someone with perfect hair. Jo, thought Dora regretfully, was not.

'You see, here's the sitting area. Isn't it great? The awning is electric, goes up and down at the touch of a button.'

'Gorgeous,' said Dora. For some reason she felt sorry for Carole. In spite of her stunning looks and lovely clothes there was an air of loneliness about her. She wondered if this Marcus was nice to her. What sort of man would leave his woman to show off his boat, unless they were married or something?

'And there's a hydraulic lift for the car,' Carole went on. 'Marcus is using it now, but it means when you arrive in the middle of the countryside, you can just drive off to the shops or a hotel. Should you want to, of course.'

It seemed to Dora that Carole did want to. The barge was probably Marcus's heart's desire and she just went along with it. More fool her.

'Very useful,' said Jo. 'Er – can we go inside now? I'm much more interested in the inside of boats—'

'Barges,' corrected Carole.

'. . . than the outside.' Jo smiled firmly.

'Of course, so am I, really,' said Carole, 'but *Hildegarde*'s got so many wonderful features, I don't want to forget any of them. This is the wheelhouse,' she announced proudly a moment or two later.

Dora had by this time seen enough barges to stop being amazed at how different from each other they all were, but this wheelhouse was something else entirely. There were no plants here, for a start.

It had what looked like a flight deck. There was a padded chair to sit on while steering, and a raft of electronic equipment that Carole was now explaining to a patient Jo.

Dora wandered down the stairs, wondering vaguely why there was no one else looking at it. She would have assumed that most people would leap on to this barge as soon as possible. She liked the interior. The saloon had tongue-and-groove panelling in a pale coloured wood. There was an unlit wood-burning stove on which Carole (it would have to have been Carole), had placed a bunch of dried flowers. There was pale carpet on the floor, but the furniture was arranged with such perfect symmetry it could have been done with a ruler. It was beautiful but soulless, she thought.

There was, however, a bookcase. Dora walked over to it

to give herself something to look at while she waited for Jo and Carole to come down. The books, she noted with horror, were in alphabetical order and there were no novels. She shuddered. She didn't think she should go into the other rooms until she was ushered, it would seem like prying, so she went to the window, which was definitely a window rather than a porthole, and looked out. Across the water she could see *The Three Sisters*. From here, she looked quite elegant, and even Dora could appreciate she had lovely lines. Inside, however, she was definitely a boat. Thick, round portholes let light into the saloon but you couldn't stare out of them. The large windows in *Hildegarde* offered brilliant views.

'Right, this is the saloon,' said Carole as she entered, Jo behind her looking tired. 'See how spacious it is?'

'There is a lot of living accommodation in these barges, isn't there?' said Jo.

'And the owner's cabin is to die for!' enthused Carole, convincing Dora that she had, if not actually died there, experienced what the French call 'the little death' in it. What was Marcus like? she wondered, pitying Carole for allowing herself to be used by him? But then she ticked herself off for being judgemental. She didn't know anything about their relationship and, after all, she was hardly an expert on relationships herself.

The bedroom was pretty wonderful, Dora had to concede. She noticed Jo wanting to hate it, too. They both thought the built-in mahogany bed was elegant, with drawers underneath that slid, in Carole's words, 'like silk'.

'To match the sheets, presumably,' murmured Jo, to Dora's private amusement.

'Oh yes, all the bed linen is silk,' replied Carole, and then she frowned, aware that something she'd said had not been quite right.

'Goodness,' said Jo.

'And all the drawers are all lined with scented drawer liners.'

'Wow,' said Jo, obviously struggling to keep up the enthusiasm.

'And this' – the ta-ra was unspoken but obvious – 'is the en suite.'

Whatever she had been expecting, and today Dora's ideas of what you were likely to find on a barge had been hugely expanded, it wasn't a sunken bath on a raised plinth surrounded by tiles featuring naked gods and goddesses, not in turquoise blue, anyway.

She glanced at Jo, hoping their eyes wouldn't meet. Her mouth was open and then snapped shut. Then she opened it again. 'How often do you have to fill the tanks to have a bath here on a regular basis?' said Jo.

There was a moment of silence. 'We only fill the bath when we've got shoreside facilites. Otherwise, it's the shower. It's a power one, of course, and has multiple settings.'

Dora and Jo both gazed at it admiringly.

'So do you go cruising with her much?' asked Jo. They had left the bathroom and were back in the saloon.

For someone who had declared herself as chronically seasick, not to mention terrified, she was giving a good impression of a person eager to take the barge across the Channel and explore the canals of Europe.

Carole lost some of her confidence. 'Not really. At least, not since Marcus and I—'

The sound of someone arriving on deck caused Carole to give a meerkat-like start.

'I'll just go and welcome the next group,' she said, and made her way swiftly up the stairs.

Dora had been expecting Jo to make their excuses and

follow her up, but she had picked up a photograph and was staring at it. When she looked up, her eyes were full of laughter.

'I think it's the same Marcus! Years older, of course, but I'm sure it's him! How funny!'

'That's weird! How did you know him?'

'I'm just trying to remember. He was a friend of a friend, I think, and joined our social group, just after Philip and I became a couple.'

'So what was he like when he was young – younger?' asked Dora.

'To be honest, if I hadn't been so besotted with Philip, I might have been tempted to have a little fling. We had a long conversation once – I've no idea what it was about – and he looked at me in this really intense way that made me feel I was the only girl in the room.'

'So he was attractive even then?' Dora asked, looking over Jo's shoulder at the photograph.

'Oh yes. I remember us girls thought he was devastating, in a sort of rugged way. Not handsome, like Philip was. But dangerous. He was rather sure of himself too, I recall. And he had a reputation as a playboy. A commitment-phobe, I suppose you'd call him now,' Jo said, putting the photograph back down.

'I could do with a commitment-phobe,' said Dora thoughtfully. 'A playboy would suit me just fine.'

Jo laughed. 'Carole must feel the same. And Marcus must be quite fit to keep up with her.' Her smile faded. 'I was just thinking, are any of those couples we used to know still couples? Michael was widowed but now has a younger girlfriend, Philip's got the Floosie, and Marcus has got Carole – although to be fair, he didn't have her then. But are all men programmed to want a new woman when their old one has passed childbearing age?'

'Goodness, what a horrible thought!'

Jo smiled. 'Never mind, I think of Philip leaving me as a lucky escape now. Come on, Carole's got a new lot of visitors to show round, we'd better leave. Where else shall we go and snoop?'

They waved at Carole, who was busily explaining how the car lift worked to another couple, and headed off *Hildegarde*.

'Do you fancy poking around that one on the end?' Dora asked.

'It's a tug and I think they're mostly engine. I'm rather tired. Let's go back to Miranda and Bill's barge. They promised us cups of tea.'

They actually had a glass of Pimm's. 'Come and rest on your laurels,' said Miranda. 'It's been such hard work, hasn't it? Being nice to people – so exhausting. We'll sit on deck and repel boarders.'

'Mm, lovely idea,' said Jo, flopping down beside her. 'Do you know when the voting happens, all that stuff?'

'Voting!' said Dora. 'What's all that about?'

'We vote for the barge we like best,' explained Miranda, 'which is sometimes connected to the person we like the best.'

'But we don't know when it happens?'

'No, I'm not sure,' said Miranda, pouring lemonade. 'Don't care, really. Oh, I know I should care, but I don't think it's hugely important. What did you think of *Hildegarde*? Amazing, isn't she?' She handed them both glasses and Dora took a seat next to Jo.

Dora closed her eyes and turned her face to the sun. It was so nice being here, she thought, far away from recriminations, arrangements, cancellations and, most of all, guilt. She couldn't abandon the guilt completely, of course. John's heart was still broken, and she had broken it when she realised that while she loved him as a friend, she didn't want him as a husband. She couldn't even pinpoint when the change had happened, she just knew she had to stop the wedding before it was too late. She couldn't be completely at peace. Still, better now than after years of unhappy marriage, with children to think about. She pushed these uncomfortable thoughts to the back of her mind and concentrated on topping up her tan, or more accurately, getting one. Her mother had told her she must look pale to get married, and had kept her out of the sun and under a very high factor sunscreen. Another sort of guilt, this time a pleasurable one, superseded the other. She even felt guilty for not wanting to cry any more. But that, she was sure, was because she'd used up all her tears. She wasn't really shallow and callous, just worn out with weeping.

'Are you asleep or just risking skin cancer?'

A male voice, familiar and jocular, woke her. She blinked up at Tom. 'I don't think you get skin cancer in ten minutes, not in England.'

He shook his head. 'Better not take the chance.'

'Where did you spring from?' she asked.

'Want a Pimm's, Tom?' asked Bill, who had appeared in the same mysterious way.

'Great! Thanks,' said Tom. 'We were in the engine room. Bill's got a bit of a problem I was trying to help him with.'

'I knew I was right not to look at it,' muttered Jo.

'And did you get it fixed?' asked Miranda. She didn't seem greatly concerned, as if sitting around in the sun drinking Pimm's was more her thing than worrying about engines.

'Mm, think so,' said Bill. 'Tom was very useful. Here you are, get that down you.'

Dora felt it would be rude to sleep now there were five

of them and sat up, blinking in the sun, still bleary from her short nap.

'So, what's on tonight?' asked Jo. 'If anything? I might opt for an early night, myself.'

'Nonsense,' said Bill. 'There's a barbecue. Bring food and wine and we all cook together. Miranda brought half a cow from home, so be our guests. You too, Tom.'

'Actually, I might take Dora away from all this, if she'll come,' he said.

Dora sat up straighter. 'What have you got to offer me that's better than half a cow?'

'And a wine lake,' put in Miranda.

'I want to show you my etchings,' said Tom. 'Or rather my gaff.'

'What's a gaff?' asked Dora.

Tom gave her a pitying look over his tumbler of Pimm's. 'It's a slang word for home,' he said.

'Oh!' She flapped at him crossly. 'I knew that. I thought a gaff was some sort of boat or something.'

'So did I,' said Jo.

'Well, it is a sort of rigging,' Tom conceded, 'and my gaff is a boat, but I didn't mean it like that. Come and see.' He drained the last of his Pimm's, took Dora's glass out of her hand and put it down. Then he pulled her to her feet.

'It looks like we're going,' she said apologetically to the company.

'Have a nice time, lovey,' said Jo. 'I know Tom will get you home safely, if late.'

'Oh, Jo! I promise not to be too late and wake you again.' Another reason to feel guilty flooded over her.

'You'll have to come back and eat,' said Miranda. 'You might as well take advantage of the free food.'

'You're not accusing me of being a ligger, are you?' said Tom indignantly.

'Yes,' said Miranda calmly.

Dora decided not to ask what a ligger was, and followed Tom up the ladder and on to the dockside.

Chapter Five

❦

Dora decided she liked Tom. He was very different from John, who was kind and gently funny, but not fun in the way that Tom was. And the joy of Tom was the fact that he was going travelling. In the unlikely event that something did develop between them, the relationship would have a natural end, which made it all the more exciting to be going somewhere with a boy she hadn't known since she was seventeen.

'Give us your hand,' said Tom, and he hauled Dora up the last bit of ladder. 'It's a little way away, is that OK?'

'Cool,' said Dora. She also liked being with Tom. She didn't feel quite so safe as she had with John, who had looked after her, but he was introducing her to new things and hadn't indicated that he wanted anything more than friendship. And that could easily be because there was no one else his age around.

'There are some people off the other boats who'll probably come over.'

'You mean, people who live on the moorings, like Jo?'

Tom laughed. 'No, not like Jo. They're nice, but – well . . .' He hesitated. 'You'll see.'

It was quite a long walk to 'Tom's Gaff'. They went out of the dockside area, with the pub, corner shop and down a road leading to some trees.

'There are some boats tied up on an island,' explained

55

Tom. 'You can't get cars to it, and it's a bit unofficial, but we like it.'

'How do you mean, unofficial?'

'It means they could throw us all off with no notice, but it suits us. Not as handy for work as my official mooring with the boatyard, but worth a bit of inconvenience,' he added, perhaps sensing Dora's horror at the thought of such an insecure life.

'I don't think I could cope with that,' she said, almost to herself.

'You should get out more,' said Tom and Dora laughed. He was right, she should.

In spite of this resolution, she still felt nervous as he led her over a very rickety wooden bridge on to the island. It was covered with tall trees, so much so that there hardly seemed space for the slimy path that led round to the other side, where the boats were. However, it was still only late afternoon and nothing too dreadful could happen – she hoped.

'It's a nature reserve really,' said Tom, 'which is why we're not supposed to be here, but we don't bother the birds.'

'How do you know? Have you asked them?'

Tom nodded. 'Yeah. They were cool.'

Dora bit her lip. It wasn't good for Tom, or indeed any man, to think that their jokes worked all the time.

Tom's boat was not easy to get on to. It was a boat of the type Dora felt should have been made of plastic and floated among the bubble bath. It was small and wide for its length and was draped in old and faded tarpaulin. She regarded it dubiously.

'Here,' said Tom, who had leapt aboard without her noticing how he did it. 'Put your foot on the gunwale. It's that bit there,' – he pointed to the side of the boat – 'and I'll pull you up.'

It took several ungainly efforts. Eventually Dora overcame the restrictions of her jeans and got her foot up high enough. Then Tom heaved her on to the boat in a jumble of arms and legs and a coil of rope that somehow got involved.

'I'm not really designed for boats,' Dora said apologetically once she'd reconnected with her limbs and got to her feet.

'Nonsense, you just need time to adapt. And looser jeans.'

Dora brushed herself down. 'If I'd known I'd be doing acrobatics, I'd have worn my leotard.'

'Oh, have you got one?'

'Of course, red with spangles,' she said, thinking of Jo's top.

'And doesn't it go up the cra— Well, never mind.'

Dora knew perfectly well what he had been going to say but was grateful that he didn't finish his sentence. He seemed aware that she was out of her comfort zone, and while he blatantly intended to stretch those boundaries, he had the sense not to move too fast and cause her to dig her heels in.

'Come in,' he said now and lifted a hatch. The steps down were even steeper and narrower than they were on *The Three Sisters*. Dora dabbed at them with her foot, not knowing if she should turn it in or out.

'Go backwards,' Tom suggested.

When Dora reached the bottom and turned round she saw that the boat seemed to have no furniture, built in or otherwise, and was nearly filled with a futon, several floor cushions and a sleeping bag. It was dingy and there was a distinct odour, a combination of unwashed sleeping bag, mildew and joss sticks. The part of Dora that was her mother inwardly recoiled.

'It's – quite small,' said Dora, hoping her nose hadn't visibly wrinkled.

'I'll open some portholes,' said Tom.'I keep them shut while I'm out because otherwise – oh, too late. I hope you like cats.'

A cat so large it had probably had people reporting sightings of it to the police or the newspapers as 'the Beast of Thames-side' oozed through the porthole and landed at Tom's feet with a thump. Then it opened its mouth and yowled.

'Horrible animal!' said Tom, nevertheless stroking it affectionately behind the ears. 'Has no one fed you?'

'I've never seen such a huge cat. Is it yours?' asked Dora, impressed.

'It isn't anyone's. It lives off us all. Talk about liggers,' he added. 'He's a real scrounger. I think his original owner left but he stayed on.'

'He probably liked living on a bird sanctuary.'

Tom laughed. 'To his credit, I've never seen him with a dead bird. And we all feed him, so what's his incentive to hunt?'

Dora shrugged. 'He's very handsome. What's his name?'

'Fluffy, or the Surveyor.'

'What?'

Tom shrugged. 'A surveyor was doing a survey on a boat once and the cat went down every gap and hole, whenever a plank was lifted, to check out conditions. Fluffy is far too kitsch a name for a cat like that, don't you think? Anyway, enough of this, would you like a drink?' Tom went to the bow of the boat where a two-burner gas stove and tiny sink indicated a galley area.

'Mm. Something soft, please.'

'I'll see what I've got.' He opened a cupboard beneath the sink and rummaged about while Dora stroked the

58

Surveyor in self-defence. He seemed as greedy for affection as he was for food and she felt if she didn't stroke him hard, he might decide she was a tasty snack that Tom had brought home for him.

'Sit down. There must be something here that isn't washing-up liquid,' muttered Tom.

'Are you feeding me or the cat?' Dora overcame her squeamishness and subsided on to a cushion, more because of the limited headroom than anything else. She could only stand up right in the very middle of the boat. Tom had to hunch over even there.

The cat moved on to her knee, spilling over the edges of her lap and on to the cushion, and Dora was beginning to notice the smell less when there was a knock on the top of the boat. Tom was still rummaging in boxes.

'Hello! Are you up for a visit? Or are you naked?' called a husky female voice with a Cockney accent.

'Come in,' yelled Tom, sounding relieved. 'Have you got any soft drinks at yours?'

A young woman came down the steps. She had hennaed hair, black footless tights and a short net skirt. She was very thin and, while not pretty, had a quirky charm, like a subversive fairy.

'Hiya, Tom,' she said as she kissed him. She regarded Dora through slightly narrowed eyes and instantly Dora felt fat and decidedly uncool. 'Who's this?'

'This is Dora. Dora, this is Bib, she lives with her partner on a boat moored at the end of the island. An old pilot cutter.'

Dora smiled and nodded, wondering simultaneously how anyone could be called Bib, and what a pilot cutter was like.

'Hi, Dora,' said Bib, regarding her in a kindly, but rather disinterested way. 'So why do you want soft drinks, then?'

59

'Dora's thirsty,' said Tom with a hint of firmness. 'I've got home-made wine for you.'

Bib stretched and yawned, exposing her very flat stomach. She had a ring in her navel and black-painted fingernails. She curled gracefully on to a cushion. 'I haven't got no soft drinks, sorry. Hamo might have some ginger beer. He likes that stuff. He'll be here later.'

'I'm popular because of the home-made wine,' explained Tom, although Dora didn't believe this was the only reason.

'Did you make it?' Dora looked around her, thinking it would be difficult to make a cup of tea, let alone wine down here.

'No. My mother picks random fruits and berries and then doesn't know what to do with them. When they start to ferment she turns them into wine. My parents can't drink it, it's too disgusting, so they give it to me.'

'Tom's parents wanted him to do law,' said Bib. 'They haven't got their heads round him being a boat boy yet, have they, love?'

'Of course they have,' said Tom. 'They don't like it but they make the best of it.'

Footsteps were heard overhead. 'That'll be Hamo. Hamo!' he roared up the hatch. 'Got any ginger beer, bottled water, anything like that?'

'Nah – Jim might have.'

Jim could have been on another planet and he would still have heard Hamo's call.

Two men came thundering down into the boat. 'Hi, Tom! Oh, company.'

'Dora,' said Tom. 'Dora, this is Jim and Hamo.'

Dora nodded, reluctant to expose her middle-class accent until she had to. Which one was Jim and which Hamo she'd have to pick up as she went along. She shifted

60

along a bit so one of the young men in ripped jeans and a T-shirt could sit next to her. He had tattooed arms, a shaved head and earrings all the way round his ear. The other one had dreadlocks, so once she'd worked out which was which, they would be easy to tell apart. Part of her wanted to go home.

'Sorry,' said Tom eventually, 'no soft drinks.'

'Not even water?' Dora didn't fancy home-made wine. She knew it was likely to be strong and she didn't want to get drunk in unfamiliar and faintly threatening surroundings.

'Make the girl a cup of tea,' said Bib. 'We don't like to drink the water unboiled,' she explained to Dora. 'It comes out of the river.'

Dora swallowed and decided that home-made wine was not such a bad idea. 'I'll have what you're having,' she said, grateful that her mother would never know she'd been here.

A selection of glasses and mugs filled with something the colour and consistency of cough syrup was passed round. Dora was given a glass and decided she was honoured. It had the remains of a cartoon character on the side and had once contained peanut butter.

'So, Dora, you new round here?' said one of the men.

'Yes. I'm staying with a friend on one of the barges. *The Three Sisters*. It's a Klipper.' She looked at Tom.

'They're big, they are,' said the other man.

'So why stay on a barge, Dora?' asked Bib, her eyes narrow and enquiring.

'I'm staying with my best friend's mother. I wanted somewhere near London, so I could look for work.'

'Your best friend's mother? Why not stay with someone your own age?'

Dora couldn't work out if Bib was being hostile, or if it

was her own insecurities that made her think she was. Dora did sound rather prim, even to her own ears. 'I didn't know anyone else near London, and she offered.'

'Cool,' said Bib. 'Cheers!' She raised her glass.

Dora was forced to join in the toast and took the tiniest sip she thought she'd get away with. It made her cough.

'It's OK after the first few sips,' said Bib, watching her.

Dora took a bigger sip. 'So how do you all come to live here?' She guessed that Bib wouldn't leave her alone until she'd asserted herself a little.

'Hamo an' me heard about the island and got the boat towed up. Jim was already here. It's a good community. Safe.'

Instinct told Dora that Bib didn't mean 'safe' in the normal sense but she just nodded.

'That means it's a nice place to live,' said Tom.

'Pass that jug around again, mate,' said the one who Dora thought was probably Jim.

Tom dragged a demi-john from behind him and there was a lull while more wine was slopped into glasses and mugs. Dora's glass was still clutched in her hand.

'So what sort of work are you looking for?' asked Bib, obviously determined to squeeze Dora for every bit of information she could.

'Office work, mainly.'

'So, can you do computers and all that?'

'Yeah,' said Dora and buried her nose in her glass again.

Bib looked around at the group. 'Cool.'

The men started talking about boats: which one was where, and why. Dora looked at the plywood revealed by the gap in the ragged carpet. She wondered why Tom had been so keen to show her his gaff – it wasn't all that marvellous. Maybe if his friends hadn't turned up he'd have told her his plans for it. Now she looked more

62

carefully she noticed some of the planks looked new, and had been fitted very carefully in place. She was a bit surprised he hadn't mentioned his suggestion that she work in the boatyard, but then guessed that he hadn't in case it made her feel awkward. It would have done, and she was grateful for his silence on the subject.

Eventually she began to relax a little. Following the conversation she began to work out who was who and although these men were unlike any she'd ever met, she felt they were good-natured, even if they were people her mother would describe as members of the counter-culture. Bib's initial hostility was probably to do with her being the only woman in the group, and she had to make sure that Dora was no threat. The thought of being a threat to anyone made Dora bite the corner of her lip. She didn't want to be caught smiling at her private thoughts.

Tom sipped his drink. 'Ugh,' he said. 'I'd forgotten how foul it is.'

Jim, with the dreadlocks, reached into his back pocket and produced a tobacco tin, every inch of which was painted. He then produced a packet of papers.

Dora felt her stomach clench. Of course she'd been around people who smoked a bit of dope but she had never fancied it herself. Was she suddenly going to be in a situation where she couldn't refuse without looking incredibly middle-class and snooty?

Tom glanced at her and said, 'You lot stay here if you like, but Dora and I have got to go to a barbecue.'

'Ooh!' said Hamo. 'I've never been to a barbecue,' he simpered. 'Can I come with you?'

'No,' said Tom firmly. 'Come on, Dora.' He took her hand and heaved her to her feet with more strength than courtesy.

'Sorry about that,' said Tom when they were crossing the

bridge back to reality. 'They're really nice people, but I'd forgotten they can be a bit scary to girls like you.'

Dora was indignant, although she knew exactly what he meant. 'What do you mean? I'm a grown-up, you know.'

'But you need to get out more. We've agreed that.'

Dora didn't answer. They'd reached the mainland now and she felt more confident. 'Let's go to the barbecue. That's getting out, isn't it?'

'Not really. I'm not sure I really want to go now.'

'Well, I do need to check in with Jo.'

'Why don't you go and find her and then meet me back here and we can decide? I need to blag a shower off someone.'

Dora was leaning up against the rail of a barge when Tom found her. She had seen Jo and they had both made sure the other was all right, and now she had begun to get bored and was very pleased to see him. He smelt of shower gel and toothpaste and looked slightly damp but very clean. It seemed that his shower had given him extra bounce and enthusiasm.

'Hello,' she said.

'Hello yourself. Listen, why don't we go downriver to this pub I know?'

'Aren't we supposed to be going to a barbecue?'

'Well, yes, but there's only so much of the middle classes I can take.'

Dora smiled at him. 'I'm middle class. And so are you.'

'I know, but I'm trying to get over it.'

'So why did you come to the rally?'

'I thought I might pick up some work on something that actually moves. Now, do you want to come or not?'

Not entirely sure if going with him meant handing in her membership card of the Middle Classes he so much

64

despised, Dora considered. She didn't want to disappoint Tom, and nor did she want him going off without her. It wasn't as if she wanted to go to the barbecue either. 'What's the pub like?'

'Nice.' He took this question as her agreement. 'Listen, I'll just go and ask Bill if I can borrow his tender and he can tell Jo where you're going.'

Dora decided she would go with Tom to the pub. Recently, her resolutely middle-class, middle-England roots had started to bother her. But although she liked Tom, and he was very easygoing, she didn't feel entirely comfortable being alone with him. The trouble was, she'd forgotten – if indeed she'd ever known – how to be with a boy who wasn't John. She didn't want to give out the wrong messages by mistake. John, she considered, had hardly ever been a boy – he was always a young man. Tom would have called him a Young Fogey, she knew. Which would have made her, she supposed, a Young Fogeyette. She shuddered.

'Right,' said Tom, bouncing into view. 'I've got Bill's tender. We're going downriver a bit.'

Dora didn't ask what a tender was, assuming, correctly, that she would find out soon enough.

Tom was very good at rowing. Dora sat back in her seat in the stern and watched him pulling the oars, some-how making the little boat go where he wanted it to, with only the occasional glance over his shoulder for direction. At first Dora felt a bit nervous about being in the middle of a big river in such a tiny craft, but Tom quickly brought it into the side a little, where she felt safer.

'We just had to get out of the current. We're fine here, in the eddies.'

Dora decided she didn't need to know what an eddy was, and thought she'd more or less worked it out anyway.

'So, tell me about this pub. It'll have to be good to make it worth all this exercise.'

Tom grinned. 'I haven't noticed you taking much exercise, madam.'

'Watching you is quite enough for me.' She made a face and hoped it wasn't a smirk.

He laughed and pulled more strongly at the oars, his heels pressed against the stretcher in the bottom of the boat, his thighs taking the strain.

'You'll have to row home again,' she said, as at last he directed the boat into a slipway.

He glanced over his shoulder to see where he was going. 'Oh no, it'll be your turn then.'

'But I've never rowed a boat in my life! We'd capsize or go round and round in circles.'

'That is probably what would happen, but how have you got to be your age and not learnt to row? Now you stay sitting down while I get the boat up.' He leapt ashore and pulled the boat until the stern was ashore. Then he came and helped her out. 'Well?' he said.

Dora, who thought it had been a rhetorical question, put her nose in the air. 'I'm very young and I've led a sheltered life.'

Tom laughed. 'Maybe I should unshelter you. We'll start with getting you a drink you've never had before. Are you OK for sitting outside? It's a lovely evening.'

The pub was crowded and almost all the tables outside were taken but Tom spotted one where the people were just leaving and nipped over to it. 'Right, I'll get us some drinks.'

While he was gone, Dora watched the people around her and then the birds swooping and diving, catching insects. She tried to identify them; they were swallows, swifts or martins, but she could never remember which was which.

66

They reminded her of Tom a bit, swooping and diving on life, apparently at random, yet purposeful.

He put a drink down on a mat in front of her. It was in a half pint glass and was cloudy.

'It looks like an enlarged version of a very dodgy urine sample,' she said. 'What on earth is it?'

'Scrumpy, rough cider. Actually, it's a bit of a tough one to start with.'

Dora took a sip. It tasted of vinegar that might have been apples a very long time ago. 'It's vile.'

'But it's cheap.'

'It's not fair,' said Dora, risking another taste. 'You invite me for a drink and then give me something only fit to clean brass with. Now that's something I know a lot about.'

'What?'

'Cleaning brass. My mother used to make me go and clean it for an old lady when I was a Brownie.'

'How sweet. I can just picture you in a Brownie uniform.'

'I had those culotte things and a yellow baseball cap. My mother used to help out. She made me sew on all my own badges, although the other girls' mothers always did it for them.'

'Was your mother quite strict, then?'

'Depends what you mean by strict.'

'I mean – did she let you bunk off school to go to Glastonbury? Things like that.'

Dora put down her glass so she could react with appropriate horror and disbelief. 'You have got to be joking! My mother wouldn't have let me go to Glastonbury even if it didn't involve bunking off. And she made my dentist appointments during the holidays so I wouldn't miss a second of school. It might have been because I'm an only child, she only had me to focus on.'

'Right, a full-on mother then. I'm an only child too, but

fortunately, my mother was a bit more laid-back. I went to my first festival when I'd done my GCSEs – it was after my exams so Mum was fairly cool with it.'

Dora took time to imagine a mother as relaxed as that. Now she came to think about it, Karen used to go to festivals, but maybe that had been after Dora had started going out with John. She took the tiniest sip of cider she could manage so she couldn't actually taste it; it came a close second to the home-made wine. 'I haven't ever been to a festival. John wasn't into that sort of thing.'

'John?'

She hadn't meant to mention John, but as he was largely responsible for how she'd spent the most recent part of her life, he had been bound to crop up. 'Ex-everything. We went out for ever, were engaged. Not any more.'

'So, are you suffering from a broken heart?' he asked with a lightheartedness that took away any embarrassment Dora might feel.

She shook her head, laughing at his directness. 'Certainly not. Look, would you mind if I didn't drink that? It really is foul.'

'I'll get you something else.'

'No, it's my turn. Here – here's my purse. Take it and get us both drinks.'

Tom ignored her outstretched hand. 'Dora, have you ever bought a drink in a pub before?'

Dora felt herself blush. 'Yes, of course, but not in London.'

'I don't think this counts as London.'

'It has a tube station, which in my book means it's in London. Now, do you want a drink or not?'

'Tell you what, if you come up to the bar with me, I'll pay, and you can have what you really like – a gin and tonic or something. Or a shooter. They do tequila slammers.'

Dora had it in her mind that to drink a tequila slammer, you had to slam the glass down on the table and catch the tequila in your mouth as it flew upwards, but she didn't think she wanted to share this with Tom just now. She'd revealed quite enough naivety already. 'Fine, what are you having?'

'A pint. The Tangleberry – it's the one at the end. Here, take some money.'

'It's my round,' said Dora and got up before she could think better of it.

She'd told Tom that she'd bought drinks before, but actually she hadn't very often, and when she had, it had been in the local she'd been going to since she first pretended to be of drinking age. She wasn't that innocent, she argued as she edged her way through the crowd to the bar, but there were many more things she hadn't done than rowed a boat and bought a drink.

It was a lot easier than she'd feared. The barmaid spotted her straightaway, she didn't have fifteen men pushing in when it was her turn, and no one looked remotely surprised to see her. It was a bit of an anticlimax, really.

She came back, carrying his pint and her own half of lager carefully through the crowd. As a stroke of independence, she'd bought a couple of packets of crisps too.

'Really, Dora,' said Tom, 'is that all you can think of to have? How am I going to get you pissed if you only drink lager?'

'I should tell you, Tom, there's no point in you getting me pissed. I'm really not up for anything apart from a jolly night out. As friends.'

Tom grinned. 'Fair enough. If we're friends, we should play a game. What about Truth or Dare?'

Dora nearly spluttered into her drink, something she seemed to have done a lot of that evening. 'No!'

'Oh, go on. I've been thinking and I just reckon you should do a few dares.'

'What sort of dares?' Dora had always faintly despised herself for being so law-abiding, and wondered if it was too late to change.

'I don't know – dares that would make you braver and feel better about yourself.'

'What, now?'

Tom became thoughtful. 'Actually, I was thinking we should do it over the next few months, before I go travelling.'

'Do what? Your dares?'

He nodded. 'I wouldn't ask you to do anything I wouldn't do myself – or hadn't done – but for instance, I could dare you to go and camp at a festival.'

'Well, of course I'd do that. I'd probably take something to make sure I didn't have to go to the loo for the entire time, but I'd certainly dare.' She laughed merrily, hoping to give the impression that she'd find this so unchallenging it was hardly worth asking her to do it. She pictured herself wallowing around in mud up to her armpits wearing bin liners and getting trench foot.

Tom regarded her speculatively, and it made Dora feel uneasy. Possibly he'd read her thoughts. 'Tell you what,' he said, 'I bet you wouldn't do five things that I dare you to do.'

'I said I'd go to a festival!'

'OK, that would be one thing, but there'd be four others. Bet you won't agree.'

'Well, what are the four things?'

'I'm not going to tell you. I haven't thought them all up yet.'

'But you can't expect me to agree to things when I don't know what they are!'

'That's where you have to be brave and trust me. You have to undertake the five tasks.'

In spite of her common sense and her conditioning, Dora felt intrigued. 'But why should I?'

'For the reward.'

'What's the reward?'

Tom threw up his hands, laughing. 'Questions, questions – I don't know yet! I'll have to think of something.'

'Well, I'm not doing anything if I don't know what the prize is.'

'You're just a scaredy-cat. Miss Half-a-Lager-and-a-Packet-of-Crisps.'

'No I'm not!'

'You are!'

'Oh, go and buy me a shooter, then. I'll prove to you I'm not a scaredy-cat.' Miss Tequila-Slammer did sound a lot better than what he'd just called her.

'You can have the most expensive drink on the menu, and bearing in mind I'm a poor working boy that's quite an offer. But you have to agree to my challenge.'

'OK, Poor Working Tom, I'll take you up on that. But the prize had better be worth it!' She started to giggle, partly from nerves.

Tom picked up her mood and laughed too. 'Oh, it definitely will be. Now you've got to drink a margarita.'

'Is that one of the dares?'

'No! Way too easy, but it's nice. More crisps?'

'No thank you. I'm trying to give them up.'

'Tell me something you've never done that you think you ought to do,' Tom said as he came back with two margaritas, a lager and another pint of beer – to keep them going.

71

'I don't see why I should help you,' she grumbled. The margarita was a definite improvement on the scrumpy.

'You're helping yourself, really. Well?'

Dora thought and realised there were so many things. 'I've never flown on my own. I've never eaten in a restaurant on my own. I have been to the library on my own, but not the movies. You've got loads to choose from. This is way too easy for you.'

They went on teasing each other until the time came for another drink. Tom turned out his pockets and his wallet and came up with a voucher for a Happy Meal and fifty-seven pence.

'I'll have a look at what I've got,' said Dora. She delved into her bag and came across the letter from her father. She still hadn't opened it.

'What's that?' asked Tom while she looked at it as if it might bite.

'A letter from my dad. I haven't had the courage to open it yet.'

'Why on earth not?'

'It'll be full of reproaches. I know it.'

'Come on, open it. You're pissed, you can roll with the punches.'

'OK. Oh,' she said as she drew two slips of shiny cardboard and a letter out of the envelope. She peered at them. 'It's two invitations to a race meeting at Cheltenham.'

'What's the letter say?'

'*Darling, thought you might find a use for these. Mummy and I can't go. Enjoy! Love, Dad.*'

'Ah,' said Tom, and Dora couldn't tell if he genuinely thought it was sweet, or was mocking her for calling her mother Mummy.

'We could go! Could you get time off work?'

'Should think so. I hardly ever take time off.'

'Or should I ask Jo? She might have a friend she'd like to take.'

'No. Your dad wants you to go. And me, obviously,' he added, mischievously.

Dora giggled. 'Of course. When is it? Yikes! It's the day after tomorrow.'

'I don't think I know anyone else who'd say "yikes",' said Tom.

'You see, I'm broadening your horizons.'

'And I'm going to broaden yours. You'll have to place all the bets for us.'

Dora pretended to prevaricate. 'I'm not sure I should go. It's such short notice.'

'Dora! We're going. And you're taking my bet and placing the bets.'

'Is that one of my tasks?' She drained her lager, feeling that Tom's tasks were going to be easier than she thought.

'Not sure. It's no good if you're not really challenged.'

'And you expect me to do all this without knowing what my reward is?'

He nodded. 'It'll be worth it. Trust me.'

'That's such a gamble and I'm not sure I approve of gambling. I don't really know you.'

'Life's all about gambling, Dora, and if you don't do it, it'll pass you by.'

Dora was silent for a moment and then said, 'You're quite the philosopher, aren't you?'

'Not really, but I can come out with the pop psychology when I have to.'

'And the pop festival, presumably.'

'There are loads on during the summer, but there's one I really want to go to. I'll see if I can get tickets.'

'Triffic.' She hoped her smile didn't look too false. She

shivered, it was getting cooler. 'Shall we go home now?'

'If you've promised you'll do my dares. Five Dares for Dora. It sounds like the title of a school story.'

'I hadn't got you down for an Enid Blyton fan.'

'When you agree, I'll take you home. Otherwise, I'll make you row.'

'OK then, I give in. To be honest, though, I'm not sure I can walk straight, let alone row.'

They were in the boat and making good time when Tom said, 'Actually, rowing home's a piece of piss. We're with the current all the way.'

Chapter Six

Jo tipped her paper plate covered with chop bones and steak scraps into a black plastic bag. Then she found her plastic mug of red wine and was going back to where Miranda and Bill were sitting when she spotted Carole, from *Hildegarde*. She was on her own so Jo went up to her.

'Hello. Do you know many people here?'

'A few.' Carole regarded Jo as if she didn't want to be taken pity on by a fifty-year-old woman. A fifty-year-old man would have been quite different.

'Is Marcus here?' Jo was aware that Carole didn't want to talk to her but was determined to get some sort of conversation out of her, just for the challenge. She was also a bit curious to meet her old acquaintance after all these years.

'Oh no. He's on the Continent, on a job.'

'What kind of job?'

It had seemed a reasonable question but Carole looked at Jo with incredulity. 'He's delivering a yacht. It's what he does. Don't you know that?'

Only slightly tempted to tell Carole that she had known Marcus before she was born Jo said, 'No.'

Carole made a disbelieving gesture. 'But he's famous in the barge world. He delivers everyone's boats. He's in Monte Carlo at the moment.'

'On a barge?' A picture of *The Three Sisters'* broad and sweeping lines in such an exotic setting made Jo smile.

'No – what Marcus calls a gin palace.'

'Ah. It's a shame you couldn't be with him.'

An expression crossed Carole's face indicating that perhaps there'd been a discussion about her being with him and that the answer had been no. She shook her head. 'I have to look after *Hildegarde*. At least, during the rally.'

A man wearing a yachting cap came up. 'Hi there, Carole.' He kissed her firmly on the cheek and put his arm round her waist. 'Where's Marcus these days then? He never answers his phone when I ring him.'

'He's in Monte Carlo. I was just telling this lady. He's very busy.'

'Oh, I know he's busy,' said the man, not looking at Jo. 'But I need him. I've got to get *Lucretia* down to Faversham for some cosmetic work.'

'Couldn't you put her in a taxi?' said Jo quietly.

Carole looked at her in horror and confusion while Miranda, who had joined the group, chuckled.

'Sorry,' said Jo, 'is Lucretia not your wife?'

The man finally acknowledged Jo's existence. He looked at her for a few seconds while he worked out what she'd said, and then laughed. 'No, she's my barge, but that's quite a good joke.'

'He'll be turning it into one of his own any minute,' muttered Miranda in Jo's ear. 'You wait.'

The group seemed to enlarge, everyone asking or talking about Marcus. 'Of course, he's expensive,' said a man who seemed to be a friend of Mr Yachting-Cap, 'but he's the best. If you've got three hundred grand's worth of vessel to move from A to B, you don't want to make mistakes.'

Jo gasped and then said, 'Surely if you own a barge, you want to drive it yourself? I don't mean I would want to, I'm only renting. But if I'd bought one . . .' Her voice tailed away.

76

Only one of the group agreed with her. 'Me too. I wouldn't pay an arrogant sod like Marcus to take my boat about.'

So he was an arrogant sod, was he? Well, he'd had that potential, even back then, thought Jo, although she noticed Carole hadn't even blinked at the man's caustic remark.

'It's all right for you,' said Mr Yachting-Cap, who was squeezing Carole without apparently knowing he was doing it, 'you're a Navy type.'

'Nothing to do with that. I just like to paddle my own canoe, or steer my own barge, whichever applies.' He smiled at Jo and Miranda, who realised she knew him.

'Bruce! I didn't see you arrive! How lovely to see you!' Miranda said excitedly. 'Is Angela with you?'

'She's sorting her mother out. I didn't bring *William* – that's my barge,' he said to Jo, quickly.

'So you see, you're not so hot as all that,' said Mr Three-Hundred-Thousand-Pound's-worth-of-Barge.

'She's in France at the moment and we're only here on a flying visit,' said Bruce. 'We've got a very nice mooring on the Canal du Midi.'

Jo felt suddenly tired but realised she was actually bored of all this boat talk.

Miranda, probably feeling the same, said, 'Bruce, come and say hello to Bill. He'll be furious if you and he don't have an opportunity to chew the fat. Come on, Jo.' Expertly, Miranda gathered her chosen people and led them away from the group.

'God, I hate Sebastian,' she said. 'Just because he's a multi-millionaire he thinks he's God's gift to women. He'd sleep with anyone.'

Not me, thought Jo. He showed no interest in me whatsoever. It was galling, she decided, to be spurned by someone who'd sleep with anyone, even if she wouldn't have slept with him if he were the last man between her and childlessness.

Later that night, Jo heard Dora come in and settled down to sleep. Her mind was whirling: while she was not exactly sure of her new vocation she felt she had lots of possibilities and it was just a matter of finding her favourite. She and Miranda had discussed the subject once again when they had retired to *Hepplewhite* with Bill and Bruce for a nightcap. Miranda had been full of ideas, from her training to teach English as a foreign language to becoming a matron at a boys' prep school, 'and end up marrying Mr Chips'. Jo had protested that she wasn't young or pretty enough and even if she had been, she didn't want a husband, but as she did like mothering people, the idea had some merit. Her last thought before she fell asleep had been that cherub-restorer did have a nice ring to it.

The following morning over breakfast Dora told Jo about her evening with Tom and their planned day at the races.

'The races! That sounds such fun!' said Jo.

'You wouldn't have wanted to go, would you? I've said I'll take Tom now.'

'Of course, take Tom. Honestly, Dora, the thought of just pottering around by myself for the day after all this sociability is just bliss. You go and jolly well enjoy yourselves.'

'I should be job-hunting, really, not "gadding about" as my mother would call it.'

'Your sense of duty is too strong and your father did send you the tickets, you have to go.' Jo patted Dora's hand. 'If it will make you any happier, you could look up the addresses of some job agencies on the Internet today and then you can go and visit them after the races.

Assuming, that is, that you don't win your fortune and never need to work again.'

Dora smiled. 'I am quite tempted by the boatyard idea, actually, but I can't help feeling it's a bit of a cop-out. I think I need to look at all my options.'

'Well, have a look round in London and then you will have done your duty in that direction, too.'

They spent the day sorting themselves out and generally recharging their batteries.

'Well, this is fun,' said Dora, looking at Tom as they sat opposite each other on the train the next day. He was looking strange in a borrowed suit and shoes that were too big for him.

'It's all right for you, your clothes are your own.'

'Only some of them! The skirt and little top are mine, but the jacket is Jo's. It is a bit big, but I quite like the drapey look myself.'

Tom grinned. 'You look great. And thank you for paying for my train ticket.'

'Well, thank you for coming with me. I probably should have taken Jo, of course, but she said she wanted some time to herself.' Although Jo had been very convincing, Dora did actually suspect that she'd just wanted Dora to spend some time with someone her own age. 'A day out will do you good,' she had said, and had heaped much praise on Dora's dad for sending her the tickets, especially when they realised they included eating in a corporate tent.

They enjoyed their train journey. It was easy to spot fellow race-goers, although this wasn't a specially laid-on train.

There was a party of women in diaphanous summer frocks and hats, sharing bottles of champagne to get them in the mood. There was a foursome of businessmen, going to meet important shareholders, hoping to soften them up for more major investment. And there were couples who hadn't been to the races before, and, like Dora and Tom, were not sure what to expect.

They discovered all this quite easily. The women and the businessmen were in the same carriage and the couples were spotted as first Tom and then Dora went to the buffet car for coffee and a 'nose', as Tom put it. One of the things Dora discovered about Tom that she really appreciated was his fondness for people-watching. She loved it herself, but John had always got annoyed if he'd taken her out for a meal and she hadn't given him her undivided attention. Often Dora was more interested in the conversation going on behind her. Settling back into her seat for a bit of a rest, Dora realised that was another reason it was as well she and John had split up.

There was a bus waiting for the train that took them through the leafy streets of Cheltenham to the racecourse. By this time there was a feeling of camaraderie between the people who had all come by train and Dora and Tom had got used to being thought of as a couple. As long as we know we're not one, thought Dora, it's OK.

'I've just thought of another dare for you,' said Tom as they walked through the ticket gate.

'Already? Can't it be one dare a day? I've already agreed to put the bets on. Not that we can really afford it.'

'I'm afraid I've decided that putting bets on here is just too easy for it to count as a dare. No, what you've got to do now is to get us a really good tip.'

'Sorry?' Dora stared at him, not entirely convinced she understood.

'You've got to find some grizzled old jockey and ask him if he's got any tips. It doesn't have to be a jockey, of course, a shiny-suited tipster would be fine, as long as you think you can trust him.'

'Tom—'

'Listen, Dora, we're at the races. It'll be much more fun watching if we've got a little interest in them, but as you said, we haven't got much money, which means we can't afford to waste it. You must find out which horse has got the best chance in which race.'

'That's really tough.'

'You know perfectly well I'd do it. You're jolly lucky I'm not asking you to find a sugar daddy to actually give you money to bet with.'

Dora gulped at the thought. 'OK, but let's have a good look round everywhere first and get our bearings. There are lots of retail opportunities too – we can look, even if we can't spend.'

Dora waited until they'd had a drink before she set off on her mission. Tom would wait for her somewhere back in the drinks tent. She left him quite happily reading the paper, a pint in front of him. She wasn't a great one for talking to strangers, unlike Karen who had once just asked a man for five pence to get a car park ticket without even offering him the pennies in return. Karen would have found it easy to find the right sort of man to give them a winning tip. Dora was much less confident and had been happy to trot along behind Karen while she did all the brave stuff.

However, now she was on her own with her challenge she did feel curiously elated. After all, she didn't absolutely have to do it, if she really didn't want to, but she found she did want to.

She went first to the Tote but she didn't think there were any real gamblers there. She wanted a dyed-in-the-wool professional, someone who earned his living from his wits, who knew how to pick a horse without sticking a pin in a list or because they liked the name. She went outside, to where the bookies called out the odds, did tick-tack over their heads and offered complicated bets there didn't seem a hope of winning. They were a colourful crowd. Dora spotted the businessmen from the train. They had a couple of anxious-looking men in pale grey suits and obviously new trilby hats with them. Dora guessed that they weren't English and this was their first time on a racecourse.

Dora didn't think she'd find her tipster here. There were too many people making too much noise. She went to look for the horses.

She had never been horsey as a child. They were too big and slippery to her mind, and her mother hadn't encouraged her. It was, after all, a very expensive hobby. However, she had always appreciated the animals from an aesthetic point of view.

The saddling enclosure was filling up with horses for the first race. It was too late for that race, Dora decided, partly because she wanted not just a tip for Tom's challenge, but a winning tip – for her own satisfaction.

She watched the horses being led round the ring, mostly by girls, but also by the occasional young man who seemed to be wearing clothes too old for him – the ubiquitous trilby and tweed jacket, or shiny suit.

She was admiring a dark bay horse being led by a girl who looked too slight for the job when she spotted a man on the opposite side of the ring. He was looking at the horses with a knowing eye and made notes on his racecard from time to time.

She edged round so she was standing near him. She wasn't certain yet that he was her man. She wanted to check him out a bit more first.

Fortunately for her dubious abilities as a spy, another man came up to her quarry and started talking to him. When he opened his mouth he revealed himself to be Irish. Dora knew it was probably a stereotype but she had always believed that the Irish could pick a good horse when they saw one, especially if they were at a racecourse.

She couldn't get much information from their conversation because it seemed to be about someone they both knew who'd fallen off a horse and was now in plaster 'from his toes to his tush'.

Having decided to ask these two men what they thought of the next race, which horse was likely to finish and which would still be running by teatime, she just had to think up what to say. Eventually she took a deep breath, put on her bravest, most Karen-like smile and went up to them.

'Good afternoon, I'm so sorry to bother you but I need your advice.'

Both men stopped talking and looked at her. She couldn't really tell what they thought of her but as they smiled politely and didn't run off in the opposite direction she valiantly ploughed on.

'The thing is, I've a wager to carry out.'

'Oh yes?' one of them asked.

'My friend bet me I couldn't pick a winner for the next race – not this one, I know I'll be too late – and I really need some help.' Another Karen-like smile caused them to smile back with just the right hint of indulgence. Dora didn't care if she was patronised if they gave her the information she needed; after all, she didn't know one end of a horse from another, they had every right to talk down to her.

'Well, my dear, were you hoping for a horse to win or an each-way bet?' said the man she had spotted first.

'I'm sorry, you're going to think I'm awfully ignorant, but what's an each-way bet?'

'It's a place – first, second or third. You have to put on twice the stake, but your chances are better,' said the other man.

'Um – I think an each-way bet. My friend didn't specify.'

'What sort of a friend would make you do something like that when you don't know much about it?'

Dora smiled. 'A friend who's hoping I won't do it,' she said, although she knew this was a bit of a slur on Tom, who probably did want her to achieve the goals he set for her.

'Right now, let's have a ponder,' said the first man, getting out his card. 'What do you think, Jerry?'

Jerry got his card out too. 'You don't think we'd better discuss this over a drink? Will you have a drop of something with us, my dear?'

Dora hesitated. There was no way going for a drink with two strange Irishmen was part of the bet.

'C'mon now, if your friend is happy to let you run around the racecourse picking up tips, he can't object to you having a quick one while you're doing it,' said the one who wasn't Jerry. He put his hand into Dora's. 'My name's Gene.'

'I'm . . . Dora.'

'You don't sound too certain of that, Dora. Are you sure you're not called Dorothy or something instead?'

She laughed. 'Oh, I know I'm Dora, I'm just not sure if I should go for a drink with two men I've never met before in my life.'

'If you don't mind my saying so, Dora,' said Jerry, 'you did pick us up. It was not the other way around. If we're prepared to trust you, I think you should trust us.

'Now, we'll go to that bar over there. You'll be surrounded by hundreds of people so don't worry. Then we can study the form and win you some money.'

84

Dora weighed up the odds and decided going for a drink in a public place was indeed fairly safe.

'So, tell us, Dora, do you come to the races often?' said Gene.

'I've never been before. My father sent me tickets. He and my mother were invited to some corporate entertainment thing and couldn't go, so my friend and I came instead.'

'So, what will you have to drink?' shouted Jerry when they reached the bar, which was so noisy Dora was surprised he could hear her answer which was, to her shame, 'Half a lager.'

'Not at all,' said Gene. 'Have a wee whiskey. It'll do you no harm at all.'

As it was too noisy a place to have a proper argument, Dora accepted meekly.

They found a corner that was a bit quieter, and the three of them nursed their drinks while Gene and Jerry studied their racecards, and then their copies of the *Racing Post*.

'We've missed the first race, but we can do something with the others,' said Gene.

'I like the look of Jordan River, myself,' said Jerry.

'Let's not have any of your deviant fantasies,' said Gene. 'We all know Jordan River is not half as good as she looks. What about Swiss Chalet, now?'

Dora tuned out, sipping her whiskey, which was neat and quite large. She felt so reckless, drinking strong drink with men she didn't know while they picked a horse for her. It was a good feeling. Tom would be proud of her.

'Well, my dear,' Jerry said after what seemed like an age. 'How much of a gambler are you?'

'And you don't have a lot of time to make up your mind,' added Gene.

*

It was over an hour before Dora found Tom again. He was sitting surrounded by the women who'd been on the train, and was decidedly anxious.

'What happened to you?' said one of the women.

'Tom here thought you'd been kidnapped,' said another, waving a bottle of champagne at her.

'Have a drink,' said a third.

'I don't think I should,' said Dora, feeling her whiskey, rather. 'I'm sorry to have worried you, Tom. But I did my dare! Now, did you see who won the second race?'

'No,' he said. 'At least, I can't remember who won. Why? Did you have money on it?'

'In a manner of speaking. Did I miss the finger buffet?' Dora realised she was hungry and felt she ought to have something to sop up the whiskey anyway.

'Oh no, it's all in there,' said one of the women. 'We left you the fish-paste sandwiches.'

'That was crab pâté,' said her friend, who was now, for some reason, wearing a cowgirl hat. She must have seen Dora looking at it. 'We're on my hen do,' she explained. 'The hat's obligatory.'

'Hen do's were not like this the first time I got married,' said one of her number, who was cheerful and Scottish. 'We just got plastered in the pub and tried to pull the barmen.'

'Just because you didn't have a hen do the second time you got married, you mustn't rain on my parade.'

Dora remembered that she and Karen had been going to spend a day at a health spa for her hen do, but she'd cancelled the wedding before they could go. She brushed that thought hurriedly aside.

'I've nothing against hen dos, hen,' said the Scottish woman confusingly, 'it's just if you're a hen when you're a chick, by now we must be old boilers.'

The others hooted with laughter.

'Enough with the poultry, let's have another drink!' shouted the Chief Hen.

Tom took Dora by the arm and led her out of earshot. 'What happened to you?' he repeated.

'Well, like you said, I found someone to give us a tip. Only there were two of them and they took me for a drink first.'

'Dora! You shouldn't go for drinks with strange men! Did your mother teach you nothing?'

'I'm trying to shrug off the shackles of what my mother taught me, and you're helping me. You told me I needed to be more adventurous . . .'

'You know what I mean. Anyway, how much money did you put on?'

Dora felt it wasn't the right moment to tell Tom that she'd had to visit a cashpoint machine before she could go to the betting office. 'Oh, nothing to worry about. Tell me how the food thing works? I'm starving.'

'The girls told me you just have to show your ticket once and then turn up as and when.'

'The girls, Tom? That's not very politically correct.'

'Oh no, they're definitely girls. They referred to themselves as that. After all, they're on a hen do.'

Dora laughed and headed towards the food tent.

'So, are you hungry?' Tom asked as they showed their tickets. 'Or did your tipsters feed you as well as fill you with strong drink?'

'How do you know it was strong drink?'

'I can smell it.'

'Oh, sorry. I'd better eat something, but we must be quick. It's almost time for the next race.'

Tom couldn't understand why Dora got more excited and

yet more anxious as each race was run. At the end of the last race she shouted herself hoarse.

'You've really got into this, Dora. I'm surprised.'

'Don't distract me,' she yelled at him. 'If I lose concentration he won't win!'

'Who won't win?'

'Our horse!'

'So is this the race you put the bet on?'

'Yes. And no. And all the others.'

'What?'

'I'll explain later. Come on, Jim Boy!' she yelled, jumping up and down.

'It's an accumulator,' said an Irish voice in Tom's ear. 'If this one comes home, your girlfriend's won you over a hundred pounds.'

'Cool,' said Tom. 'Come on, Jim Boy!'

They fell into *The Three Sisters* that evening just as Jo was contemplating making herself a sandwich.

'It was fantastic,' said Dora, kissing her cheek, aware that she was a bit drunk.

'Really cool,' agreed Tom. 'Dora won us loadsa money.'

'How did you do that?'

'She chatted up these two Irishmen and they worked out an accumulator for her.'

'That sounds very brave, Dora! Good for you.'

'Oh, it was one of my dares.' Seeing Jo's blank expression, she went on, 'Tom is determined to turn me into a brave new woman. He's got five dares for me and I have to do them all. Then he'll give me a diamond tiara as a reward.'

'In your dreams, sweetheart,' said Tom. 'I'll give you something as yet unspecified.'

'You said that very well,' said Dora. 'Not sure I'd

attempt a word like – like "unspecified" in my condition. Oh, that came out OK.'

'We had a few drinks on the train coming home, to celebrate,' Tom explained confidentially.

'I think I'd worked that out,' said Jo, amused at their high spirits.

'And the fish and chips are on me!' said Dora, producing a plastic carrier and dumping it on the counter.

Chapter Seven

The following day Dora felt rather flat. 'I had such a lovely time and now I've got to face real life and go job-hunting.' She looked without enthusiasm at the list of agencies she had printed off the previous day. They had both woken up early.

'You could just take the job at the boatyard,' said Jo, who was wondering how to set about repairing plaster cherubs, wishing she could just use butter cream. She'd spent yesterday pottering about, quite enjoying the peace and quiet, emailing Karen and contemplating her future, a little more optimistically, she realised, since her chats with Miranda.

'I know,' said Dora, 'but I feel I should look elsewhere first. I might not want the job when I know more about it and my reason for coming to live with you – or at least the one I'm telling everybody – is because I wanted a job in London.'

'Tell you what, why don't I come up to town with you? I've got to buy some materials anyway. When we've both done our chores we can have lunch somewhere. I could do with a day out myself. The trouble with having a lovely time is you can feel quite down afterwards.' She sensed that Dora's day at the races had had this effect on her.

'I could perfectly well go on my own . . .'

'Of course! But I want to come with you.' Jo laughed.

'And perhaps I don't want to go all the way up to London without a minder.'

Dora giggled. 'OK.'

'Make a couple of appointments, then. It'll give us something to work round.'

After Dora had made her calls they disappeared to their separate cabins to get ready. Jo was horribly aware that she didn't have any clothes remotely smart enough to go to London in, and then remembered that it was Dora who needed to look smart. She could look 'arty'. She added another string of beads and put on some earrings in the form of parrots and then went back to the saloon while she waited for Dora.

Dora was wearing linen trousers and a fitted black T-shirt. 'Do I look all right? It's been ages since I was last at an interview.'

'What did you wear then?'

'A navy-blue suit. My mother bought it for me.'

'Did you bring it with you?'

'No. Apart from what I wore yesterday, which definitely needs washing, this is the smartest outfit I've got.'

'Then you look fine. After all, it's only an initial consultation, you're not going for an interview at an embassy. You look pretty and tidy, and casual. Fine.' Jo sensed that Dora was nervous about having to sell her skills to strangers and although she personally would have added a jacket or something, to make herself look a little more businesslike, she wasn't in her twenties. Dora was. It was right that she should look youthful.

'You're right. But if I'd thought, I'd have kept my best clothes for today and not wasted them on going to the races.'

'You had fun though.'

'Yes I did, and doing Tom's first dare gave me confidence. Let's hope it lasts all day!'

They sat on the train opposite each other. Dora looked out of the window at the suburban gardens they went past, each one different, some immaculate showpieces, others a place to dump old bikes, leaking paddling pools and rusty barbecues.

'I love train travel,' she said, 'when I'm not weighed down with stuff, and not sure where I'm going.'

'So do I,' agreed Jo.

'So we could both end up as happy commuters,' Dora said.

'Mm. Not sure I'd like to actually commute. But I love days out.' Jo burrowed in a faded straw bag and produced an *A–Z*. 'Let's work out where we want to go. What are the addresses of the agencies?'

Dora handed over the sheet. Anxiety bubbled up and then subsided. Yesterday, after she'd accomplished her first challenge so spectacularly, she'd felt full of confidence. Maybe when she'd done all five dares the confidence would last a bit longer.

'All fairly central,' Jo said. 'Have you got appointments at all three?'

'Only one. The other two said just swing by. Where do you want to go?'

'Miranda told me there's a little shop near the British Museum that sells artists' materials. We'll only be a few tube stops away from each other. You phone me when you're done and we'll find somewhere nice for lunch.'

'Mm, that sounds lovely. Like having treats after going to the dentist.'

'Exactly,' said Jo. 'I always give myself treats when I've been to the dentist, doctor, or anything like that. We could take in Selfridges later if we're feeling strong.'

'And spray ourselves with scent? Bliss! This is going to be such fun.'

Jo remembered similar trips in the past when she and Karen would come up to London for the day and try on make-up and clothes; she did miss her daughter although Dora was a good surrogate.

Dora didn't find it much fun when she was seated in front of a computer and made to do a typing test. She was a very fast typist, she knew she was, but somehow the presence of a very tanned woman with aggressive highlights made her fingers slippery and her mind go all over the place.

She'd gone to the agency where she had an appointment, feeling she could 'swing by' better if she'd got one under her belt. She should have told Tom she hadn't been to an agency before and persuaded him it would have been a good dare. Now she was suffering the tortures of the damned and no nearer to Tom's as yet unnamed reward.

The trouble was, she had a very short CV, having only had one job, and her qualifications didn't include a degree. It seemed something of the sort was required for high-powered personal assistants these days.

She knew she was dressed all wrong the moment she got through the door and cursed herself yet again for wearing the only clothes suitable for an interview yesterday.

First of all it had been the aggressive air conditioning that hit her. It was a sunny day, but not that warm. She'd been fine in the sunshine but the office felt like a fridge the moment she walked in. The girl behind the desk was wearing a silk vest top and had stringy arms. She had rather wide blonde streaks in her choppy hairstyle and apparently had a season ticket at her local tanning salon. She obviously didn't feel the cold.

'Yes?' Her glance took in Dora's not-quite-right clothes

and lack of confidence immediately, and did nothing to make Dora feel better.

'I have an appointment. I rang earlier. It's for ten-thirty,' she added.

'Name?'

Dora gave her name, just managing not to say, 'Yes, I have got one,' instead.

'Right, I'm Charlene. Give us your CV. Oh, you'd better sit down.'

Dora sat, thinking that this woman needed to brush up on her people skills quite badly.

Charlene glanced at Dora's CV for a second before saying, 'You'd better do a typing test. Go to that computer over there. Here's the test.' She pulled a sheet of paper out of her drawer without looking at it.

Dora went over to the computer and realised instantly that it wasn't a program she was used to. Keep calm, she told herself, it'll be easy really. Computer programs aren't designed to catch people out in tests, they're designed to help. Although she told herself this with all the conviction she could manage, in her heart she knew that this particular program, on this particular computer, was in fact a massive trap. She dried her hands on her trousers, no longer considering the air conditioning too vicious.

Eventually she worked out how to bring up a new file.

'You ready?' called Charlene.

'Yes,' squeaked Dora.

Charlene clicked her stopwatch. 'OK, go for it.'

Dora went slowly for accuracy and tried to concentrate but kept getting distracted by the abysmal English of the letter she was typing. She yearned to cut out the tautologies and bad punctuation but thought she'd better not. She had taken over all the letter-writing where she used to work about a week after she started. Grammar and punctuation were among her few skills, which, she realised, were not abilities likely to set the world on fire.

Charlene clicked her stopwatch again and once Dora had printed out her test and handed it to her, she cast a perfectly made-up eye over the sheet.

'Right,' she said, tossing the test on to a pile of papers and not bothering to tell Dora how she had done. 'So what sort of work are you looking for?'

Dora was tempted to say, 'In a small estate agent's office where I'll know what I'm doing,' but thought the blonde would look down her ski-jump nose at her if she did. 'As you will have seen from my CV my experience is all with estate agents—'

'One estate agent, in fact.'

'Yes, so that would be my first choice, but I'm open to suggestion.' She smiled, hoping Charlene would smile back.

Maybe a recent Botox injection made this impossible because Charlene just drummed her talons on the desk while she stared at Dora. Dora wondered if she'd applied correction fluid to her nails while she was bored but realised that it was more likely she'd spent a lot of money making them look so square, the ends flaring out like white-tipped spades. 'Well, we've got nothing like that on our books at the moment. The trouble is, your experience is very limited, isn't it? You stuck in the first job you were offered. You didn't even have a Saturday job anywhere.'

Dora wanted to say that it wasn't her fault she wasn't allowed a Saturday job because 'her school work was too important', and also that it wasn't the first job she was offered at all, that people all over town had been begging for her to join them but it wasn't true. 'I liked my job. I was good at it.'

'So why did you leave?'

No way was she going to unburden herself to this woman. 'I said. I wanted something in London, a bit more – challenging. After all, you can't stay in the same job all your life, can you?'

Charlene couldn't disagree with this. 'I have to warn you that you've shown a lack of ambition by staying at the same place for so long. London businesses don't work in the same way as sleepy little village offices do.'

'Don't they? I would have thought—'

'So we may not be able to offer you anything on the same level.'

'Well, naturally, I would expect to work my—'

'We do have a lot of vacancies in retail,' Charlene cut her off. 'Would you consider shop work at all?'

Dora pondered this. She and Karen had loved playing shops but she suspected that she wouldn't be put behind the counter of a friendly deli, or somewhere fun to work, but instead she would be made to sell vastly expensive underwear, which no one really wanted and certainly didn't need. 'No,' she said firmly.

'Fair enough. Bar work?'

'No, not unless it was very near where I live.'

'Where is it you live again? Ah yes, hmm . . . that's quite far out. You're going to have to travel quite a way in each morning. Used to commuting, are you?'

'Not really, but I'm prepared to give it a go.'

'Fine. There's just one thing, most of our clients like their staff to dress smartly. You're not very well turned out, are you?'

'Aren't I? I mean, I just called in for an initial interview. If I was going for a job I'd wear a suit, or something.'

'And proper shoes. Not sandals for an interview. And you could do with a manicure. I won't arrange any interviews at too short notice, to give you time to give yourself a bit of a make-over. First impressions are so important.'

Dora felt smaller and smaller as her marketability faded further and further into the distance. 'Yes,' she said meekly.

'Have you thought about temping, at all? It would be a good way of getting more general experience.'

'No,' said Dora. 'Not at all. I don't think I'd like it.' She got up, admitting defeat. 'Is that all?'

'Yes. We'll be in touch if we get anything suitable.'

Dora didn't so much 'swing by' the next agency, she more tottered in and sank on the offered chair, sure she was about to go down with a chill. This girl was much more friendly, gave Dora a glass of water and then a cup of tea. She did tut over the conciseness of Dora's CV, but acknowledged it meant she must have been good at her job if she'd stayed with the same firm and been promoted several times. However, the end result was the same, 'We haven't got much on our books at the moment unless you're prepared to travel over Canary Wharf way. It would be quite a trek, looking at your current address.'

Dora sipped and nodded.

'I will get in touch if anything remotely suitable comes up.'

'Thank you.'

'You wouldn't consider temping, would you? It's an excellent way of getting a broader span of experience.'

'I'll definitely give it some thought if nothing permanent turns up, but I really don't want to spend my Monday mornings travelling round London looking for random addresses.'

'You've got a point. On the other hand, it's a good way of learning your way round London.'

Dora sighed and put her mug down on the coaster. 'I'll bear that in mind too. One day, when I've got used to not working in my home town, I'll be a temp, but I don't think I'm quite ready for that now.'

'Well, you did an almost perfect typing test so we'll definitely consider you for any permanent vacancies that come up.'

Dora got to her feet and decided not to bother with the third agency. She felt she'd done enough and honour was satisfied. She'd just have to hope the job at the boatyard was still available and suitable.

While Dora was being tortured for not having changed jobs often enough, or not going to university, or not dressing appropriately, Jo was enjoying herself looking for shops selling artists' materials. Miranda had been fairly vague about where in this elegant part of London the shop she thought existed might be, but eventually, having resisted the temptation to go into the British Museum, or any of the many emporia selling prints and antiquarian books, she found a little shop that seemed to be what she wanted. The moment she went through the door, her eye was caught by the rows of products that rose from floor to ceiling – works of art in their own right. It even smelt promising.

Jo liked to consider herself a feminist, an independent woman who could look after herself, but really, she acknowledged, she got what she wanted (most of the time) by being nice. Now, she went up to the counter and smiled. The middle-aged man behind the counter smiled back reassuringly.

'Good morning. I wonder if you can help me? I have a small cherub I need to repair.'

'What sort of cherub?' To Jo's relief, the man wasn't at all fazed by this statement.

'It's on a mirror frame, so it's very small. His foot's come off.'

'And what's the frame made of?'

'Wood, I think. It's gold.'

'Ah, an old carved mirror frame. And you're trying to repair it?'

'Mm. I've never done anything like this before.'

'Why start now?'

She regarded the man and saw that he was taking her perfectly seriously. 'I'm taking a bit of a gamble – fortunately not with my own money, or at least, not really. I want a career change, something I can do at home, that's creative, and, well – satisfying.'

'And you've got this old mirror?'

'I've got several bits and pieces actually. My friend was going to give them to a jumble sale but I asked if I could have a go at repairing them. I thought I'd start with the mirror.'

'You didn't bring it with you?'

'No, I'm afraid not.' She looked around her, fascinated by the shelves filled with strange-sounding products: gesso, rabbit-skin size and something that seemed to be called rottenstone, although she thought she'd probably misread that.

'Was it his only foot?'

Jo was puzzled. 'Well, no, he had two originally.'

'That's good. Then what you need to do is take a mould of the existing foot, rejig the toes a little, then stick it on.'

'How would I do that?'

'Well, you could use a little plaster of Paris, if that's what you used to make the foot. Or, if you used a patent moulding material, you might want to glue it.'

'So, how would I take the mould in the first place?' Jo felt herself getting more and more interested.

'Well, you have two options. You could take a mould of the existing foot, using Plasticine, or latex moulding powder.'

'It all sounds very complicated.'

'It isn't really, once you get started,' the man reassured her. 'It's rather fun.' He twinkled at her as if confessing a secret. 'I repair bits and pieces myself when I come across something really delicious that needs a little TLC.'

Jo smiled back. 'So what's the other option?'

'You carve another foot out of lime wood.'

'I did carve some quite sweet little bits and pieces for my daughter's doll's house.'

Jo remembered the little wardrobe she had carved. It hadn't been exactly Grinling Gibbons, but she had been working on a very small scale. 'OK, so once I've made the foot, and there are various other little curlicues I'll have to copy too what do I do then? Presumably I don't just paint it gold.'

The man shook his head. 'Oh deary me, no. You'll need to apply gold leaf, or an imitation of it, at least. What you probably need first is a good book. Then you need to decide if you want to use proper, old-fashioned techniques or more modern, less authentic ones.'

'I think I should be authentic,' she said after a moment's thought. 'I want to learn new skills not how to botch things up.'

'That's my girl!' he said. 'Now, do you trust me to tell you what you'll need? It will be quite expensive. I'll give you some off-cuts of lime wood to make it better value.'

'Thank you,' she said meekly and decided to trust him.

When she left half an hour later she was in a state of mild shock. She had a carrier bag with many of the arcane materials she had seen on the shelves, a slim but well-illustrated book about gilding, and an envelope, on the back of which were as many extra tips and wrinkles as she could get down. It also had Peter's (they were on Christian name terms by then) telephone number. 'You'll love applying gold leaf,' he had assured her as he held the door open. 'It's like alchemy!'

Then her phone rang. Dora had finished her interviews. They discussed a rendezvous and, feeling self-indulgent and extravagant, she hailed a taxi.

When Dora found her, Jo was sipping a cappuccino in a café nearby, glad of a bit of a rest. She was flicking through a magazine and obviously enjoying the sunshine that filtered through the window. She had a couple of carrier bags by her side and she smiled enthusiastically when she saw Dora.

'How did you get on? Do you want a coffee or something?'

Dora collapsed on to the chair opposite Jo, grateful for the cool of the café, eager to take the sting out of her ordeal by relating it. 'Water please. That was ghastly!'

'Oh? Why?' Jo got up and went to the counter. 'Still or fizzy?'

'Fizzy.'

Jo carried over the water. Dora could tell she really wanted to offer Dora a Knickerbocker Glory or something, and was restraining herself. Jo truly was a very motherly person.

'What happened?' Jo asked.

Dora considered. 'Well, nothing actually happened but the first woman was so hostile. She made out that I was only fit to work in a shop because my job had been in a small country town. I ran that office!'

'How horrid!' Jo said, handing Dora a bottle of fizzy water and a glass.

101

'And she suggested I tried temping, to give me more experience.'

'You don't think that sounds quite a good idea?' Jo was tentative. She obviously didn't want Dora to think she wasn't on her side.

Dora shook her head. 'Well . . . probably, but I'm just not ready for that sort of excitement. I don't know my way round London, for a start, and the thought of having a new job every week or whatever is just too stressful at the moment.' She imagined legions of women with white nails and permatans and felt weak with inadequacy.

'I must say it sounds ghastly. Although I did a bit of temping and really liked it. Everyone was so surprised and pleased if you actually did anything, like taking a telephone message, they mostly loved you. But that was a very long time ago.' Jo regarded her young friend. 'I tell you what, let's find somewhere lovely for lunch. Have a glass of wine. You'll feel a lot better. One always feels depressed if one's blood sugar gets low.'

Dora laughed. 'The technical term for that is hungry.'

'Call it what you like, I've just spent over a hundred pounds on materials – I need a drink!'

They found a wonderful little Italian place down a side street, which had a courtyard covered with a vine and flirtatious waiters. They seemed determined to give them such excellent service the women probably wouldn't need to actually cut up their food, but just open wide as the fork approached. They were ushered to a table in the courtyard that was just the right temperature, not too hot, but not chilly, either.

'I love going out to lunch with an attractive young woman,' said Jo when her napkin had been tenderly laid over her knee for her. 'The waiters are so attentive!'

'They're being attentive to you, too,' said Dora, already beginning to recover from her interviews.

'Only because I'm with you. It's never like this when I'm by myself.'

Dora frowned. 'I've never eaten in a restaurant by myself, or even a café. I only ever meet people in pubs if I can guarantee they'll be there first.' Dora remembered Tom's dares and wondered what he would spring on her next.

Jo broke into her thoughts. 'Well, you're young.'

'I'm pathetic. That horrible woman in the interview made me realise how pathetic I am.' She looked at the menu. 'But strangely, I'm also terribly hungry.'

'Told you so,' said Jo with a laugh. 'I promise you, nothing seems so bad after a good meal. Now, what shall we have? If we shared a starter, we'd probably have room for pudding. I see they've got zabaglione, which you hardly ever see but it's just wonderful!'

'Signora – the wine list.' The younger of the two waiters handed it to Jo who took it as if it might burn her.

'Oh goodness, I don't know anything about wine. Shall we just have a bottle of house white?'

'A whole bottle?' Dora was horrified.

'It's much more economical than buying it by the glass and I've already taken a taxi today. I need to save where I can.'

Dora put an elbow on the table and rested her head on her hand. 'You're amazing. No wonder you and my mother were never really friends.'

'Oh, but I like your mother very much!'

'Yes, but she'd never suggest sharing a bottle of wine on the grounds that it would be cheaper.'

'That's because she's sensible and I'm not. Now, what shall we eat? I think maybe I won't be on a diet today.'

103

'Do you think I'd be copping out if I checked out the job in the boatyard?'

Dora and Jo had nearly reached their station. They hadn't discussed Dora's job prospects since her first description of her interviews, but it had obviously been in the back of her mind all the rest of the day as they rather merrily tripped round Selfridges and walked off their lunch.

'I mean, I'm not going to get paid very much, am I? The money would be far better in London.'

Jo took a breath, to give the impression she was thinking about her answer and not just replying impulsively – although the answer was the same. 'The thing people forget is that it costs money to go out to work. There are your fares, lunches out, smart clothes, all sorts of things. Which is not to say people – for example mothers – shouldn't go out to work, but they should make sure they've done their costings if they're only doing it for the money.'

'So what are you saying?'

'I'm saying that taking a local job, for less money, when it's unlikely they'll want you to wear sharp little suits and have French manicures, could work out almost as well paid as temping in London. And far less stressful.'

Now Dora sighed. 'Should I be going for "less stressful" at my age? I'm young!'

'Yes, but you have just had a trauma of sorts, and working in a boatyard isn't exactly going into a convent for a life of contemplation. You'll be having all kinds of stress. Probably. Just not the same kind.'

Dora warmed to this idea. 'And maybe I should break myself into my new life. I mean, I'd had the same job ever since I left college. Now I'll get a new one. Maybe I'll only

104

stay there for – a couple of years. Hardly any time at all, really.'

Jo laughed. 'Have you got a number for them?'

'No, but I've got Tom's number. He'll have theirs,' Dora said as they headed to the mooring.

'Give him a ring now. No time like the present.'

Dora hadn't telephoned any boy other than John for a hundred years; or at least, that was how it felt. But she was asking for a job, not a date, and with Jo watching her, she felt obliged to be brisk about it.

'Hi, Tom, it's Dora.'

'Yes I know.' His voice was amused. 'Your name came up on my phone.'

'Of course. Listen, you know that job you told me about? Do you think it's still going?'

'Yeah. Sure.' He sounded enthusiastic.

'Well, could you give me the number of the boatyard? I want to ring them first thing tomorrow and arrange an interview.'

There was a short, scary silence. 'Tell you what, come out to the pub with me for a drink later and I'll give it to you then.'

'Are you that pushed for company?'

He chuckled. 'Yes, as it happens.'

She couldn't help laughing back at him. 'OK. I'll check with Jo. I can't come if she's got anything planned.'

'She could come too, if she wanted,' he said.

'Jo? Tom has invited us to go to the pub with him this evening?'

Jo shook her heard. 'Sorry, love. After a day in London shopping, I'm not really up for going out again. Could you go by yourself?'

'Of course! If you don't mind. If you'd rather I stayed in and cooked you scrambled egg on toast, I'll do that.'

Jo was touched and patted Dora's shoulder. 'Make your arrangements with Tom. I can make my own scrambled egg and some for you too, if necessary.'

Chapter Eight

❧

'There's been a change of plan!' said Tom, the moment he saw Dora.

He was at the doorway of the pub, and Dora hoped her relief didn't show. On the way there she'd remembered how nervous she usually was about meeting people in them.

'Hello, Tom,' she said.

'I've borrowed a car,' he said.

'Why? The whole point of local pubs is that you walk to them. Don't drink and drive and all that.'

Tom seemed unreasonably excited. 'We're going to a different pub.'

'It's a different pub every night of the week with you, isn't it?'

Now she studied him more closely she realised that Tom was disgustingly pleased with himself for some reason.

'I saw an ad in the paper and thought of another dare for you,' he said. 'That's why I had to borrow the car.'

Dora stopped. 'What is it?' she asked warily.

'You'll see. Come and see the car.'

'Is getting in it the dare?' she asked when they'd come to a halt in front of a very old, bright green VW Beetle.

'Nope, although driving it's fairly hairy. If you offer to drive home, that could be a dare.'

He was obviously testing the water, not sure if she could

drive at all, let alone an ancient but venerable vehicle like this.

'I'll drive home!' She was a good driver and the thought of driving a strange car didn't faze her, although she didn't even know if this one was third-party insured.

Tom shook his head. 'I've changed my mind. You're too keen, which means it won't challenge you, and you certainly won't want to do what I have in mind sober.'

'What is it?'

But Tom just shook his head and opened the door of the car for her. This wasn't so much an act of chivalry but necessity. It was a big and very heavy door, and slightly stuck. Dora slid on to the cracked and peeling leather seat and was overwhelmed by the smell of Old Car, which included petrol, very ancient cheese sandwiches and something indefinable that was probably derived from animal origins.

'Can you manage your seatbelt?' Tom watched as Dora untangled miles of webbing and strapped herself in.

'Just about, although I'm surprised this car is young enough to have seatbelts. Who did you borrow it from?'

'Hamo. It is insured and so am I, in case you were wondering.'

'You must think me a total worry-wart,' she said, admitting to herself that she was.

'I'm going to cure you of that. And some of your old-fashioned expressions whilst I'm at it, endearing though they are.' And they lurched off into the night.

'I hope it's not far,' Dora said. 'I want to be able to walk home if we break down.'

'Oh, ye of little faith! We won't break down. They're dead reliable, these old Beetles.'

After a few yards of incident-free travel confirmed this for Dora she said, 'Tom, you haven't forgotten about me needing the boatyard number, have you?'

'Well, to be honest, Dora, I've already rung Fred. I'd told him about you before. I had to speak to him anyway, about something else, so I just mentioned you were interested.'

'Tom! That was very high-handed of you!' Indignation and relief vied for dominance. 'How did you know I'd want it, and anyway, he'll think I'm a complete wimp, not applying for my own job.'

'No he won't. It's all very casual. Honestly. He wants you to come in for a trial next week. It's not quite a run-of-the-mill office job.'

'That's OK. I don't want run-of-the-mill, as long as I'm not required to have Tipp-Ex nails and a fake tan.'

'What?'

'I mean, as long as it's not terrifically high-powered.'

Tom started to laugh so much he was shaking, although that might have been partly due to the car's dodgy suspension. 'Not exactly.'

'What's so funny?'

'You'll see when you get there. And you'll be paid by the hour to begin with, but eventually he'll want to put you on a salary. I should try and be paid by the hour for as long as possible.'

'Oh, why? I mean, if I have to work out the wages, it's probably less work if I'm on a salary.'

'Most of the men are self-employed and get paid by the hour. You'll end up doing loads of overtime. If you're on a salary, you won't get paid for that.'

'Oh. Right. Well, we'll see how it goes. He might not like the look of me.'

'Oh, he'll like you all right. They all will. Do you mind doing the wages?' he added before she could reply. 'It sounds like hard work to me.'

'I used to do them before. I'm good at figures and if

109

you've got the right computer program, it does most of the work for you.'

'You may have to be firm with Fred. He's not much into computer programs.'

Dora smiled. 'I'll try to persuade him.'

Tom grinned. 'I don't suppose you'll have much problem. Ah, here it is.'

There was nothing about this particular pub that was noticeably different from any other and Dora got out of the car feeling moderately confident. Maybe he wanted her to take a turn behind the bar or something. That would be quite embarrassing, having never pulled a pint in her life, but she was good at mental arithmetic, and anyway, tills did it all for you nowadays.

When she saw what was written on the blackboard outside, however, she allowed herself a small, restrained scream. 'No, Tom, not never, nohow.'

'It's not life-threatening. I'd do it. In fact, I'll do it first. Come along. You can have a stiff drink before you get up there.'

'But, Tom,' she wailed, as he dragged her into the pub, 'I can't do karaoke!'

He didn't let go of her wrist until they had got to the bar and were so hemmed in by people her chances of escape were nil. 'Now, what's your favourite strong drink? No point in having lager, there's just not enough alcohol in it.'

Dora had had time to think. It would be useless telling Tom she point blank refused, at least, for now. She would appear to go along with it and devise an exit strategy. 'I'll have a double whiskey – Irish, please.'

'Oh. Expensive.'

'You said it had to be strong, and I got a taste for whiskey the other day. And it serves you right, you deserve to pay a lot for my drink.'

He chuckled. 'Fair enough. But you've got to do it! I don't want my investment wasted.'

'Just as long as I'm wasted,' she muttered.

He bought their drinks and they made their way to a table that had two spare stools. They perched on these and Dora looked at the stage.

The karaoke hadn't started yet but the equipment was being sound-tested and people were writing their names down on a list. Discovering that this was necessary, Dora looked at Tom. He had arranged a job interview for her, had he also booked her a karaoke spot? She asked him.

'No. Couldn't, or I would have done. Have you ever done it before?'

Dora considered lying. If she declared herself to be an old hand at singing he-done-me-wrong songs, would he change his mind about the dare? No. She hadn't a hope of being convincing. She shook her head regretfully.

'You may love it!' He sipped his pint and she sipped her whiskey.

'I'll hate it. But I will do it. I hope nothing else you ask me to do will be as hard.'

Tom's brow crinkled a little. 'Don't do it if it will make you miserable.'

She looked up at him. 'No. It's a dare, I said I'd do it, and I survived a typing test today. It couldn't be any worse.' She frowned suddenly. 'You don't have to remember the words, do you?'

Tom relaxed again. 'No! They have coloured words that move as you're supposed to sing them. It gets tricky if it's too high and too fast, so don't get too drunk or you'll never keep up.'

'So you're an old hand at this then?'

'I've done it once. It's cool! Look, they're starting. You'd better get your name down.'

111

The first few acts were stunning. They had obviously done this many times before and they seemed to a terrified Dora to be practically professional. She sipped her drink and sank lower in her chair.

Tom sent her an anxious look. 'They're good, aren't they?'

She nodded.

'You'd be better off getting it over quickly, or you'll just get more and more nervous.'

'Probably.' She didn't move.

'After all, you don't want to sit here all night until it's only the no-hopers.'

She frowned at him. 'What do you mean, no-hopers? It's not a competition, is it?'

He looked very shame-faced. 'Might be. I think if you do well you get to go on first next week. But I may be wrong.'

Dora finished her drink. 'I'm going to the loo,' she said. 'I may be some time.'

Fighting her way through the crowds she contemplated getting a taxi home or, better, stealing the Beetle and letting Tom get a taxi home. Those old cars would be pretty easy to break into. She'd just ask a passer-by to help her open the door, and then give her a bump start. Could you do all that without the keys? she wondered.

Then, as she reached the door marked 'Venus', which, after a moment's thought, she realised was the Ladies, she concluded that doing karaoke would be easier than all that malarkey.

There was no respite, even in the Ladies. There were two girls checking their make-up and their identical wigs and they'd spread themselves over both washbasins and on to the floor. They were obviously an act. Dora slipped into the cubicle. They were still there when she came out, and she had to edge her way to a tap.

'Sorry, love,' said one of them, gathering up a make-up bag from the sink. 'We're taking up all the space.'

'It's OK,' she said huskily.

'Hey, are you all right? You look kind of pale.'

'I'm all right! It's just nerves.'

'Nerves?'

Dora nodded, knowing these feisty, confident women would not understand. 'Yes. I said I'd do karaoke for a dare but I don't dare, really.'

The two women exchanged glances, obviously wondering what sort of an idiot they were sharing the Ladies with.

'We could ask,' said the one who had talked to her. 'Listen, we're a band. We're just trying out some new numbers, to see how they go down. Covers, obviously.'

Dora took time to wonder how a new number could also be a cover. A cover was an old song by definition, surely?

'There are three of us usually, but Christine couldn't make it tonight. We've got a wig and dress and everything. Do you fancy going on with us? It would look better with three. We've got a guy who'll sing the verse, but the chorus is more important, really.'

Dora forced enough saliva into her mouth so she could swallow.

'Can you sing at all?' asked the one who hadn't spoken yet. 'It's no good asking her if she's tone deaf,' she muttered to her friend.

'She doesn't have to sing at all,' said her mate. 'She only needs to mouth the words.'

'I was in the choir at school,' said Dora, trying to sound as if she actually wanted to get up on the stage and sing. Part of her felt that she wouldn't have agreed to the dare if she really couldn't sing.

'That'll do,' said the one who'd first taken pity on her.

113

'We only want you to sing the chorus, with us. It's "Hit The Road Jack". Do you know it?'

'Ray Charles?' Dora said tentatively.

'That's it.'

'Well, I don't know the verses—'

'You don't need to know them. You don't even need to know the words, it's karaoke, isn't it? What size are you? Get your kit off. It might be a bit tight.'

Dora looked for Tom the moment she got on stage. He was drumming his fingers on the table and constantly looking around. Would he recognise her when he did look up at the stage?

She was wearing a stiff black wig, glossy as paint, that didn't move and made her look completely different. The dress was very short and the shoes very big, high, with platform soles. She'd had to borrow a disposable razor to deal with some stray armpit hairs and had submitted herself to the combined make-up bags of both women. The fact that her own mother wouldn't recognise her was a relief, but she did want Tom to realise what she'd suffered for his stupid dare.

'Remember, you don't have to sing, you can just mouth the words,' said the girl closest to her through the side of her mouth. 'But try not to look at the words if you can help it.'

'OK, we're on.'

A man in a Teddy-boy draped jacket, drainpipe trousers and a wig quite similar to the ones the girls were wearing appeared from the other side of the stage.

He started to sing. ' "Oh woman, oh woman don't you treat me so mean . . ." '

The girls tapped their feet and swung their hips and Dora tapped and swung along with them. When the time

114

came, Dora sang with feeling, ' "Hit the road, Jack . . ." '

She saw Tom and realised he'd seen her. At first he was a picture of incredulity, but then admiration took the place of disbelief. He raised his glass to her and in return she sang, ' "Don't you come back no more, no more." '

They were a hit, Dora had to acknowledge, and she also had to acknowledge that she'd really enjoyed herself. It was wonderful being someone quite different to who you were normally. She came off the stage with the others and went to Tom's table.

'The prize for these dares had better be good,' she said.

Tom sprang up from the table and hugged her. 'You were fantastic! I couldn't believe my eyes when I realised it was you up there. That skirt length is really you, darling,' he added wickedly.

'I'm going to get changed,' she said firmly. 'And then I'd love a drink of water.'

'It should be champagne, really, but I can't afford it, and it would be crap here, anyway.'

'A pint of water and half a pint of lager will be fine. I've been sweating golf balls.'

Dora was quite sad to say goodbye to the brassy, loud and dominant woman she had been for a few minutes, and was very sad to say goodbye to her fellow backing singers.

'You were good,' they said. 'You should do more of it.'

'I don't think so, thanks, but thank you so much for saving me. I could never have done it alone.'

'Well, make sure your boyfriend comes up with something good as a reward,' said one.

'Otherwise, you know what to tell him . . .'

Dora laughed and sang, the others joining in, ' "Hit the road, Jack . . ." '

'Now I'm going to get pissed,' she said.

*

115

The following Monday, Jo insisted on making Dora sandwiches for her first day at work. 'You don't have to eat them, you can just keep them in your bag, but if you find that everyone has produced snap tins at lunchtime, you'll be embarrassed as well as hungry.'

'What's a snap tin?'

'Oh, you know, a sandwich box. Now what would you like? I've got ham, cheese, some salad, or shall I just make something?' she added, sensing that Dora was more concerned with getting there and what she might be asked to do when she did.

'If you don't like it you can just come home,' insisted Jo, waving her off. 'That's the joy of being able to walk to work.'

Dora wasn't the only one feeling excited and nervous. In a different way Jo was starting a new job, too. First of all she cleared the table and all the worktops. She didn't want to run out of places to put things. Then she spread newspaper over the table and put on an apron. She was aware that some of these preparations weren't really necessary for the work, but she wanted to prepare her mind as much as anything.

Then she got out the box of oddments she had undertaken to restore and her bags of materials and equipment.

There was the mirror that had first caught her eye, with the gold carved frame and the injured cherub. It was very badly damaged. Jo didn't really know where to start so decided to admire her materials, first, including the bag of off-cuts.

There was the gilder's pad, knife and tip which were used to lay the loose gold leaf. Water gilding was extremely tricky, but Peter, her mate at the shop, had

116

persuaded her it was the way forward and, if she could do it, a valuable skill.

The gilder's tip was like a fat, almost square paintbrush with soft bristles. This was used for catching up the gold leaf, which, Peter had told her, could fly away on a breath and was dreadfully prone to tearing. The pad had a guard round it, to help stop this happening. The knife was just like an ordinary knife with the top sliced off at an angle and she had resented having to buy it. But as all the knives on the barge were Michael's she didn't really have a choice. She wouldn't need much of this today as she had to apply several layers of gesso, which had to have time to dry first, but she couldn't resist looking at everything.

Her favourite piece of equipment was the agate burnisher: a wooden-handled tool with a piece of polished agate on the end. This was what got you your reward, Peter had told her. This little piece of kit would turn your fairy-fragile gold leaf into something resembling sunlight, shining and strong.

'Right,' she said out loud. 'Let's get the frame cleaned up.' She put on some rubber gloves and got out the wire wool. 'When I've got all the dirt off, I'll start warming my gesso.' Peter had encouraged her to buy ready-made gesso. 'You don't want to be messing with rabbit-skin granules,' he had said. 'They smell dreadful.'

Half an hour later she had applied her first coat of thinned down gesso to the mouldings that she had built up with a bit of filler. While she was waiting for it to dry, which might take a couple of hours, the book said, she got out her carving tools and scraps of lime wood.

It took her a while to get used to using the tools again, but eventually she produced a very acceptable little foot.

Encouraged by her success, she started modelling the scalloped edge of the frame she had created earlier and

117

added two quite impressive segments. She was nearly convinced that when everything was painted and gilded it would look good enough to sell.

Although the radio had been burbling away to her in the background, she hadn't really taken in anything that had been said. Gently, she tested the gesso for dryness and applied another thin coat. It would be a while – maybe not even today – before she got to the gold-leaf part, when she would stroke the gilder's tip against her arm and use it to catch up the gold leaf. It would fly to it like iron filings to a magnet, Peter had told her.

So as not to get impatient, Jo got out another item, the little dish that had a figure supporting a bowl, the head of which was missing. If she cleaned everything in readiness, she could set up a production line. She sighed happily. If she could get this right she wouldn't have to be a barmaid – something that would be a relief to her ex-husband and her daughter. She took an acorn-sized piece of Fimo and set about modelling a tiny head, humming happily to herself.

Chapter Nine

Dora set off along the towpath, wearing, as instructed, clean but not new jeans. It went against all her ideas of correct clothes for the office, and would have horrified Ms Scary-Nails, but Tom had been firm. 'If you turn up in a little suit and high heels everyone will have a fit and you won't get the job,' he had said.

'That's good. I didn't bring any clothes like that with me.'

Her sandwiches and bottle of water were concealed in her shoulder bag along with a dictionary and bottle of Tipp-Ex. Jo had handed her a Red Cross parcel, having found a paper shop nearby that supplied these things; they had both agreed that while it probably wasn't entirely necessary, and there would be a gleaming new computer waiting for her, One Never Knew. 'It could be a battered old Underwood,' said Jo, and then reflected that battered old Underwoods had gone out even before her days as an office temp.

It was a lovely day, which helped; the sun was sparkling on the water and, further along, through the trees. She was to carry on walking until she reached the outskirts of the town where there was a riverside pub, Tom had told her. She had then to keep to the towpath and walk round the front of this. The boatyard was on the other side of the river.

She was expecting a bridge or something, because she knew the boatyard was on another island. But there wasn't

119

a bridge; there was Tom. He was down at the river's edge, holding on to the painter of a small rowing boat.

'Hi, you made it all right, then?' he asked, looking up at her.

'What are you doing here?' said Dora, not all that pleased to see him. 'I am supposed to be meeting the boatyard people and having my trial day, aren't I?'

'Oh yes. I'm here to take you to work.' He indicated the boat that bobbed against the slipway. It seemed a long way down and very muddy.

'I really don't want to go by boat, Tom. I'll get covered in mud.'

'Don't worry about that, we're all covered in mud. And as for not wanting to, well, I'm afraid there's no choice. At high tide, anyway. For a couple of hours either side of low tide you can walk.' He smiled encouragingly.

Dora looked at the boat, at Tom and then at the boatyard. For what she could see, it seemed to consist of a lot of old barges and boats, a building that looked like a barn with the side missing, and a sign that could have done with a touch-up. She had heard that it had a terrific reputation – not for presentation, obviously. She opened her mouth to make her apologies.

Tom interrupted her. 'Don't be a wuss.'

He was looking at her challengingly and she remembered she didn't have to stay if she found she hated it. 'OK, then.'

'It's not called a slipway for nothing, is it?' she said as she slithered her way down to the water's edge.

'Now you know why I told you to wear jeans,' said Tom. 'I hope they're not too tight. Get in.'

'It's too late to tell me my bum looks big in these,' she said. Very gingerly she stepped into the little boat and sat down hurriedly as it tipped under her.

Tom pulled at the rope until a mud-covered weight appeared. He heaved this into the boat and picked up what seemed to be the only oar. He didn't sit down.

'How are you going to row with only one oar?' she asked a little nervously.

'Like this.'

Tom dipped the oar in the water, first on one side of the boat, then the other. In no time they were across.

'How will I get over if you're not here?' asked Dora, getting to her feet and taking Tom's hand so he could steady her as she got off.

'If there isn't a boat, you'll have to bellow and someone will get you, but there usually is one. You'll get used to it.'

Convinced that she wouldn't, Dora said nothing. In spite of being careful, there was a fair bit of mud on her jeans, but she'd just have to trust Tom that it wouldn't matter.

She followed Tom up the slipway and along to a ladder. They went up this and followed a series of planks that ran along the side of the barn that Dora now realised was a temporary workshop rigged up over a barge. From under the tarpaulin covering could be heard the sounds of banging and sawing, whistling and Radio 2.

'Sorry about the radio,' said Tom. 'The oldies like that easy-listening stuff and the rants.'

Someone stuck his head through a gap in the canvas. 'Not so much of the oldies, young Tom. Oh, is this our new girl in the office? Does it mean we'll get proper pay slips at last? Great!' The man had thick blond hair like teased rope and a gap in his teeth revealed by his broad smile. 'Will she be in charge of brewing up?'

'No,' said Tom. 'Come on, Dora, no need to take any notice of the riff-raff.'

Dora smiled at the riff-raff and continued to follow Tom

along the planks to where there was a small wooden building. 'Fred?' he called. 'I've brought Dora.'

A small man with grey hair and a worried expression appeared at the door. 'Morning, Dora, welcome to Paper Hell. I'm Fred. Tom, put the kettle on.'

Dora followed Fred into the shed. It consisted of two desks, several filing cabinets and a couple of office chairs. The walls were papered with charts, notes, drawings, notices, calendars and blueprints. Both desks bore tottering piles of files, catalogues, magazines and unopened letters. Fred's description of it being Paper Hell seemed an understatement.

'Sit down,' he said, removing a pile of ring binders from a chair so that she could. 'How do you like your tea? Or would you prefer coffee?'

'Either,' said Dora to an enquiring Tom. 'Milk no sugar in whichever.'

'Well, Dora,' said Fred, when Tom had disappeared into what looked like a lean-to. 'I hope you like a challenge.'

Dora found that she did and returned Fred's smile. 'Have you got a computer?' she asked.

'Over there. State of the art. None of us knows how to use it.'

Dora pushed up her sleeves, actually and meta-phorically. 'Where should I sit and what would you like me to do first?'

'That's up to you, love, but there's some post that should be opened, I suppose.'

'Can I have a free hand? I won't throw anything away unless I'm absolutely sure, but I will sort stuff into piles.'

Fred's relief spread over his face, erasing several years of worry as it did so. 'You do exactly what you like!'

Jo had known that she wouldn't be able to apply the gold

leaf for a few days, until the coats of gesso were really dry, and was grateful. She was nervous of ruining such an expensive product. She cleared away her materials, stroking the cold, smooth end of her agate burnisher tenderly against her cheek for a moment before putting it in its box. Was she enjoying herself so much just because she liked the tools involved? It probably was part of it. She wiped the table, reminded of the times she'd wiped the table after Dora and Karen had made Valentine's cards, plaster models or later, jewellery. She was obviously still a little girl at heart.

As it was still only three, she decided she had plenty of time to check her emails when she'd stored everything away. She wanted to email her daughter Karen, to tell her how Dora was getting on. Karen would be impressed to hear that Dora was having a trial at a new job and completely amazed that she'd been talked into performing karaoke. Jo was amazed herself. It wasn't something she could ever have done, however drunk. She made a cup of coffee while the computer warmed up, and then clicked her way through to her Inbox and was surprised and a little unnerved to see one from Michael. He hadn't been in touch since just after she'd moved on board. Was he saying that he needed to come back immediately?

Dear Jo, Hope all is well with The Three Sisters *and you. Can you look in the boat file and tell me when she's next due a Boat Safety Examination? The file's in the case in the desk. The insurance is always due about the same time. I'll phone in a few days if you haven't read this message by then. You did say you went on-line most days. Best, Michael.*

Well, she wasn't going to be made homeless immediately, which was good. Jo found the case and in it the file.

123

The Boat Safety Certificate was due to be renewed in a couple of weeks. This was a bit unnerving because it might involve her in doing something boaty – something she really didn't want to do. She shuffled through the papers until she found the insurance certificate. That was due soon too. She took both bits of paper to her laptop and started replying to Michael's email. Then she looked at the date of the Boat Safety Certificate again. She was out by a year. *The Three Sisters* hadn't had a valid certificate for eleven months. Feeling slightly sick, she checked the insurance. That at least was still valid, although only had a few weeks to run.

Dear Michael . . . She told him of her discoveries.

To her relief, she had her reply almost immediately.

Dear Jo, What a bloody nuisance! I can't believe I didn't check before. You'll have to dry dock her and have a survey to get the insurance renewed. It's best if she can go where she went last time. She needs some work done to her too. I'll arrange it. I'll be back with more details shortly. Stay on-line. Best, Michael

Jo went to make another cup of coffee to replace the one she had let go cold. She tidied the galley whilst she was waiting for the kettle to boil. All the joy she had felt modelling the little cherub's foot had been replaced by anxiety. Where would she and Dora live? And it might be very difficult for Dora, if she had just found a job she could get to love. A ting from her laptop warned her there was another message – from Michael.

All sorted. She's booked into the dry dock and they can do the work. Very lucky to get a slot as it is a bit urgent. Just as well the insurance is still valid. Best, Michael

It's all right for Michael, thought Jo. He doesn't have to actually do anything about any of this. He can just stay in his luxury villa with his trophy mistress and direct operations. She pressed Reply again.

You know I'm really grateful to you for lending me The Three Sisters *but I'm a bit worried about having to deal with this. I did tell you I wasn't boaty! I don't suppose you could put it off for a few months, could you? Or even a few weeks, just so as I can find somewhere to stay. Jo*

Jo was not normally so relaxed about things like insurance, but, she reckoned, no one would know if *The Three Sisters* was insured or not, except her and Michael. It would be a different matter if she was going to go anywhere, but just sitting on the mooring shouldn't alert anyone to their uninsured presence, surely? She pressed Send and hoped Michael would listen to her pleas. After all, he'd surely want to supervise things when he was in the country? He wouldn't want his middle-aged female lodger in charge.

She chopped some onions as a displacement activity. Her laptop pinged again.

So sorry, failure of communication! No need for you to worry about any of this. I'll sort it.

Jo was mortified by her relief. She knew her daughter would have taken on the challenge of getting a barge into dry dock with enthusiasm. Karen had acquired some courageous genes that had skipped a generation and passed her mother by, unless they came from her father, of course.

Reluctant to admit that Karen's father had had anything

125

to do with her daughter, she decided to capitalise on her displacement activity and chop carrots and celery too. She'd make a nice lasagne for supper. Dora would need something familiar and easy to eat after her first day at a new job.

Dora came home exhausted, muddy, but happy. 'I've had a brilliant time!' she said. 'They're all so sweet at the boatyard.'

'So you're going to stay?' asked Jo, infected with Dora's enthusiasm.

'Definitely. It's great! They haven't had anyone working there for ages so there's masses to do. I'll have to devise a system for them. They have got a computer but they only use it for typing letters on. I'm going to get them into order. I love that sort of challenge,' she added, sighing blissfully. 'Tough, but not actually life-threatening.'

'Goodness.'

'Well, you know how it is: when things have been absolutely dreadful, anything I do is going to seem brilliant. It's a win-win situation. Like you said it was when you were temping. I am so tired though!'

Jo handed her a mug of tea and a rock cake she had made in case she couldn't repair decorative objects and needed to open that teashop.

'So, how was your day?' Dora mumbled through half a cake.

'Well, I started on the picture frame, the one with the broken cherub and the broken moulding? I really got into it. I just hope I'm good enough to make the things sellable.'

'Oh, let me see,' Dora said.

'They're drying under cover – I'll show you later.'

'And? What else happened today?'

Determinedly, Jo put the smile back on her face. 'Michael

126

emailed asking me to check the insurance and the Boat Safety Certificate.'

'Were they OK?' Dora had spent time checking similar things all day and felt she had a professional interest.

'The insurance was. The Boat Safety's about a year out of date. But I don't think it will matter. After all, we're not going anywhere, are we?'

Dora shook her head. 'These cakes are lush.' Jo sounded relaxed but Dora sensed some disquiet about living somewhere without all the relevant documents.

'I think it will be all right,' Jo went on, almost to herself. 'What time do you think you might be hungry again?'

Dora's hand stopped halfway to her mouth. 'Um, not terribly soon. These cakes are just too delicious. Sorry! Oh, and I've just remembered.'

'What?'

'I've invited Tom for supper.'

'That's nice. I've made a big lasagne.'

'I know I shouldn't have without asking you and I'm perfectly happy to cook, but I felt I had to ask him.'

'Why?'

'He met me this morning and rowed me across to the boatyard.'

'He rowed you? You mean there's no other way of getting there? Dora, that's awful!'

Dora smiled happily. 'You only have to row when the tide's in. When it's out there's a really muddy set of stepping stones you get over.'

Jo rolled her eyes. 'That's OK, then!'

'Can I email Karen?' asked Dora, pulling the laptop towards her. 'I want to tell her what's going on.'

'Good idea. I was going to do that before I got that email from Michael.'

Karen replied quite soon.

Hi, Dora, great to hear from you! I'm writing this in my lunch hour. Brilliant about you getting a job so soon. It sounds fab. Is Mum OK? Is she in a stress about the boat being uninsured? She used to be really hot on that sort of thing. She may be putting a brave face on it, but worrying really.

By the way, could you ask her if she could find my fork-lift truck driving qualification? They won't believe I've got one here and I need it to move the big installations around. (The fork lift, not the certificate!) I don't want to take another test here! It's in a file at home somewhere. I know that's a bit of a bind, but I do need it. You could go home with her and protect her from the Floosie. Oh, got to go. Bye! Love, Karen

'I'm not sure I want to go home,' Jo said when she'd read her daughter's post. 'Even with you to protect me.'

'Why not? Shall I set the table for supper?' Dora asked, shutting down the computer.

'Yes, and open a bottle of wine. In the cupboard. Because I've sort of made my statement.' Jo returned to the subject at hand. 'I don't want to have to go back. Although as it is for Karen's certificate, and Philip won't mind. It's just me.'

'Couldn't he get it for Karen?'

'Not a cat in hell's chance. He'd never find it, or she'd have asked him.'

'What a nuisance!'

'On the other hand' – Jo hunted in a drawer for the bottle-opener – 'there are some clothes I need to collect. We could do that at the same time, I suppose.'

'Is it only clothes?' said Dora as she laid the table.

Jo considered. 'I expect there are other things. I left most of the utensils and I could do with some of them.'

'Let's go on a raid,' suggested Dora. 'Next weekend. I

wouldn't mind seeing if you've got those old tapes of me and Karen.'

'That's a good idea. Now, where's that Tom? Supper's just about ready,' Jo said, peering into the oven.

Just at that moment, Tom's voice could be heard hallooing. Jo shouted up out of the porthole and he came down.

While they were eating, Jo's phone rang. She got up from the table and answered it. It was Philip.

'Jo? I've had an email from Karen. She says she needs her fork-lift truck licence and that you've got to get it.'

'I could try and tell you where it is—'

'Don't bother. I never could find anything in that rats' nest you call a filing system. Karen says Samantha and I have got to go out for the day. She's very protective of you, I must say.'

Jo was silent, giving Philip time to realise why Karen was protective of her mother.

'It won't take you that long to find, will it?' Philip went on.

Now he seemed to be grudging her time in her old home, Jo felt indignant. 'I do need my summer clothes and I would prefer it if – you weren't there.' Jo was surprised at how shaky she felt at the prospect of seeing her husband's new woman.

'Better for Samantha too. I don't want her getting upset.'

Jo's shakiness became anger. 'Of course not.' She bit out the words with more emphasis than was really appropriate.

Dora and Tom looked at their plates.

'No need to get antsy. The house is immaculate. Samantha has redecorated the spare room and it looks lovely.'

It looked lovely when I decorated it, thought Jo,

129

outraged at the thought of her humorous toile de Jouy wallpaper being removed. 'Dora and I will come next weekend, if that's all right. But do please arrange to be out. I would hate to upset Samantha.'

Chapter Ten

꩜

'Well, that's told him,' said Dora a few moments later.

'He always was irritating,' said Jo, sitting back down and piercing a piece of lettuce rather fiercely. 'But since he left me, I haven't bothered to suppress my feelings. But don't worry, Dora, they'll be out when we go. You won't have to face a dreadful scene. Eat up, both of you.'

'So, Tom, what's all this about you making Dora do karaoke?' she asked after a calming few moments of companionable munching.

'She was excellent. I was well impressed.' He shot Dora a look of admiration that only Jo noticed.

'Good for you, Dora. Now, could one of you open some more wine?'

They had a jolly meal and Jo managed to put all thoughts of her ex-husband, his new partner and her anxieties about going home to the back of her mind, but afterwards she wanted some time to herself. Unsure how to get this, it was Tom who came to her rescue.

'That was fantastic, Jo. Can I repay you by taking you out for a nightcap?'

'What, now?' asked Jo and Tom nodded. 'Dora, are you willing ever to go to a pub with Tom again?'

Dora looked at Tom and then back to Jo.

'I mean, if a friend of mine made me get up and sing in public I wouldn't let him within a hundred miles of me,' Jo went on. 'But if you could find it in you to take him up on his offer, I would be fine on my own.'

'But you made supper,' protested Tom mildly. 'You should have a reward.'

'And we couldn't leave you with the washing-up,' added Dora.

'We have a dishwasher and I would really like a few moments to get my head round various things. Quite a lot of things.'

There was a pause before Tom said, 'If you're sure?'

Jo nodded. 'Do go – they'll be calling time soon.'

Tom and Dora looked at her pityingly. 'They don't do that at the local these days,' Tom explained. 'It always stays open until midnight.'

'Oh goodness, I'd forgotten. I really hope I don't need to get a job as a barmaid.'

'Come on, Tom,' said Dora. 'I think Jo needs some peace.'

As they were saying their goodbyes, Jo's bra buzzed. She turned away and reached into it.

'Does she always keep her phone in her bra?' she heard Tom ask as he and Dora went up the steps.

'Anything she doesn't want to lose, she told me,' said Dora as they disappeared into the night.

'Hi, Jo?' said a male voice. 'Michael.'

She was immediately anxious. 'Oh. Hello.' She paused, waiting for his reason for calling. First an email, now a phone call. He hardly *ever* rang her.

'Yes – um – I thought I ought to call you, rather than reply on email. I wasn't sure when you'd be on-line again.'

'Oh?'

'Yes. It's about the dry dock.'

Something in his tone of voice made her move to where she could sit down. 'What about the dry dock?'

'It's quite a serious situation. The thing is, the moorings company won't let us stay without a Boat Safety Certificate and up-to-date insurance. One of the reasons I remembered is because I'd had an email from Steve.'

Frantically Jo trawled her brain for a Steve and couldn't find a match. 'Sorry, who's Steve?'

'He's the man at the office. You may not have met him, anyway, he's a good guy and told me they're having a crackdown. It's to get people to move those half-sunk old wrecks from down the end.'

'Oh. But we're not a half-sunk old wreck from down the end.' Jo felt her anxiety increase.

'No, but we have to have our paperwork up to date,' Michael insisted. 'I also want to get the hull shot-blasted and a coat of epoxy put on.'

'Oh.'

'The thing is, Jo, I want *The Three Sisters* to go to Holland for that.'

'Holland!'

'Yes.' He paused. 'It's part of the EU, you know, not the other side of the world.'

'But it is the other side of the North Sea!'

'I'm not expecting you to take her there, Jo!'

'Good!' Her voice became very quiet and high. Hearing it, she strived to sound light-hearted and bantering. 'But where am I going to go while *The Three Sisters* is visiting windmills and red cheeses?'

Misinterpreting the reason for her mouse-like tones, Michael strived to be reassuring. 'You'll stay with her, of course. There's no need for you to move off the barge. Go along for the ride! Do the cooking. Be useful,' he added.

Jo moistened her lips. 'I think I should explain, Michael. Although I've really loved living on the barge and might even consider buying one of my own, I really do not want

133

to go anywhere on it. The thought terrifies me. And I get seasick.'

'There's no need to be anxious. She's as safe as houses; you could go anywhere in her.'

But I don't want to, Jo said to herself. 'Really, whoever is taking her to Holland doesn't want me around, getting in the way, worrying about it capsizing all the time.'

'You're not like that, Jo! You'd be an asset.'

Jo wondered where he was getting his information from. 'How? How can I be an asset? I said, I know nothing about boats, I get seasick, and I'd be scared witless.'

'You can cook. Make cups of tea, keep everyone happy. It's a vital role. It's miserable if you've been on watch for hours and hours and have to heat yourself up some ghastly ready meal.'

'Ready meals have come on a lot recently,' muttered Jo.

'If you won't go, I'll have to find another cook.'

'It's not just a matter of me not going,' said Jo, lying through gritted teeth, 'it's that I can't. Dora, my temporary lodger, has just started a new job at the boatyard on the island.' She waited for Michael's approval, but it didn't come. 'She can't just go off to Holland, and she lives with me.'

'I'm sure she could find alternative accommodation. But be that as it may—'

'That sounds very pompous, Michael.' said Jo, stalling for time.

He chuckled and said, 'Be that as it may again, the boat needs to go into dry dock, and I really want her to get her hull done in Holland. They know her, they're reasonable, and it's very hard to get it done in England.'

Jo sighed, resigned to the fact that *The Three Sisters* had to go to Holland – with or without her. 'OK. I'll try and find a cook and somewhere for me and Dora to live.

When do you need to go and how long would it all take?'

'I've booked her in for mid-June. It should take about three weeks if all goes well. That's just under a month away, near enough. You should have got it all sorted by then, shouldn't you? But you really ought to go with her. It would be the trip of a lifetime. I'd go myself like a shot,' he said quickly, anticipating her next question, 'but I'm so tied up at work.'

Jo sighed again. Her dreams of becoming a restorer and gilder might turn out to be only dreams and a lot of expensive equipment. 'I wish I could say the same, but maybe all I'm fit for is to cook for people on boat trips.'

'So you're going? Brilliant! I knew you wouldn't let me down.'

'No, I never said I'd go!' Jo exclaimed. 'And I'm not letting you down and I won't. I'll find someone else.'

'I'll get in touch with the skipper. He might be able to change your mind.'

'I doubt it.'

'Well – you might remember him. It's Marcus.'

'Oh, the famous Marcus!' How interesting, thought Jo. 'Everyone was going on about him at the rally.'

'Well, he is the best. Do you remember him from when we used to meet every Saturday lunchtime, before most of us got married?'

'I never knew him very well. He was a latecomer to the group, wasn't he? Didn't you introduce him?'

'That's right. We used to row together when I was at university and he at a naval college. He always spoke very highly of you,' he added and Jo was sure she detected a note of mischief in his voice. She also suspected she was being soft-soaped.

'Oh?'

'Really. I think he was a bit put out that you were spoken for at the time.'

'Right.' Jo's disbelief was audible. The girls in their group all agreed Marcus was a handsome devil but that only a fool would go after him. Even if she hadn't been with Philip, he had been way out of her league.

'But you do remember him?'

'Oh yes.'

'Good, because he wants to come over, tonight.'

'Tonight!'

'They're taking *Hildegarde* back up the Thames tomorrow. He wants a recce tonight.'

'You've already set all this up, haven't you?'

''Fraid so. I'll tell him it's OK to stop by, then?'

Jo squeaked her confirmation and then disconnected. She got up and pushed her fingers into her hair for a few seconds, trying to massage some of the tension out of her scalp. Then she looked at the state of the place and reached the conclusion that it was a mess. Now she wished she hadn't dispatched Dora and Tom to the pub. With three of them they could have had it looking shipshape in a jiffy. On her own she had very little time to decide on priorities. She'd had enough shocks today. Now a man who had rather unsettled her all those years ago, and who quite a few people thought of as arrogant, was due any minute. What's more he was coming to check out the barge and it was a tip. She braced herself and a moment later was throwing things into the dishwasher with one hand and filling the kettle with the other. A few rapid passes with the Hoover and the barge was nearly presentable. Then she took five minutes to attend to her own appearance. She was spraying herself with scent when her phone went.

'Marcus Rippon here. I'm going to take your barge to Holland.'

Jo suddenly realised that she remembered his voice: sexy, humorous and just a little bit unnerving. 'Michael said you'd ring.'

Jo looked up when she heard his call from the pontoon. She was in the bow, cleaning out the scuppers with a stiff brush, finding some excuse to be on deck so she wouldn't be taken by surprise when he came. She recognised him instantly. 'Marcus,' she said quietly, putting down her brush and going to meet him.

'Joanna,' he said as she reached him. 'I'd have known you anywhere.'

'Really?' She was instantly suspicious. A lot of years had passed since they had last seen each other, and they had never known each other well. She must look very different now – but then she'd have known him anywhere, too. 'Did you come to my wedding? I can't remember.'

Marcus shook his head. 'No. I was abroad. Can we go in? I want to check things out before I take *Hildegarde* away, as I'm here anyway,' he said rather brusquely.

'It was a shame you missed the rally,' said Jo as he climbed on board.

'Not at all. I was lucky to escape. Carole loves showing off the barge. I hate it.'

They went into the wheelhouse and while Marcus immediately swung himself down into the engine room, Jo wondered about him.

He hadn't changed much, she realised, although because she'd seen a photo of him, she was prepared for what changes there were. His hair was grey, when it had been very dark, but it was still thick and curly. He was taller and broader, she thought, but realised it was probably just broader, and only felt taller because they were in the relatively confined space of the wheelhouse. He did have a rather arrogant, curt air about him but perhaps he was just being efficient and didn't have much time. And judging by the fact that he didn't have a wife and several children, he was still a commitment-phobe. And still, although she hated to admit this to herself, very attractive. Poor Carole!

She left him in the engine room and went down to sort out refreshments. Would he want coffee, or wine? It depended, she supposed, on whether he was going anywhere tonight. If he only had to go back to *Hildegarde*, he might like a glass of something. Except that he couldn't have been home long, and Carole would have been waiting for him, so he probably wouldn't linger.

Jo felt awkward and shy in a way that she hadn't done for years. She wasn't shy normally but Marcus had always made her feel slightly fluttery and stupid, she remembered, and she supposed her brain had just gone into the old pattern from habit. Michael had said he'd always spoken well of her but she hadn't believed him. Now she did recall an incident at a party – it couldn't have lasted more than a couple of minutes – when they'd collided in a doorway. He'd apologised and said something to her that made her stop and look at him. She couldn't now remember what he'd said, but his look had seemed to absorb her, to take in every bit of her. Then he'd said, 'But you're with Philip.' She had agreed and carried on towards the kitchen.

Now, he called down to her. 'Has Michael got any charts?'

She went to join him in the wheelhouse. 'Only what's under those cushions, as far as I know.' She lifted one of the seat cushions revealing a pile of plastic-covered sheets.

Marcus lifted them out, took a pair of reading glasses out of his top pocket and put them on and then began flicking through the sheets on the small table. 'No, none of these are

138

what we want, but never mind, I can bring charts with me.'
He put down the charts, took off his glasses and turned to
Jo. His gaze was rather disconcerting.

'Would you like a cup of coffee?' she said, hoping she
hadn't blushed. 'Or a glass of wine, or something?' Was he
thinking how much older she looked? It was nearly thirty
years since he'd last seen her, after all.

He took time over his decision but then said, 'I do need
to check out the accommodation. If I'm the skipper, I need
a decent cabin. Where do you sleep?'

'I sleep in the original cabin but I can move out – in fact I
probably won't be coming on the trip anyway.'

'Won't you? Why not? Shall we go down?'

They went down into the saloon and she poured him a
glass of wine.

'So, what have you been up to since we last met?' he
asked, sitting down and stretching out his legs in front of
him.

Jo sighed. 'It doesn't amount to much. I got married to
Philip as you know, had a lovely daughter, who now runs
an art gallery in Canada, and came to live on a barge.' She
didn't want commiserations from him about Philip
abandoning her and he must know – Michael would have
told him – so she didn't mention it. 'What about you?'

'Well, I was at sea for years, as a deck officer. Never
married. Got bored with deep-sea sailing and so retrained
as a surveyor, but now I mostly make my living by moving
other people's boats about. I also buy the odd bargain and
sell it on.'

Jo smiled. 'Was *Hildegarde* a bargain?'

He nodded. 'Actually, yes. The man needed to sell it very
quickly and offered it to me at a price I couldn't refuse. I'll
sell her eventually, but for now, she's comfortable to live
on.'

Jo laughed. 'We saw just how comfortable.'

He smiled back at her. 'Don't mock! It's all top of the range. The guy spent a fortune on her.'

'I wasn't mocking!' But she was glad he thought that she was. Somehow she felt it would be good for him not to be praised all the time. He was obviously rather used to it.

He got up, put his glass down and started prowling around.

'It doesn't matter how things are arranged down here, does it?' she asked.

'Not really, but why wouldn't you be coming to Holland? There is plenty of accommodation, after all.'

She thought he hadn't noticed her saying that but she realised he was the sort of man who would remember all those tiny details most people would forget. 'Well, to be quite honest, I hate the sea. I get terribly seasick and frightened.'

'We'll need a cook.'

'And I can't cook, either.' The lie came out glibly and she didn't want him to believe her.

'You used to cook extremely well.'

She frowned. 'Did I?'

He smiled broadly. 'Yes. Can't you remember?'

'No. What?'

'It was a dinner party, before you were married. You and your friend invited Philip and me for dinner. You and Philip got engaged shortly afterwards. He told us in the pub later he was checking out your cooking before he made up his mind.'

Jo shuddered. 'I think I'm very glad he left me.'

'I think I am too,' said Marcus.

'Why?' Jo didn't really want to go there, but asked all the same.

'Because if you were still together you wouldn't be on a barge, about to go to Holland.'

Was this a good thing? she wondered. 'True, but as I really don't want to go, there's nothing very good about that.'

He took a sip of his wine, put the glass down on the side, and then sat down again. She noticed that the banquette was a bit disarranged from when Tom and Dora had been sitting on it. 'But it will be fun.'

Jo sat down opposite him and curled her fingers into her hair. I must stop doing that, she thought. No wonder my hair is always such a mess. 'I don't think so.'

He continued to look at her in a way that made her twitchy. Was he surveying her, looking for signs of damage, pitting, patches of her hull that were thinner than others? The last thought made her smile but eventually she had to break the silence.

'Carole seems very nice,' she said, going on the offensive. 'Very young.'

'Yes, too young, really.'

Suddenly she stopped feeling awkward and relaxed a little. 'Well, I'm glad you can admit that! It's not right, these young women throwing themselves away on men nearly old enough to be their fathers! It's a topic I'm sensitive about, of course.'

'Philip always was a fool.' Before she could react to this provocative statement, he went on. 'But I don't like the "throwing themselves away" part of that. I'm much sought after, I'll have you know.'

Ruefully, she accepted this was probably true but she wasn't going to pander to his already more than adequately sized ego. She raised her eyebrows, alight with merriment. 'By whom?'

'By many young women who've tried to catch me.'

She chuckled. 'I'm sure that's true, but what are they after? Your massive bank balance or your renowned boat-handling skills?'

'Well, with the women, it's the former, but the men, definitely the latter.'

'So you're sought after by both sexes, are you?' Jo reflected that there were advantages to being middle-aged. You could say what you liked without any danger of being taken seriously.

'For different reasons, yes. Are you jealous?'

'Mystified,' she said solemnly. 'Unless of course you really have got a massive bank balance.'

He narrowed his eyes. 'I have, actually, but why are you being provocative?'

She shook her head, still smiling. 'I'm not! I'm just saying I don't know why all those people should pursue you. At least, I understand about the men. There was a man here the other night who said you were expensive, but if you had three hundred thousand pounds' worth of barge, you were worth it. Damn!' she added, cross with herself. 'I shouldn't have told you that. Now you'll be more bigheaded than ever.'

A smile started reluctantly at the corner of his mouth. 'Whoever said I was bigheaded?'

'No need to state the obvious.'

'Is my bigheadedness so apparent?'

'Now don't look all affronted, I dare say not everyone would notice.' She managed to stop herself patting his hand just in time.

He shook his head slightly and turned away, possibly hiding an answering smile. 'So, if you know that I'm the best skipper around, why won't you come to Holland with me?'

Now it was Jo who was on the back foot. She sighed as

she tried to explain when she didn't understand why she was so nervous about it herself. 'It's nothing to do with your skippering – your reputation precedes you. I'm just frightened at the thought of being in a small boat on the sea.'

'It's quite a large boat. It has a very well-maintained engine, going on what Michael has told me, although I will make more checks, of course. It's perfectly seaworthy, and we'll pick our weather. What is there to be frightened of?'

'Drowning, maybe?'

He dismissed this possibility with a gesture. 'Not at all!'

'Well, seasickness, definitely. I'm a terrible sailor.'

'You could take pills.'

'They knock me out. Then I certainly wouldn't be able to cook for you, although I could make up lots of dishes you could just put in the oven. There's quite a large freezer compartment in the fridge.'

'So you can cook?'

She realised she'd been caught out. 'Yes, but badly.' She smiled at him. Now she'd got over feeling she was nineteen and was back to being fifty, she was beginning to relax and enjoy his company. Not enough to go to sea with him, of course, but enough for now.

He looked at her with a hint of mock sternness and got up. He went to where the leftover lasagne was cooling, prior to being put in the fridge. He found a spoon from the cutlery container, and took some. He ate it thoughtfully. 'Mm. Not bad at all.'

Jo rose too, her instincts to feed on full alert. 'Would you like some? I could easily heat it up in the microwave. It never occurred to me you might not have eaten.'

'I have eaten,' he acknowledged, 'but not very much. Carole is very careful about my diet.'

'But you aren't?'

143

'I don't need to be, with her to do it for me.'

Jo, who had found a plate and a serving spoon, hovered over the lasagne. 'So do you want some or not?'

'Yes please.' He picked up the bottle of wine and refilled both their glasses. 'I'll bring you some wine tomorrow.'

'There's no need for that.' Jo pressed buttons on the microwave. 'It's only supermarket plonk.'

'I know. I've got some really nice wine on *Hildegarde*.'

'I thought you were taking *Hildegarde* away tomorrow. That's what Michael said.'

'Nothing's set in stone.' He took another sip of wine and grimaced slightly.

Jo took a few moments to decide whether or not she should be offended, then she laughed. 'Go and sit down. I'll bring this when it's ready.'

She was aware that she had let down the Sisterhood, that feeding a man like that was against every rule. But she liked seeing him sitting there, reading a copy of the Dutch barge magazine while she heated lasagne and added a bit of tomato and cucumber to the leftover salad. It must be because, at heart, she was a provider, a wife and mother, most fulfilled when caring for others. It was a salutary thought.

'Here you are,' she said. 'It's ready.'

She sipped her wine and watched him eat, wondering what Miranda would say if she could see her. Would she chide her for falling back into her old ways of being wifely? Or would she understand that seeing someone eating with evident pleasure the food you had cooked was satisfying?

'Well, you've definitely blown your cover, I'm afraid,' he said. 'You cook better than ever.'

'Perhaps I didn't cook it!' She challenged him with her eyes.

He gave her a sidelong smile. 'Oh come on. Of course you cooked it.' He wiped his plate with a bit of bread.

'Well, possibly,' she conceded. 'There's a bit of Eton Mess for pudding if you'd like it.'

A look of sheer ecstasy flickered across his face. 'Yes please. Don't tell Carole.'

'I won't if you won't, but do make sure you take that bit of ragù off your shirt.'

He looked down quickly and then scrubbed at a tiny spot of tomato. Jo reflected that Carole taking care of his diet was the reason his middle-age spread was kept to a minimum. Maybe younger women were good for men after all. But what would become of the older ones?

'Here's your pudding,' she said, adding a sprig of mint from the pot she had brought down from the wheelhouse to the dish on impulse. She didn't care that some restaurant critics thought it was common – she liked to eat it. 'Would you like some coffee?'

'I've still got some wine, thank you.' He handed her his dirty plate and accepted the pudding in return.

'Even though it isn't very nice wine.'

'I didn't say it wasn't nice. I just said I've got some that's much nicer on *Hildegarde*. This pudding, however, is to die for.'

'I hope you don't mean that literally. Do you have a problem with your cholesterol?'

He laughed. 'Not at all.'

'Probably thanks to Carole.' She was aware she probably sounded snippy, but she couldn't help it – her recent experiences made it impossible to be completely normal about such things.

'Maybe. She doesn't really appreciate good wine.'

'Perhaps that's something that comes with age? Like opera?'

He snorted. 'I've never liked opera.'

'Perhaps you're not old enough. I only like some of it.'

'I'm older than you,' he said.

'Well, it's an acquired taste. Like boating, probably.'

'You probably just need to make an effort,' he said sternly. 'With opera or boating.'

'I don't think that would work with me. I'm just too frightened.'

'What, of opera?'

She laughed but shook her head. 'No!'

'I think you should give it a go. I promise not to do anything that could possibly frighten you.'

'Does Carole like boating?' Perhaps he'd taken her out on small trips to begin with, so she could gain her confidence.

'Oh yes. At least, I think so. I haven't actually asked her.'

Jo opened her mouth to tell him he was very selfish but as she wasn't absolutely sure this was true, shut it again.

He got up. He put down his dish with a clatter. 'I'd better go. Carole will be wondering where I am.'

Jo stood up too, and realised Marcus was much taller than Philip. She moved past him to the door to the stairs, opened it and went up them. The fluttery teenager in her couldn't help wondering if he was looking at her bottom and thinking how big it was. Carole's bottom was of the pert, tight, high variety. Hers no longer was and possibly never had been.

They reached the wheelhouse and he turned to her. 'Do think carefully about coming on the trip. It could be really interesting. I never usually encourage owners – they can be a bloody nuisance. I'm making an exception for you.'

She laughed, feeling a bit lightheaded, possibly because of the wine. 'But I'm not the owner, Michael is.'

He smiled. 'That probably explains it.'

146

'Well, on behalf of Michael, I'll thank you for coming to look at *The Three Sisters*. Will you email him or shall I?'

'I will. I need to ask him if the fuel tanks have been cleaned out within living memory. If not, it'll have to be done before we go. There are a couple of things as well. I didn't look at the navigation lights.'

She felt guilty. 'Oh. I shouldn't have given you lasagne. I distracted you from your job.'

'Yes you did,' he said. 'But I was happy to be distracted. Goodnight, Joanna.'

She watched him walk away thinking that most men would have kissed her cheek. The fact that he hadn't was more disturbing than if he had. She went back down into the saloon contemplating her feelings. He wasn't the first man she'd entertained by herself since she'd been on the barge. She never had been the sort of woman who assumes every man is making a pass at her, even when she'd been of an age to be made a pass at, but she'd found Marcus both unsettling and exciting. 'Perhaps they're the same thing,' she said aloud as she cleared up his plates and glass.

The week whistled by for Dora as she struggled to bring a little order to the chaos that was the boatyard's office. It didn't take very long before she became much loved and depended on. She made tea twice a day for everyone, and people gathered in her little office space to collect it. When she wasn't chatting, she was filing, sorting and recycling forests' worth of paper. She set up a program so she could do the wages quickly and efficiently and even acquired a wall planner and made everyone decide when they were going on holiday.

Jo was putting the whole dry-dock business out of her mind, or at least she tried to. She was concentrating on her gilding.

Although she was not frightened of the gold leaf in the same way she was frightened of crossing the North Sea in a barge, she was anxious.

All her little bits of carving had been glued on, sanded, gessoed, coated with glue size mixed with clay. Her friend at the art shop had told her to mix up a combination of size, water and a drop of vodka for the final layer and to arrange the surface she was using to be slightly sloping so the water couldn't run back over the gold she had laid. Then she opened her book of gold leaf. It seemed about half the thickness of tissue paper and threatened to float away. It was like trying to catch a strand of gossamer. Just managing to catch it on her gilder's tip she watched it float down to the suede where it would be safe for a few moments. She divided it into two and then brushed her tip over her arm a couple more times, as instructed, so the oil from her skin would help the gold adhere to the bristles. Then, carefully with her clean sable brush she wetted an area a little larger than the space the gold would occupy. Finally, her tongue between her teeth, she caught the gold leaf and offered it up.

Like magic it leapt from the brush and attached itself to the carving.

'Wow,' she said out loud. 'That really is alchemy.'

A little braver now, she wetted the next section, brushed the tip over her arm and caught up the next piece of gold leaf.

After applying two pieces she had to make herself a cup of tea to help calm her down. She hadn't done anything so exciting for years. Later she would rub it smooth with the agate burnisher until it looked as if the wood was made of gold.

She tried to convey her excitement to Dora when she came home but she realised, as she saw Dora's somewhat glazed expression, that you had to have been there, really.

Tom, who'd become a regular guest at mealtimes, worried away at the two women about the dry docking with the persistence of a particularly obsessive terrier.

'You two should definitely go. It'll be brilliant! I'm going to go, if I can persuade Marcus to take me.'

'What was he like, Jo?' asked Dora. 'What did you think of him?'

Jo was glad she'd had a second to think of an answer. The trouble was, she didn't really know what she thought of him. He was confused in her mind with the Marcus she'd known before. Had he changed? Or was he still a bit arrogant, a bit of a womaniser, someone she didn't have the confidence to be natural with? She decided to be economical with the truth until she was clear in her own mind. 'He seemed very professional. He took a lot of trouble to check things.'

'That's reassuring,' said Dora, putting plates in the dishwasher.

Tom was wiping the table. 'The blokes with boats that cost the same as London flats wouldn't let him move them about unless they trusted him.'

Perhaps I should trust him too, thought Jo. Although probably only where boats are concerned.

Over the following days, Dora and Jo got tired of hearing how much fun going to Holland would be, how brilliant Marcus was, at least by reputation, and how they'd be mad to miss the opportunity to go on the trip.

Dora, who had become used to Tom being there to row her across the creek when she finished work, was aware she'd miss him if he wasn't around. Her loyalty to the boatyard had been instant, and knowing she might want to take leave so soon focused her mind. She stayed late several nights and was making huge progress. She couldn't decide if she wanted to go to Holland or not.

Jo was only concentrating her attention on her gilding and her trip to her old home, planned for the weekend. It would be the first time she had gone back and she wasn't looking forward to it. She made lists of things she wanted to collect, aware that she might not remember anything once she got there. 'I'm bound to forget Karen's fork-lift truck certificate,' she warned herself, 'which is the whole reason for going!'

As they set off down the motorway in Jo's little car, Dora was aware that Jo had been unsettled since the trip was proposed and Marcus had visited. She couldn't tell if it was the thought of seeing her garden again, or the house infiltrated by the Floosie. It was bound to be emotional. She had emailed Karen about it, who had railed against her father all over again.

Now, Jo put the radio on and they travelled the thirty odd miles mostly in silence.

'They're not going to be there, are they?' asked Dora, as they drove through the village. Suddenly anxious herself, she was on the alert in case she saw anyone she knew and had to duck. She still wasn't ready to go back, she realised, and didn't know if Jo was either.

'I insisted that they shouldn't be,' said Jo. 'I don't want to have to be polite when I see what she's done to my home. I can't believe she got rid of the wallpaper in the spare room. It was terribly expensive! It was toile de Jouy – you know? It's a French thing. There are little drawings of people ploughing and tending their sheep usually. But this was modern. It was a city, with road-menders and diggers and even a man throwing up in the gutter.' She made a noise very like a growl.

150

'Oh, there's Mrs Thing!' said Dora in alarm. She hunched down in her seat before allowing her head to rise enough for her to see. 'It's OK, she hasn't spotted me.' Dora felt herself go hot and cold.

'Mrs Who?'

'I don't know her name, but she came up to me in the shop and told me I was a very selfish young woman.'

Jo tutted supportively. 'Take no notice. Here we are. Hop out and open the gate, will you?'

Chapter Eleven

❦

As requested, Dora hopped and Jo drove in. The climbing rose up the side of the house was just coming into bloom and summer shimmered on the threshold, about to descend into her full glory.

Jo noticed the rose and wondered, as she always did, why yellow roses were always the first to bloom. Then she noticed a planter. It was a miniature wheelbarrow full of brightly coloured primulas, egg-yellow, shocking pink and mauve. Jo loved old fashioned polyanthus, with their wonderful, old-fashioned names, and there was a bank under a hedge that was starred with wild primroses in the spring, but she didn't like these artificial hybrids. She wasn't keen on miniature wheelbarrows, either.

'Come on, let's go in,' she said to Dora after a moment, and then got out of the car.

There was an arrangement of silk flowers on the hall table. Jo had always had something real there, even if it was only twigs with a few optimistic buds. Of course, silk flowers could be very pretty and they didn't need attention, they didn't drop or die or run out of water. She glanced at the mixture of blooms, which wouldn't have been flowering together naturally, and passed on.

'Let's go into the kitchen.'

As she stood on the threshold she was overcome with despair. All the feelings of loss and abandonment that she thought she'd got over came welling up as she saw the room that had been the heart of her home. It had changed from a farmhouse-style centre of comfort and pleasure to a hotpotch of styles that was more like a showroom than a working kitchen.

The table under the window was made of stainless steel, with two spindly-legged chairs under it. It was round and tiny, only big enough for a couple. Jo had had a solid pine table, scarred by the years and used for everything, for rolling out pastry, for sticking and pasting, for Karen's and often Dora's homework. Her favourite sort of dinner party happened there too.

Now she turned to where once her Rayburn had been the source of so much warmth and nourishment ever since they'd moved into the house, over twenty years ago. It had been replaced by a range cooker, but one disguised as a real range. It had matt-black doors and there were covers to the burners; Jo half expected to see fake flames flickering through a mica panel, like something on a stage set. Over the top of this black and silver monster were stencils of cornflowers and poppies.

'I suppose stencils have come in again,' said Dora, peering at them closely. 'They're not very well done. I wonder if she did the cupboard doors as well?'

The cupboard doors were also decorated with some sort of paint effect. 'I think that's dragging,' said Jo. 'I remember reading about it.'

'It's awful,' said Dora. 'If the Floosie did it, she's not very handy with a paintbrush.'

'No,' said Jo. 'Dora, would you mind if I went outside for a moment? I need to get my head together. I think coming back was a bit of a mistake. Why don't you rummage round in the attic and see if you can find those tapes of you and Karen?'

Jo sat on a bench in the garden, the back part of which

was as yet unchanged. Reality had hit her in the face and she needed to recover. When she'd first left Philip and gone to live on the barge she'd felt in charge, pro-active, but although she knew she was leaving the home she'd created over the years and the husband she'd had for nearly thirty, she hadn't really taken in that those things were gone for ever.

'I should have stayed,' she muttered. 'I shouldn't have left my house. I made it.' Every stick of furniture she had either bought or restored or loved into usefulness. Now her kitchen table was exchanged for a spindly metal monstrosity and her lovely Rayburn, nurturer of everything from people to kittens, was replaced by a fake version of itself. It was horrible.

A tear slid down her cheek and as she brushed it away she forced herself out of her pit of grief. This was not the way forward; she couldn't afford the indulgence. She'd done her weeping, her raging, now she had to live.

She took a deep breath, got up and went to find Dora.

Jo found her in the sitting room. French windows looked out onto the garden via a large paved area. The garden beyond was beginning to look glorious.

Dora remembered that Jo used to spend a lot of time gardening and thought she probably had very mixed feelings looking at it now.

'Nice patio furniture,' said Dora.

'Yes. Shall we take it? We could put it on deck. It would be nice to have something to sit on.'

'Would it go in the car?'

'Probably not, and you're right, we can't take anything I haven't arranged to take.'

'I never said that!' Dora protested.

'I know, but you thought it. Let's go and find my clothes. He knows I'm taking those. Also the biggest saucepan and my omelette pan. They'd be useful for the trip to Holland . . . for whoever is going. Did you find those tapes?'

'Yes, they're in my bag. And you mustn't forget Karen's certificate, although you could definitely take more than that,' said Dora, relieved that Jo wasn't going to do what would feel very like stealing.

'I'll get it now. It's in a file in that little bureau.' Jo crossed the room to the little piece of furniture she had saved for ages to buy. 'I've no idea why Philip couldn't find it.' She opened the front of the desk and a lot of bits of paper fell out. Jo made herself laugh – it was better than crying. 'See! Perfectly easy – put my hand right on it.'

To Dora's amazement, Jo did have her hand on a pale mauve folder with 'Valuable Documents' written on it.

'I hate to think I'm not being supportive,' said Dora, 'but I think I might not have found that straightaway.'

Chuckling, Jo extracted Karen's certificate.

'I'll take that for you,' said Dora, who still had her bag slung round her neck.

'Thank you. Now, let's go and find a drink of water. I'm suddenly dreadfully thirsty.'

'It's probably stress,' said Dora.

'It's summer!' said Jo, not wanting to acknowledge her feelings even if Dora was meaning to be kind.

They went into the kitchen and Jo found glasses and filled them from the big American-style fridge that had a water dispenser.

'We would have loved this when we were little, Karen and me,' said Dora, doing the same. 'Oh look, it does crushed ice. We could have played cocktail bars.'

'I like cocktails,' said Jo. 'Do you want some more water?'

'I'm fine for now.'

'Come on then, let's hit the bedroom.'

Dora had no way of knowing how much had changed when they got upstairs but judging by Jo's expression the bed hadn't been covered in fluffy toys when she had had it.

'So what do they do when they want to get in at night? Take them all off, I suppose,' said Jo. 'I wonder what Philip thinks about all this?'

Dora found herself wandering over to the dressing table, which was antique and very pretty. 'Was this yours?'

'Yes. It was my mother's. I will take it back when I've got a house. It's got glass on it, and so shouldn't get damaged if the Floosie spills her nail varnish. Golly, I've changed since I last looked in a decent mirror.' Jo laughed. 'I need a haircut!'

Dora came up behind her. 'I remember me and Karen going through your make-up, trying it on. Were you furious?'

'I don't remember if I ever found out. You couldn't have done much damage with it.'

'There was a lipstick that got broken.'

Jo laughed again. 'Oh yes. Very bright red. It stayed on the towels forever. I had to dye them in the end.'

Dora was abashed. 'I'm so sorry! What a pain!'

'Not at all. I was into dyeing at the time. Right, now, which cupboard did he say?' She opened one of the fitted cupboards, then another, until they were all open. 'Well, they're not here. Where are they?' She took out a hanger with a rectangle of black leather hanging on it. 'The Floosie must be tiny.'

'Haven't you met her?'

Jo shook her head. 'Philip wanted to show me a picture on his phone, but I didn't want to look. He said she's just like I was when young. I didn't want to see the difference to how I am now.'

'You're lovely now.'

'I was never that size,' she said, putting the rectangle back. 'OK, let's go and see if my clothes are in the spare room. Oh,' she said a moment or two later when they had crossed the landing. 'This is so boring. I had such lovely paper in here, it was quirky and fun. Now it's just – chintzy. I don't know why, but I never like having matching wallpaper, curtains and bed linen and this has got just too many roses.'

'I'm not sure I'm that keen, either,' said Dora. 'In fact, Samantha – is that her name? – seems to have quite retro tastes. Are these your clothes, do you think? In these bin liners?'

Jo appeared to take her possessions being stuffed into bags like so much jumble quite calmly. She opened one. 'Yes. I must say, as I had taken all my winter clothes, I do think she could have left these in the wardrobe.'

Dora pulled out a sundress. 'They're awfully crushed. Is there an ironing board on the boat?'

'Don't think so. I haven't really needed one up until now. I used to have a wonderful woman who did my ironing for me. She was brilliant at it and did it all in about five minutes.' She lapsed into silence and when she spoke again she sounded tired. 'Still, I suppose you wouldn't really want to see the first wife's clothes hanging there every time you open a cupboard door.'

'You're being awfully reasonable,' said Dora. 'I'd go ballistic if I found all my clothes scrunched up into rubbish bags!'

Jo sighed. 'I'm trying very hard not to go ballistic. It doesn't achieve much. Now, let's go through these to make sure I'm not filling the boat with clothes I can't get into.

157

'I should have done this years ago,' she went on a few minutes later, pulling off a cotton sweater that was definitely too tight. 'I haven't worn that for years.'

Dora picked up the jumper. 'This is really nice.'

'Do you want it? Help yourself. I'm always very flattered when Karen takes my things, although they are usually my cashmere jumpers.' She paused suddenly. 'I might not be able to afford cashmere jumpers soon.'

'Why not?'

'Well, Philip's bound to stop being so generous eventually. He's still feeling guilty, but that'll wear off. I'll have to earn my own living. I really hope I can earn enough from restoring collectables and antiques.' She hugged a striped Breton top to her. 'Philip bought me this from France, years and years ago. I couldn't convince him that horizontal stripes weren't a good idea for a woman of my shape.'

'Put it on! I think it might look nice! Or does it remind you of the good old days?' Dora bit her lip, afraid that she'd been lacking in tact.

Jo pulled off the T-shirt she'd been wearing. 'I'm not at all sure,' she said through the top as she pulled it down.

'It does suit you, really it does. It sort of nips you in at the waist.'

'Does it?' Jo considered her reflection. 'Mm, perhaps you're right. Let's put the clothes I'm taking in this bag and the ones that need disposing of in that one.'

'That's such lovely fabric,' said Dora, looking at a wrap-around skirt.

'Does anyone wear skirts like this these days?' asked Jo. 'It would make lovely cushions.'

'Have you got a sewing machine?'

'Yes I have actually, in the attic. I don't think Philip would mind if I took that. It is mine, after all.'

158

'Let's go and look, then we can make cushions out of the clothes you don't want to keep and sell them.'

Jo laughed. 'It would take a lot of cushions to buy a cashmere sweater.'

'Never mind! Many a little makes a lottle – or something.'

'I think you mean "many a mickle macks a muckle",' said Jo, starting to giggle.

'Do I?' Dora giggled too and picked up a pair of linen trousers. 'I think you should wear these.'

'I think one leg should wear them, though I'm not sure what the other leg would wear, they're tiny. In fact, they're Karen's. You have them.'

Dora was struggling into them when they heard a car pull up on the gravel outside. Jo rushed to the window.

'Oh no! It's Philip and – Samantha! What are they doing here so early?'

'Oh God, I've got stuck in these trousers!' said Dora, trying in vain to pull them off. 'How old was Karen when she had these?'

'I told him we'd be here this morning. He promised he'd keep away until twelve though he'd said I could have a whole day to begin with. He is the limit! Shall we run out through the back?'

'I can't run anywhere!' declared Dora. 'I'm hobbled by these wretched trousers. I can't pull them up or down!'

'I'll have to find something to cut them with. Here – there's a manicure set. It's bound to have scissors.'

The tiny scissors made no impression on the cloth.

'Oh God, this is so awful,' said Dora. 'My circulation is being cut off. They'll have to amputate my legs, let alone the trousers.'

Jo felt a bubble of laughter rising and fought it down. 'There'll be some better scissors in the kitchen. I'll run down and get them.' They both heard the front door open. 'Too late. They're here now.'

Both women stood, Dora swaying slightly in an effort to keep her balance, listening. They heard the sounds of things being tossed on the hall table, keys jangling, the door shutting, and then, a moment later, a female voice.

'Where is she, then?'

The voice was tense and a little on the shrill side.

'She must be upstairs,' said Philip. 'Jo!' he called up the stairs. 'Are you there?'

After a quick glance at Dora, frantically struggling again, Jo went out on to the landing so she could talk to Philip. To her irrational relief, his companion had gone into another room. 'Yes. I thought you'd arranged to be out. Until twelve. I was going to have a whole day, then a morning, now it's only about an hour!'

'Samantha forgot something. It is her home, she can come and go as she wants.' He sounded angrier than the pre-arranged presence of his ex-wife in his house really warranted.

'Dora's here,' said Jo, staying calm. 'We need some scissors.'

A small scream was heard from the kitchen. 'She's cutting up my clothes! Philip! Do something!'

'Jo! How dare you?' demanded Philip, one foot on the bottom step.

Jo looked down at him, unable to credit what she was hearing. 'I'm not cutting up anything – except a pair of Karen's old trousers. No, don't come up. I'll come and get some scissors out of the kitchen.'

She went downstairs and met her husband's new love drinking a glass of water. She was very young, moderately pretty, with long bare legs shown off to their best advantage by a miniskirt. Jo had to concede Samantha did

160

look a little like she had done when she was that age. Samantha undoubtedly drank many litres of water a day. Had she been a friend of Karen's, Jo probably would have liked her, but as her own replacement in Philip's bed, liking was impossible. Maturity was the only advantage she had in this situation and Jo did her best to sound grown up. 'Hello,' she said, holding out her hand. 'You must be Samantha. I'm Joanna.'

'But everyone calls her Jo,' said Philip, coming up behind them.

Jo ignored him. 'Would you mind if I found a pair of scissors from the kitchen? My friend is upstairs. She tried on a pair of my – our – daughter's trousers and she can't get them off or on.' She smiled, still trying to keep up her role as a benign headmistress on speech day – terribly polite and terribly patronising.

Philip and the Floosie exchanged glances but didn't move as she went to the drawer where she had always kept the scissors. Thankfully, they were still there. She picked them up and they felt familiar in her hand. She'd made cardboard castles, Romeo and Juliet's balcony, model theatres, produced any amount of Christmas cards and cut enough wrapping paper to encircle the earth, all with those faithful scissors. Now she had to ask to borrow them.

She cleared her throat. 'Excuse me,' she said to Samantha, who was blocking her way.

Samantha wouldn't move. 'What are you going to do with those scissors?' she demanded.

'I told you, rescue my friend from a very tenacious pair of linen trousers.'

'You're not going up there!' said Samantha, highly agitated. 'I've read about people like you, taking revenge. I don't know what you might do! My clothes are all designer labels. I don't want you cutting them to pieces.'

161

It seemed to Jo that the younger woman was on the verge of hysteria. 'Why would I want to do a thing like that?'

'Because you're jealous! I've taken your husband!'

Jo took a deep breath. There was no doubt that she was the injured party, but she was not going to spend time placating this young woman and as Philip would doubtless object if Jo threw water over her, she'd have to try and cool her off by other means. Thanking God for her part in a WI play many years ago, Jo got into her role.

'Darling,' she drawled in the most patronising manner she could manage, 'one isn't jealous of the bin men when they take away your rubbish. One is grateful, and gives them a tip at Christmas.' Wondering if she'd overdone the 'ones' she smiled graciously, and, as Philip and Samantha instinctively made way for her, went back upstairs.

'Mad woman!' she muttered to Dora who was hiding behind the bed. 'She accused me of wanting to cut up her clothes because I'm jealous!' She turned her attention to Dora's predicament. The waistband of the trousers were cutting deep into her thighs, just below the hip. 'I don't want to cut you by mistake.'

They heard footsteps outside. 'Oh God,' said Dora, 'they're coming in! Hurry up! Please!'

Jo eased the blades of the scissors between Dora's flesh and the fabric and cut. As Philip and Samantha entered the room she tugged hard at the nick. A ripping sound filled the silence for long seconds.

'I knew it!' screamed Samantha. 'She's up to something. What's she hiding?'

Philip stood by looking anxious. Jo leapt to her feet, aware that Dora didn't want to appear half-naked in front of Philip. 'I'm not hiding anything – at least – not anything in the sense you mean.'

'I don't believe you!' Samantha screeched. 'There was a tearing noise. You're tearing my clothes. Or my new curtains – something!'

'My dear, while good taste suggests that cutting up the curtains and duvet cover in this room would be an excellent idea, I haven't done it. Now, if you could give us a moment or two of privacy we'll be able to set your mind at rest.'

Samantha was not to be pacified. 'I don't believe you! You're up to something ghastly! Of course you're jealous! It's only normal!'

'Sweetie, don't upset yourself,' said Philip, trying to sound soothing but actually sounding a little hysterical himself. 'Your hormones are all over the place. Jo wouldn't do anything spiteful. We've just found out,' he added to Jo confidingly. 'Samantha's pregnant! It's why we came home so soon. Isn't that wonderful?'

Jo's head swam and for an awful moment she thought she was going to faint. She moved round so she could sit on the bed. Stars danced around her head and her blood was pounding so loudly it seemed to be running through her ears. She shut her eyes.

'Jo! Are you all right?' Dora, setting aside her modesty, got up and perched on the bed next to her.

The blackness cleared and Jo pushed her hair back from her forehead. 'I'm fine. I just suddenly felt hot. Must be *my* hormones!' Her smile, though brave, was very brittle. 'Philip, could I trouble you for a glass of water?'

'I'll get one immediately.' He nodded a hello in Dora's direction and turned to leave the room.

Jo was touched to see genuine concern in his eyes and felt a little better. 'No, it's all right, I'll come downstairs. Dora and I have more or less finished sorting clothes, haven't we?'

Samantha, apparently not convinced that her designer clothes were not in danger from the rather blunt kitchen scissors, didn't move. Philip waited, putting a hand under Jo's elbow as she got up.

Dora, obviously longing to be left alone to get her own trousers on, said, 'Why don't you go down? I'll get dressed and tidy up here.'

'I'm sorry if it sounds neurotic,' said Samantha, 'but I'll stay upstairs, too.'

Dora really would have preferred to get her own trousers on in private. She didn't know Samantha, didn't like her, and didn't want her seeing her putting her less slim and less brown legs into her slightly grubby combats, but she smiled. 'Be my guest.'

Samantha opened the wardrobe doors and ran a hand over her clothes just to be sure. Seemingly satisfied, she turned to Dora. 'So, is Jo very bitter?' she asked. 'She's bound to be. I don't blame her, I suppose, but she'd got very boring, Philip says. She can't have been surprised that he found another woman.'

'I don't think you could say she was bitter at all,' said Dora defensively. 'She's been very upbeat about the whole thing.' She laughed. 'In fact, she said that *Philip* had got very boring, so maybe they'd just fallen out of love with each other. I don't think she's jealous of you at all.' Dora didn't know if this was entirely true, but Jo had been putting a very brave face on things and she didn't want to give the Floosie any more ammunition.

'But I've got her house. My mother would never have let Dad have the house. He had to go and live in a ghastly little flat when he and Mum split up.'

'Jo's a very special person,' said Dora, 'and although I probably shouldn't tell you this, I wouldn't be surprised if she was snapped up by another man very soon.'

Samantha made a face. 'But how could she be? She's old!'

'She's younger than Philip, she told me, and she's a very attractive woman. The men on the moorings have been flocking round her. Some men like the more mature woman,' she added.

'But her figure's gone, her hair is a disaster, and while I do admit she's got good skin, I mean . . .'

Aware that Samantha wasn't capable of expressing what she really meant, Dora said, 'But don't you think it's the person that matters? I mean, Uncle Philip – sorry!' She laughed artificially. Actually, she'd never called Karen's father anything except Mr Edwards. 'Philip – I used to call him "Uncle" when I was a little girl – is quite a lot older than you are, but you don't notice his turkey neck and saggy stomach, do you? You love the real Philip, the one inside.'

Samantha bit her lip. 'Yes, of course . . . hey, you wouldn't like to come and see my wedding dress, would you?'

'Your wedding dress? But Philip and Jo aren't divorced yet, are they?'

'Well, no, but we're going to have a special party to tell all our friends about us being together and everything. Now we can tell them about the baby too.'

Feeling that Jo might want a bit of time alone with her ex-husband, Dora reluctantly followed Samantha back into the master bedroom.

While Samantha and Dora were upstairs, Jo sat down at the kitchen and accepted a glass of water.

'Do you think I could have my sewing machine?' she said quietly once she felt able to speak again. 'It's in the attic.'

'Of course,' Philip said. 'Shall I get it down for you?'

'That would be kind. You bought it for me when Karen started to need costumes for her dancing lessons. Do you remember?'

'That's right! She was a talented little thing, wasn't she?'

'Still is, only not as a dancer.' She was aware that he must miss talking about his only child. Samantha wouldn't want to hear how well Karen was getting on, running an art gallery in Toronto. 'You'll have another baby to think about soon.'

'Yes, but Karen—'

'Is your first child, the only one we had together.'

He swallowed, as if remembering the heartbreak that subsequent attempts at parenthood had caused. 'At least I know . . .'

'That it wasn't your fault,' Jo finished for him. 'That's very nice for you. Now would you be a dear and get the sewing machine for me?' She needed space alone more than she needed any amount of machinery.

'Of course.'

Jo was still sitting at the table when Dora and Samantha appeared. 'Philip's gone into the attic to get my sewing machine.'

'A sewing machine!' said Samantha. 'I've always wanted one of those.'

'I'm sure Philip will get you one if you ask him,' said Jo, her patience wearing thin.

'Or you could buy your own,' suggested Dora, who was a different generation.

'I'd like to make the baby little clothes,' Samantha said confidingly. 'I used to make dresses for my Barbie.'

'Did you?' Reluctantly, Jo felt some respect. 'Now that's really fiddly. I would have thought you'd have had to do

166

most of it by hand. I once made a suede jacket for Karen's Sindy—'

'I was so jealous of it!' said Dora, her youth coming back to her in a rush.

'It was only fake suede,' said Jo. 'Oh, here's Philip.'

'Sweet cakes! I was just saying, I really want a sewing machine.' Samantha was obviously remembering a happy childhood playing with dolls too.

'Could you put that into the car for me?' Jo asked Philip. 'I'll take the clothes.'

'I can take them,' said Dora, 'or the machine.'

'It's all right, I'll take it,' said Philip. 'Sammy, darling, you wouldn't like to think about making some lunch, would you?'

They all trooped outside, including Samantha, who obviously felt the need to be near Philip, just in case.

Philip put the sewing machine in the back of the car. 'I hope you're going to be all right, Jo. I do worry about you.'

'I'm going to be absolutely fine,' said Jo firmly.

'And you're not going to go on this ridiculous trip to Holland, are you? Michael told me all about it. I was appalled. It sounds grossly irresponsible. You're very welcome to stay with us, both of you, while someone else takes it.'

Samantha's expression of horror at her new man's sense of duty would have made Jo laugh in normal circumstances. Now, she couldn't remember what normal circumstances were.

'A trip like that' – Philip went on solicitously – 'is not really the sort of thing a woman of your age should undertake.'

For a ghastly moment, Dora thought she was about to witness a murder, but Jo seemed very calm.

'Oh, I don't think my age means I should miss out on a

167

chance of an adventure, do you? I mean, I only have myself to worry about now and it would be a shame to miss what could be the trip of a lifetime!'

'But you know how sick you get and you'd hate it.'

'Oh, I'm definitely going.' She got into the car, slammed the door and opened the window. 'I've got the chance to live a bit now I'm no longer married. I want to take full advantage.' She smiled. 'Oh, and by the way, remember Marcus? He's skippering.'

Jo felt a wicked pleasure in seeing Philip's look of bewilderment and then slight displeasure. It made up a little for the horror of the last half-hour.

'Thank you for getting my sewing machine,' she added sweetly as she started the engine.

Dora saw from Jo's and Philip's expressions the way the conversation was going, and leapt into the car with alacrity, a black plastic bag clutched to her bosom.

A little way down the road, Dora said, 'That Samantha is a piece of work! It must have been utterly horrible for you. Shall I take you out to a pub for lunch?'

Jo sighed. 'That would be lovely! Somewhere with a garden where we can take our shoes off. I'm awfully hot.'

After they had found the perfect pub and were settled under an umbrella in the garden, their food ordered, she said, 'This is so kind of you, Dora, you don't need to pay for me. It could come out of your rent.'

'Not at all. I'm a wage-earner now. I can afford some treats. Besides, I've got a bit of a confession to make to you.'

'Oh, what?'

Dora sipped her spritzer. 'I said that the men on the moorings were flocking round you.'

'You did? Why?' Jo asked, raising her face to the sun and feeling the stress of the morning gradually ease.

'Because Samantha said you must be jealous of her, and

I couldn't bear it, so I said you had no need to be jealous and that Philip had got very boring and she had no need to pity you. Although actually,' she went on thoughtfully, 'I think she is jealous of you.'

Jo didn't speak for a few moments. 'To be absolutely honest, I was a bit jealous of her for a few moments. It's why I nearly fainted.'

'From jealousy?' Dora was appalled.

'No, shock, more. It was when Philip told me they were going to have a baby. It just hit me.'

'But you wouldn't want another baby!' Dora was aghast. 'Would you?'

'Good God no! Not at my age! But we did try to have another after Karen, in fact Karen took about five years to turn up. We – well, maybe it was just me – really wanted another baby. Now Philip's going to have one. He was a very good father,' she added.

Dora found herself unbearably saddened at Jo's plight. The longed-for baby was going to Philip, who was the one in the wrong. It did seem that his bad behaviour was being rewarded, while Jo's good manners were doing her no good at all. They sat in silence for a while and then Dora said, 'Did you mean it when you said you were definitely going to Holland?'

Jo took a deep breath and released it again. 'Oh, I think I'd better now, don't you?'

'Yes!' said Dora, punching the air in a restrained way. 'Then I will too! Tom will be so pleased!'

'Do you want to please Tom, Dora?' Jo looked at her questioningly.

'Well, sort of, but it's mainly because it would be a challenge. Tom thinks I'm awfully pathetic.'

'He can't think you're pathetic now. You've got racing tips and done karaoke.'

'Those dares are different. Going to Holland on the barge would be a real challenge, don't you think?'

'Deffo,' said Jo and Dora laughed.

Chapter Twelve

Jo awoke the following morning with a sense of doom so deep she had to check that no one had died. The moment she was properly awake she realised why: her ex-husband was going to be a father again and she had committed herself to going on a trip that genuinely terrified her. She got up, determined to clamber out of this Slough of Despond before anyone noticed she was in one. Her strange, personal ladder was to cook an old-fashioned Sunday lunch. It involved soothing, familiar tasks and the stress at the end always gave way to a sense of triumph. She needed to feel in control again.

Dora, unaware of Jo's different priorities, was intent on planning the trip to Holland.

'So, where are we all going to sleep?' she asked. 'If Marcus has your cabin – are you sure you have to give it to him?'

'Yes,' said Jo, who was peeling carrots. 'He has to be near the action, and it's quiet and comfortable.'

'OK, then you must have my double cabin, I'll have the single, but where will Tom go? On the sofa?'

'He could, but I'm not keen. I suppose we should clear out the glory hole.' She bit her lip at the prospect. She had managed to more or less ignore this space since she'd moved on to the boat, apart from the few ghastly times when its door had been opened during the parade of boats, and didn't really want to attack it now, when she had so many other things on her mind.

'But where would we put all the stuff?' Dora asked. 'If it's Michael's, we can hardly throw it away. If only boats had attics. I don't think we saw a single barge with attic space, although they had everything else.'

Jo smiled in spite of her preoccupations. 'I'll email Michael and ask him. Really,' she went on, sounding less amused, 'I hate to sound ungrateful, but if Michael had lent me a country cottage he wouldn't have been able to ask me to move it, or with it.'

'No, but he could have asked you to have the dry rot seen to, or some such. That would have been much worse.'

'True.' Jo wondered if she should confide her terror to Dora but decided not to. 'But this trip to Holland is causing us both a lot of work.'

'But it's going to be such fun!' Dora insisted, trying to conjure up some enthusiasm for them both. 'Tom was so thrilled when I rang him about it last night. He's coming over later to see how the plans are going.'

'He's coming to check that I haven't chickened out, more likely,' said Jo. 'But if he's coming, he can help us shift stuff. His reward is Sunday lunch.'

'I'll ring him. Why don't you email Michael and ask if we can chuck his rubbish?'

Jo regarded her young friend with her head on one side. 'I don't remember you being this bossy when you were a little girl, Dora.'

'I've grown up a lot since then,' said Dora, 'and I learnt a lot from Karen.' She frowned. 'I think the real reason was that I let my mother make all those wedding arrangements, and I never argued with her once. She chose the style of dress, the flowers, what sort of a reception we should have, everything. This was her day, I thought, John and I have the rest of our lives. Then I realised that I didn't want the rest of my life with John, and that I must take control a bit.' She grinned. 'Which was why I ran away to live with you. A surrogate mother cooking Sunday lunch!'

Jo laughed. 'Except there seems to have been a bit of role reversal,' she said. 'Go and ring Tom. I'll try emailing Michael.'

Dora went up on deck, where the reception was better, to do this. She reflected what a really good friend Tom was. He not only made her have a lot of fun but he was really supportive, sort of like an older brother. Of course, Dora reminded herself, she didn't want anything else from him – that would make things far too complicated.

As Jo had declined help with peeling the potatoes, Dora decided to tidy her cabin, which hadn't had much attention since she'd started her job. She stowed away the bits and pieces that she had bought yesterday, wondering what would happen between her and Tom if either of them did want a relationship. He was a normal, healthy male, he was bound to want a girlfriend sooner or later. He wouldn't want Dora hanging around then.

A bag of woolly socks that she had last worn at school got filed neatly in the waste-paper basket. Her mother had made her take them, convinced that boats were all freezing cold, even in summer. She must be on the alert. If she got any hint from Tom that he fancied anyone else, she must make it clear that it was fine by her – she just wanted to enjoy being single for a while.

Jo came to her door. 'Michael was on-line, luckily, and he says we can throw away anything we like as long as Marcus doesn't think it might be useful.'

'For goodness' sake! How are we expected to second-guess what Marcus will think! I wish I'd met him,' Dora added. 'It would make it much easier.'

Jo laughed. 'I expect we'll be able to tell if there's

anything we might need to keep. Michael says we can put things we're not sure of in the forepeak.'

'What's that?' asked Dora, horrified.

'It's a tiny little cabin up the front end. It's a vertical glory hole. Instead of stuffing things in, you just drop them down. Like an oubliette, only for clutter, not people. There's stuff that's been there since before Michael bought the boat, I'm sure.'

'You know what Karen would say . . .'

'And what you're going to say . . .'

'We should clear out the forepeak as well, and then we've got it if Marcus needs to bring anyone else along.'

Jo sighed. 'Let's consult with Tom, and I'll cook lunch.'

'You're just trying to get out of clearing out the forepeak!'

'You've got it, sweetheart, but I took a lovely joint out of the freezer yesterday. I thought I might need to cook a proper roast today.' Aware that her strategy was working and she was now feeling a lot more cheerful, Jo congratulated herself on her foresight.

Dora, who had finally picked up the fact that Jo was doing a roast dinner for therapeutic reasons, hoped it would include Yorkshire pudding, even if it was lamb.

Tom joined Dora when she was standing in the corridor of the barge, surrounded by bits of plywood, old life jackets, several rusted navigation lights that could have come off the *Queen Mary*, piles of rope and tins of patent rust remover.

'Hi!' she said. 'You're just in time to tell me how much of this we can chuck and how much is useful.'

He looked at the heaps around her feet. 'Well, I wouldn't actually chuck anything, just sell it on eBay.'

'We haven't time to fiddle about selling things on eBay! And do you think we should clear out the forepeak?' It was a relief that she didn't have to explain what this was. 'Do you think we might need it? How many people will Marcus want helping, do you think?'

'Well, he won't want passengers, that's for sure. But he'll want people who can steer, as well as handle a rope.'

'Can you steer?'

'Think so. Haven't tackled anything this size, though. It shouldn't make a difference, but it might.'

'This lifebuoy looks terribly old,' said Dora, picking up a shabby orange horseshoe-shaped item with grey nylon tapes dangling from it.

'Marcus will say, and I agree, it looks ancient. I'm not sure if they have use-by dates, but if they have, that's definitely past it. What else have you got in there?' He peered round the corner of the door. 'There's still a lot of stuff in here.'

'Lots of that is Jo's. I'm only dealing with the stuff that's obviously boat-orientated. Do you want to look in the forepeak? It may be beyond us.'

'Nothing is beyond us,' said Tom grandly, and disappeared.

He reappeared with the air of someone who'd just decided to row the Atlantic single-handed: he might live to regret it but it was the right thing to do. 'I do think we should clear it out. It could be a useful cabin. I think Marcus quite often brings someone he knows, in case no one on board can do anything.' He sighed. 'Now that's a job I'd like.'

'What?'

'Working for Marcus.'

'I thought you were a boat-builder.'

'I am, but anything to do with boats suits me.'

'As long as that includes clearing them out,' Dora teased.

He grinned. 'I'm afraid I'll need help with the forepeak.

I'll need someone to help haul the stuff up. We'll make a pile on the deck and decide what to do with it. If necessary, I'll borrow Hamo's van and take it to the tip.'

'Hamo has a lot of vehicles,' said Dora, remembering the VW Beetle.

'Yes. He sort of collects them. Or rather, people let him have them and he does them up. He's supposed to sell them on but he can never bring himself to.'

Having reassured Jo that they weren't just abandoning work on the cabin and were going to sort out the forepeak, they went upstairs and out on to the deck.

'I wonder if Jo knows how many people Marcus will need or if he'll bring his special person,' said Dora, peering down the hatch of the forepeak dubiously.

Tom chuckled, 'I don't suppose he'll be that special. Just a horny-handed old salt.'

'It might be a glamorous girl who's a dab hand at steering.' She chuckled. 'Or Carole.'

'I'm sure Carole isn't a dab hand at steering.'

'You don't know that! Just because she's young and pretty, it doesn't mean she's an idiot.'

'I know that—'

'And I'd have thought with your encyclopaedic knowledge of the Dutch barge world, you'd know who he usually took with him.'

Tom sighed, obviously peeved that this top item of barge-gossip hadn't ever reached him. 'I haven't actually met Marcus. I only know him by reputation.'

'Well, if you're just all talk, let's get this cabin sorted out. Then we can put all the stuff for the tip together. You go down.'

Between them they hauled a large amount of what Tom defined as 'used timber', which meant off-cuts and sheets of marine ply with sections missing. Eventually the forepeak was sufficiently empty of everything – mouldy mattresses, rotting rope and a huge quantity of paint, the lids permanently seized to the cans – for Dora to join Tom in it. She picked her way down the ladder carefully.

'It smells,' she said, looking around.

Tom was indignant. 'You'd smell if you'd been full of all this junk for years.'

'I wasn't being insulting, I was just stating facts. We need something to wash it all down with. Oh, hand me that dustpan would you? Is it damp because something's leaking, or because it was full of damp stuff?'

'I don't know! What do you need to clean it with? You stay here and I'll go and ask Jo for it.'

Jo was feeling red-faced and harassed when Tom arrived in her kitchen demanding cleaning products. It was a definite improvement on feeling frightened and depressed.

'Have a look in that cupboard there. I can't help you, I'm afraid, I've just discovered I've got to peel a whole lot more potatoes.'

'Right.' Tom, apparently missing the significance of this, crouched down and began sorting through bottles of highly fragranced fluid guaranteed to get rid of stubborn limescale and kill all known germs. 'You don't happen to know who Marcus is bringing with him on the trip, do you? If he's happy with just me, we probably won't need the forepeak.'

'You can ask him yourself,' said Jo, not feeling nearly as calm as she sounded. 'He's coming to lunch.'

'Yikes,' said Tom, borrowing an expletive from Dora's vocabulary. He removed his head from the cupboard. 'When did this happen?'

'He just rang up. He wants to check things, the fuel tanks mostly. Michael says they should be fine but Marcus won't take chances. I do wish Michael was here.' Ever since the break-up of her marriage, Jo had told herself she couldn't rely on men and didn't need to. But maybe doing without them completely took practice and she hadn't been single all that long. 'I didn't have to ask him to lunch, of course, but as I was cooking it, the invitation sort of came out.'

'Shall I get Dora?' Tom had straightened up and was looking at her with such concern, Jo made a big effort to smile.

'Oh no. You two carry on. But if there was a moment to get the things out of the corridor down here, so the bathroom's accessible, that would be terrific.'

Tom left, clutching a barrage of bottles, a scrubbing brush, a bundle of rags that Jo had rescued from the engine room, and the news that the myth that was Marcus was soon to be made flesh.

Jo stood in her galley considering lunch. There would be enough meat if she carved thinly. She'd already peeled extra potatoes but was it lunacy to try and roast them when she only had one oven? Sunday lunch therapy, which had worked for her so well when she lived in a house with a Rayburn and a conventional oven, seemed to have lost some of its beneficial properties. Was it because Marcus was coming and she wanted to live up to the reputation he had bestowed on her that she was a good cook that she was extra worried?

She certainly wanted to be good at something when she was going to be so utterly useless on the boat trip. She looked at her watch for the hundredth time, hoping it held the answer to all her questions.

'Would you like me and Tom to go to the shops for you?' said Dora, who had appeared while Jo was audibly going through her store cupboard in her head. 'Tom told me that Marcus is coming for lunch too. We need some hard-core cleaning products in that cabin, which includes gloves.'

'Oh yes, could you? I've been caught on the hop, rather. It would have been fine if it had just been you and Tom but Marcus – well, Marcus is a guest. He'll need pudding.' She remembered how much he had liked the Eton Mess. It was a shame she couldn't do it again – it was so easy.

'I'll make a list.'

'Do you think he's a custard or a cream man?' Jo asked a few moments and half a shopping list later.

'I haven't met him, Jo. Why not get both? Then if he doesn't like cream we can have strawberries another day.'

'Thank you, Dora, you're a star. Now, you'd better take my card to pay for all this, and you'd better get some cash as well.'

'But you can't tell me your pin number!'

'Darling Dora, I've known you since you were a little girl. I think I can trust you.'

After Dora had gone, Jo rushed up on deck and shouted across the water to her and Tom. 'Gravy granules! I can't do without Mother's Little Helpers.'

'I do wish Jo had been a bit more specific than just "red wine" ', said Dora, looking at the rows of bottles in the wine aisle. 'I don't know much about wine.'

'I'll choose it if you like,' said Tom.

'You drink home-made wine a lot of the time. I'm not sure I trust your palate.'

'My palate is fine, we just don't want to spend too much of Jo's money. Although I will buy a bottle. I ought to. I'm always having meals with you two.'

'That would be nice but we still haven't decided what to

179

have. John always chose the wine when we went out. I just drank it.'

'Mm,' said Tom speculatively, in a way that made Dora glance anxiously at him.

'But I can read a wine list as well as anyone! Honestly, you've got me so I daren't say anything in case you turn it into a dare.'

He laughed. 'I promise to give you lots of warning when I do it next time. I do admit that the first two were rather sprung on you.'

'Kinda!'

'You know one of them is to go to a festival?'

'How could I forget?' said Dora trying to sound breezy and unconcerned.

'So you can't say I've sprung that one on you. It's just a shame I haven't managed to get tickets for the one I really wanted to take you to.'

'That is a shame.'

Tom gave her a sideways glance but let the subject drop. Dora was sure he knew exactly how unenthusiastic she felt about music festivals. She was glad that he changed the subject. 'Do you know why Jo decided to cook Sunday lunch today? It seems a bit barking to me, when she obviously doesn't do it every Sunday.'

'Well, I'm not a mind reader, but I think it's to do with yesterday.'

'Yesterday?'

Dora nodded, picking up a bottle of red that was part of an offer. 'What about this? It's a bogof.'

'I'm all for buy-one-get-one-free.' He took the bottle from Dora and inspected the label. 'So what did you do yesterday?'

'We went back to her old home. It was horrid for her. She didn't say much but I could tell she felt as if her past had

180

been swept away by her husband's new girl. It really shook her confidence. I think the big meal is a way of reminding herself that she does have skills.'

'But of course she's got skills! What about that restoration stuff she's doing?'

Dora shook her head and loaded the trolley with bottles. 'I know. I think the cooking thing represents what she did before and she wants to prove she isn't rubbish at it, or something.' The fact that Jo hadn't been able to have more than one child probably made her feel pretty worthless, she reflected, although she didn't share that thought with Tom. She also didn't think he was very interested in Jo's psyche but he was polite enough not to look bored. 'If we get six bottles there's quite a good discount, and it'll come in handy.'

'I don't know if we should buy six bottles of wine with Jo's money,' Tom objected. 'I know, we'll buy three and she can buy three, then we don't have to feel guilty about eating with her all the time.'

'I don't feel guilty,' said Dora primly. 'I'm a lodger. My meals are thrown in.'

'I'll pay for the extra wine then. What else is on the list?'

'Something to make crumble with, but we mustn't be too long. There's still all that stuff in the passage.'

The stuff had all been crammed back into the glory hole. The cabin had been hoovered and the table was set. Jo was kneeling on the floor staring into the oven as if it contained the secrets of the universe when Dora and Tom came back.

'What are you hoping to see?' asked Tom curiously.

Jo sighed, slammed the oven door shut and got to her feet. 'The meat is already resting and now I'm trying to decide if the potatoes will ever brown or if I should take them over to Tilly's. She's got a fabulous state-of-the-art cooker. Did you get the wine? Goodo. Let's open a bottle. I'll need it for the gravy, anyway.'

'We bought six bottles. There was a discount. But Tom's paying for three of them.' Dora looked at Tom, waiting for him to get his wallet out.

'Oh no, don't pay for the wine!' Jo flapped at him as he reached into his back pocket. 'You're clearing out the forepeak, and coming with us to Holland – if Marcus agrees of course. I think you've earned some wine.'

'Oh God, Jo! You've cleared the passage! We were going to do it!'

'I got in a panic. He'll be here in a minute. You could organise it a bit better in the glory hole, so it looks as if it could be somewhere to sleep, eventually.'

'I bought some flowers,' said Dora. 'They definitely are a present. They were reduced,' she added. 'So I bought two bunches.'

'You honey! They're just what we need! Thank you so much. Put them in a jug. I think there's one that would suit.'

Dora put the irises in a jug, as instructed. Tom opened a bottle of wine and stowed the other bottles in the rack that was built into the worktop. Jo opened the oven door again. 'It's no good,' she said. 'I'm going to Tilly's with these. They're never going to get brown.'

Dora edged Jo out of the way and had a look. 'He's not even here yet. You're not going to put lunch on the table the moment he appears, you'll give him a drink first. I should think you've got time for them to brown. Why don't you take a glass of wine into the back cabin and make yourself tidy?'

Jo looked at Dora. 'You know, I think it's a good thing you've got bossy since moving in with me. Tom, pour me a glass of something soothing.'

It was cooler in her cabin. Jo put down her glass and burrowed in a locker for her make-up bag. Since the parade of boats, she had kept everything hidden away. When Marcus had inspected his quarters, she'd set up her dressing table again. It was only the surface area of a box of tissues, but she liked having a hairbrush and a lipstick to hand.

Now she tipped her make-up out on to the bunk and found the tube of cream that Karen had given her: 'Guaranteed to lift your eye-bags, Mum.' Sadly, she felt nothing could do that but as the cream did seem to encourage her make-up to stay on a bit longer, she found it useful.

Next she applied another expensive product, paid for by her, this time. This 'contained light-reflective particles', and a whole list of technical-sounding chemicals which promised youth-enhancing improvements 'to the dark circles and puffiness' under her eyes. She didn't really think you could apply youth from the outside, via a beautiful little pot, but she did it anyway, more from superstition than anything else.

Meeting her ex-husband's new woman yesterday, and knowing that Marcus also had a very much younger partner, made the normal insecurities that every woman has about their appearance even worse. She wasn't just keeping her end up with other women of the same age, she was trying not to look like a hag, knowing it was almost impossible, given her age. Compared to Samantha and Carole, she was bound to.

She sprayed herself with Chanel No. 19. As Karen had used to borrow this from her, she presumed it wasn't an old-lady scent. Then she dipped her fingers in a hair product also filled with gravity-defying properties, and teased at her curls. Why hadn't she noticed sooner how badly her hair needed cutting?

'Jo?'

Dora's tentative voice made Jo put down the nail scissors just in time. 'Yes?'

'A pinger has just gone. Do you want me to do something?'

'No, I'd better come.'

Hastily, she hid everything again, and then went to see what had gone on in the galley while her back had been turned.

Chapter Thirteen

❧

'I'm sorry I'm late,' said Marcus, over an hour after Jo had applied her make-up. 'I got held up.'

He didn't seem sorry but he did seem annoyed. Hm, thought Jo, adding 'moody' to her list of his characteristics.

'That's fine,' said Jo airily, as if she hadn't spent the previous half-hour agonising about the meat getting cold, the potatoes burnt and the Yorkshire puddings dried to a crisp. After all, it wasn't his fault she'd elected to undertake Sunday-lunch therapy for her own reasons.

She made the introductions and then got everyone to sit down so she could serve. Even while she was pulling dishes of vegetables out of the oven, pouring gravy into a jug and generally getting the meal onto the table, she heard Tom trying to ask Marcus if he could come without actually saying it.

Fortunately for Tom, he seemed to make a good impression on Marcus and they were soon discussing plans for the trip. Dora was joining in womanfully and Jo allowed herself to remain silent. She'd done what she'd set out to do, produced a meal that, even by her high standards was a success, in spite of the waiting around, and everyone was eating enthusiastically.

And then, when the last Yorkshire puddings and roast potatoes had been distributed, and Jo was thinking about serving the pudding, Marcus said, 'I know you've said you're coming, Joanna, but I want to know the real reason why you're so reluctant.'

Had she been expecting this question she'd have prepared an answer, but as it came completely out of the blue she had to fall back on the truth.

'Because I'm terrified. I keep telling people, but no one seems to believe me.'

There was a silence; everyone seemed to have stopped chewing. 'Right,' said Marcus calmly and got up. 'Dora, can you see to whatever needs seeing to? Joanna and I are going for a walk.'

Tom and Dora exchanged glances but kept quiet.

'But I can't just abandon everything!' Jo said, aware of the tottering heaps of greasy dishes and baking tins that were now piled on every surface.

'Yes you can,' said Marcus. 'Come.'

She went. She didn't appreciate his commanding tones, but something in his look made her realise it was safer to comply. She told herself it was so she could give him a piece of her mind without an audience. As she went up the steps, Tom and Dora started clearing plates and stacking the dishwasher.

Marcus didn't speak until they were both off the barge and out of the gate.

'I really don't feel—' said Jo, not at all sure what she did feel.

'I want to find out why you're so frightened,' said Marcus quietly. 'And then I'm going to put your mind at rest. Tom seems a good lad,' he went on, so Jo couldn't protest any more.

'Oh yes. He's really keen to come. I hope you'll let him. And Dora, I feel responsible for her.'

'Is she reasonably calm? Unlikely to get hysterical, able to make a cup of tea?' He was striding purposefully along and Jo was having a job keeping up.

Feeling slightly hysterical herself, Jo laughed. 'All that. She and Tom are getting to be a bit of a team.'

'Are they going out?'

Jo frowned. 'Don't think so. I'm fairly sure they're just friends, but who's to say if they'll stay like that? Where are we going?' she added, borrowing his technique of sudden subject-changing.

'Just for a walk. We'll go along the river for a bit and then find an unoccupied bench.'

Instead of going in the direction of the pub and shops, he led her in the other direction, crossed a bridge and along a lane until they were on the towpath.

'Do you often have to talk people round to the idea of going on barge trips?' asked Jo when they could walk side by side.

He laughed and shook his head. 'No. I'm usually telling people they can't come, can't bring their girlfriend, can't sell tickets to all their friends.'

'People don't do that, do they?'

'No, but they are keen to see these trips as pleasure jaunts, and while everyone wants to enjoy themselves, having too many people is distracting and dangerous.'

'You don't want me then, I'm distracting and dangerous.'

She was teasing him and expected him to laugh but he didn't. 'No you're not. Well, not in . . .' He was looking at her disconcertingly again. 'Anyway, it's not so much that I want you to come because you're a good cook and would keep everyone happy but because I don't want you to be frightened of the sea.'

'If I didn't come I wouldn't have to be.' Really, he was so hard to read. Philip had always been so transparent she'd got used to knowing what he was about to say and when. Marcus on the other hand was difficult to pin down.

He ignored her comment and took her arm. She had to lengthen her stride again to keep up with him and neither of them spoke until Marcus stopped at what he obviously considered to be a suitable place. It was a bench that looked out over the river. Jo suspected that the trees they were looking at were Tom's island, where his boat lay among the other diverse vessels that rotted and decayed until they merged with the river and the surrounding vegetation.

'Now,' he said, 'what are you frightened of exactly?'

Jo considered. It was very hard to put irrational fears into words – whatever you said sounded silly and weak-minded. 'I don't know. I think I'm just frightened. I do get seasick, and that doesn't help, and I don't like being on small boats, even ferries, very much. The sea is so big, so endless, so utterly relentless.'

Marcus didn't speak immediately. 'The sea is big, true, but if you think of the little boats and ships that have travelled across it since man hollowed out logs. It's also quite useful.'

'Useful?' After the huge, expansive language she had used to describe the sea, 'useful' seemed a little niggardly. 'No, really,' she decided to make light of it. 'I can't see that catching on. *The Useful Sea, The Wide, Useful Sea*, "I must go down to the useful sea, the useful sea and the sky . . ."' She misquoted book titles and fragments of poetry, trying to prove what an inappropriate word 'useful' was.

Although he chuckled, he was insistent. 'But it is useful. Rivers are useful. Towns have always sprung up on the banks of rivers. Look at London.' He gestured towards the island, covered in trees and not looking at all like a vast metropolis. 'And think of tides, how useful they are. If I'm dealing with a slightly underpowered craft, I motor for twelve hours when the tide is with me, and then anchor while it's against me.'

Jo opened her mouth to say that it was different for him but he went on before she could. 'I know millions of people used to drown but not nowadays. *The Three Sisters* is a very seaworthy little ship. You can't come to any harm in her. I won't let you.'

Unexpectedly, Jo did start to feel calmer at the prospect of setting off across the ocean.

'I have a lot of experience. I take precautions some people would think are obsessive. I'll have Ed, who's been at sea even longer than I have, with me, and all sorts of kit that wasn't even invented a few years ago. I'll keep you informed of what's happening at all times, and I might even make you steer. I promise to keep you and *The Three Sisters* entirely safe.'

Jo made a little sound, a sigh of resignation; her fears were going to be wrenched from her whether she liked it or not.

'So, do you feel better now?' he asked, and Jo detected a slight edge of concern in his voice.

She sighed again and nodded. 'Why did you want to make me feel better? Why didn't you just let me stay at home?'

He smiled. 'Apart from the fact that you might not have anywhere to stay? I don't want you to be frightened of anything, if I can prevent it. And it's important to me that you like boating.'

'Why?'

There was a tiny pause. 'I have my reputation to keep up. If it got out that people were refusing to go to sea with me, my reputation would be in pieces.'

Jo couldn't tell whether he was joking or not. Maybe keeping up his reputation was the only reason he wanted

189

her to come to Holland, and her cooking of course. 'But everyone knows I don't own *The Three Sisters*, that Michael does,' she said.

'Even so. Michael might ask some awkward questions himself. We don't want him losing faith in me.'

Jo laughed and took the opportunity to change the subject. 'I can't remember – were you at university together?'

He shook his head. 'No, we were in the same rowing club. I was studying for my second mate's ticket – exam to you – and he was in his first year at university. We go back a long way.'

'I can't remember how he and Philip got to know each other.'

'Is it important? Now?'

Jo bit her lip and shook her head. 'No, not really.'

He took her hand but not in a romantic way, more as if he wanted to stop her running away. 'So, what made you decide to come on the trip, feeling as you do?'

His hand was warm and dry and a little rough. Her own felt small and childlike in its grasp. 'Philip. He knows how frightened I am – was – and said I couldn't possibly cope with it. It's amazing how contra-suggestible I am!'

He laughed. 'I must remember that. So you saw Philip yesterday?'

'Mm. I went home with Dora to pick up some things. He and Samantha, his new woman, were supposed to stay out of the way but they came back early.' She debated telling him about Dora's debacle with the trousers but decided it wasn't her story.

'So, what's she like, Philip's new woman?'

'Oh, I'm sure you can imagine. Young, thin, pregnant.' She hadn't intended to tell Marcus about Samantha's pregnancy, it just came out. She sighed, managing to refrain from adding, 'Everything I never will be again.'

'Pregnant? That's a bit sudden, isn't it?'

'I don't know if they planned it.'

'Hasn't Philip heard of contraception?'

He seemed remarkably indignant about it. 'It's not always a good idea to put off having a baby for ever, you know.'

'I just think . . .'

'What?'

'It's a bit lacking in respect, to start another family so soon after leaving you.'

Jo didn't respond immediately. 'I don't suppose they thought about that.'

'Well, they should have done.' He got to his feet and pulled her up. 'Did you make a pudding?'

Surprise made her laugh. 'Of course. I'm a nurturer and provider. Puddings are what I do.'

'I don't think they're all that you do, Joanna, but shall we go back?'

Jo was relieved their conversation was over. All this talk of Philip and her old, beloved house, not to mention the way Marcus kept looking at her, had made her feel rather unsettled.

Their timing was perfect. All the detritus of the meal had been cleared away or washed up and the crumble sat in the middle of the table surrounded by bowls and spoons. There was also a jug of custard.

'Oh Dora,' said Jo. 'You've made custard!'

'I made the custard,' said Tom. 'I'm good at it.'

'So, where do you think you'll go into Holland from?' asked Tom when everyone was happily eating again.

'Flushing, probably,' said Marcus. 'You can go into the system sooner, but that's the way I know best.'

'And how many people will you need?' Tom went on, possibly needing his place on the trip to be confirmed.

191

'Four good reliable ones. Me and you, my mate Ed, Dora and Joanna.'

Tom smiled with relief.

'That's five,' said Jo quickly.

'I don't mind if I don't come,' said Dora, suddenly aware that she did mind.

'I'm not going without Dora,' said Jo. 'Although she could be the cook and I could stay at home.'

Dora was about to protest loudly when Marcus did it for her. 'You're both coming,' he stated. 'Will there be enough accommodation? I can't remember.'

'Thank God you cleared out the forepeak,' said Jo aware that she was at last feeling an inkling of excitement. Perhaps this trip would be fun after all.

'Think so,' said Tom, obviously doing the sums. 'Two people in the forepeak, one in the glory hole, when we finish clearing it out. Dora's got her cabin –'

'Except Jo will need it, if Marcus is sleeping in hers,' said Dora.

'I can sleep in the glory hole,' said Jo.

'Will the person you're bringing – Ed – mind sharing?' she asked.

'Ed? No, he's very easygoing,' said Marcus. 'Is the glory hole fit for Joanna to sleep in?'

'It will be,' said Dora quickly. 'And anyway, I'll sleep in it. Jo can have my cabin. It's larger.'

'I know I've put on a few pounds since I was seventeen, but I don't need a double bunk all to myself. Even if Marcus does,' she added.

'Who said anything about needing it all for myself?' he said.

Jo started gathering plates, not sure if he was flirting with her or not. Then she saw a couple of disappointed faces. 'Oh, did you want more crumble?'

'Shall I make coffee?' asked Tom a moment later after Jo had served seconds. He was obviously dying to get the meal over and the table cleared so real plans could be made. 'Then we can discuss what's happening.'

'Black, two sugars, please,' said Marcus, throwing his spoon into his empty bowl. 'That really was excellent.'

'I won't be doing roast dinners while we're going along,' said Jo. 'I'd be terrified of hot fat spilling all over me.'

'Really, Joanna, we're not going out into the Atlantic, there won't be a lot of movement most of the time. Still, I agree, meals like this are better kept for when we're in port.'

'I've always wanted to make this sort of passage,' said Tom. 'Shall I find some paper?'

'There's a pad in the desk, Tom,' said Jo.

'Right.' Everyone hastily sat down again so they could listen to Marcus.

'When we do set off, we'll leave about two hours before high water at London Bridge then we'll get maximum benefit from the ebb tide.' He looked at Jo and smiled. 'But this barge isn't underpowered. I just don't like wasting fuel. It's bad for morale too, bashing against the tide.'

Dora made a mental note to grill Tom about all this afterwards. Although she'd picked up a fair bit about boat-building and repairs since she'd been working at the boatyard, she only knew about tides when they affected her getting to or from work.

'We'll probably stop for the night at somewhere like Queenborough, near Sheerness,' Marcus went on.

'Why stop?' asked Tom. 'With plenty of us, we could just carry on overnight, couldn't we?'

'We could, but we wouldn't cover much distance. Better to have a good night's sleep and set off early the next day.'

'How long will it take to get to the dry dock?' asked Jo.

'It's about sixteen hours from Queenborough to Flushing and about another twelve hours from there to Dordrecht.'

'Right,' said Jo, trying not to sound daunted. 'I must say, I'm relieved we don't have to travel at night.'

'Although in some ways navigation is easier at night than in the day,' said Tom. 'You can tell where you are better, from the light buoys.'

Marcus glanced at Jo. 'Don't worry, we've got lots of bits of kit that will tell us where we are, even in daytime.'

Jo managed a feeble laugh.

'OK.' Marcus carried on telling them his plans. 'Then, if weather permits—'

'What's the maximum force you'd go out in?' asked Tom, who had his own bit of paper and was making notes like mad.

'Force four, maximum. Ideally we'd set off during a settled period of high pressure.'

'What about fog?' asked Jo.

'If there's fog, we won't go. Right – any more questions?'

Dora resisted the temptation to put up her hand before asking, 'What are we all going to do while we're in dry dock?'

'Go home, if you've any sense. Dry docks are not fun places to be, although—' He glanced at Jo, and seemed about to say something but then stopped.

'So we'll come back and get her when she's ready to come out?' asked Tom.

'You can if you like, but Michael might come over and give Ed and me a hand.' He paused. 'Anything else? Joanna?'

'No, I think that covers it.' Jo sighed and then smiled. Although she felt a lot better since her talk with Marcus, she wasn't completely cured of her phobia.

He smiled back at her, as if reading her thoughts. 'It'll be fine, Joanna, really it will. Now, I need to have a good poke around so I'm going to put on my boiler suit and get going.' Marcus got up from the table.

When he had gone up to the wheelhouse, where he had presumably left his boiler suit, Dora said, 'Now, you have a rest, Jo. Lie down and shut your eyes while we finish clearing up.' Dora had noticed that Jo liked to doze for twenty minutes or so and obviously felt she deserved to even more today.

'I couldn't relax with Marcus here,' she said. 'He might want to ask me things.'

'But you won't know the answer!' Dora's honesty was brutal. 'If you can't chill here, go and see Tilly. If Marcus really needs you, I'll shout across or come and get you.'

'I'd come with you if I could get away,' said Tilly, handing Jo a tall glass full of ice cubes and fizzy water. 'But some of us have to work for a living.'

'I have to work for a living!' Jo was already nervy from having this whole trip to Holland made horribly real. 'I'm restoring some bits and pieces for Miranda. Did you meet Miranda and Bill? On *Hepplewhite*?'

'Think so. They've got an antique shop, haven't they?'

'Well, Miranda part owns it, but she said if I can learn to restore little collectables it would be really useful for them. And good for me, too.'

'I know it's too late for you, Jo, but I would never give up my ability to earn my own living.'

Tilly, Jo remembered now, was a high-powered management consultant who appeared to work smart not hard. Jo sighed. 'The trouble is, I didn't have much ability to earn money. I always had jobs, not a career. All I wanted were babies, really.'

'And you've just got the one daughter?'

'That's right. Karen. I'm terribly proud of her! I've just posted her fork-lift truck driving certificate to her; she needs it in Canada.'

'Oh wow. She's got skills, then!'

Jo laughed. 'Oh yes, she's quite different from me.'

Dora appeared on the pontoon.

'Oh, come aboard,' said Tilly. 'Have a spritzer.'

Dora took a moment to wonder if people on boats really drank more than their shore-side equivalents, or if it just seemed that way. 'Better not. I'm in the middle of a job. Jo, Marcus wants to know when you last had the fuel barge round.'

'The fuel barge?' Jo's brow wrinkled in thought.

'Yes,' said Tilly. 'To fill you up with diesel. It hasn't been round for months, Dora.'

'Why does Marcus want to know?' Jo sounded agitated and put on the spot.

'He wants to know how much fuel is left in the tanks.'

'I've been as economical as I can,' said Jo. 'I turned off the central heating as soon as possible. There should be plenty left because the tanks were nearly full when I arrived. Michael told me.'

'Oh.'

'Oh? Isn't that good news?'

'I don't think so. Marcus wants to drain the tanks.'

Jo drained her glass and reluctantly got up. A 'rest' had been too much to ask for, obviously. 'I'd better come. I can't relax over here when God knows what is going on over there.'

Tom and Marcus were in the engine room. Marcus was wearing his boiler suit, and Tom a lot of grease. Jo and Dora peered down the hatch at them.

'What's the problem?' asked Jo. 'There should be plenty of fuel. I've used as little as possible.'

196

'That's the problem,' said Marcus. 'Whatever Michael says about them being clean, I want to check for myself. That means we have to drain the tanks.'

'What, now?' Jo felt that reality was slipping away. 'It's six o'clock on a Sunday evening.'

'If I can drain the tanks I can see if they need cleaning. Tom's undertaken to do that for me if it's necessary.'

'What, now?' Jo said again, obviously still aghast.

'Well, no,' said Marcus. 'Over the next few days. When is the fuel barge due to come again?'

Jo opened the wheelhouse door and yelled across to Tilly, who, fortunately, was still relaxing on deck. 'When's the fuel barge due next?'

'You'll have to book it. If several people need diesel, it'll come. Otherwise you have to go round to it. Or you could go on to the river. Lots of barges need filling up there. The fuel barge goes up and down all the time.'

Jo came back inside. 'Fine.' The time had come for Marcus's attempts to cure her of her terror to be tested.

'OK!' Marcus called up. 'I've found the gauging stick.' There was a tense silence while Jo and Dora imagined having to take the barge out on to the rolling Thames, which, in their minds, was enduring a hurricane at the time.

'There's not too much in there, but I want it all out.' This was directed at Tom. 'Is there a pump? Oh yes. Now, is there something we can empty it into?'

Marcus had stopped asking Jo questions and was concentrating on Tom.

'Don't think so, not on the barge, but my mate's got oil drums. I could borrow a couple.'

'Now?'

'Pretty much. I'll go and ask.'

'You'll need a hand to get them back.'

There was a silence. Jo and Dora were listening from the wheelhouse, both tense.

'I'll get my mates to come back with me. I don't want to take Dora,' he added in a lower voice.

In the wheelhouse, Jo and Dora exchanged relieved glances. Jo was relieved that Dora wasn't going to leave her with Marcus, and Dora because she didn't want to walk miles with an oil drum clutched to her chest – and also because she was a bit nervous of Tom's mates. They were definitely scary to a nice middle-class girl from the Home Counties.

Tom emerged from the engine room. 'I'm going to—'

'We know,' chorused Jo and Dora. 'We heard.'

'Oh. I'll be off then.'

He was halfway down the pontoon when Dora suddenly called after him. 'Wait! I'll give you a hand.'

As she hurried to catch him up she wondered why and realised that being a nice girl from the Home Counties was quite a boring thing to be, and that she wanted to stretch her boundaries a bit.

Marcus joined Jo in the wheelhouse. 'He's a good lad, that Tom. He has initiative.'

'He'd be thrilled to hear you say that. He's so keen to come with us to Holland.'

'And how do you feel about it now?'

'Better, but I won't know if I'm frightened until we actually set off. Do you want to sit down?'

'Have you got a newspaper or something for me to sit on? I might be a bit oily.'

Jo instantly produced a newspaper from under one of the cushions, glad for once that she hadn't got round to recycling recently. 'So, what's the plan?'

'I'll help Tom pump out the tanks, to see what they're like, and then he said he'll clean them out over the coming week. I'll be back next weekend and we'll go to the fuel barge and refuel.'

'But if you pump out all the fuel, how will you get to the fuel barge?'

'We'll filter enough from what we pump out to get us there.' He hesitated. 'It's very messy, Joanna.'

'Why do you insist on calling me Joanna?'

'Because it's your name, and I like it.'

'Oh.' Jo considered for a minute and decided she liked it too. On the other hand, she would never get people to stop calling her Jo, not now.

'But what about the mess?' Marcus went on. 'Diesel gets everywhere and it's horrible stuff. We'll need to make sure we've got loads of rags, newspaper, kitchen towel, things like that.'

'There's quite a large bundle of rags that I purloined from the engine room so Dora and Tom could clean out the forepeak.'

'Newspapers?'

Jo patted her seat. 'Several under here, and there's a recycling section for them with the other bins. We could raid that.' Jo looked at her watch. 'Won't all this make you late back?'

He looked at his watch too. 'A bit, I suppose.'

'Does Carole worry? It must be hard for her.'

'How do you mean?' Marcus shifted on his newspaper.

'Well, if you're away a lot, taking random boats about the place. I'd worry.'

'To please you then, I'll ring Carole.'

To prevent herself wondering too much why he should want to please her, Jo went down to the main cabin and put the kettle on.

'She's fine,' he said a little later, as Jo was making tea. 'She and I'll set off first thing tomorrow. We've got a few days to get back in, so there's no need for her to fret.'

'I thought you were going back down the Thames when you came before.'

He looked enigmatic and to Jo, maddening. She'd have to give up trying to work him out – it was quite clearly a lost cause. 'We were but we didn't. And Carole doesn't mind either way.'

She wasn't going to ask him why. 'I wasn't being critical, only saying how I'd feel. Did you want tea? You don't have to drink it if you don't want to.'

'No, I do want tea.' He took a sip from the mug Jo handed to him. She sipped her own. There was a slightly awkward pause.

'Did I not manage to convince you that you're not going to drown?' he asked after a few moments.

'Oh yes! Well, nearly.'

'So why are you looking so anxious?'

'Am I?' Jo tried to assume a calm expression but only partially managed it. He seemed to have an unsettling effect on her.

'Yes.'

'Oh, well – life in general can be a bit anxious-making. More tea?'

'Changing the subject?'

'Yup!'

'Why?'

'You're very . . .' She searched for the word. 'Inter-rogatory.'

'Tell me what makes you worry.'

'And demanding.' She kept trying to lighten the mood, but he wouldn't co-operate.

His expression was as demanding as his words. She sighed, and gave in. 'OK, it's because I don't know if I can earn my own living.' She decided to go for the part truth. It was easier. 'I haven't done for many years and although I have restored some things for Miranda to put in her shop, I don't know if there's a living in that. Philip has been very generous, but his girlfriend is pregnant. Things will change. Michael will want his barge back eventually and then I'll be homeless.'

'You could live on another barge.'

'They don't cost nothing, and it's difficult to get a mortgage or a loan for them.'

'Philip could increase the mortgage on your old home. He owes you half the value of the house, at least.'

'Does he? Really that much? After all, he paid for it.'

'I'm sure you made a contribution,' he said matter-of-factly.

'Oh yes. I made it the house it is now – or really, the house it was when I left. But it wasn't a financial contribution. Isn't that what counts?'

'I don't think so, but you should see a solicitor, find out the facts.'

Jo smiled and shook her head slightly. 'It's all right, you don't have to offer solutions. It's a very male thing to do, I know, but I'm only moaning, really. And I certainly don't expect you to be able to solve my problems.'

'I want to solve them.'

Fortunately for Jo's peace of mind, they heard footsteps on the pontoon and then the sound of something landing on the cabin roof.

'They were quick,' said Marcus.

'Tom lives quite near. He has a boat. I expect his mate has a boat in the same place. But it's really handy that he happened to have oil drums, isn't it?'

Chapter Fourteen

❧❦❧

Tom and Dora were standing next to a large green container that looked to Jo like a water butt.

'What's that?' asked Marcus.

'It used to hold lemon juice, apparently.'

Marcus appeared unimpressed. 'It's a bit bulky and hard to handle.'

'Absolutely! We've just handled it from the island and it was jolly hard,' said Dora, meaning a tougher word than 'jolly'.

'Not ideal,' said Marcus.

'But it's all we've got. And it's Sunday night. Beggars can't be choosers.' Dora wouldn't normally have been so outspoken but the container had been very difficult to manipulate.

'It won't melt if we put diesel in it, will it?' asked Jo.

'Probably not. We'll have to try and see.'

'But will we get that huge thing down into the engine room?' asked Jo, not wanting to disparage Tom and Dora's efforts but expressing her doubts anyway.

'Let's try,' said Tom, obviously a bit fed up with this lack of enthusiasm.

The two women stood on the deck and let the men wrangle the huge tub into the wheelhouse, through the narrow door, and down into the pit of the engine room.

'How will they get it down the ladder?' asked Dora.

'Just drop it, I expect.'

'They'll never get it back up again, not full.'

'I think the plan is to filter some and put it back, using the pump.' She sighed.

'Are you still dreading the trip, Jo?'

'Actually no, not really. Marcus talked me out of my fears a bit, and while I can't see myself wanting to go round the world in a boat, I don't feel quite so hysterical about it.'

'He's much less scary than he seemed at first, isn't he? Less Alpha Male.'

Jo laughed. 'I think our opinion was formed by what other people said about him. Always foolish. Let's go down and make a cup of tea. Marcus and Tom seem to be getting on OK. He's such a nice boy.'

'Huh! You should see his friends! They're the kind of dropouts from society I should have brought home to my mother! That would have taught her!'

'When did you last speak to your mother, Dora?'

'Not for ages. I sent her an email about the job.'

'Why don't you ring her now?' Jo suggested. She didn't want to boss Dora, but she knew Dora missed her parents, despite what had happened between them all.

They'd reached the saloon now and Dora crossed it to put on the kettle. 'Because . . . she'll have a go at me. Or put Dad on the phone. Something.'

'Wouldn't you like to talk to her?'

'I'd like us to be able to be more normal with each other, but I really don't want to have the conversation. She'll expect me to apologise.' She turned to Jo. 'I am truly sorry about all the upset I've caused; I couldn't be more so. But I'm not sorry I pulled out of the wedding. I don't think she'll see it like that though.'

'These things don't happen by magic. You'll have to give your mother a chance to see things from your point of view,' said Jo, reaching for the tea bags and assorted mugs.

'I know.' Dora picked up a cloth and began wiping the perfectly clean counter.

'And if your mother won't ring you, you have to ring her. You're both adults, even if one of you did give birth to the other.'

'But I don't know how she feels about me. She was so cross and disappointed.'

'I'm sure she feels she'd like to have contact with her daughter,' said Jo gently. 'You're an only child, remember. I would hate it if Karen and I weren't speaking. I couldn't bear it, in fact.'

'But you and Karen, you have quite a different relationship.'

Jo laughed. 'You mean she bosses me about and not the other way around?'

'Well, yes . . .'

'I found out very early on which of us was the stronger character, but she never took advantage of my weakness.'

'No, I remember her saying that she couldn't do anything that would worry you because you were so soft.'

Jo sighed. 'I used to worry so much that I was such a pushover, and yet I couldn't be a different sort of mother. I don't think one can.'

'But Karen's done very well,' Dora insisted.

'I know, I'm terribly proud of her. But even if she was living in a squat, living off social security, as I imagine some of Tom's friends do, I'd still really love her and want to keep in touch.'

'I suppose so,' said Dora, reluctantly conceding that Jo had a point.

'Your mother loves you just as much. Give her a ring. After all, if we're all going to drown on this trip to Holland, it would be nice if you two were friends again.'

204

'Oh all right.' Dora rinsed out the cloth and dried her hands. 'I give in. I'll go and give her a ring. It'll give me something to do while the boys are playing with pumps and diesel and things.'

'I wouldn't describe Marcus as a boy, exactly,' said Jo, but Dora had already disappeared into her cabin to find her phone.

'We need some kitchen towel,' said Tom, landing in the cabin looking flushed and as if he was in his element. 'The pump's working fine now, but quite a bit got spilt at the beginning.'

Jo handed him a new roll, making a mental note to buy it in bulk before the trip to Holland. 'What about newspapers?'

'I'm going to ask Dora if she'll raid the paper bank by the bins.'

'She's phoning her mother. I'll ask her when she gets off and we can go together.'

'Oh. Fine.'

When Tom had disappeared, Jo reflected that the person she most wanted just at the moment was her own daughter. Karen wasn't nearly so law-abiding and would manage to break into a recycling bin without a glimmer of guilt or doubt. She switched on her laptop and banged out a quick email.

It's all hell here! Marcus (old friend of Michael's – and me. Dad knew him too, years ago) is draining diesel into a lemon-juice barrel and I've got to get newspapers to mop up the spills. Wish you were here!!!! Love, Mum

Dora emerged holding her phone. She looked as if she'd been crying, but basically happy. She came up to Jo and gave her a hug. 'You're so wise! We had a good chat and I

205

feel so much better now. I'm not going home, though,' she added.

'Did your mother ask you to?'

'Yes, but I explained that I'd started a new life and would come home for a weekend or something soon, but not for good.'

'How did she take that?'

'Well, she obviously didn't like it, but she had to accept it. I'm a grown-up now!' Dora grinned. 'Let's go and play!'

'Well, I think I'm satisfied that the tanks are clean,' said Marcus when Dora and Jo appeared. 'I'd better be getting back. Carole will be wondering what's happened to me.'

'I feel awful!' said Jo. 'I should have thrown you out ages ago.'

'I'm responsible for myself,' he said. 'You don't have to monitor my comings and goings.'

'No, I suppose not. For a moment there I thought that you and Tom were friends of Karen's who I'd allowed to stay far later than their parents would have.' Jo's thoughts were full of mothers because she and Dora had been discussing hers. 'Have you decided on a date yet?'

'There's still quite a bit more planning to do, and then we can't really decide on a date until we know what the weather's likely to do.'

'Oh. I was just thinking, Dora will have to arrange to take holiday. She'll need to give some notice. And you, too, Tom.'

'Oh, Fred'll understand,' said Tom glibly.

'I hope so,' said Dora. 'I don't want to let them down.'

Dora chose her moment to ask Fred about taking some holiday. She had tackled a particularly large batch of filing, and now this was out of the way, there was a spare chair in

206

the office. He was sitting on this, at the end of the day, when she brought up the subject.

'Fred, I know I haven't worked here very long—'

'You're not thinking of leaving are you, Dora?' His face was a picture of shock and disappointment.

'No, no! Of course not. I love it here. I was just going to ask if I could have a bit of holiday.' Her voice tailed away, unwilling to cast Fred into a further state of gloom.

'Holiday! Of course, everyone's entitled to some holiday.' He didn't sound particularly thrilled by this accepted truth though.

'I wouldn't if I could get out of it, but I have to go for Jo's sake.'

'Go where?'

'Go to Holland on *The Three Sisters*.'

'You want to go on a barge trip?

Dora nodded. 'Well, not so much want as need. Although I suppose I do want to go.'

'Has this got anything to do with young Tom?'

'Well . . .'

'I can't think of anyone going anywhere and him not trying to get himself a berth.'

Dora laughed. 'Yes, he is coming. He's really keen. And apparently *The Three Sisters* has to go to Holland for dry docking.'

'Ah,' said Fred knowledgably, 'you'll be wanting grit blasting. We'd do it here if it wasn't for the noise pollution.'

'So is it all right? Can I go?'

'Of course. I said.'

'The trouble is, I'm not exactly sure when and for how long. We have to wait for the right weather and things.'

Fred sighed. 'That's all right. I know how it is with these trips. Very difficult to make definite plans. You never know what you're going to find when you're in dry dock, and if the weather turns nasty, you're stormbound on the other side of the North Sea.'

Dora didn't want to think about being stormbound and changed the subject to something she knew about. 'Will you organise cover? Someone to do my job while I'm away?' She really hoped not. She didn't want to think of a Tipp-Ex-tipped temp, a clone of the woman who had interviewed her, messing about in her newly set-up systems.

'Far too expensive, but don't you worry. You've done so much since you've been here,' he said. 'And we didn't have anyone for ages. We'll manage. And I'll tell you what, if that lady you're staying with –'

'Jo.'

'That's right. If there's anything we can do to help before she sets off, just let us know.'

'Oh, that's so kind!' Dora had flung her arms round his neck before she remembered that he probably wasn't used to hugging, but having got that far it was hard to back off. 'Sorry. I thought you were my dad for a moment.'

'That's all right.' Fred patted her arm in a fatherly way. 'I reckon you should go home for a visit before too long.'

As Jo had said much the same thing, when they were making hot chocolate one evening, Dora sighed. 'I know. But there's so much to do before this trip to Holland.'

'I'll give you the day off, if you need it. So when roughly are you going?'

'We're getting everything ready then Marcus is going to look for a spell of settled weather in the middle of June.'

'Oh, yes.' Fred's faith in weather forecasts was obviously not huge.

'Apparently you can get a six-day prediction. Marcus says.'

Fred sighed at the folly of youth and then said, 'Take

young Tom with you to meet your parents. He needs some civilised company. He mixes with those dropouts all the time.'

'Have you got children, Fred?'

He nodded. 'Grandchildren, too.' He smiled nostalgically. 'They really are grand. I miss them. My two eldest boys live abroad and we don't see as much of them as we'd like. You don't like to think your grandchildren are growing up, and you not there to see it.'

'OK! I'll go! And I'll drag Tom along too, if I can. Now could you be a love and put up this new noticeboard? I want it to be absolutely impossible to forget a single bill while I'm away.'

Fred grumbled off to get his tool kit. 'You'll only be away a few days. They could wait!'

Jo wished she'd warned Miranda she was planning to visit her shop just after she'd found somewhere to park her car and was walking down the pretty high street. When she'd set off her plan had been to check out the shop before she went in, to see if what she'd done was of the quality required. Now that felt stupid and she didn't want to fall back on the old, I-was-just-passing-so-I-thought-I'd-call-in lie, because where could she possibly be going to?

She saw the shop from across the road. It looked, even from a way away and through traffic, decidedly upmarket. Miranda had obviously just been being kind when she suggested she could possibly restore things that were good enough to sell there. Still, she might as well put herself out of her misery. She could go and see Miranda, or Miranda's partner, show her stuff, then take it away again and go shopping instead.

Procrastinating desperately, she took time to cross the

road. But at last, in spite of all her efforts, she found herself outside the shop. The windows were screened off from the rest of the shop and while what was displayed was extremely attractive, it meant that Jo could only see the choice pieces on display.

On one side a blue-painted dresser held a collection of creamware. Jo looked for a while and decided that her favourite was like a little openwork basket, only made of china. Someone had filled it with redcurrants and the splash of scarlet, in among the white dishes and jugs with the blue background, looked like a work of art.

In the other window was a complete contrast. Here quantities of old painted sweet tins, tea caddies and biscuit tins, a glorious range of rich colours and intricate patterns, filled a table. Behind these was an old storage jar filled with cow-parsley. Jo gave a little sigh of ecstasy. It was definitely her sort of shop. Some of her anxiety faded. She opened the door and went in.

It took her a moment or two to recognise the elegantly suited woman who was coming towards her with out-stretched hands. Miranda looked so different from the woman who drank large quantities of wine and Pimm's and wore linen slacks and faded shirts.

Different or not, she hugged Jo warmly. 'Jo! Why didn't you say you were coming? We could have gone out for lunch. As it is I'm stuck here.'

Jo returned the hug with equal warmth, taking strength and comfort from Miranda's firm embrace. 'I came on the off chance you'd be here. Things are quite busy on the barge and I wasn't sure when I could get away.'

'Well, it's lovely you're here. So, *The Three Sisters* is going to Holland?'

'How on earth do you know that?'

'Word gets around. Come and have some coffee or

something and tell me all.' She noticed the bag Jo was carrying. 'Is that what I think it is?'

Jo nodded. 'I'm really not sure if I've done a good enough job, Miranda. Your shop is so full of lovely things.' She put the bag down by the desk where Miranda had been sitting. 'Can we have the coffee before I show you?'

'I'll put the kettle on. Have a look round!'

Jo looked, exclaiming, either to herself or out loud, at the plethora of items which ranged from the dainty, the quirky, the sweetly pretty to the kitsch, with all styles in between.

Unsurprisingly to Jo there was a section of model boats of all kinds. There was a paddle steamer, its hull brightly painted in black and red, various yachts, obviously designed to be sailed on village ponds, and a scale model of the *Queen Mary*. The star of the selection, to Jo's eyes, was a diorama in a glass case depicting some ancient drama involving a two-masted ship, a paddle-steamer and two little dinghies. Quite why all those vessels were in the same place at the same time was not explained.

Around the boats were various related items: carved whales' teeth, a ship in a bottle, a selection of telescopes, sextants, shackles and other mystifying bits of tackle.

Everywhere Jo looked were lovely things. In the corner was a rocking horse, dapple grey with a flowing mane and a real, tiny saddle.

'I love this shop,' said Jo. 'It's heaven encapsulated in prime real estate.'

Miranda laughed as she edged the tray on to the desk, pushing aside a pile of papers as she did so. 'I'm so glad you like it. I have to confess to being quite fond of it myself. Have a seat.'

Jo pulled out a little chair she faintly recognised as being Art Nouveau.

211

'I'm hoping I'll find a couple more of those chairs, to make up a set,' said Miranda, pouring coffee, 'but until I do, it might as well be useful.'

'What was it William Morris said? "Have nothing in your houses that you do not know to be useful, or believe to be beautiful"?'

'I think that's right. Have a biscuit.'

'This is so civilised. I've spent too much time worrying about fuel tanks and navigation lights recently.' Jo bit into her shortbread with a hedonistic sigh.

'You shouldn't be worrying about things like that, surely? I thought Marcus was in charge.'

'Well yes, he is, and he's obviously very efficient, but it all goes on at my house, so to speak. Although *The Three Sisters* is not my house, really.'

Miranda sipped her coffee and regarded her friend. 'You went back home?'

Jo nodded. 'How did you guess?'

'Not hard. How did it go?'

It was lovely to have a woman of her own age to talk to, thought Jo. Dora was a dear and Marcus was a contemporary, but, however hard they tried, they couldn't really relate to Jo's fears and disappointments. Miranda listened attentively, taking occasional bites out of her biscuit. Then she let loose a short, fluent statement full of foul language that Jo found immensely satisfying.

'Oh Miranda, I love you!' said Jo.

'Likewise. Now, enough of that,' she said briskly, sensing it was time to change the subject. 'What have you got in that carrier bag?'

'I may have to take back my last statement about loving you. These little items represent hours of painstaking work, practice, research, and goodness knows what else.'

'You missed out "blood, sweat and tears".'

'They're a given.'

'So, let me look.'

Jo reached into her carrier and took out the first tissue-wrapped parcel and handed it to Miranda. She unwrapped it carefully and took out the little mirror.

'Oh my God! I can't believe it,' she said. 'You've worked a miracle.'

Relief made Jo laugh. 'It was no miracle, it was all those other things, including the blood and tears.'

'But it's exquisite! My goodness, you've gilded it properly, with real gold leaf! I can't believe it!' Miranda said again, lowering the mirror. 'You are ambitious.'

'Foolish, more like. I fell in love with the technique when I was in the shop, buying supplies. I knew I had to try it. It sounded so much like alchemy.'

'You've done an amazing job, Jo. I'm so impressed. I'm going to send everything that needs repairing to you from now on.'

Jo felt some of her confidence return. 'Do, although I'll need more space if I'm going to do it for a living.'

'There're a couple of rooms upstairs. They're full of junk now, but we could easily turn one into a little workroom for you.' Miranda paused. 'There's a little bathroom too. If you ever need a place to go, there's one here.'

Jo patted her friend's hand, unable to speak for a moment. 'That's really kind,' she said huskily. 'I might well take you up on that.'

Jo got back after her visit to Miranda feeling satisfied and calm. She did have saleable skills, she had taught herself a new and difficult technique so she still had a brain and hand–eye coordination, and, if all else failed, she had a place to live.

All this made her feel a lot less vulnerable and

dependent on Philip's generosity. While Marcus may well be right in saying that half the value of the house was hers by right, it could take a long time to organise. And much as she found it hard to think of Philip living there with the Floosie, the thought of her old house being sold to strangers made her very sad.

Dora arrived home late, but relieved that Fred had taken her impending holiday so well.

'He was very understanding about me not knowing how long the trip would take.'

'I suppose, being a boatyard, he must know about waiting for weather windows, cleaning out fuel tanks and all that stuff.'

'Of course he does.' Dora paused. 'He also thought I should go home for a visit before we went. He said I should take Tom with me.'

'Oh yes, that's a good idea. They won't be able to do anything or say anything that will bring shame on the family if a stranger's there,' she said.

'Well yes, Mum's not likely to make a scene while he's actually there, but I can't rely on her not to send Dad and Tom out for some reason.'

'She will want to see you on your own, but so will you, really.' Seeing Dora was ambivalent about this proposed visit she went on, 'You can borrow the car if you like. It would make it easier to get away if it all goes pear-shaped.'

Dora laughed, but protested. 'I'm not insured!'

'I'll ring up so you will be.' Jo was sprinkling cheese and breadcrumbs over a gratin dish full of pasta and vegetables.

'There's just one thing I'm worried about.'

'Yes?'

'I don't want Mum thinking me and Tom are an item. That could be really embarrassing, and hurtful to her, if she

214

falls in love with him straightaway, like she did with John.'

'I'm sure she's not so fickle as to fall in love with someone else so soon,' said Jo, thinking in fact that Dora's mother might easily transfer her affections to Tom, so keen was she to see her daughter married.

Dora laughed, possibly thinking the same thing.

'Just make it clear from the beginning that Tom is only a friend,' Jo went on.

'I've just thought. I'll have to think of an excuse to bring Tom.'

'Tell your mother I made you. That I wouldn't let you borrow the car unless you had a responsible adult with you.'

'Jo! This is Tom we're talking about!'

'I know, but . . .' She paused.

'What?' demanded Dora, instantly aware that Jo was pausing for reasons of tact and diplomacy.

'I don't want to say anything about your mother that might sound like criticism . . .'

'But?'

'While she must know that you're a good driver, she would probably think you were safer if you had a man with you. She can't help it. It's her conditioning.'

Dora chewed her lip. 'And I could say I wanted him to navigate.'

Jo laughed. 'After all, it's well known that women can't read maps.'

'And that most men can't walk down the street and chew gum at the same time!'

'Give your mum a ring. It'll give her plenty of time to plan lunch for you.'

Dora paused. 'I wish we could go out. Restaurants are less stressful, don't you think?'

'Your mother will want to cook for you. The good thing about Tom is that he eats a lot. Mothers like that in a boy.'

Chapter Fifteen

'OK, you know the way?' asked Jo, a few days later.

'It's only getting out of London that's the problem,' said Dora, not for the first time. 'I've got my list of road numbers and places to look out for, and Tom's got the map.'

'Sorry, I'm fussing.' Jo smiled in self-reproach. 'I'm such a mum!'

'It's perfectly understandable, I'm taking your car.' Dora picked up her bag. She patted Jo's arm and smiled. 'I'd better go – Tom's waiting by the car. What are you going to do while we're away?'

'Cooking for the trip. I shopped till I dropped yesterday. I'm going to fill the freezer, and then the fridge, with meals that can just be bunged in the oven or microwaved. I'll enjoy myself,' she added.

Reasonably convinced that this was true, Dora kissed Jo's cheek and went out to meet Tom, jingling Jo's car keys in her hand. It was a beautiful summer's day and her spirits lifted. She was nervous and excited at the same time. It was fun to be going off for the day with Tom, but the thought of seeing her parents for the first time since her escape was a bit daunting.

Tom was as relaxed as ever. 'When did you last drive, Dora?' he asked, getting in the passenger door.

'I didn't have a car of my own but I used to use Mum's quite a lot.' She looked in the rear-view mirror and adjusted it slightly.

'And John's?'

She shook her head. 'He always had cars it was too expensive to insure for me to drive. He wasn't a good passenger. But it did annoy me. I'm a far better driver than he is – was.' Her brow wrinkled, remembering how they used to share the driving before he got his own car, but afterwards he was so critical she always let him take the wheel if they were together, whatever car they were in.

'OK,' said Tom after a moment's pause. 'Turn right out of the car park.'

'I think I could have managed that bit on my own.'

'If I'm here as your official navigator, I've got to do my job. Think of me as sat-nav.'

Dora relaxed. Tom wasn't John, he wasn't going to keep his hand on the handbrake and suck his teeth whenever she changed gear. 'Sat-nav gets people into all kinds of trouble, it's well known for it,' she said, beginning to feel confident and in control behind the wheel of Jo's car. She just hoped she went on feeling confident and in control when she got home.

'The advantage of the human kind is that they can read maps too,' said Tom.

Later, when they were on the last stretch of the journey, Dora said, 'Now Tom, there are a few things I need to tell you about my mother.'

'I'm sure there aren't.'

'Yes! For example, you mustn't breathe a word of our bets—'

'But your dad gave us the tickets to the races.'

'Yes, but he didn't tell Mum about it first. She'll know by now, obviously, but you must not tell her that you made me get a tip for a race.'

'Or that you picked up two Irishmen, did an accumulator, and won a hundred quid?'

217

'No. And don't mention the karaoke.'

'I really don't see that there's anything wrong with it,' said Tom, resting his knees on the dashboard.

Dora sighed, wondering if Tom was being deliberately obtuse or just winding her up. 'And if you mention us going to a music festival—'

'Oh, didn't I tell you? I tried again, but I really couldn't get tickets for the one I wanted to take you to.'

Dora struggled to disguise her relief. 'Oh! Shame! Perhaps you'd better think of some other way of torturing me, then.'

'Maybe. I'll see what I can think of. A music festival would be so fun.'

'Yes. I'm really disappointed too. Especially if it involves lovely camping, and pyramids of poo in the loos.'

He nudged her elbow, even though she was turning a corner. 'Liar!'

'Darling!' Dora's mother ran out of the front door the moment the car pulled into the drive. 'How lovely to see you! And this must be Tom.'

As she and her mother hugged, Tom, Dora was embarrassed to note, got a head-to-toe inspection.

'We're just friends, Mum, I told you,' Dora whispered as they released each other. 'Tom helped me map-read,' she added more loudly.

'Not that she needed help,' said Tom, obligingly. 'She's an excellent driver.'

'Yes she is,' Dora's mother acknowledged, somewhat surprised.

'Where's Dad?' asked Dora.

'In the garden. He's just getting the grass clippings off his feet. Or at least I hope he is. He mowed the lawn in your honour, Dora.'

'I expect he mowed it because you told him he had to.'
Aware that there'd been quite a rift in their relationship,
Dora took her mother's arm. 'Let's go in.'

'You haven't introduced Tom properly.'

Dora suppressed a sigh, determined to make the day a
success however much her mother got on her nerves. She
said, 'Mum, this is Tom. Tom, this is my mother, Mrs—'

'Do call me Sukie,' said Dora's mother graciously. 'I'm
sure we're going to be friends.'

'Let's find Dad and a glass of wine,' said Dora, ushering
her mother firmly inside.

'You'd better have a spritzer, darling, if you're driving.
So what do you do, Tom?' Sukie carried on as Dora led the
way through the house and out of the French windows into
the garden.

There was a bottle of wine in a cooler set on the table
under an umbrella. Dora's father was waiting by it, his
arms open. Dora ran into them, smelling his familiar Dad-
scent that made her momentarily tearful. His arms closed
tightly about her. 'How's my little Flora-Dora then?'

She couldn't speak for a while, but eventually she
managed a squeaky 'Fine.' Then, 'This is Tom, Dad; Tom,
this is Cliff.'

'How do you do?' said Tom, and Dora remembered that,
however much he teased her, his parents were probably
like hers, and that he knew how to behave.

'Glass of wine, everyone?' asked Cliff. 'Darling, are we
eating inside or out?'

'I thought out,' said Sukie. 'Dora, you could come in and
give me a hand.'

'Let the girl have a drink first,' said Cliff soothingly.

Sukie tutted. 'She's driving, don't forget. I'll get the
canapés.' And she hurried off.

Cliff poured the wine. 'So, Tom, you work in a boatyard,

219

Dora told me in her email,' he said as he handed Tom a glass, but with, Dora was relieved to notice, only polite interest.

'Yes,' said Tom as they all sat down. 'It's like an apprenticeship, really. I studied at Falmouth but it took a while to find somewhere to take me on. I do anything boat-related that I can.'

'Why don't you study to be a surveyor or something?'

Tom made a face. 'I may do that eventually but I got really fed up with studying and I want to go travelling for a bit before I settle down to a real career.'

'Quite right,' said Dora, sipping her drink. 'I want to travel too.' The more she thought about it, the more she felt that this was true.

'Do you? Then why don't you?' said Cliff.

'I will,' said Dora firmly. 'When I've saved up enough.' Although she would hardly have admitted this to herself, she was quite glad her mother was out of earshot when she said this.

Sukie reappeared with a dish divided into compartments, each one containing a different sort of nibble. 'Have an olive, Tom,' she said, putting the dish on the table. 'Or a cherry tomato with cheese. Those are stuffed vine-leaves, and those are just green beans tied with a bit of leek. Oh, and I've got some nice crisps, the ones you like, Dora.'

'Thanks Mum, that's really kind,' said Dora. 'And of course I'll give you a hand with lunch in a minute.'

'This looks like lunch to me,' said Tom, helping himself to a miniature kebab of chicken, tomato, cheese and pimento.

Cliff laughed. 'These are just a few little snacks before we eat. We're having coronation chicken with salad. Have a napkin, Tom.'

'You've gone to so much trouble, Mum. You needn't have.'

'Well, it's not every day your runaway daughter comes home, is it?' Sukie's eyes were bright, and Dora realised that while she might have gone over the top with the hospitality, it was for all the right reasons.

'I didn't exactly run away from home,' said Dora.

'Let's not get into that now,' said Cliff. 'Have something else to eat, Tom.'

'Thank you,' said Tom, speaking with his mouth full.

'So, tell us about your new job,' said Sukie, pulling up a chair near Dora's.

'Well, it's in a boatyard, in the office. It was a complete muddle when I joined. I'm having such a good time sorting it all out.'

'But, darling, a boatyard! It doesn't sound quite as good as an estate agent. Do you meet nice people?'

Dora glanced at Tom, who winked at her. 'Oh yes, very nice.'

'Tell me about this trip you're going on,' said Cliff. 'To Holland, isn't it?'

'That's right,' said Dora.

'I don't understand why the boat can't be repaired in England,' said Sukie, sipping her wine. 'Why can't it be taken somewhere a bit nearer?'

'It doesn't actually need repairing,' said Tom. 'It has to have a survey for its certificate – rather like an MOT, I suppose. And while it's out of the water, it's going to have its hull gritblasted and given an epoxy coating.'

'Really?' asked Cliff. 'That's a good idea, is it?'

'Lots of surveyors recommend it nowadays,' said Tom, oblivious to Cliff's rather bewildered look. Once he was on to the subject of boats there was no stopping him. 'Our boatyard wanted to offer the service but because it's in a

221

residential area, they weren't allowed. Noise pollution,' he explained.

Sukie caught Dora's eye. 'Do come and look at this new outfit I've bought. It's for Hannah's wedding.' She turned away, obviously trying to avoid looking reproachful. 'I couldn't bear to wear the outfit I bought for yours.'

'OK, Mum, let's have a look. But I hope you haven't bought anything that's too old for you. Lots of those Mother-of-the-Bride outfits are terribly ageing . . . Sorry! I didn't mean that quite like it sounded.'

To her surprise and relief her mother managed a laugh. 'It's being the mother of the bride that's ageing, sweetheart, nothing to do with the clothes.'

Dora pulled her mother to her feet and kissed her. 'Let's go and look.'

Upstairs in her mother's bedroom, Dora put her arms round Sukie. 'Mum, I know I've tried, but I've never really managed to say sorry for all the awful trouble I caused you. I do think I did the right thing not marrying John, but I should have found that out a bit sooner.'

Sukie patted Dora's arm. 'It's OK, after I got over the upset, I understood that it was better just before the wedding than just after. John's got a very nice new girlfriend now. We met her when we went there for drinks.'

'That's nice.' Dora wandered over to the dressing table and started picking up bottles, reading the labels and sniffing them. Although she was pleased for John, she couldn't help feeling it was rather pathetic of him not to stay single for a while and just find a replacement for her immediately.

'So you and Tom . . .'

'No. I've said. He's a lovely friend but there's nothing else between us.'

'You don't think anything could – develop?'

222

Dora sighed. 'John obviously doesn't feel the same about this as I do, but I think it's a bit soon to start rushing into a new relationship. Now, let's see this outfit.'

Sukie moved across the room and opened the wardrobe. 'You're absolutely right. Men are so pathetic about being alone, aren't they? Even quite nice men, who really loved their wives, seem to find new ones really quickly if they're widowed. Jo's still on her own, isn't she?'

'Apart from me, she is. Now, what have you bought yourself? Oh! Fab! I bet that was expensive,' said Dora as her mother laid a confection of peach and pale grey swirls on silk chiffon, palazzo pants and a long coat tenderly on the bed. 'Much nicer than what you bought to wear at my wedding!'

'Perhaps I'll save it for when you do decide to get married.' They exchanged glances in the mirrored wardrobe door.

Dora decided to risk teasing her mother. 'I wouldn't bother. You're bound to have put on weight by then. And you wouldn't want people thinking you were mutton dressed up as lamb.'

'Cheeky! But you do like the outfit? I thought I'd wear the same hat as I got for yours. It was so expensive.'

'Put it on. Let's see the whole effect.'

'I feel it's important to look good, for my pride's sake,' said Sukie, twiddling with her hair under the hat.

'But, Mummy' – Dora reverted to what she had called her mother as a child without noticing – 'no one thinks it's anything to do with you. They're all blaming me.'

'I know, but it's not very nice having everyone think your daughter's a flibbertigibbet who can't make up her mind.'

Dora swallowed. She hadn't really thought about this aspect of it. 'Well, anyway, that's a really super get-up. All

223

your friends will envy you and the best man will run off with you.'

Her mother laughed and took the hat off. 'I must say I think it's awful what's happened to Jo. That girl must be half her age!'

'I don't think quite half.'

'And is it true she's pregnant?'

Dora considered. There was no point in pretending ignorance. 'Yes, but don't spread it about. Jo's quite upset, although she's not showing it.'

'Too late for discretion. The whole village knows.'

'Oh dear. I can see why Jo left – and me. It would be awful to stay here and know that everyone is talking about you.'

'Well, dear, one does have to be aware that the reason we've managed to keep our village shop when so many have gone is because of the gossip.'

'Hm. I can't decide if that's a good or a bad thing. I never picked up any useful gossip when I lived here.'

'Oh, they wouldn't talk about you to your face, darling. Now, let's go and see if your father and Tom have stopped talking about boats. I can only take so much of that sort of chat.'

As she followed her mother downstairs, Dora reflected that she was quite interested in boats, now that she lived on one, worked in a boatyard and was planning a voyage. Just as well, really.

Jo had borrowed Tilly's state-of-the-art food processor and had Radio 4 on loudly. Her eyes had stopped streaming since she'd created a pile of chopped onion the size of a large melon, one of celery nearly as big, and now she was decimating several pounds of carrots. Minced beef was browning in a frying pan and she was enjoying herself.

She switched off the machine and consulted her list. 'Now,' she muttered, 'If I make a basic mince and tomato thing I can add beans and turn it into chilli, but I won't bother using a dish for that, only those plastic containers—'

She screamed.

'Sorry,' said Marcus, coming into the galley. 'I did knock but you obviously didn't hear me.'

Appalled to think she'd been caught talking to herself, Jo ran her hands through her hair and somehow managed to get onion juice into her eye at the same time. 'Oh God, now I'll have to run my eye under a cold tap.' She managed a very feeble smile and rushed for the bathroom. 'Keep an eye on the mince!' she called before slamming the door shut behind her.

Inside the bathroom she ran the cold tap and started splashing her face before she had a chance to look at how red and puffy her eyes were. How could he creep up on her like that? It was an outrage! Then she remembered that the water supply was not inexhaustible and turned off the tap. She dried her face on the hand towel and took stock before finding some moisturiser that was probably Dora's.

The trouble was, she suspected she had conjured Marcus up just by thinking about him as she peeled and chopped and fried. She had meant to think about the new set of challenges that were waiting for her at Miranda's shop, but Marcus had just drifted into her head, through Radio 4 and her thoughts about cooking. She had begun by wondering what he liked to eat when he was on a passage and it had gone on from there. He intrigued her, and she had to admit he really was very attractive, but he did seem to have a rather dark side. She just hoped it stayed away whilst they were on their trip. Now here he was in her galley, stirring the mince. Or at least she hoped he was.

She applied Dora's make-up as artlessly as she could. It

225

wouldn't do to let him see that she had applied full slap just because he had appeared. She had had a good reason for running to the bathroom but she couldn't emerge too thoroughly painted.

'Sorry about that,' she said. 'I'm dreadfully sensitive to onions and have been fighting them all day. Would you like a cup of tea?'

Just at that moment, Jo had no idea of the time. Was tea an appropriate suggestion? A glance at the ship's clock fixed to the bulkhead assured her that it was. 'I've made a cake.' Quite why she added this rider, she didn't know. She'd made it for Dora and Tom when they came home, in case the visit had not gone well.

'I didn't come for tea and cake,' said Marcus. 'But if you're offering it, I won't say no.'

Jo put the kettle on, less flustered now she had a task to do. 'So why did you come?'

'I brought a life-raft. It's on deck. You would have heard me getting it aboard if you hadn't had the radio on so loudly.'

'I had to have it on loudly or I wouldn't have heard the play over the sound of the mixer.'

'Is it yours?' He regarded the machine, which was about the size of a small fridge, with misgiving.

'Don't worry, it's only borrowed. It's fantastic, but I agree there isn't really room for it.'

'I didn't say that.'

'No. Your thoughts are very loud.'

He laughed. 'You look as if you're planning to feed an army.'

'I am. I know I'm going to be seasick, so I don't want to have to do more cooking when we're under way than I absolutely have to. I'm going to fill the freezer and the fridge. You'll all be able to come down and just pop something into the microwave.' She paused. 'Don't worry, you can tell Carole I'm keeping the salt and fat down. Oh, I'd better drain that mince, now.'

Wondering why people always stood in front of the sink when there were acres of other space for them to stand in, she edged him out of the way.

'What did Miranda think of those bits and pieces you repaired for her?'

Jo nearly spilt the mince into the sink. 'How on earth do you know about that?'

'Bill rang me about something and mentioned you'd called in at the shop. He didn't tell me if the pieces were all right.'

The boat world bush telegraph was even more active than her village one had been, she thought wryly, slightly taken aback by his interest. 'They were more than all right, actually,' she said. 'Miranda wanted to give me a whole lot more stuff to tackle only I made her keep it until we're home again and I've got a bit more space.' She frowned slightly, blotting at the mince with a bit of kitchen towel.

'Well, that's good, isn't it?'

'Of course.'

'But you look worried.'

She looked up at him in surprise. 'Well, I am a bit.'

'Why?'

'Why the interest? I can't have looked all that worried.' She found his questioning unnerving. Why did he care?

'I was just asking,' he said more gently.

Unaware until that moment that she didn't want to talk about her fledgling new career in case it all came to nothing she got a grip on herself. 'I'm sorry. I think the onions are making me irritable. Why don't you go and sit down and I'll make you a cup of tea.'

'So what are you cooking for us?'

'Lasagne, chilli, moussaka, though I should have used lamb mince for that really.' She smiled at him. 'I'm thinking of writing a cookery book: *A Million Ways with Mince.*'

'Not really?'

Jo raised an eyebrow. 'No, but I could have done. When we were first married, Philip and I didn't have much money. I managed to do very elegant dinner parties that were either vegetarian, or used mince. Just as well we hadn't heard of BSE in those days.'

He smiled reminiscently. 'There were still plenty of mad cows about.'

'Nowadays it's politically incorrect to refer to women as cows,' she said sternly.

'Whatever else you may or may not expect of me, you can't expect me to be politically correct.'

This made her laugh a little. 'That much I do believe.'

'Will you have tea with me? Or am I too politically incorrect?'

She swallowed, trying to make sense of her feelings. In one way she had to admit she found Marcus very attractive and he was being very nice to her, interested in her goings-on etc. But she couldn't help remembering that he was used to getting his own way, was a bit arrogant and had a much younger girlfriend. What's more, she just couldn't trust men at the moment. If Philip could leave her after nearly thirty years of marriage, a man like Marcus couldn't possibly be interested in her as a woman. So what was he up to?

'Marcus, we may not know each other very well, and it may have been a very long time since we first knew each other, but your lack of PC-ness comes as no surprise. I will have a cup of tea, though. Do you want some cake?'

'Mm. Yes please.'

So was she giving him cake because he was a man she

wanted to impress or because she saw him as a boy she wanted to indulge? She'd had too many shocks lately, she decided, it had addled her brain – even her thoughts were gibberish.

Jo made two mugs of tea and then found the cake, which was hiding under a recipe she'd printed off the Internet. She brought the tea and then went back for the cake. Could she ask him outright why he hadn't just dumped the life-raft?

'So, was there any other reason for coming round? Apart from the life-raft, I mean.'

He seemed to find her directness amusing and was equally direct. 'I came – with the life-raft – to see how you were getting on and to bum a cup of tea off you. I also thought you might have cake.'

She found his directness funny too, and she laughed. 'But, Marcus, it means we have to make polite conversation while you drink the tea and eat the cake.'

He raised his eyebrows in mock horror. 'I never thought of that.'

'Don't worry. I'm good at thinking of uncontroversial topics of conversation. Tell me about Ed,' she said, dragging a subject from some previously unplumbed depth.

That surprised him. 'Ed? What about him?'

She made a throwaway gesture. 'Well, you know, I'm going boating with him. I ought to know what he's like.'

Marcus apparently sensed that while Jo was being glib about her social skills, underneath it all she was unsettled and uncomfortable. 'Joanna, what's wrong?'

'Nothing's wrong. I'm fine!'

'No you're not. You seem anxious again. I wonder why?'

Jo took a breath. She thought she knew why but there weren't enough wild horses in the universe to drag the information from her. She was annoyed with her brain and her body being so out of sync. Her brain didn't trust men, especially men like Marcus, so her body should jolly well do the decent thing and reject them too.

'So – what does Ed like to eat?' Jo didn't want him to start counselling her again.

Marcus shook his head slightly, apparently giving up his attempts to get Jo to unburden. 'He'll eat anything, sleep anywhere, and takes his turn at the washing-up. He's very house-trained. I've known him a long time.'

'He sounds like good news for lots of reasons. We'll definitely have him on the trip.'

Marcus smiled. 'He's also got years of ship-handling experience; he can steer. What about Tom, since we're interrogating each other on our choice of shipmate?'

'You know about Tom, and as you've already told him he can come, you can't change your mind now.'

He studied her for a few seconds before answering. 'You fight for those you're fond of, don't you?'

'Of course! Don't you?'

'I'm not often fond of people. It's hard to tell.'

Suddenly her tension disappeared. She patted him firmly on the wrist. 'Oh, have some more cake, you miserable old misanthrope.'

He laughed and lifted his hand as if to cover Jo's, but just before Jo could panic, they heard Tom and Dora arrive. Marcus replaced his hand on the table and they both listened to the clattering down the stairs.

'Hey, Jo! What's that enormous suitcase doing on deck? Oh, hello, Marcus,' added Dora.

'It's a life-raft,' said Marcus.

'I could have told you that,' said Tom.

Chapter Sixteen

❧❧❧

'Cup of tea?' Jo asked, putting the kettle on without waiting for an answer. When Dora came over to help her she added, 'How did it go?' sotto voce while Tom sat down next to Marcus and started talking to him about weather patterns.

'Fine, really, although I think Mum would have been happier if Tom had been the new man in my life.'

Jo scooped a wet tea bag out of a mug and put it in the bin. 'I suppose that's only natural, in the circs.'

'It was lovely seeing them again in a slightly more normal way though, after how we parted last time.'

'I knew you'd feel better if you did. And your parents didn't try to make you go back and live at home, did they?'

'Nope. I think they realise I've fled the nest.'

'I think you mean "flown", don't you?'

'No, "fled" is the word.' Dora chuckled. 'I was definitely fleeing. Or maybe I was chased out.'

'Either way, I'm so glad you've made it all up. It must have niggled you.'

'Yes it did. Mum and I have had our ups and downs over the years but I think we've reached a more equal point in our relationship now. We're beginning to see things from each other's point of view more. Oh, and John's got a new girlfriend.'

'Oh . . .' Jo checked to see how Dora looked; she seemed quite calm about it all. 'How do you feel?'

'Strangely, fine actually. I realise that I really did make the right decision. I think Mum and Dad do too, now.'

'And they're not too miserable without you?'

'Don't think so. They may even like having some time alone together. Mum's got some lovely new clothes.'

'Although I would have much preferred Karen to stay in the same country, before it all went wrong for me and Philip we were enjoying each other's company. Or at least I was. I didn't realise he was enjoying someone else's more.'

Dora waited a tactful moment before saying, 'Has Marcus been here long?'

'Not terribly. Long enough to have a cup of tea.'

'And it's been OK? I still find Marcus a bit scary. He's so knowledgeable and a bit brusque. I feel I might make a mistake when he's around.'

'So do I really. Not sure why. He's perfectly polite.' But was he perfectly polite? Wasn't his rather intense questioning a bit rude? Jo chewed her lip. She felt like she'd been through a job interview and wasn't sure how she'd done. But at times it felt as if he might have been flirting with her. It was all very confusing.

Dora moved nearer. 'So did you talk about old times or something?'

'Not really. Only in an abstract way. When we knew him I always thought he despised us for tying the knot and settling down so young.' She gave a small, wry laugh. 'Perhaps he could tell it wouldn't last.'

'What are you two muttering about?' said Tom.

'We're discussing what to do about supper,' said Jo instantly, improvising fluently. 'Because I said I absolutely refuse to cook it. And Dora said she couldn't cook it because the galley is covered with half-made lasagne and chilli.'

'Yes,' said Dora, feeling that, personally, she didn't want to eat again for some time.

'Oh,' said Tom, obviously convinced by this string of lies. 'Tell you what, why don't we go to the pub for a bar meal? I'll pay.'

'That's a brilliant idea,' said Jo.

'I must be getting back,' said Marcus, closing the charts and rising from the table.

'We can't tempt you with chicken-in-a-basket?' asked Jo. Now she knew she couldn't, she felt free to ask.

'What's "chicken-in-a-basket"?' asked Dora.

'It's a seventies thing,' said Jo. 'You had to be there.'

'Not at all,' said Marcus. 'It was disgusting. But even a home-made meal couldn't tempt me tonight. I've left Carole on her own.'

Thinking, but not saying, that she must be used to it, and yet still rather confused about Marcus and Carole's relationship, Jo said, 'Well, I certainly won't press you, but I will see you out.' They both went up into the wheelhouse.

'Oh,' said Jo, 'what about the fuel?'

'We'll get it as we go down the river. It's easier than arranging for the fuel barge to come here.'

'Fine,' said Jo. Then, not knowing what else to say, she added, 'Thank you so much for bringing the life-raft.'

He looked down at her. 'Thank you for the tea and cake.'

'It was a pleasure.'

He continued to look at her and Jo willed him not to say or do anything else unconventional or controversial. Her life as a wife and mother hadn't prepared her for being with large men she was not related to in any way in small, intimate places.

Eventually he said, 'I'm looking forward to this trip.'

Relief made her garrulous. 'Oh yes! I suppose it will be exciting, going to Holland.'

233

He laughed and stepped out of the wheelhouse down on to the deck. 'I've been to Holland dozens of times. That wasn't what I was talking about at all.'

Jo attempted a light smile and then said, 'Right. OK then. I'd better go. So had you.' Then she retreated to the wheelhouse and watched until he had walked away.

Jo didn't immediately go and join Tom and Dora. She wanted to calm her breathing and wait for her complexion to return to normal. She knew she couldn't retire to her cabin because Tom and Dora would wonder what on earth was up with her so she took deep breaths and fanned herself for as long as she could.

The trouble was she had realised – to her horror – while she was plying him with tea and cake, that she fancied Marcus in a way she hadn't fancied anyone for years and years. And although she couldn't be sure, she had felt he'd been flirting with her. She gave herself a mental shake 'It's my hormones, or my age, or my feelings of rejection projecting themselves on to the first man that comes within six feet of me,' she told herself sternly. 'It's because I'm a frustrated old bat. It's not because I like him or anything. God! I hardly know him! But my hormones are out of order because of my imminent menopause, or something. It's making me react strangely. It's like developing an allergy. I really must take no notice and try to behave normally.'

When this very sensible lecture had had time to take effect, she went back downstairs.

'It's still early,' she said. 'Why don't you two go off to the pub while I finish making up these dishes for the freezer?'

'Tom can go to the pub,' said Dora firmly. 'I'll help you here. You look tired.'

'Tired' was one way of putting it, thought Jo.

'I'll help,' said Tom. 'I am a new man, you know. I know how to wield a saucepan.'

'Well, that's very good to hear,' said Jo. 'If Dora and I are prostrated by seasickness, you can take over in the galley. At least we know you can make custard if necessary.'

Later, after all three of them had worked hard, assembling dishes, washing-up, finding storage containers, she said, 'Well, I think that should take a small army across the Russian steppes without them going hungry. Let's go to the pub.'

Knowing that she'd made all the preparations she possibly could, Jo went over to see Miranda again. The plan was that they should clear one of the spare rooms over her shop so Jo could use it as a workroom when she got back from Holland.

They enjoyed themselves and worked hard all morning until Bill came to take them out to lunch.

'What would be really good,' said Miranda, tucking into her Caesar salad, 'would be if you could come with me to an antiques fair that's on soon. We could see how good a saleswoman you are. They're such fun, those fairs. Especially this one, the atmosphere's terrific.'

'It does sound fun,' Jo agreed, 'and it would be good for me to get away from the barge for a bit. We've worked so hard to get it ready for the trip. A little holiday would be wonderful.'

Miranda laughed. 'It won't be a holiday, exactly.'

'But infinitely preferable to crossing the North Sea in a barge.'

'Each to his own,' said Bill. 'I'd prefer the barge trip myself.'

Both women looked at him. 'But you like boating,' said Jo. 'I don't, especially.'

They bickered gently about how they liked to enjoy

235

themselves until Bill noticed what the time was. 'Do you girls want another drink?'

'Pre-women, Bill,' said Miranda, as if she had said it many times before. 'It's politically incorrect to call women "girls". It's pre-women now.'

He smiled and sighed. 'Do you pre-women want another drink?'

'Yes please,' said Miranda. 'Then we must get back to work.'

While Bill was at the bar they went back to discussing the forthcoming antiques fair. 'It sounds heaven,' said Jo. 'If I can manage the dates, I'm definitely on for it. Oh, thanks, Bill. That is kind.'

'A pleasure. If you go with Miranda to the wretched antiques fair, a drink is the least I can reward you with.'

It was over a week later when Marcus telephoned to say that the weather forecast was good enough for them to make the first leg of their journey.

'We need to leave very early tomorrow, I should warn you,' he said, curt to the point of rudeness.

'Oh.' Jo quickly collected herself. 'That's fine. We'll do all the final preparations we need to do tonight.' Jo thought he must be on edge because of the trip and tried to think of something comforting to say – and failed.

'Goodbye, then.' He disconnected, leaving Jo slightly taken aback. He'd been so cheerful. What could have happened to make him so grumpy, suddenly?

'I hope he snaps out of that mood,' she muttered, 'or this isn't going to be any fun at all.' She realised that although the trip still terrified her, part of her had been looking forward to being with Marcus.

She went to find Dora. 'Marcus has rung. We're on for tomorrow.'

Dora nodded. 'So Fred was right? He said yesterday he wouldn't see me for a little while. Maybe he gets the same weather forecast as Marcus does.'

'Or maybe he has a piece of seaweed that is just as accurate,' said Jo, unwilling, at that moment, to give Marcus credit for anything. His curtness had rattled her.

'Right,' said Dora, 'we'd better get on.'

They sprang into action like a well-trained pair of soldiers going into battle and Jo felt pleased that she hadn't mentioned Marcus's shortness. Dora was obviously well into the trip and Jo didn't want to spoil that.

They checked beds for clean bedding, they counted towels and speculated on the chances of Marcus and Ed bringing their own. They allowed the massive fruit cake that Jo had made for the voyage to come out from its tin and be tested; they checked the bathroom and hid all but the basic essentials from critical masculine eyes. When they had done all this, and Tom had arrived and demanded it, they secured everything that might move. They took the plants out of the wheelhouse, sending the tomato plants and geraniums for a holiday with Tilly on the next-door barge. The herbs came down to the galley.

Then they slumped on the sofa, nursing glasses of medicinal sherry – stronger than wine but weaker than whisky, since they would need reasonably clear heads. They were both exhausted.

'I've gone off the idea of going to Holland,' said Jo. 'Let's just stay here and eat the cake and all the other food. I wouldn't have to cook again for weeks.'

'I'd be disappointed if I couldn't go,' said Dora. 'Although now we've got all that lovely food, chocolate and crisps—'

'Cans of lager,' added Tom, who was sitting on the chair opposite them holding one.

'We could just stay here and have a holiday,' finished Jo. 'I need a holiday.'

'You have been working very hard to make everything ready,' said Dora. 'You could rent the barge to rich tourists now.'

'No!' wailed Jo. 'I couldn't! At least, not unless I just left them to it.' She closed her eyes, hoping to sleep and then wake up and find it was all a dream, she wasn't going anywhere on *The Three Sisters* and could go to the antiques fair (which was also due to start tomorrow) and have a lovely time.

She did drift off into a light doze. It was one of her skills, catnapping. Ten minutes with her eyes shut could keep her going for many extra hours. She prided herself on being able to do it almost anywhere.

She was awoken by voices and realised that Marcus and Ed – she assumed it was him – had arrived. Tom and Dora had obviously gone up to give them a hand with their baggage. They seemed to be taking a long time, so she went up to join them. She was surprised – and not terribly pleased – to see Carole with Marcus in the wheelhouse.

Before she could say hello, Marcus said, 'You still here?' to her.

She frowned. 'Yes, still here. Shouldn't I be?'

'I expect you're going later?'

What was he talking about? His mood clearly hadn't improved. 'No, I'm spending the night here, thank you very much,' then she turned away, ignoring bad behaviour like a good mother should. 'Carole! How nice to see you. Did you give them a lift? That's very kind of you. Why don't you come down and have a glass of wine or something while they sort themselves out. Will you eat with us, or do you need to get back?' While she was saying this she was aware of Tom disappearing with the man she realised was indeed Ed, and whom Marcus should have introduced. Honestly, Marcus had no bloody manners at all!

'I'm not going back,' said Carole, who appeared both frightened and defiant. 'I'm coming with you.'

Jo swallowed, thinking even more badly of Marcus, springing an extra person on her without notice, especially when he didn't approve of people bringing their girlfriends along. Typical double standards. 'Right. Good, I'll show you your cabin. You are sharing with Marcus, aren't you? Otherwise I don't know where you'll sleep. I'll have to find some extra pillows.'

'Of course I'm sharing with Marcus,' she said, looking at Jo oddly. 'We're partners.'

'Is Tom showing Ed where to sleep?' Jo asked Marcus.

Marcus nodded. 'I'll check his accommodation is suitable.'

Concealing her mental description of him as a sulky child behind a smile, Jo said, 'Come with me, Carole.' She opened the door to what had been her private space a few hours before. 'You might prefer to go backwards, but do mind your head.' Where, she wondered, was she going to find half-decent pillows at this stage? Tom would have to be a hero and sacrifice his. He could probably manage with a sofa cushion.

'Oh. It is quite small,' said Carole, when she had made her way down.

'Just the usual size. You and Marcus are a bit spoilt on *Hildegarde*.' Jo concealed her defensiveness behind a Brown-Owl bracingness. 'This is the original living space, although in the old days they had to cook and eat in here as well as sleep.'

'Yes, I suppose so. Is this the bathroom?' Carole peered into the adjoining cupboard. It's minute!'

'I only use it for the loo and tooth-brushing. I haven't

quite worked out how the shower works. I use the other bathroom, up the fore end.'

'Not very convenient.'

'It's fine when it's just me and Dora.' Jo kept up her bracing tone by sheer effort of will. To think that she'd given up her haven, her sanctuary, to two people who didn't appreciate it. One was a spoilt brat and the other was moody, arrogant and too rude to live! 'I'll leave you to get yourself organised,' she added, thinking longingly of her sherry, still unfinished in the saloon. Would this trip turn her an alcoholic? she wondered as she made her way up the steps and into the wheelhouse.

'Shall I open the wine?' said Dora, seeing the look on Jo's face.

'Yes.' Jo threw herself full length on to the sofa, aware she'd have to spring to attention any second. She no longer cared about becoming an alcoholic – it was probably inevitable.

'You didn't have any idea Carole was coming, did you?' Dora placed a full wine glass next to Jo's half-finished sherry.

'Nope.' She kept her eyes closed.

'I wonder if she can cook,' said Dora.

'I'm sure she can. Anyway, she won't have to. She might do the heating up though. That could be very useful.'

'I can't help wondering—' Dora began before the sound of feet on the steps stopped her.

Jo sat upright and knocked back her sherry in one, dizzy-making action.

'The men won't be long, will they?' Carole stood in the doorway, sounding nervous.

'I don't suppose so,' said Jo. 'There's not much to see up there. Come and have a glass of sherry or wine; we've got both.'

'Marcus is always very insistent that Ed gets a decent berth,' said Carole.

'Well, it's as decent as we could make it. Though I did omit to put flowers on the dressing table.' Jo sounded less welcoming now.

'Oh, it's all right,' said Dora. 'I did that.'

Carole and Jo stared at her.

'Not really. Only joking. Let's get to the wine!' Dora said brightly.

'Do sit down, Carole, we mustn't stand on ceremony if we're crossing the ocean together.'

'The North Sea's not an ocean,' said Dora. 'Red or white, Carole?'

'Nothing, thank you.'

'Of course, this will be a very run-of-the-mill trip to you, Carole,' said Jo after a moment. 'You must have been to Holland dozens of times with Marcus.'

'Actually, I haven't been before. He doesn't usually let me come on trips.'

'But he let you – asked you to come this time?' The reasons for this buzzed round Jo's head like angry flies.

'No, he didn't ask me, but he said I could come.'

Mortification flooded over Jo. He must have let Carole come because he had sensed she fancied him. It was for protection from a frustrated perimenopausal woman. It was probably also the reason for his extreme rudeness – he was fending her off. When she became aware she was using nautical expressions in her head, she sipped her wine to ward off despair.

Dora took over the role as hostess. She opened another bottle of wine and retrieved a few cans of lager from the fridge. She opened a packet of handcut crisps and put them in bowls. There was a chicken casserole all ready to serve. She peeked in the oven and counted the baked potatoes that were to go with the casserole. Thank goodness for Jo's tendency to over-cater, she thought.

As there was nothing else constructive she could do, she poured herself a glass of wine and took a handful of crisps. She glanced across at Jo, who looked tired, and felt very sorry for her. Poor Jo! She was anxious enough about this trip without having to deal with Carole too.

Then she noticed the table that she had set earlier and added another place. It was going to be a squash, but too bad. No one should mind too much; after all, they were on a barge, about to do a job, not socialising on a yacht in the South of France.

Carole, she couldn't help thinking, would be more at home in the Cap d'Antibes than chugging down the great greasy Thames to the coast. There was an awkward silence. Jo, usually so socially conscientious, didn't break it, and Dora couldn't think how to. Carole didn't speak either. To everyone's relief, they heard footsteps approaching.

Dora bounced forward, feeling like a Labrador puppy, friendly but a bit over-enthusiastic. 'Come in, both of you. I'll get you a drink. You must be Ed – what would you like?'

'How do, all,' said Ed. 'And beer for now, if you've got it. A drop of rum later.' He was tall, silver-haired and, Dora decided, gave one confidence. A different confidence to Marcus's, who seemed rather sullen all of a sudden. Ed was happy in his skin and knew what he was doing. He was either unaware of the atmosphere or dispelled it by his jovial presence.

'Glass or can?' Dora asked.

'Can. Let's save on the washing-up wherever possible!' He laughed merrily and Dora felt he was going to be a good catalyst for the disparate group of people on board.

'Oh, thank you for doing the honours, Dora,' said Jo, who seemed to have returned more or less to her old self.

242

'What would you like, Carole? You must have something while we're all swigging away.'

'A glass of still mineral water then, please. I don't need anything complicated.' She aimed for a smile but didn't quite manage it.

'I'm afraid that's a bit of a problem,' said Jo after a moment. 'We haven't got any. I've got lots of fizzy water, all kinds of soft drinks and alcohol, including rum' – she glanced at Ed – 'but no still mineral water. You might have told me, Marcus,' she finished. Marcus had told her that Ed liked rum. Marcus didn't respond.

'There's some orange and mango juice,' suggested Dora. 'It's lovely with some fizzy water.'

'Carbonated water is connected with osteoporosis,' said Carole.

'Not at your age, surely!' said Jo.

'It's never too early to start taking care of oneself,' said Carole. 'You should be really careful.'

'What about you, Marcus?' Jo went on, ignoring this and making an effort to speak to him when she felt like spitting. The combination of Marcus's sullenness and Carole's fussiness was getting on her nerves. How would she last an hour, let alone a few days with them?

'Wine – no – make that a lager.'

'You're going to have to drink my wine eventually,' said Jo, almost to herself. 'It's perfectly nice. It was on offer and Dora and I have been test-driving it.'

Carole frowned.

Aware that Carole was still drinkless, Dora said, 'Why not have the orange and mango with just a splash of sparkling water? I'm sure a little drop can't do you any harm. You could take a calcium pill or something.'

'OK, that would be fine,' said Carole with a rare smile. 'I did bring all my supplements with me.'

'But how are you going to manage when all you really want to drink is water?' asked Jo, who thought she'd considered every single requirement anyone could possibly have. Her heart sank.

'I'll pop along to the Eight-'til-Late,' said Tom, who had come in quietly and helped himself to a can of lager. 'Dora can help me carry it.'

'Well, let's eat first. Everyone must be hungry. Oh, thanks for setting an extra place, Dora. Just sit anywhere, all of you.'

There was a lot of shuffling and jostling and you-go-firsting and then Carole said, 'I'm a vegetarian.'

Jo thought about the dishes and dishes of non-vegetarian food she had prepared. 'Oh well, would you like me to make you a quick omelette or something?'

'Yes, please.'

Jo had offered but she hadn't expected Carole to accept. She had expected her to say, 'Just a baked potato is fine.'

'Carole, don't put Jo to that trouble,' said Marcus quietly.

'It's no trouble,' said Jo, struggling to her feet.

'I'll do it,' said Tom. 'I'm nearest.'

Jo and Dora sent him looks of gratitude that almost conferred sainthood.

'Thank you so much, Tom. Now, shall I serve out? I'll do it for this first meal, but you'll have to look after yourselves after that.'

Everyone began eating except Carole, who regarded the baked potato and peas on her plate. They were possibly not toxic, but they were certainly high on the glycemic index – or perhaps low. Dora didn't know which, she only knew that from Carole's point of view they were 'Bad'. When Tom laid a perfectly golden omelette next to them, Dora felt he was due a round of applause. Jo obviously agreed because she gave him a very warm smile and patted his arm affectionately. Dora caught Marcus noticing this with distinct lack of approval. He was probably embarrassed that it was his girlfriend who had made the omelette necessary.

'This is delicious, Jo,' said Ed. 'Would you pass the bread, I want to make sure I don't miss any of the wonderful sauce.'

Jo handed him the basket of bread and added a smile such as she had just bestowed on Tom. 'There's plenty more if you'd like it later.'

'Oh, I'm fine, love. Better wait till everyone's finished before doling out a second lot of rations.'

'How's your omelette, Carole?' asked Jo warmly. Possibly only Dora could tell that Jo might have said something very rude had the answer not been positive.

'It's wonderful. Thank you so much, Tom.'

Strange, thought Dora, Marcus didn't seem to notice Carole's beaming smile of gratitude.

Carole rejected the homely crumble that oozed black-currant juice over the edges and had a crisp, buttery crust that Dora could have eaten by itself as a biscuit it was so good. She didn't want tea or coffee, either.

Ed stood up. 'That was thoroughly enjoyable, Jo. I can see we're going to get good vittles on this trip. Now we'll just get this washing-up out of the way—'

'Well thank you so much for offering, Ed,' said Jo, 'but there's a dishwasher and I expect Marcus wants to talk things over with you. Dora and I will do this in a jiffy.'

'OK then, I dare say the boss does want a bit of a conference, but I don't hold with the womenfolk doing all the domestic chores, so put me down for cooking duty sometime.'

'I certainly will, Ed. Thank you so much!' Jo's gratitude was perhaps enhanced by the fact that Carole had gone on deck, possibly for a cigarette, and Marcus looked pre-occupied, a frown of concentration on his face.

Tom tagged on to the planning meeting that was going on round the table while Jo and Dora dealt with the detritus of the meal.

'I'll leave this dish to soak a bit, shall I? Those bits won't come off in the dishwasher even if we could fit it in,' said Dora.

'Oh yes, we can finish in the morning.' Jo yawned hugely. 'What time do you want us ready for action tomorrow, Marcus?' She'd decided she had to try and treat him normally. They couldn't set off with her hating him, she had enough to feel stressed about.

He looked startled. 'Why? Are you coming then?'

His question hung in the silence. 'Of course I'm coming,' said Jo after a second. 'Why shouldn't I be? Would you rather I didn't?'

Now he hesitated before speaking. 'I thought you'd changed your mind, that's all.'

'Well, I hadn't,' said Jo, thinking now was not the time to demand how on earth he'd got hold of that idea. 'So what time?'

'Er, well, high water is at seven, I want to set off about two hours before to get the benefit from the ebb. That means leaving at five – so I suppose we should get up at about half past four.'

'Fine,' said Jo, hoping her horror didn't show as Dora gasped.

'Not everyone needs to be up then,' said Ed soothingly, 'Marcus and me and young Tom here will be able to manage.'

'No, I'll get up when you do,' Jo insisted, yawning widely, 'but I might slope off to bed now. I'm quite tired.'

246

'We'll go and get the water then, shall we?' said Tom. 'We can carry it between us.'

Jo considered. Maybe a bit of fresh air would do her good before bed. 'No, I'll go and take the car. I'll give you a ring from the car park and you can help me carry it back.'

'We'll all three go,' said Dora firmly. 'It won't take long.'

As Dora, Tom and Jo walked along the jetty to where the car was parked, Dora said, 'What are the chances of Carole having finished the washing-up before we get back?'

'Low,' said Tom. 'She's a high-maintenance woman.'

Dora looked across to him. Was there a hint of admiration in his voice? And if there was, why did she mind?

'I feel quite sorry for her,' said Jo. 'She's going to sea with a lot of people she doesn't know. It would be daunting.' *And her boyfriend is a moody boor*, she added silently. She wondered if his earlier friendliness had just been to make sure she came along and he had a chief cook and bottle-washer on board. When he thought she wasn't coming he'd obviously felt peeved he hadn't got everything the way he wanted it. How childish. She had more sympathy with Carole.

'You're just too forgiving,' said Dora. 'She probably invited herself, we're all in the same boat – if you'll forgive the expression – and she's an adult. She can just make an effort to fit in.'

'I should have thought of water,' Jo went on. 'After all, it can taste a bit funny out of the tap after a few days.'

'The water in the tap is fine,' said Tom firmly. 'It only gets stale if it's been there a while and we're not going away for long, it's only just a hop across the North Sea.'

'Nothing's ever that simple, Tom,' said Jo. 'Trust me. I'm an eccentric old woman. I know stuff.'

Chapter Seventeen

Having been to the bathroom, Jo went into the little cabin formerly known as the glory hole. It didn't make sense to move Dora, she had insisted, and it was only for a short time. She'd soon be back in her stateroom, about to be occupied by Marcus and Carole.

The glory hole was glorious, thought Jo, as she shut the door. When they'd first been clearing it out and making it nice, she'd had it in mind that Tom would be sleeping in it. Once they'd realised that he would be sharing the forepeak with Ed, and it was going to be a woman who lived there, they'd made a special effort with it. Now, Jo noticed, Dora had put a selection of creams and potions on the shelf, tucked a teddy bear into the bunk and put a copy of *heat* magazine on the little bedside cabinet. On top of that was a miniature bottle of Famous Grouse whisky. Jo laughed, and hid the bottle away behind her pillow. She really hoped things wouldn't get so bad that she became a secret drinker but if all else failed it was nice to have a fallback position.

Jo felt a bit guilty going to bed before everyone else. She was the hostess, she should stay up in case anyone needed anything, put the lights out, find extra bedding or whatever. But she had done all the cooking they were likely to need for the entire trip, made so many trips to the local shop she called the boy who helped her pack her bags by his first name. She had organised all the bedding, which meant buying extra. And if she was to be up at the un-godly hour Marcus suggested she needed to get her head down immediately. Marcus was an excellent skipper, she told herself, everyone said so. If he was behaving a little frostily then she'd just have to live with it. So what if he hadn't even said goodnight, that was his problem. At least she had Ed, Tom and Dora. Touched and amused by Dora's presents, she snuggled under the duvet and went to sleep with a smile on her face.

She woke early and got up immediately, hoping she was the first. Without doing more than pulling a sweater on over her pyjamas she went up on deck to see the dawn on the water. She knew she must hurry – everyone would be up very shortly.

She had always loved early mornings and when she lived in her old home, she used to steal out in her nightie into her garden and revel in the beauty of the dew on the lawn, the flowers, the way the light stole in behind some of the plants creating strange, pale shadows. She would stay out until her feet got cold and then go in, make a cup of tea, and come back out to drink it, sitting on a bench, watching the day emerge and the magic fade. It was as if the earlier moment had been just for her, a secret revelation of beauty.

The dawn was almost as beautiful today, only she wasn't alone to enjoy it. As she stepped down from the wheel-house, she saw Marcus up at the bows, clutching a cup of something that steamed. She stayed still, hoping he wouldn't notice her, planning to hop back up the steps into the wheelhouse and then back down below again. She couldn't face any hostility this morning. But something must have alerted him to her presence and he turned.

Quickly, he edged round the boat towards her and was with her too soon for her to be able to go back without it

249

looking like she was running away. Pride forced her to stay where she was.

'I seem to have been under a misapprehension,' he said.

'Oh?' She tensed, trying to guess his mood.

'Yes. I thought you'd decided not to come.'

'Why on earth did you think that?' Jo felt herself bristling all over again.

'It was something Bill said. He said – I'm sure he did – that you were going to some antiques fair with Miranda and were about to start work there.'

This did explain, to some extent, his surprise at seeing her on the barge. 'Well, only if I could. We didn't know when we were going, did we?'

'No.' He paused. 'I think I owe you an apology, Joanna. I thought you'd abandoned this trip, and after all my coaching.'

'I'm surprised you thought that. I would have thought you knew better than to think that of me.'

'I have said I'm sorry.'

'No you haven't!'

The tiniest smile nudged the corner of his mouth. 'OK, I'll say it now. I'm truly sorry for misjudging you.'

'And listening to gossip.'

'It wasn't gossip, precisely . . .'

'Hearsay then.'

He sighed, getting impatient with this protracted apology. 'It was just that Bill said the antiques fair you were going to with Miranda was starting tomorrow.'

'I would have very much liked to have gone,' said Jo primly. 'It would have been very good for me, career-wise. However I had arranged to come on this trip some time ago. It was my priority.'

He touched her shoulder. 'I really have said I'm sorry now. Can we be friends?'

Jo considered. It was a bit like being asked to be friends with a panther – while it seemed impossible, it was a much safer option than being enemies. He was so unpredictable, who knew what else might set him off, but they were about to go on a journey together and she had to trust him. 'Of course.' She made to go but he put his hand on her shoulder again. 'Don't go just yet. Ed will be up in a moment and he'll get Tom up. What about Dora?'

Jo glanced at her watch. 'I'll give her another ten minutes or so, let the others use the bathroom. What about Carole?'

'She'll stay out of the way until things are under way. She's not much good at boats.'

Jo couldn't ask why he'd brought her – it would be rude, even if she was curious. Jo was rarely, if ever, rude. 'There's no point in her dragging herself out of bed, then.'

'No.'

'I'll make some tea for the others.'

'I would have done it but I couldn't find a teapot.'

'Oh, no, well, there isn't one.'

'Which explains why I couldn't find it.'

Jo sighed. 'I should have got one. I seem to have forgotten so much.' In spite of his apology, Jo still felt out of sorts with Marcus. His thinking that she could duck out of such a long-standing engagement was hurtful and it didn't exactly warrant such frosty behaviour. She would get over it, of course, but just now, she felt at odds with him.

Possibly sensing this, Marcus was insistent. 'No, you haven't forgotten anything. You've done brilliantly. As Ed said, there's vittles for an army and liquor for the Navy.'

'I like Ed. I'm so glad you brought him. He's going to make everyone feel better.'

Marcus didn't seem to approve of this accolade. 'I hope he's going to be my first mate.'

'But he'll do the other thing just by being here. I'm going to make tea, now.'

Once in the galley she congratulated herself on sounding really quite normal. She put the kettle on feeling that maybe everything would be OK after all.

Dora was woken by the sound of the bathroom door closing. Although there was light coming in through the porthole she could tell it was still very early. She must get up. They were setting off that morning.

Excitement flooded through her. She was going on an adventure and Tom was there. He was amusing to go adventuring with and fun just happened around him.

Briefly, she allowed herself to think how John would have been on a trip like this. He would have been fine, she told herself firmly, if he'd actually come. There just would have been a million, unarguable excuses why he shouldn't. About the only times they'd been away together had been to visit his relations.

She pulled on her jeans and a cotton sweater. She could hear swooshing and spitting and a few ecstatic groans coming from the bathroom and realised it contained an enthusiastic strip washer. Feeling guilty for the quick swipe of deodorant and fingerful of moisturiser that comprised her own ablutions that morning, she went to the galley.

Tom and Marcus were there, drinking tea. Jo was making toast under the grill and indicated a mug. 'I was going to take that in to you. Ed's in the bathroom.'

'I know. I decided it was too early to wash. I'll do it later. Good morning, Marcus. Oh, hi, Tom.' Seeing his wide smile made Dora wish she'd had a chance to brush her teeth. The moment Ed was out of the bathroom she'd go and do it.

'Butter that lot for me,' said Jo, 'there's a dear, and think of what people might like on it. There's marmalade, Marmite, honey, jam.'

'Too much choice,' said Tom firmly. 'Just put marmalade on it. Or peanut butter, my own favourite.' He winked at Jo and then started buttering alongside Dora.

Jo put another four slices of bread under the grill.

'Just the one loaf should be enough,' said Tom and Marcus laughed.

'I don't want anyone going hungry,' she said calmly, 'but maybe I won't do this lot until the first lot has gone. Marcus, are you going to take some to Carole, or doesn't she eat toast?'

'Hm?' Marcus looked up from his charts. 'Oh, I'll take her some, if you insist, but I don't know if she'll eat it.' He got up, took a plate from the drainer and put a couple of slices of toast on it.

'Who's that getting breakfast in bed?' asked Ed, appearing from the bathroom, slightly damp and full of enthusiasm. 'Oh, young Carole. Sleeping with the boss has its advantages.'

He laughed so cheerfully that no one could take offence; in fact, Dora thought, no one appeared to notice, but he'd said what she, and probably Jo and Tom, were thinking. Jo was appearing to debate whether or not to make yet more toast.

'I'll eat another bit,' Dora said, 'and Tom will.'

Tom, who had his mouth full, nodded.

'OK, all hands on deck,' said Marcus, putting down his tea with a thump.

'OK, Skipper,' said Ed. 'High water's at seven?'

'Yes, we should get going. Can you start the engine, Ed? I just want a final look at the weather map before we lose our Internet connection.'

253

'Wonderful these modern fandangles,' said Ed, going up the steps. 'In my day we just used to check the seaweed hanging outside the wheelhouse.'

'He's joking,' said Tom to an open-mouthed Jo and Dora.

'We knew that,' they said in unison a moment later.

The engine juddered awake and a vibration that was both new and unnerving to Jo and Dora rumbled through *The Three Sisters*, turning her from a comfortable suburban home into a thing that moved, travelled, and possibly bucked about a bit.

'You go and help Tom,' said Jo to Dora. 'I'll do the washing-up.' She didn't want anyone to notice how nervous she felt. This was it. They were finally about to leave the safety of the mooring.

'No,' said Marcus firmly. He did have an uncanny ability to read her mind. 'You go up on deck. You're bound to get sick if you're down here all the time. Wait until you've got used to being on the move. The mugs will wait until the next round of tea is required, which in Ed's case will mean in about ten minutes. Don't bother to ask him if he wants one, just bring it every time you can bear to make it. Three sugars,' he added, then disconnected Jo's laptop and leapt up the steps.

'Lucky Carole,' said Jo.

'What, being allowed to stay in bed?' asked Dora, washing mugs too quickly for proper hygiene, but not caring.

'Mm,' said Jo, being non-committal.

'Here, hold this fender,' said Tom as Dora arrived beside him. They had now left the safety of the mooring and were out in more open water. They were waiting to be allowed into the lock. Docks were always at a higher level than the river, Tom had explained, so they had to lock down. Dora had decided life was too short to ask him how a lock worked and hoped she'd just learn as they went along.

'I don't know what to do with it!' Dora protested, taking the fender's rope as if it was a poisonous snake.

'Just hold it between the barge and the side if we look like hitting anything. And when we get into the lock you might need to hold it a bit higher.' Tom was very calm. 'Just watch me. It's easy. Trust me, even Carole could do it.'

'Don't be nasty about Carole,' said Jo as she appeared. 'I reckon she has a hard life.'

'Being shacked up with Marcus?' asked Dora.

'I don't imagine he's easy to live with,' said Jo.

Later, as they eased their way into the lock without having hit anything, or indeed gone nearer anything than was absolutely necessary, Tom said, 'Man, that Marcus can handle a ship!'

'I should jolly well hope so,' muttered Jo. Nerves were making her edgy and she still hadn't quite forgiven him.

'Did you see the way he turned the corner? A gust of wind came just at the wrong moment, but he had the wheel over before it could do any damage.'

'I thought there wasn't supposed to be any wind,' said Jo. 'I thought the whole point of waiting for ever to get this thing over was to get a period of settled weather, with no wind.'

'You always get the odd stray gust,' said Tom confidently. 'Right, now, Jo, cop on to this fender and move it if you need to.'

Tom bounded up to the wheelhouse, wanting to be in on the action.

'I wasn't supposed to be doing anything boaty,' Jo grumbled mildly. 'I was supposed to be keeping everyone fed and happy.'

'And keeping Ed supplied with tea.'

'Exactly. I wasn't supposed to be holding fenders and deciding whether or not to move them. Oh, look, Dora. I think maybe you should shift yours a bit more to the front.'

Dora laughed. 'I think the expression is forrard.'

At last, *The Three Sisters* had been lowered down to the level of the river. Marcus could be seen in the wheelhouse, turning the wheel first one way, then the other, and then they were in the Thames, the great artery of England and centuries-old trading route.

'It is quite romantic,' said Jo. 'If a bit scary.'

'Mm,' said Dora. 'I think I might get to quite like boating.'

'Well, that's a relief,' said Tom, who, having taken their fenders from them, was now making sure there were no stray bits of rope anywhere to be tripped over.

'No danger of a cup of tea, is there?' said Ed, appearing behind them. 'The boss wants one.'

Dora laughed. 'And would you like one too?'

'All right then, if you insist.'

As Dora made to go with Jo, Jo held up her hand. 'You stay here. I can make the tea on my own.'

Dora stayed. There was plenty to see: all sorts of barges, converted lifeboats and tugs. Over on the other side of the dock was a tall ship. It was new and all its masts and spars caught the morning light.

'That's a sail-training ship,' said Tom, appearing at just the right moment to answer Dora's unspoken question. 'It's aluminium. Light but strong.' He looked at her speculatively, in a way that suddenly made her feel nervous.

'No time to get me to go up the rigging, Tom,' she said, trying to sound unconcerned.

He laughed. 'You're all right, I know that.'

'I feel I should be doing more to help.'

'There's nothing much you can do at the moment. Just be

256

ready with the fenders and take them to wherever looks like hitting.'

'I think I can manage that.'

'Are you enjoying yourself?'

'Oh yes! More than I expected to, really. There's so much to see! Look at the garden on that boat. It's like something you'd see at Chelsea.'

Tom gave her a look that made her realise he probably didn't regularly watch the Chelsea Flower Show on television. She laughed. 'I'll give Jo a hand with the tea now. She won't manage it all in one trip.'

Carole was in the wheelhouse when they got up there with the tea. She was cuddling Marcus. 'Ooh, tea!' she said. 'Can I have a cup?'

'I'll make it,' said Dora, sensing Jo's reluctance to go back down below so soon.

'I'm sure Carole's quite capable of making her own tea,' said Marcus, disentangling Carole's arms from around his waist.

'Oh, Marky!' Carole's reproachful eyes gazed up at him.

'Don't bother. I'll do it,' said Dora. 'I might find a biscuit.'

'Oh, biscuits. Now you're talking,' said Tom.

'Biscuits have hydrogenated fat in them,' said Carole.

'Not these, I checked,' said Jo and then hated herself for sounding smug.

'It's a lovely day,' said Carole. 'I slept really well in that bunk.'

Jo waited for her to thank her for giving it up for them but then decided life was too short to wait that long.

'I'm going to get my shorts on and top up my tan,' Carole went on.

'But it's still a bit chilly, isn't it?' Why do I have to treat

257

everyone as if I was their mother? Jo chided herself. Why would she care if Carole got cold?

Carole sprang back down to her cabin a few moments before Dora arrived with the tea. Dora knocked on the door. 'Do you want me to bring it down there?'

'Oh. No thanks. I've just had some water. I'll be fine,' Carole called up.

'There's a spare cup of tea,' said Dora, showing, Jo thought, remarkable restraint.

'Ed will drink it,' said Marcus.

'I'll go and put sugar in it,' said Dora.

'I'll do it!' offered Jo, who didn't want to be left alone with Marcus. She still felt odd about him and didn't want to have to analyse why just yet.

'No, you stay up here.' Dora was firm and beginning to treat Jo much like Karen did.

Rather than make stilted conversation, Jo speculated on how Carole could be so completely self-centred when it came to everyone else, and yet be so devoted to Marcus and his comfort. Love, she supposed, had a lot to answer for.

About ten minutes later, Carole appeared in a canary-yellow bikini designed to reveal a maximum amount of flesh and to prove the myth that some women's legs went from waist to feet without any connecting hips. She was carrying a large beach bag.

'You don't need anything, Marky?' she asked him as she passed by. 'I'll just be out there if you do, but I'm sure Jo or Dora will get you anything you want.'

Having made this announcement, she climbed up on deck. Before everyone's fascinated gaze, especially Tom's, Dora noted, she laid out a huge beach towel and sat on it. Then she produced a sunhat, sunglasses and several bottles of suncream. She applied the cream in a thick layer, rendering the surface of her skin almost white, and then rested her head on a life belt. But only for a moment.

'This is a bit hard, can you throw me a cushion?' she called.

Jo and Dora both leapt to obey but Dora got there first.

'Why don't you do a little sunbathing?' Jo suggested to her, 'if you're going out there anyway?'

'I haven't got anything suitable to wear,' Dora said. 'I left my dental floss in the bathroom.'

Tom and Marcus shot her confused glances and Jo frowned. 'Well, just get a bit of sun while you can,' she said firmly. She didn't think it was fair to make disparaging remarks about Marcus's girlfriend in front of him. Especially when he didn't understand the reference.

'I wonder if Ed would like another cup of tea?' said Jo rhetorically and went off to make one, in spite of hearing Tom's protest that he'd been given one only moments before.

Jo decided that Ed would be her source of information. She would have used Tom, but he was in the wheelhouse, steering, and Marcus was with him, making sure he could do it, she presumed. Ed obligingly drained his mug and took the full one that Jo offered.

'So, what's going on, Ed? I don't want to distract Tom.'

'It looks like he's making a good job of steering. Marcus will be pleased.'

'Tell me where we are, and everything.' Jo felt she could reveal her ignorance to Ed without being embarrassed.

'You've watched the Boat Race on telly, have you?'

Jo nodded.

'Well, we'll pass the same landmarks, Harrods Depository, all the bridges. We'll be down in Westminster in a couple of hours, that's where we'll get fuel. It's grand seeing the Houses of Parliament from the water.'

'Goodness me! Now that does sound exciting,' said Jo, still teetering between the near-phobic stay-at-home she had been before and the slightly more confident seafarer Marcus had made her. On reflection, it did explain why Marcus had been so off with her. If he'd really thought that she'd chickened out when he'd gone out of his way to make her feel less terrified – well, it would have made anyone grumpy, especially a man used to getting his own way. And he was disturbingly attractive.

Ed was unaware of Jo's little revelation. 'You'll get used to being on the go,' he said. 'Although it must be a bit strange when your home just casts off and moves.'

'It is! It's unsettling for someone like me who hasn't done much travelling, or anything. I got married too young,' she added, speaking her thoughts.

'It's never too late to catch up. Young Tom was telling me how he plans to go travelling. Now, a handy person like him could get a lot of work as boat crew. I reckon that'd be a grand life for a youngster. I got married young too,' he added. 'Although I went to sea and everything, I always had a wife and family to support. I've got lots of grand-children now.'

'Oh, that's nice.'

'It is. I don't envy Marcus,' he lowered his voice somewhat, but not, Jo thought, quite enough. 'That Carole takes a lot of upkeep, I reckon.'

'Have they been together long?' Jo almost whispered.

'He doesn't usually bring her on trips, so I don't know.'

'Oh.'

'He doesn't really like women being on board at all. He says they panic and get in the way. Maybe because you and Dora had to be here, he thought Carole would be – company.'

'I see.' Jo didn't know quite how to take this. Why, when

he'd never felt the need of Carole on a trip before, did he decide to bring her this time? To warn her off perhaps? But he'd thought she wasn't coming. 'I wonder what time Marcus thinks we should have lunch?' she went on, saying the first safe thing she could think of.

Ed grinned. 'It's not ten o'clock yet. You weren't planning on doing a roast, were you?'

Jo laughed. 'No. Home-made pizza, brown rolls, cheese, salad. Tom said that's all anyone would want.'

'Home-made pizza sounds grand to me. But not for a few hours yet.'

They'd taken on fuel and had set off again when Dora told Jo that the pizza should be served cold.

'Heating it will make it go all floppy, and it's a lovely day. We don't need warming up, nor does the pizza. Carole will have salad on its own, I expect.'

'Oh?'

'We were chatting. She doesn't do dairy and has a wheat allergy.'

'I wish Marcus had told me she was coming!'

'She said that she gets annoyed when people take nut allergies really seriously, but think that wheat allergies are just faddiness.'

'That does seem unfair.' Jo was frantically trying to think how to keep Carole alive over the next few days. Fortunately she was so slender she probably wouldn't need a lot.

'I told her that having an allergy to nuts was really dangerous, just a sniff of one and you could die. I don't think the effect is quite so dramatic with wheat.'

'I don't know,' said Jo. 'I just hope she doesn't have a problem with citrus. Fruit is about all she's going to be able to eat.'

261

'I think it's people with arthritis who should avoid citrus,' said Dora. 'I don't suppose Carole qualifies.'

'I wouldn't mind, really I wouldn't. I want people to be happy, to have what they like to eat . . .' Jo lowered her voice, although they were in the galley and couldn't be heard on deck. 'But why isn't she down here telling us what she needs? Why do we have to second-guess all the time?'

'She's put stuff on her hair now, for highlights.'

'Can't remember when I last had my hair done,' said Jo. 'I might just buy a bottle of something.'

'You could go to a hairdresser,' said Dora. 'That's what Karen would say,' she added, knowing this would have the desired effect.

'Do you think so? Maybe you're right. I'm going to take this lot up. Do you want to bring those rolls and the salad?'

Tom was in the bow when the food arrived in the wheelhouse, but it didn't take him many seconds to join it. 'Wow, this looks great!'

'There isn't room for everyone in here,' said Marcus sternly. 'Why don't you take that lot outside, after Ed and I have had some pizza, of course.'

'You could take the tray out to Carole, to see what she'd like,' said Jo to Tom. 'I'll get the lagers. You would like one, wouldn't you?'

'Actually, have you got something soft?' asked Marcus.

'The skipper doesn't like us to drink while we're working,' said Ed, taking another slice of pizza with gratifying enthusiasm.

'There's no reason why you lot shouldn't have a beer,' Marcus went on. 'But it's not professional to drink and drive.'

'Don't worry, Jo, lass, we make up for it when we're safely tied up,' said Ed.

262

'I'll go and find something non-alcoholic – or would you prefer tea?'

'Tea for me,' said Ed, 'but I can wait until everyone's having a cup.'

'I'll go and gather up the mugs,' Jo said, trying not to sigh, worrying that the huge box of tea bags – a year's supply in normal circumstances – might run out. The gallons of milk might not hold out either.

Jo rinsed out approximately twenty mugs, wishing she had a teapot, to save on tea bags. She also wished that Carole would occasionally do a tea round. Dora and Tom had been assiduous about taking turns, but Carole just lay on the deck in her bikini, lightening her hair, complaining about the food, being high-maintenance eye candy. Trust Marcus to have a trophy girlfriend, he was just that sort of man, she thought crossly. And then felt even crosser with herself for minding.

She had just fitted the mugs on to a tray when Dora came dashing down.

'Oh my God! The River Police have just radioed – they're coming aboard!'

Tom came down behind her, a lot calmer.

'What does this mean?' demanded Jo, her little sins crowding her mind – *heat* magazine, the miniature of whisky, various other weaknesses that might contravene some unsuspected by-law.

'Well.' Tom spoke solemnly. 'I think it may mean more tea.'

Chapter Eighteen

A second after this serious pronouncement, Jo threw a tea towel at Tom and he put the kettle on again.

'What will really happen?' asked Dora.

'They'll check the papers and the boat for explosives and what not, and it'll all be fine. I gathered from what they were saying over the radio that they know Marcus. I suppose they would. Ooh, cake.'

Without commenting, Jo passed the open tin that was full of a rather crumbly but fruit-filled cake, which was going to do as pudding if she couldn't manage anything more exciting. 'Do you think the others will want it?'

Tom nodded, his mouth full. 'Deffo,' he said eventually, blowing crumbs.

Dora followed Jo up the stairs carrying the cake, the sugar and the teaspoons. The wheelhouse was more crowded than ever, full of laughing men carrying radios and trading insults with Marcus. After she'd had time to mentally disentangle them she realised there were only three.

'Tea?' said Jo, and Dora was horribly reminded of her own mother, when faced with a fellow committee member she didn't know well.

'Joanna,' said Marcus, making Dora wonder why on earth he called her that when no one else did, 'these chaps are from the River Police. They just need to check us over since we're going past Westminster.'

'I don't know why you're risking your life going anywhere with this old renegade, madam,' said one.

'Believe me, I'm not here by choice, but do please have some tea and cake.'

Dora turned away. If she caught Jo's eye, they would both start to giggle – Jo had sounded so like someone on television.

'Wow, look at that,' said one of the younger policemen, looking at the sunbathing Carole through the window.

'That's Marcus's girlfriend,' said Jo sternly.

'Oh, sorry, mate,' he said. 'No offence.'

Marcus was chatting to the more senior officer and didn't seem to notice what was going on.

'I'll go and see if Carole wants any tea,' said Dora, and left, hoping that Carole wouldn't suddenly find caffeine an acceptable substance, or worse, demand fennel, or camomile, or any other fluid that reminded Dora of cats.

'The police are here,' said Dora to Carole's sunglasses.

'Mm. I saw the launch pull up. Would you mind looking at my hair? Do you think the product's done enough now?'

'It depends how blonde you want it. Doesn't it go on working for a bit?'

'Mm. I like a good bright blonde though.'

'You don't want it to go brassy,' said Dora bluntly. 'And you have to think about the condition.'

'I do have a wonderful conditioner I use. It's horribly expensive but worth it, I think.'

Dora sat next to Carole and stretched her legs in front of her. Then she rolled up her jeans. 'My hair is always rather boring. My er – ex-boyfriend liked the natural look, so I never played around with colours.'

'Did you go out for long?'

'About four years too long. I might try some highlights.'

265

'In my experience men don't care what you do to make yourself look good as long as you look good.'

'So have you and Marcus been together a while?' Carole had asked the question first, so Dora felt it was all right for her to ask the same.

'About eighteen months.'

As Carole seemed perfectly relaxed about this question, Dora probed a little deeper. 'Marcus is awfully attractive, I can see that, but don't you find he's a little old for you?'

'Oh no. I like older men. I feel safe with them. I also find Marcus terrifically sexy.'

'Oh.'

'The trouble is, lots of other women do too. Which is why I have to keep myself in tip-top condition. And make sure I'm there to head off the competition. I don't usually come on these trips, you know.'

'No?'

'No. I was quite surprised when Marcus said I could.'

'So why do you suppose he did that?'

Carole yawned. 'Dunno, really. It's possible he wanted everyone to know he's spoken for. I reckon he gets hit on a lot by needy females.'

Dora took off her deck shoes and wriggled her toes in the sunshine, feeling insulted and eager not to show it. Between her and Jo, whom did Carole perceive the 'needy female' to be? Well, she could set her mind at rest about one of them.

'I have to admit that although I love my dad to pieces I wouldn't want to go out with anyone even near his age.' Dora closed her eyes, to simulate a lack of concern about Carole's reaction. It was just possible that if she declared her disinterest, Carole might get off when they got to Queenborough, where they were mooring for the night. Surely she couldn't suspect Jo of having her eye on

266

Marcus? Just because she was single, it didn't make her needy.

'Maybe when you're a little older yourself you'll come to appreciate the older man. He's more likely to take you to nice places than a younger one. Although your Tom's very cute.'

'He's not my Tom,' said Dora, wishing after all that she'd never got into this, 'we're just friends.'

'Oh? Well, it's nice to know where everyone stands.'

Carole was still apparently concentrating on topping up her tan, but a twinge of unexpected jealousy shaded the sun a little for Dora. Did Carole fancy a bit of young flesh on the side? And if so, why did she care?

The day progressed. Dora and Jo watched London slip past: the South Bank, Tate Modern, London Bridge, the infamous Millennium Dome. It was all rather exciting as they hadn't seen these parts of London from this vantage point before. Gradually the river widened as they got nearer to the Estuary, so that the landmarks, warehouses and executive flats became scarcer and scarcer until eventually Tom told them that Queenborough was coming up. Although it was only early afternoon, Dora could tell that Jo was flagging and said, 'Once we get there, you must stop looking after everyone and let them look after themselves. You slope off for a nap. We're bound to be starting early again tomorrow.'

'I'll certainly try. I feel as if I've been up for days, and as if weeks have past since we set off from the moorings.'

'Yes! Weird, isn't it? What have you planned to eat for supper? I'll help.'

'Moussaka which I've done already, with carrots, peas and rice. Carole can have carrots, peas and rice. Did you get to know her a little today?'

'Not really. She's been with Marcus for eighteen months,

267

apparently. One thing she said was odd, though. She more or less implied she was here to keep an eye on him.'

'In what way, keep an eye on him?'

'So he doesn't go off with other women, which is pretty much us. Or worse, he thinks we're needy and after him. She says it happens a lot.'

Jo's expression hardened. 'So we're needy, are we?' She knew she was right not to trust his olive branch that morning.

'I don't think she meant that we were in particular, just that single women in general are.'

'I think that makes it worse! It's bad enough when men stereotype women and say and think patronising things about them but when women – young women – do it too, it's just too bad.'

Dora nodded. Although she was indignant for a slightly different reason, she was happy to follow on in the tide of Jo's. 'I know! She just assumed me and Tom were a couple and said he was cute. When I said we were just friends, she said it was nice to know where everyone stood.'

'Well, he is cute, Dora, and you can't blame Carole for noticing.'

Dora shook her head. 'I don't know what's going on in her mind, to be honest.' Or was it her own mind that confused her? 'I do know what she does to her hair though,' she added on a more frivolous note. 'But she's not very easy to get to know.'

'You couldn't get through the factor fifty-five sun-cream, you mean? Oh my goodness, I can't believe I said that.'

Dora laughed. 'I think Karen would be proud to think that you've discovered your inner bitch.'

'Karen might be, but I'm not. She's just a child, I shouldn't be making unkind remarks about her.'

Noises from above indicated that they might be arriving very shortly. 'Let's go up and look at Queenborough,' said Jo.

There wasn't a lot to see. They were tied up to a concrete hulk moored in the river and there was no way of getting ashore. Carole was standing on deck, staring out. Dora and Jo joined her, as extra fender-holding didn't seem to be required.

'No shops,' said Carole.

'No,' agreed Jo, who'd wanted to stock up on water and various other Carole-friendly products.

'Retail therapy will have to wait until we get to Holland,' said Marcus, who chose that moment to emerge from behind the wheel.

'I personally don't regard grocery shopping as therapy,' said Jo, still rattled by him.

'Marky, darling, I wanted to buy some chocolate,' said Carole in a tone only a hairsbreadth away from a whine.

'Surely you don't eat chocolate, do you, Carole?' asked Jo in surprise.

'Chocolate has anti-oxidants, provided it has enough cocoa solids in it,' Carole explained kindly.

'Oh,' said Jo, who knew that, and went down below.

Dora was about to follow her when Carole said, 'What's got into her?'

'Being up since before dawn and having to cater for people with peculiar food fads, probably,' said Dora and went down to join Jo in the galley.

'That animated Barbie doll is getting right up my nose,' said Dora.

'Have a good blow and you'll feel better,' said Jo, laughing, and feeling better herself. 'It's bloody Marcus who's getting on my – nerves.'

'Jo, I really hope you weren't going to say "tits",' said Dora. 'What would the Flower Circle think?'

'They'd agree with me, to a woman. Now I'm going to have what my mother would have called "a nice lie down".'

When Jo got up, a couple of hours later, she found that Tom and Dora had organised supper. A panful of prepared carrots was waiting and there was even a salad. 'Go up on deck and have a drink. Marcus and Ed are up there.'

Jo didn't particularly want to sit with Marcus, especially as she knew Carole would be there too, but nor did she want to spend any more time in the galley than she had to. Her pre-trip cookathon had used up all her enthusiasm for the moment.

She had had a quick shower after her nap and put on make-up and a long white linen shirt, which probably made her seem the size of a house, but was comfortable and fresh-feeling – suited, she felt, to sitting on deck drinking white wine. So, having checked her make-up, she went to join the others.

Any concern she might have had about having to make polite conversation with Carole, whom she had very mixed feelings about, and Marcus, whom she was still annoyed with, and Ed, whom she loved for many reasons, were dispelled the moment she joined the group. Marcus was talking shop.

'We'll have two people on watch at all times. We should get there in daylight, but if for any reason we don't, the same applies. Four hours on, four off, alternating one hour steering periods.'

'I don't have to do that, do I?' asked Carole.

'We're all shipmates together, love,' said Ed cheerily.

Jo, who had been about to ask to be excused, as she was the official ship's cook, kept quiet.

270

'There's no point in people crowding the wheelhouse,' said Marcus. 'Tom seems a capable lad. I'll go on with Tom. You can choose between Dora, Joanna or Carole.'

'You've put me in a right spot, Skipper. I'll have young Dora. Jo's working hard enough already, producing meals fit for seagoing kings.'

'What about me?' asked Carole, obviously feeling left out.

'You can do what you're best at, darling, looking decorative,' Marcus said, with a hint of sarcasm Jo noticed.

She regarded Carole, wondering why she didn't slap Marcus, or at least give him a filthy look. But Carole just simpered. She was obviously as simple as she looked. 'Would you like me to get you another beer?' she asked.

'If you're offering and I think Ed would like another one too,' Marcus said.

Carole got up and stretched, revealing a stomach you could have ironed sheets on if it hadn't been for her belly-button piercing. She went to the top of the stairs and called down to Dora and Tom, 'Could we have another couple of beers up here, please?'

'I don't think that's quite what is meant by getting someone another drink,' said Jo, as mildly as she could, seeing as she was feeling anything but mild.

'I expect they want some fresh air anyway,' said Carole, 'I'm sure I would if I had to cook.'

'We'll be organising a cooking rota later,' said Jo, 'so you'll find out.' Jo had never been prone to bitchiness but she just couldn't help it. Carole just had that effect on her.

Tom appeared at the top of the steps, holding cans of beer and a bottle of wine. 'Would we like to eat up here, in the fresh air? Or downstairs at a table. It's quite hot down there.'

271

'What would you like, Joanna?' asked Marcus, causing her to start. She'd been deeply annoyed with him, finding him arrogant and high-handed, and now here he was, being considerate.

'It would be quite an effort to drag everything up here, wouldn't it?'

'Not if everyone helps themselves to what they want and then brings it up,' said Tom. 'I could bring up some sofa cushions.'

'That sounds lovely!' said Carole. 'I'll just have the vegetables, or salad, whatever it is that hasn't got a face.'

'The plan is we're going to help ourselves,' said Jo gently, hoping she didn't sound too patronising. 'If you're going to be here, with us all, you have to join in properly.'

Carole and Jo looked at Marcus, both hoping for support for their separate causes. They were both disappointed. He was up the bows with Ed, looking at navigation lights. Jo wished he'd take his girlfriend in hand for all their sakes.

Dora was woken by Ed going to the bathroom. It was the following morning and as Marcus had insisted on everyone having a reasonably early night, and not drinking too much, she felt sleepy, but not desperately so. She stood on her bunk and looked out of the window. Another perfect day, the dawn making even the mud flats look rose-tinted and romantic. She decided to take Jo a cup of tea in bed, hoping to find her still there, and not yet up and doing.

The previous evening had been spent playing Monopoly, which Jo had bought specially, 'in case everyone's rubbish at making their own entertainment'.

Marcus didn't play. He retired to his cabin with the charts and, presumably, a good book, but everyone else had. It had been fun. Well, Dora insisted to herself that it had been fun, but she was aware of being niggled. Was it because Tom was so helpful to Carole, assisting her to win, or was it because Carole was so coy and giggly with him?

Now, she pushed it out of her mind. If Tom liked giggly, clingy women, did she want to have anything to do with him? As she pulled on her jeans she reminded herself firmly that they were just friends, and so who he chose to flirt with was nothing to do with her.

Jo was grateful for the tea. 'I was up really early yesterday; today I feel as if my limbs are made of lead.'

'Well, there's no need for you to get up yet. I'll see the chaps get breakfast.'

'I suggest you just give them toast and cereal. They can have bacon butties for elevenses.' Jo sank back on to her pillows. 'I should have thought about buying soya milk. Lots of people have allergies to dairy products.'

'Yes, but they usually tell you about them beforehand. They don't just turn up demanding special food.'

'Poor Carole,' said Jo, sipping her tea with her eyes closed. 'We mustn't be horrible about her.'

'Why not?' said Dora and nipped back to the bathroom, having heard Ed leave it.

Everyone was a little quieter that day. The first excitement of being on the move had worn off and maybe people felt daunted by the prospect of crossing the North Sea. Marcus delivered a safety lecture, talking about life jackets, what to do if anyone fell overboard, how to launch the dinghy – which fortunately Tom seemed to know all about – and the importance of everything being tied down in the galley. Dora and Jo confessed their anxiety to each other while they were preparing lunch, having debated fixing the tomatoes with elastic bands before they cut them up. They didn't want to share their worries with anyone else.

'After all, if Carole's not bothered, we don't want to put ideas into her mind,' said Jo.

'Yes, ignorance is bliss,' said Dora, 'or it seems to be in her case.'

'I don't think she's actually that happy,' said Jo.

'Don't you? She's got Marcus, who she adores, doesn't have to lift a finger, looks like a supermodel, what more can a girl want?'

'A bit of fulfilment, possibly,' said Jo. 'Although before when I said that about her not being happy, I hadn't really thought it. I'm probably making things up. Take no notice. I just wouldn't fancy being hooked up with Marcus myself.'

'Really? I think he's very attractive, for an older man.'

'Oh, he's attractive all right; I just wouldn't fancy being his girlfriend.'

What Jo did fancy being she kept hidden even from herself, throwing herself into domestic activity as a distraction. How could a woman of her age, approaching the menopause with the speed of a flying bullet, have such inappropriate feelings for a man she wasn't sure she even liked? However attractive the cause, it must have some chemical reason. When she got back on dry land, she'd go and see a doctor and sort out some medication. She sighed. She hadn't always disliked Marcus. When he took her for a walk and talked her out of being frightened, she'd liked him very much.

'Well, that's the last we'll see of land for a while.' Dora had delivered Ed his hourly cup of tea. It was about two o'clock in the afternoon. 'Now we've got to miss the Goodwin Sands, all the ships in the shipping lanes, and then we're laughing.'

'Aren't the Goodwin Sands terribly dangerous?' Dora asked him. 'I think I've heard of them.'

'They're all right if you keep a good lookout and pay

attention. It's not foggy, or windy, and we've got a good crew. Nothing can possibly go wrong. Cheers!' Ed downed half a mug of hot tea in one.

About an hour later Jo decided to confront her mixed feelings about their skipper and join Ed and Marcus in the wheelhouse. Tom had been steering for the past hour and had gone to find Dora. Carole was lying on deck, wearing more than a bikini now they were on the sea and it wasn't quite so warm, and Jo was bored. She realised she hadn't felt sick or terrified and grudgingly put this down to Marcus's ability to calm her nerves. It would be a good idea to find out where they were, where they were going and to practise being normal while close to Marcus – something she found disconcertingly difficult.

'It's a bit crowded in here,' said Ed when Jo came up.

'I'll go, I just wanted to see where we were, on the chart,' said Jo apologetically, glad to have an excuse to leave, really.

'No, you're all right. You have a look at the chart and I'll get my head down for a bit, now we're through the shipping lanes. That big container ship on the port side is clear of us now.'

'Go and get some kip! It'll be your watch in a couple of hours,' Marcus said.

Jo remembered the state of the forepeak before Dora and Tom cleared it out and felt a surge of pride and gratitude towards them both.

'I'll just take some of these mugs down—'

Suddenly the barge lurched heavily to the right and Ed fell against the door that opened under his weight. The next thing Jo saw was Ed clutching at nothing, and then he was gone.

'Oh my God!' said Jo.

'Man overboard,' snapped Marcus, pulling the control

275

lever right back, and then he shot past Jo, lifted the lifebuoy from its cradle and threw it over the side. 'Now I want you to watch that lifebuoy and don't lose sight of it,' he barked. 'I'm going to turn the barge first one way and then the other so I come back to him and can get him aboard. But don't let it out of your sight.'

'I can see him! His cagoule is holding him up a bit.'

'Good. Now call Carole and get her to get Tom up here.'

Now the first shock was over, the lecture Marcus had delivered a lifetime before began to come back. Her eyes watered with the effort of staring at the lifebuoy and she called Carole without looking at her.

'Carole! Get Tom up here. Ed's fallen overboard.'

'What?' Carole unplugged her headphones.

'Ed's fallen overboard!' Jo was shouting and her mouth had gone dry. 'Get Tom!'

Fortunately he appeared from the forepeak, Dora behind him. He raced up to Jo. 'What's up? We heard the engine slow. Oh fuck!' he finished as he saw the lifebuoy and near it, Ed.

'It's Ed,' explained Jo to Dora. 'He's fallen in.'

Marcus was very calm. 'I'm turning the barge and getting it into position so I can pick him up. I want you two to get ready to launch the dinghy and tie it securely at each end so it's a platform we can get him on to. We'll get him on to the barge from there. Do you understand?'

'Yup. I did a man-overboard exercise when I was on a sailing course,' said Tom.

Marcus put the engine ahead and turned the wheel in big movements. Gradually the barge swung round. Jo's eyes never left the lifebuoy and Ed, just beyond it. As the barge moved, so Ed appeared to move also, although Jo realised she was in more or less the same place. 'Thank goodness there's no wind.'

Then Marcus swung the wheel in the opposite direction. Why is he doing that? she wondered, knowing better than to ask. He answered her unspoken question. 'If I'd carried on round, we'd have overshot; this way we'll come straight up to him.'

Now the lifebuoy and Ed appeared to be in front and, to keep them in view, Jo ran up to the bow and pointed to him. Oh God, please don't run him over, she muttered under her breath.

'Lower the boat, Tom, Dora. Make sure the ropes are really tight so the dinghy can't move around,' Marcus called out.

When Jo realised that Marcus could see both the lifebuoy and Ed she went back to help Tom and Dora.

'Carole!' called Marcus. 'I want you to get the heaving line from the forepeak entrance, throw it as near to Ed as you can and then make it fast once he's got it. Clear?'

Jo looked at Carole and realised she didn't understand. She went to get the line herself and took it to Tom. 'I can't throw!' she said to him, anxiety turning her voice into a whisper.

'Give it here,' said Tom, sounding remarkably calm. 'There we go, he's got it. Now tie it on to that cleat.' He pointed. 'Right now, take a round turn and then just wind it round in a figure of eight.'

Jo did as she was told and then watched as Tom and Dora tried to heave Ed aboard. Dora leant over the side to him and water came rushing in, nearly capsizing the dinghy.

'Keep your weight as far inside as you can,' gasped Tom.

Marcus came up with a thicker line. 'Tom, can you get this round Ed's arms and tie a bowline? Then we can heave on a single line.'

Miraculously, Tom seemed to know what a bowline was

277

and everyone watched as he flattened himself on the waterlogged dinghy to get the rope under Ed's arms. But eventually the line was round him and Marcus heaved. Tom and Dora caught whatever bits of Ed they could reach and at last he flopped into the boat.

'You should have seen the one that got away,' said Tom to him.

Ed, gasping and short of breath, said, 'Maybe we should splice the main brace, Skipper. For medicinal reasons.'

Chapter Nineteen

❦

Jo went into full mother-mode. 'A hot shower, not a strip wash. Tom, get him a change of clothes. I'll put the kettle on, or would you prefer some soup, Ed? I've got some leek and potato I could defrost?'

'There's no need for all this fuss,' said Ed, shaking his head from time to time, like a dog. 'I'll just change me gear and carry on.'

'You can have a tot of rum when you've done everything Jo said,' said Marcus firmly. 'Then you're for your bunk and a couple of hours' kip.'

Everyone except Marcus and Carole clustered round Ed when he emerged from the shower, warm and dry, to drink the soup. 'The catch on that door is weak,' he said. 'When the wash from that container ship hit us I just lost my balance for a moment. Then splash.'

'Thank goodness Marcus knew what to do,' said Dora. 'He was a hero!'

'Just doing his job, lass,' said Ed, to Jo's secret approval, 'but I do reckon I owe my life to him.'

'That is quite heroic,' muttered Jo, buttering another of her home-made brown rolls for Ed. Seabathing had obviously given him an appetite.

'I did a sailing course when I was in the sixth form,' said Tom. 'We had to practise man-overboard techniques. Bloody difficult! Were you terrified, Ed?'

'Well, I had several things on my side: it's summer, so

279

although the water's freezing cold, it's not as cold as in winter; it's daylight; and we're out of the shipping lanes.' He took a huge slurp of soup, draining the mug. 'I reckon I got a bit careless because we'd done the difficult bit.'

'I've made you a hot-water bottle,' said Jo. 'When you've finished your rum you're to go to bed and sleep. Captain's orders.'

'I'll go up and see if Marcus wants me to steer,' said Tom.

'Good idea, lad. He'll be glad of a break too, I reckon.'

Dora went with Tom. Seeing him help rescue Ed had made her see him in a slightly different light. She'd known he was thoroughly capable, handy about boats, but now she'd seen him being brave as well. She felt a glow of pride.

'Would you like me to relieve you?' Tom asked Marcus almost shyly.

Seeing how the two men related to each other, Dora realised that everything had changed, not just how she saw Tom, but how Tom regarded Marcus. He had been promoted from 'man who has the perfect job' to something approaching a god.

'That would be kind. I'll get my head down for a while. You see where we are on the chart? Dora will spot buoys with you, and there's the GPS as well.'

'I don't think Ed approves of the GPS,' said Tom. Although Marcus had stepped away from the wheel, he hadn't yet disappeared to his cabin. He chuckled.

'"Log, lead and lookout" is what he prefers,' said Marcus, 'and he's right. When all your fancy equipment goes wrong, you have to rely on your eyes.'

'Sorry, but I don't understand,' said Dora.

'You explain,' said Marcus to Tom. 'I'll just be down there, Tom. Don't hesitate to call me. I'll only be cat-napping.'

When they were alone there was silence. Dora wanted to

acknowledge Tom's part in the rescue, but she couldn't quite think of the words. She had just decided to keep it simple when Carole appeared.

'What a commotion! You were great, Tom!'

Dora felt a stab of something that felt like jealousy, and not because Carole had used the very form of words Dora had just decided on.

'Just doing my job, ma'am,' said Tom, sounding like an American cop film.

Carole laughed and pushed his shoulder playfully.

Dora winced. Why was it that Carole, who hardly knew Tom, could tell him how she felt and be so easy with him? And yet she'd been easy with him when they'd been playing backgammon in the forepeak, before they heard the engine note change.

Determined not to let Carole take over the conversation, she said, more forcefully than she'd meant to, 'What's this log and lead business?'

'Er, well, it's not an expression I'm familiar with—'

'If you're going to talk about ship-handling, I'm going,' said Carole. 'Would you like a cup of tea, Tom?'

Dora was fairly sure this was the first time she had heard Carole offer to make anything for anyone else except Marcus. 'I'd love one, too,' she said quickly, determined to make Carole actually do something.

'Oh God, I wasn't going to make everyone tea!'

'Go on, there's a good girl,' said Tom.

Carole bridled charmingly and went down below.

Dora bit her tongue to stop herself saying something bitchy and, at that moment, nothing unbitchy occurred to her. 'So, the log thing?' she managed eventually.

'Right. Well, presuming he's not talking about the ship's log, which is where they write down everything that's happening—'

'Like people falling in.'

'That's right, only it'll be things like "man overboard – altered course to starboard" and explaining how Marcus manoeuvred so we could pick Ed up.'

'So not a great read then?'

Tom acknowledged her gentle teasing and Dora was relieved to feel their old ease returning. 'You learn to read between the lines. Logs can be gripping.'

'OK, so what's the other sort of log then? When it's not part of a tree, that is.'

'Obviously it was originally part of a tree – they used to trail one behind the ship – oh, never mind. What it means in Ed's terms is a sort of wheel that counted how many leagues or nautical miles you'd travelled.'

'Not fathoms?'

'No, that's depth, and it's metres now. That's the "lead" part. That used to be a bit of lead on a long line that was marked out in fathoms. Sometimes they used to put tallow on it so it would pick up sand or shale or whatever so they could tell what the bottom was like. Then, if they wanted to anchor, they knew if it would hold or not.'

Dora found herself surprisingly interested. Tom really did know his stuff. 'So that's working out how deep the water is. How does that help?'

'The least depths are marked on the chart so you know that at any stage of the tide you've always got a bit more water than that. The lookout bit is self-explanatory.'

'So what it all means is that you have to have old-fashioned methods to check your new-fangled machinery. I didn't realise navigation was so low tech.'

Tom laughed. 'It involves a lot of calculations which fortunately I don't have to do. Oh, here's Carole with the tea.' He smiled warmly at her and she smiled back. 'That was quick.'

'Oh, Jo had already made it. I just brought it up. Here.' She handed Dora a mug, slopping a bit over her hand. Fortunately it wasn't desperately hot.

'Has Marcus gone for a nap?' she said, putting Tom's mug down carefully. 'I might slip in and join him.'

She gave a little giggle and Tom and Dora exchanged pained glances as she went below.

A moment later she reappeared. 'He doesn't want to be disturbed,' she said importantly. 'I'm going to get a drink of water.'

Dora thought she seemed tense and wondered if there'd been time for a row in those few minutes she was in the cabin with Marcus.

'I hate to be fussy,' said Tom, oblivious of any tension, 'but this tea is really cold. You wouldn't make me another cup?'

Carole smiled winningly. 'Anything for you, Tom, if I can work out how to do it.'

'On the gas,' snapped Dora. 'It's quite simple.'

Jo was still clearing up when Carole joined her in the galley. 'I've got to make more tea for Tom,' she said. 'At least he wants me,' she added in a mutter so soft Jo could ignore it.

'Oh, OK. Shall I do it for you?'

'I'm not stupid, you know. I can boil water.'

'It was just that I'm over here.' Jo sensed hurt behind this somewhat belligerent statement. 'Of course you're a very capable young woman, Carole.' Jo didn't know this for a fact, but she had run Marcus's life for him for a while. She must be capable or he wouldn't put up with her.

Carole filled the kettle and banged it on to the stove, slopping water over the burners so that when she tried to light the gas, it spluttered and refused to co-operate.

'What's the matter?' asked Jo gently.

'Everything! I wish I'd never come on this horrid trip. Everyone hates me. Marcus is being vile. I just wish I could go home!'

'Well, you can, quite soon. Don't get upset, Carole. No one hates you.'

'I think Marcus does.'

'I'm sure he doesn't.' Jo's words were automatic but she thought something must have caused Carole to feel like this, and she blamed it on Marcus. It wasn't fair to bring Carole on this trip, when he must have known what she'd be like, and then be unkind to her. Jo had noticed that he was rather dismissive of her and their relationship wasn't exactly loving, in public at least, but she did hope they could hold it together until the end of the trip. Being a ship's agony aunt wasn't part of Jo's job description.

'Do you think he's too old for me?' Carole's question seemed more of a plea.

Jo took a breath to give herself time to consider her answer. 'Well, it's a very personal thing, of course.'

'But do you?'

'Carole, love, it's nothing to do with me.'

'I know! I just want your opinion. Dora thinks he is.'

'Did she say that?' It was unlike Dora to be so outspoken. Karen, now, she'd have said exactly what she thought.

'Not exactly. She said that as much as she loved her dad she couldn't go out with someone remotely his age. How old is Dora's father?'

'I don't know! I should imagine he's a bit older than Marcus, though.' Jo swallowed, having done a few sums and come to the wrong answer. 'Do *you* think he's too old for you?'

'Maybe. I mean, he's very sexy, but sometimes he's quite bad-tempered.'

'Younger men can be bad-tempered too, you know, but I

admit they tend to be more tolerant.' Jo didn't want to think about Marcus's sexiness at that point.

'Tom's really nice.'

'Yes.' Jo really didn't know what to say now. In her mind, Tom was Dora's. But Dora always maintained they were just good friends.

'I think he fancies me.'

Jo bit her lip. 'I'm sure he does, but I really don't think you should flirt with Tom on this trip. It would be awful if he and Marcus fell out.'

'But it might make Marcus jealous, then he'd want me again.'

'Nothing is certain where men are concerned,' said Jo, with feeling. 'Look what happened to me!'

'What happened to you?'

'On the other hand, I don't suppose that's very unusual. My husband left me for a much younger woman.'

'Oh.' Carole certainly didn't seem surprised.

'Who's now pregnant.'

This caused her to be a bit more animated. 'Oh, that's nice.'

'I suppose it is.' Jo suppressed a pang of jealousy. 'For her. Carole, do you want children?'

'Oh yes. I'd love a baby.'

'Leave Marcus then – he's far too old to be a father.' She had spoken without thinking, but the thought of Marcus tolerating a demanding toddler with the patience demanding toddlers required was too unlikely to be considered.

'Quite old men become fathers these days,' said Carole, pouting a little.

'I know, but because it's biologically possible doesn't mean it's desirable. I think if Marcus wanted a family, he'd have had one by now.'

Carole considered. 'Hm. I think you may be right. Maybe

I'll finish with him.' She moved as if to go and do it that very moment.

Jo put out a hand and would have physically stopped her had it seemed necessary. 'But not till this trip is over, please! We don't want a lot of upset.'

'I won't be upset. I don't mind dumping people. I've done it lots of times.'

'But Marcus would be! Think, his glamorous girlfriend leaving him, in front of a whole lot of people! It would be awful!'

'But that would serve him right for being so horrible.'

'Was he really horrible? I don't see he can have had time.' Jo drew Carole to the table and pushed her gently into a chair. Tom would have to wait for his tea.

'Just now. He was a bastard!'

'Everyone else seems to think he was a hero.' Jo teetered between disliking Marcus, because that seemed the safe thing to do, and wanting to stick up for him and stop his girlfriend leaving him.

'Well, he wasn't heroic to me! I thought I'd snuggle up with him while he had a nap and he told me not to disturb him!'

'He's probably very tired. He's been on watch more or less all day, with only the odd hour off here and there. He needs some rest, Carole.' He's old, she could have added, but didn't.

'He could have rested with me there! He never seems to have any trouble at night, snoring away!'

'Older men do tend to snore more. Don't know why,' said Jo, reflectively.

'Well, it's disgusting. I'm sure Tom doesn't snore.'

'You'd have to ask Ed,' said Jo, whose mouth was fighting for permission to smile. 'Although not now!'

'Do you think I'm being silly?'

286

'A bit. I think you should just wait until you and Marcus are home. I'm sure you'll find the magic comes back into your relationship.' The thought that she actually could find work as an agony aunt flitted through Jo's mind as this platitude emerged.

'I don't think there ever was much magic. I think he just wants me because I'm so young and pretty.'

'Those are not bad things to be,' said Jo, wishing she herself was above wanting to be those things. 'And he wouldn't have done more than take you out to dinner if you were only that.'

'And I did fancy him rotten. Still do, really.'

Jo didn't reply. A 'me too' from her at this point would not be helpful.

'But maybe a younger man would be more fun.' Carole rested her chin on her hand, thinking hard.

'You could have some space on your own. Have fun being single, for a while.'

'I've never been single,' said Carole, sounding as if this was an achievement.

'I definitely think you should try it. I'd never been single, either, before my husband did what he did, and although that was absolutely awful, I've had a lot of fun since.' Saying the words out loud made her realise just how true they were.

'I think I'd feel weird, not having a boyfriend.'

'You should talk to Dora about this. She was engaged for years—'

'Engaged? She didn't say she'd been engaged.'

'Didn't she? Then maybe she didn't want anyone to know, but that's not the point. She had a boyfriend for years and now she's single. I think she's having much more fun.'

'So she and Tom really aren't an item?'

To Jo's immense relief the kettle chose this moment to boil over and Dora appeared. 'Where's this tea, then?'

'The kettle's only just boiled,' said Carole, who hadn't got up and wasn't now making the tea. 'So, Dora, you were engaged before, were you?'

Dora shot Jo a horrified glance.

'I'm sorry, Dora,' said Jo, 'it just slipped out. I was only telling Carole that she should try being single if she splits up with Marcus. You're having fun, aren't you?'

Before Dora could answer Carole went on. 'And then I asked her if you and Tom were an item.'

Jo could have thrown the scalding tea bag at Carole just then. 'Carole, dear, I really don't think you should keep going on about this. A boat trip is not the place to have showdowns. Ed could have died in the sea. Please, let's not have any scenes.'

'What do you mean?'

'I mean that you're not to split up with Marcus, you're not to try and ensnare Tom, and just try and fit in with everyone else.'

'Ensnare? What's that mean?' asked Carole.

'You know perfectly well what it means!' Jo's temper had finally reached breaking point. 'Now, let's just all behave like adults, stick with the men we came with and don't try and get anyone else's!'

'You know, Jo,' said Carole thoughtfully, having let this tirade pass her by, 'I came on this trip because I thought Marcus was interested in one of the women. I really don't think it's Dora.' She glanced at Dora to double-check she wasn't her rival. 'Could it possibly be you?'

Jo realised she could either lose her temper completely or burst out laughing. She laughed. 'Carole, if you think a man like Marcus would fancy a woman like me, you must need your bumps felt! Now, take your tea, everyone, I'm going to have a nap.' She grabbed a mug and hurried off before anyone could say anything else that would make her want to scream, either with hysteria, or with laughter.

Dora looked at Carole. 'Well, that's us told! Do you want some cake? If not, could you bring some up anyway? I know Tom will want some.'

'Oh, OK.'

Carole seemed a little surprised at Dora's friendly, down-to-earth attitude. Dora was quite surprised at it too, but she decided it was a good strategy. It would keep everything as normal as possible. Kind and rational Jo was obviously near the end of her tether and she was almost there herself. It was also quaintly British – have a nice cup of tea and everything will be all right.

'Don't forget your water,' said Dora. 'Or whatever it is you were having.'

When the buoys became more frequent, Tom called down to Marcus who was awake and in the wheelhouse in seconds. Carole and Dora made themselves scarce immediately.

'Let's go and see what might be for supper, shall we?' suggested Dora. 'Jo's done all the cooking so far. It's exciting to think we'll be eating it tied up against Holland, isn't it?'

'It would be nicer to eat out, really,' said Carole.

'There might not be anywhere, then we'd have to start cooking when everyone is starving and bad-tempered. My dad's always grumpy when he's hungry.' She had been about to say 'I expect Marcus is too' but she managed to stop herself in time.

The two girls went down into the galley. Dora opened the fridge to see if Jo had taken anything out to defrost. She hadn't. She opened the freezer and Carole looked over her shoulder at the array of frozen vegetables. 'I could make a salad. I make brilliant salads. I used to have a job doing it.'

'I don't know if there's much to make salad with,' said Dora peering in.

'You've got green beans and all sorts. Don't worry. I can make salad with anything.' Carole opened the fridge again. 'Look, there's celery, green peppers, a leek, lots of things in here. Don't worry, it'll be delicious. I'll forget about food combining and put croutons in it.'

'There are potatoes and carrots and things outside, in the lobby by the bottom of the steps.'

'Excellent. Marcus isn't big on salad so I don't often make them. This'll be fun!'

If anyone had suggested to Dora that preparing a meal with Carole could possibly be described as fun she would have been totally disbelieving. But it was. Carole started chopping and peeling and grating with huge enthusiasm. The wooden salad bowl was filling up with all sorts of colours, textures and, potentially, flavours.

'Now, the dressing,' said Carole. 'Has Jo got any decent olive oil?'

Dora handed Carole the bottle. 'I think that it's been pressed by the hands of virgins from trees planted on sacred ground, or whatever.'

Carole laughed. Dora was surprised. 'You're really into this, aren't you?' she said.

'Yes I am, and I suddenly feel a lot more cheerful. I've been quite depressed recently but I've started taking some new supplements and I think they've just kicked in.'

'Oh, right.'

'Or it could be that I've decided that Marcus and I are history. I'll have to find somewhere else to live, of course, but that'll be OK. I won't go until I've got that sorted.'

'You won't dump him until you get home though, will you? Imagine the upset!'

'That's what Jo said, but I think once you've made a decision you should act on it.'

Dora chewed her lip. Carole had suddenly become incredibly proactive and while it was brilliant in lots of ways, the thought of a sulking – or, worse, heartbroken – Marcus at mealtimes was dreadful. 'We don't want Marcus being all miserable though. We need him, for one thing, and for another, he takes up quite a big space as it is. If he was surrounded by a black cloud of despair there'd be no room for the rest of us.'

'What on earth are you talking about?'

'Heartbreak takes up a lot of space, trust me. When I finally broke up with John after about a hundred years, I had to leave the village. There just wasn't space for me and his broken heart in it.'

'Oh, wow,' said Carole, looking up from her chopping.

'And if you think how small a boat is, even a big one like this, well – nightmare.'

'I suppose . . .'

'And where would you sleep? There isn't anywhere else.'

'Couldn't I share with you?'

'No,' said Dora firmly. 'I don't have any problems with sharing a bed with women but mine isn't very big. So please don't say anything to Marcus until you're home!'

'Say anything to me about what?' Marcus's voice caused both women to jump and emit small screams.

'I'm going!' said Dora. 'Let me out of here!'

She pounded up the stairs to the wheelhouse where Jo and Tom were in charge. Tom was at the wheel and Jo was peering into the distance. She'd obviously had her 'nap' and Dora hoped she now felt calmer.

'What on earth's the matter, Dora?' said Tom, blithely. 'Has the beast escaped? And if it has, did you close the door behind you? We don't want it up here.'

291

'Oh God! This is worse than any beast! I think Carole is going to finish with Marcus although I begged her to wait until we got home. The trouble was Marcus appeared.'

'He wanted a cup of tea,' explained Tom. 'I did offer to make it.'

'Oh Lord, what will happen now?' said Jo. 'She is selfish sometimes.'

'Actually we've been having a nice time down there. She's made a brilliant salad, and the lasagne's in the oven.'

'Oh, fab! Did you find the garlic bread? It's next to the bags of frozen peas.' Jo hesitated. 'What did she find to make a salad out of? I haven't got any lettuce. We've used it.'

'She's really imaginative when it comes to salad.'

'That's good,' said Tom. 'I like salad.'

Jo and Dora looked at him. 'Real men don't like salad,' said Dora firmly.

'That's right,' said Jo.

'Rubbish. I like what I like.' Tom began whistling softly between his teeth, completely unabashed by the women's firm assertion that his liking for salad was somehow unmanly.

'Well,' said Jo after a moment, 'I hope we don't find the salad all over the floor, if Macho Man here is so fond of it.'

Dora chuckled. 'I do feel a bit sorry for Marcus, actually.'

'Mm, being dumped is no fun,' said Jo.

Only Tom continued to whistle, unaffected by recent dumping experiences from either the dumper's or the dumpee's perspective.

Marcus seemed fairly unaffected too when he appeared in the wheelhouse holding a mug. 'Sorry, did anyone else want tea? I very selfishly just made one for me.'

'I'm going to wait until we tie up and then have a big drink,' said Jo after a few seconds. 'I think I need one.'

'Me too,' said Dora.

'We're a good two hours away, Tom might need something before then,' said Jo, returning to her unofficial horizon-watching duties.

'I'm fine for now, thanks.' Tom smiled at Dora and something in his smile made her blush slightly.

To her surprise, it was Marcus who came to her rescue. 'If you're not doing anything else, Dora,' he said, 'I think Carole could do with a hand down there. She wanted to know if Jo had a micro-plane grater. She wants to put ginger in the salad.'

'I'll go and see,' said Dora and fled back down the stairs almost as fast as she'd come up them a few minutes earlier.

'Well! What happened?' she said to Carole when she landed in the saloon. 'Did you finish with him?'

'Yes! He was very calm about it. He said, "If you feel it's time to go I mustn't hold you back." He kissed my cheek. It was rather sweet.'

'You don't mind that he didn't beg you to stay?' Dora felt that Carole might be the sort of woman who'd appreciate a bit of begging.

Carole laughed. 'Oh, Marcus doesn't beg. No, I was just pleased he wasn't too hurt really, because as you and Jo both said, it could have been terribly awkward. I'll sleep on the sofa tonight.'

'Oh, good idea!'

'So let's get this dressing made and then we should set the table,' said Carole firmly. 'And do you think we could open the wine yet?'

'Definitely,' said Dora finding a bottle and a corkscrew simultaneously, 'although we won't be there for another couple of hours. I didn't think you did drink.'

'Oh yes, just not all the time.'

Then a door opened at the top of the stairs. 'Any tea going?' called down Ed. 'When a man's been half drowned, he needs a cuppa.'

Chapter Twenty

✦

Ed's accident had changed things, somehow, and the women decided to stay down below during the last couple of hours of the trip. They had their separate reasons. Jo was quite frankly nervous and didn't want to see the huge ships and the occasional barge that made their vessel seem so tiny in comparison. Down below she could close her eyes and sip wine from time to time and pretend they were just on a jaunt.

Dora stayed because she didn't want to hang around Tom. Ed's accident really had made her see him in a slightly different light; she'd known he was fun and capable and had always respected him, but seeing him be so efficient, so thoroughly good in a crisis, made her realise just how worthy of respect he was. The accident had brought them much closer in some ways, but for Dora, their friendship had tipped into something a bit more unsettling than their previous mateyness had been.

Dora and Carole, who was keeping clear of Marcus for obvious reasons, did take a turn up at the bow together, but there wasn't a lot to see so they came back to the comfort of the saloon.

Jo had made snacks to keep the men going until they could eat properly, and tea flowed to such an extent that Jo began to worry about her tea-bag supply again.

'Let's play cards,' suggested Carole, to Jo and Dora's complete surprise. 'Have you got any?'

'Mm! Yes I have,' said Jo, springing up. 'I bought them, just in case. What shall we play? Old Maid?'

Dora and Carole looked at her in disbelief. 'Poker,' they said together.

'I'll teach you,' added Dora kindly.

Rather to their surprise, Jo was not such a novice as they had expected and turned out to be very good at poker. By the time Tom called down to tell them they were missing all the fun, she had enough matchsticks to set her up in a nice little flat somewhere, if only they'd been exchangeable for cash.

They had heard the engine note change and their speed slacken right down and wondered what was going on. Jo used the excuse of putting all the matches back in the boxes not to rush up and see, but both younger women went up when Tom called.

The engine manoeuvres gave Jo mixed feelings of excitement and anxiety. It seemed amazing that in the early, early hours of that morning they'd still been in England, and now they were in Holland. They had another half a day to go before they reached Dordrecht, their final destination, but tonight they would tie up in a foreign country. Excitement sent her up the stairs just as they turned into the lock. She immediately went outside, not wanting to be in the way or, worse, called upon to do something she didn't understand. She stood next to Ed, where she felt safe.

'It's enormous!' she said to him, referring to the lock. 'I've only ever seen locks on canals at home, or on rivers. They seem so tiny in comparison.'

Ed chuckled. 'This is small compared to some of them we'll see later. And not much rise to it, either.'

She forced herself to stand there and watch and not scuttle back down below. The trouble was, she was tired and unsettled by lots of things, and in that mood she was extra liable to feel nervous. She glanced at Marcus in the wheelhouse. He was chatting on the VHF, and then to someone on the lock side. He was completely in control of the situation, a fact that didn't make him any less attractive.

Carole was with Tom, holding a fender, and he was making her laugh. Jo could see Dora holding one somewhere else. Did Dora mind that she couldn't join them and stop Carole snatching him from under her nose?

Jo shook her head to try and force some reality into her brain. She really must track down some good supplements when she got home, something that would control her wretched hormones that needed a Richter scale to measure the soaring highs and lows. She wouldn't go as far as having HRT, not unless she really needed it, but she'd heard good things about black cohosh, wild yams and evening primrose. She'd always been very bad about taking vitamins but if she was going to feel like a teenager in the presence of a perfectly ordinary man, she had to do something. She'd preferred it when she'd had good reason to dislike him but now she had to admit he was actually being quite nice again and it unsettled her once more.

Suddenly she said, 'Oh my goodness! There's a windmill! We really are in Holland.'

Ed chuckled again. 'It really looks like the books we all had as a child, doesn't it? It's a great country, Holland. I like it a lot. We'll be all tied up in about half an hour,' he added. 'Any chance of a cup of tea?'

Jo nodded. 'I'll make you one now, but don't tell the others. Then I'll make sure dinner's hot.'

Although it was a bit chilly, they decided to eat up on deck so they'd appreciate how far they'd travelled. Tom helped Dora and Carole bring up the table and chairs which fortunately, as Carole pointed out, had been

297

designed for outside in the first place, and so conveniently folded.

There was an air of celebration. For the first time Carole was remarkably cheerful, possibly because she'd dumped Marcus, or maybe because she'd made a contribution to the meal. Marcus was putting a brave and relaxed face on his broken heart, seeming more full of a sense of achievement than anything. Ed was full of beans, enlivened by his dip in the sea and their successful arrival. Dora and Tom were as friendly as ever, although Jo noticed that Dora didn't seem quite so relaxed around him. And Jo – well, she reflected that although they were not at their destination, the hard part was over. She had survived and even enjoyed the trip a little bit.

'That was a massive lock,' said Dora, 'but it all went so smoothly, didn't it?'

'They're very efficient on the Continent. Transporting cargo by water is much more part of their way of life,' said Marcus, 'and in a country like Holland, which is so full of waterways and rivers, it's the only sensible way to do it. Great salad, Carole,' he added with a smile that would have turned Jo's heart to mush had she been on the receiving end of it.

The women regarded him in disbelief. Carole had definitely said he didn't like salad and here he was, praising it with genuine appreciation.

Carole couldn't speak for a moment. 'Oh. Thanks.'

Was he trying to get into her good books again? thought Jo. Was this an attempt to win her back? Looking at him, it seemed unlikely. Maybe he just wanted to let everyone know he had no hard feelings about her and appreciated her efforts. If that was the case, he definitely earned a good mark in Jo's book.

'Yes,' agreed Ed, unaware of any subtexts. 'I love that

298

touch of wholegrain mustard in the dressing.' He filled Jo's glass with wine. 'Do you remember, Marcus, when we came over here the first time? We were coming the other way, we'd picked that barge up in Rotterdam. We found a completely empty quay, went for a meal at the yacht club and then turned in. You'd have laughed, Jo . . .' Just the way he said it told Jo she would not have laughed. 'At about two in the morning, wasn't it, Marcus?' Marcus nodded. 'We were woken by a hell of a row! All these fishing boats came in and started discharging. We thought we might be in one of them's way, but they didn't knock us up or anything, so we sat tight. Oh, happy days.' Another well-loaded forkful went into his mouth.

'Jo looks like a rabbit in the headlights of a boy-racer,' said Marcus with something that to Dora definitely sounded like tenderness.

'Oh, Marcus!' said Carole, 'can't you just say she looks nice?'

Everyone laughed. 'She does,' went on Marcus, 'a very glamorous rabbit, but a frightened one.'

'It's no good waiting for compliments from Marcus,' Carole confided. 'He just doesn't notice what you're wearing.'

Uncomfortable at being the centre of attention, Jo looked about anxiously. Was Carole addressing her remarks exclusively to her, or was it for general consumption?

'Oh yes, we're in for a grand time,' Ed went on. 'When you see the size of some of those craft . . . it can put you off your breakfast, thinking what might happen if there was a collision.'

Jo sipped her wine, trying to feel better. Everyone around her seemed relaxed and happy. In spite of Marcus's efforts to make the journey seem like a luxury cruise, she still felt incredibly edgy, although she was forced to acknowledge that it wasn't only the thought of travelling on a huge and much-used waterway that was causing it. It was Marcus. She'd somehow lost her ability to resent him, and without the firm conviction that he was arrogant and bossy, other feelings that she had for him, ones she had tried so hard to blame on other things, held sway.

'Still,' went on Ed, who was quite unaware of the turmoil going on in the woman on his right, 'Marcus has done it a few times, haven't you?'

'Oh yes. It was quite impressive the first time, but then you get used to it. You see great big push-tows, huge square barges with two thousand tonnes of coal each, maybe two or three of them being pushed by very powerful tugs, and tiny French peniches going right down to the South of France.'

'You make it sound positively romantic, Marcus,' said Carole.

'My trouble is, I feel romantic about the wrong things. Moonlight and roses do nothing for me, but give me a tall ship and a star to steer her by and I'm all through-other.'

There was another smile. Jo hoped that Carole didn't notice it. The poor girl would definitely be thinking she'd done the wrong thing by dumping him. 'I really hope that's not true,' she muttered.

Unluckily for her, her muttering fell into a silence and Marcus heard. 'Do you want me to be romantic, Joanna?'

'No, not at all! I just don't want you being through-other, whatever that means. I want you able to concentrate when our lives are in your hands!' She realised this sounded a bit melodramatic but it was how she felt at that moment, for all sorts of reasons.

'That's what I'm paid the big bucks for.' This time it was less of a smile and more just a roguish look, which made Jo turn away.

'It's a shame to take the money sometimes,' said Ed. 'The fun we have!'

'Falling in couldn't have been much fun,' said Jo.

'Well, no. I should have remembered the old adage, "One hand for the ship, and one for yourself." '

'I'd noticed that catch was a bit loose and not done anything about it,' said Marcus. 'I'm sorry, Ed. I feel responsible.'

'Oh, don't be daft. As I said, if I'd been paying proper attention, I wouldn't have had my hands full of mugs.'

'Tom, you did really well rescuing him. And you, Dora, of course. But Tom, you were a star.'

Tom blushed, beamed and almost visibly swelled.

'Yes,' said Jo and raised her glass. 'Here's to Tom!'

'Aye,' said Ed. 'Man of the match – or the trip, anyway.'

'You have to clink with everyone,' said Carole, looking into Tom's eyes, 'otherwise it's unlucky.'

When everyone had done this, Marcus said, 'If you ever need a reference or anything, I've got quite a few contacts abroad, if you're going travelling and want a bit of work.'

'That would be great!' said Tom. 'Thank you so much.'

Carole put her hand on Tom's in a congratulatory way. 'What a hero!'

'Um . . .' said Dora. 'Does anyone want any more, or shall I get the pudding?'

'Is there pudding?' said Jo, eager to stop Carole flirting with Tom so blatantly. 'What is it?'

'Just because you haven't cooked it doesn't mean it doesn't exist,' said Dora. 'Carole and I have concocted something.'

Wishing she could go down below, just to get away from Marcus, whose foot she seemed to bump every time she moved hers, Jo accepted she had to let Dora and Carole get on with it. They had seemed to be getting on much better,

301

although how Dora would feel about her now was anyone's guess. Whatever, she mustn't push in and be motherly and spoil it all.

Tom and Ed started talking about technical things that Jo was too agitated to concentrate on. Marcus sat in silence but whenever Jo looked even vaguely in his direction, he seemed to be looking right at her.

What seemed like a lifetime later, Dora and Carole came up with the pudding. It looked very impressive.

'We found some frozen puff pastry in the freezer, all ready rolled out, so really easy,' said Dora.

'And then we put fruits of the forest on it,' went on Carole proudly. 'And here's some ice cream.'

'It looks great,' said Tom. 'Well done, girls.'

'Are you going to let him get away with that old-fashioned, sexist and patronising remark?' said Jo, smiling to take the sting out of her words. She didn't really think Tom was sexist or patronising, but her mouth and her brain weren't really communicating properly at the moment.

'Tom can say what he likes,' said Carole. 'We love him.'

Jo saw Dora flinch and her heart blipped in sympathy. Jo's growing suspicion that Dora did rather like Tom strengthened.

'Now, Ed,' went on Carole, 'do you want some of this?'

'Never been known to say no, that's me,' said Ed, blissfully unaware of any strange atmospheres flitting about the table.

'Help yourself to ice cream,' said Dora, handing him a tub and a scoop.'Marcus, what about you?'

'Just a small portion, please. I ate rather a lot of whatever that first course was.'

Carole opened her mouth and then shut it again. Possibly she'd been about to chide him for having pudding, and then remembered his diet was no longer her responsibility.

'And salad. The salad was fab, Carole,' said Jo.

'It only takes a little imagination. Anyone can do it.' Carole smiled and Jo, whose own salads were fairly fab, tried hard not to feel patronised.

From the head of the table, Marcus said, 'At the risk of sounding like Captain Bligh, can I suggest we all turn in early tonight? I want to get off as soon as we can, soon after six, if possible.'

'Right you are, Skipper,' said Ed. 'I did tell you I've got to get off home as soon as we tie up? I'll be back to take her home again, but I'm expecting another grandchild any day.'

'Grandchildren, how lovely,' muttered Jo, wondering if she'd had too much to drink and pouring herself a glass of water.

'There's no point in people hanging around in dry dock,' said Marcus. 'I'll call you all about the return trip.'

'Well, count me in for that,' said Tom. He went on, 'I wonder if anyone's got a phone that works here? I promised I'd give my parents a ring to say we got here safely. My mother's going off on a walking holiday soon and she didn't want to go to Peru not knowing about me.'

'My phone works here,' said Marcus, pulling it out of his pocket. 'Does anyone else need to use it?'

'I suppose I should tell my parents too,' said Dora. 'I also ought to ring the boatyard, to see how they're getting on without me.'

'They were expecting that barge, weren't they?' said Tom. 'There was a lot of work to be done on the interior. It's going to be converted to a gym.'

'Well, as I said, we'll be here for about ten days with nothing much to do. Public transport's really easy. You could pop back quickly if I needed you in a hurry.'

'I must say I would like to go back to work if I could,'

said Dora. 'I'd only just started the job when I went on holiday. They were very nice about it but I do feel guilty.'

'I'm certainly going back,' said Carole. 'We can travel together, with Tom.'

'And me,' said Ed.

'What about me?' said Jo, realising that none of them except Ed and Marcus had really thought about what they would do once they arrived.

'It's rather difficult for you to go home, Jo,' said Marcus, 'because you're here already.'

Her befuddled state meant it took her a second or two to work this out. She smiled weakly.

'Here's the phone, Tom,' said Marcus. 'You asked first.'

Although Tom took the phone a little way away to use it, they couldn't help hearing the hellos, the fines and, 'Brilliant, thanks.' Then there was quite a long silence before he almost shouted, 'Sweet! That's fantastic! I'll get on to him right away.'

'This is such good news,' he said when he came back to the table. 'My mum told me a mate of mine's got tickets to a music festival, right here in Holland! We're definitely going, Dora.'

'But, Tom, I should go back to work!'

'Not at all,' he said, 'you told them you were going to be away for at least ten days. The festival's only for this weekend.'

'Oh, can I come too?' asked Carole.

Tom shook his head. 'Sorry, mate. Only two tickets and we've got to share a tent.'

'Oh, camping,' said Carole. 'Maybe not.'

For a second, Carole and Dora were in perfect agreement.

'Do we have to?' said Dora.

'Yup. You promised.'

As Dora didn't want to tell everyone about the whole dare thing and was secretly very pleased at the way Tom had stopped Carole butting into their adventure, she decided to just go with it. 'OK, I suppose I did.'

'We can take the train,' he said.

'The station's just up the road,' said Ed. 'When we get to Dordrecht.'

'What will you do, Carole?' asked Marcus, sounding concerned. 'Travel back with Ed?'

'Of course, if he doesn't mind. I can stay on *Hildegarde*, can't I?'

'For as long as you need to. I won't be there for at least a fortnight, possibly longer.'

'Thanks, Marcus, that's cool.'

A vague but persistent feeling of panic was rising in Jo and however hard she tried to squash it, it persisted. Everyone was making plans to leave, except for Marcus. Where was she going to go? She could probably stay with Tilly on *Appalachia* for a few days, but Jo knew she had a lot of guests coming soon. There were Miranda's two rooms above the shop she'd been offered, but they weren't currently fit to live in. She chided herself for not thinking ahead, so worried had she been by the journey out. 'I think I'll make coffee,' she said, in the hope that a solitary moment would give her a better idea of where she could stay until *The Three Sisters* came home.

'I'll help!' said Dora, getting to her feet, ignoring Carole pouring more wine into Tom's glass and then her own.

'Can I have a word?' asked Dora when they were in the galley.

'Yes of course. What is it? Are you worried about this music festival? You don't have to go if you don't want to, you know. Don't feel pressured.'

'It's not me, it's you!'

'What do you mean, me?'

'Are you happy to be left alone with Marcus? Everyone is going back to England when we reach Dordrecht and you're going to be left with him. Is that OK?'

Jo sighed. 'I think so. Besides, I can't think of where else to go.' She ran through her list of potential spare beds with Dora and they agreed that none of them were really an option.

'And you can't stay at your house, what with the Floosie pregnant and all.'

Jo shuddered visibly. 'Absolutely not.'

Then the door opened and Marcus appeared. 'What are you two plotting?'

They both jumped guiltily. 'We're not plotting,' said Jo, indignant but guilty.

'I do hope you're not planning to jump ship, Joanna. I still need a cook. Besides, it'll give you an opportunity to explore a bit. A bit of a holiday before the trip back.'

Dora heard Jo exhale although she knew her landlady was trying to control it. 'Yes,' Jo said weakly.

Dora made a decision. It was obvious that Marcus unsettled Jo, but in spite of everything Jo had said about him up until now, it was possible that she rather liked him. They'd known each other in the past and Jo hadn't said, 'Don't leave me alone with him at any cost,' or anything like that. And it would do her good to spend some time with a man who wasn't her husband and who did seem to value her company. Jo could do with another friend right now. 'You did say earlier it was a shame there wouldn't be time to see more of Holland.'

'Did I?'

'Stay with me, Jo.' Marcus did have a very persuasive manner, Dora noted. 'I promise I'll be on my best behaviour.'

Jo smiled vaguely. 'OK then. Besides, I haven't got anywhere else to go.'

'I won't let the fact that you're not running off at the first opportunity go to my head then.'

Dora laughed. 'They have lovely flea markets in Holland. I've read about them.'

'And Amsterdam is a wonderful city. We can hire a car and go there.'

Jo, outnumbered, admitted defeat and as she now appeared relatively happy to stay, Dora wondered if she was transferring her own doubts and anxieties about the festival on to Jo.

She also wondered if she was the only one who had a sense that life was going to change for everyone after the trip to their final destination, the old Dutch town, Dordrecht, that had been there longer than Amsterdam.

Ed was going back to a new grandchild, Carole would be on the lookout for a new boyfriend and, possibly, provider. Jo was staying with a man who had been secretly known to them as 'Scary Marcus'. How would she cope? Would she mother him into submission? Somehow Dora didn't think so. Unlike many men, Marcus didn't appear to want to be mothered. On the other hand, that might just be the bold front he put on for the world. Dora felt protective of Jo, who had been so good to her in her hour of need, but she was a grown-up, she could make her own decisions.

Dora had another opportunity to check up on Jo the following morning, after breakfast, when she found her leaning on the gunwale, watching the world pass. She'd done her packing and was all ready to leap ashore when Tom gave the word, trying to push aside her own anxieties about the festival.

'I can't believe how much like my expectations this is . . .'

307

Jo gestured to the passing scene. 'It's so satisfying to see there really are windmills, and sheep grazing the walls of the dykes, and people on bicycles.'

'Mm.' Dora didn't want to talk about the scenery, she wanted to know about the characters on the stage. 'Are you sure you're going to be all right with Marcus? I don't have to go to this wretched festival, whatever Tom says.'

Jo laughed. 'Are you looking for an excuse to back out? I don't blame you. I wouldn't fancy it at all myself.'

Dora chuckled. 'Well, I am quite anxious about it – camping with Tom's weird friends as much as anything, but I do want to go. I definitely feel stronger since coming on this trip. I hate to use the word "empowered" but I am a bit.'

'That's really good! And what about you and Tom? You don't have to tell me anything if you don't want to.'

Dora laughed. 'You're just like my mother, you say you don't want to pry, but you're desperate for the details really.'

'That's what Karen used to say. And I must say she told me the maximum she thought I could cope with, which, in her opinion, wasn't very much. You don't have to tell me any more.'

'OK, well I do really like Tom. But I don't feel I should consider another relationship so soon and anyway, I'm not sure how he feels about me. What do you think?'

Jo threw up her hands in surrender. 'Honey, I'm not Solomon! I don't know. I think you should just take it day by day and see how it works out.' She looked very anxious so Dora let her off one hook only to put her on another one.

'OK. So what about you and Marcus? Tom says the work might easily take longer than ten days. Will you be all right for that long before we come back for the trip home?'

Jo looked towards the wheelhouse, as if Marcus might hear her from over eighty feet and a noisy engine away. 'He does have a strange effect on me, but as I'm going to have the menopause at any minute, I'm not going to take any notice.'

'What do you mean?' Dora had lowered her voice too, to match Jo's.

'Just because I feel all sort of faint when I'm near him doesn't mean I fancy him, it just means I need some special seedy bread or something. A friend used to rub extract of wild yams into her breasts.'

'Oh my goodness.'

'I don't know if I could cope with that, but I can cope with Marcus. If I did fancy him it would be awkward, but it's just fluctuating hormones. Maybe I should buy a fan in case I start having hot flushes.'

Dora digested this. Aware she knew very little about the menopause and its effects she hadn't previously picked up that it might make you feel all faint round one particular man. However, she didn't feel in a position to say this to Jo, who obviously had all the facts at her fingertips.

They arrived at the old port of Dordrecht at teatime. While Marcus negotiated his way smoothly through the canals to the boatyard, all three women stood together and watched the houses pass. 'It's wonderful to have canals actually in the town like this, isn't it?' said Jo.

'They have them in towns in England,' said Dora.

'But not in the middle of them, like this. I think it's great. We can practically see into the windows.'

'It's weird that they don't have net curtains, or only in some houses,' said Carole. 'You've only got the plants to stop you seeing everything.'

'Spoilsports, aren't they?' said Dora mischievously. 'Oh!

309

They're lifting the bridge for us! But who's operating it? I can't see anyone.'

'Perhaps it's all automatic,' said Carole. 'You know, I've never been on a trip with Marcus before, and I quite like this boating malarkey. I might join a yacht club or something,' she went on. 'Learn to sail.'

'There are some very fit blokes who go sailing,' said Dora. 'We went with some friends years ago and the blokes were fab! Really fit in the way you mean, Jo, but also really fit in the way me and Carole mean, and very tanned.'

'Mm,' said Jo, 'you won't catch me doing that, fit blokes or not. And it looks like we've arrived. I'm going down below to make tea for Ed. Oh! Hear that carillon – the church bells playing a tune? I think I know that hymn.' She went below, humming to herself.

They'd all been too tired to do much more than pack, tidy up a little, plan their various onward journeys and fall into bed early.

Chapter Twenty-One

❧❧❧

'Paying-off day, it's always a scramble,' said Ed, the following morning, handing Carole's bag up to her. 'Everyone wants to get home as soon as possible, the minute they've got their wages.' He patted his top pocket. 'In euros, too.'

'You were lucky with the flights,' said Dora, partly wishing she was flying home with Ed and Carole instead of getting on a train to a music festival. Although she was happy that she was going with Tom. They had both been paid too, although they had protested vehemently that they hadn't expected anything.

'Aye. And Marcus was excellent booking it all on the Internet,' went on Ed, pulling himself up the rungs set in the dockside and joining Carole on the top. 'Is the taxi here yet?'

As it wasn't, Dora stayed chatting up to him. 'What time will you be home?'

'Not sure, but with luck I'll be there before the baby. That's the important thing. Did Marcus sort you out with a train?'

'Yes, all on the Internet too. There's one that goes direct to the town.'

'And you're sure you don't want to share our taxi to the station?'

'I've still got things to do. We'll just walk up.'

Then the taxi arrived and everyone was suddenly

waving, and saying goodbye, and 'See you in a fortnight!' and then Ed and Carole were gone.

There was hardly time to notice their absence before Jo was asking Dora for the hundredth time if she was OK camping. 'It's not the sort of thing you want to do without notice. We only went once and I spent a fortune in the camping shop buying bits of equipment.'

'We'll have to be all right, but Tom says there'll be lots of shopping opportunities.'

'Mm,' said Jo, 'but they'll be for wind chimes and didgeridoos, not useful things like baby wipes. Here you are.' Jo handed Dora a packet. 'I bought them in case the bathroom was suffering from overload,' she explained.

'I think my rucksack is suffering from overload,' said Dora, stuffing the baby wipes into an already stuffed pocket. 'It's too small for more than one night away.'

Jo, who'd helped her pare her requirements down to spare clothes, a toothbrush, a pot of moisturiser and a novel, tried to sound upbeat. 'Well, you won't get a chance to wear your pyjamas, will you? You'll be dancing all night.'

'Listening to bands,' said Tom, who was fretting to go, 'waving your arms in the air.'

'We should be back in a couple of days,' said Dora, uncertain if she was reassuring Jo or herself.

'You'll have a lovely time,' said Jo, sounding like a parent sending a child to a party it didn't want to go to.

Dora managed a smile. 'I'm sure. Just promise not to tell my mother where I'm going.'

'Well,' said Dora, sitting by the window on the train. 'We've got this far.'

'Public transport is brilliant in Holland, isn't it?'

'Mm. And so clean.' She paused. 'Do you think their festivals will be clean and well organised, too?'

312

Tom smiled teasingly at her. 'You're not looking forward to this, are you?'

'Well . . .'

'When you pretended to be disappointed before, you were really relieved, weren't you?'

A guilty smile started at the corner of her mouth. 'A bit.'

'Don't worry. You'll have a great time, and then you'll only have two more dares to do.'

'Oh, those wretched dares,' she said, laughing. 'What're they going to be?'

'Still haven't decided.' He looked around airily.

'Well, don't make them too hard.' She thought back to the karaoke night with a certain amount of horror. 'You've been a real meany so far.'

'"Meany",' he repeated fondly. 'I love the way you talk. Anyone else would have said "bastard".'

Dora smiled. 'I've been very properly brought up.' She couldn't help noticing her heart give a little skip at this slight show of tenderness.

Somewhere between Ed's falling in and the rest of the trip, Dora was aware her feelings had changed. Whether she'd always fancied Tom and had just been denying it because it was all too soon after John, or whether seeing him be heroic and Carole fancying him so obviously, or what, she now knew she wanted him to be more than a mate. She just didn't know how he felt about her and whether or not he still saw her as a kid sister.

'I've noticed,' he said. 'Now, why don't you get some kip while you can? You won't get much when we get there.'

'But I want to look out of the window and see Holland.'

'Well, do that, but if you can nod off, I would. You won't be getting much sleep over the next two days. Don't worry,' he added, 'I'll make sure we don't miss our stop.'

*

313

'I can't believe I actually did doze off,' said Dora as they waited in the door area to get off the train.

'Things have been a bit hectic,' said Tom, 'what with Ed falling in and everything.'

'We didn't talk about it much, did we? Considering how dreadful it was.'

Tom shook his head. 'No. Ed thought he'd been careless and Marcus thought it was his fault for not knowing that the catch was loose.'

'I don't see how either of them could blame themselves, it was just an accident.'

'No such thing in their book. Still, we don't need to think about it any more, we're here!'

Any doubts they'd had about finding the festival were banished the moment they got out of the station. There were signs and flags everywhere and there was a bus laid on.

'This is all going so well! I can't believe how easy it's been to get here and everything,' Dora said as they jolted along in the bus.

'Mm, it has gone well so far,' said Tom.

'What?' His tone alerted her; there was something he wasn't telling her. 'What's the matter?'

'Well, you know I said my friend had got tickets for the festival?'

'Yes?'

'Well, we haven't. We have to go over the fence.'

Dora wondered if she'd ever be able to speak to Tom again, she was so cross. This was jacking up the terror-factor in a bet that was already enormous. It was too much! She forced herself to take a few calming breaths.

'Tom, I can't. I just can't gatecrash a festival. You can call me a wimp or a piker or any other term you can think of, but I just cannot go in without paying. It's stealing.' She could just see herself banged up in a foreign jail. What would her mother say? She'd never forgive her.

Tom fended off her outrage. 'Whoa, Dora! That's a bit of an overreaction, isn't it?'

'Maybe, but I don't care. I have my limits. I don't mind being brave – or at least, I do, but I admit it's a good thing. Being dishonest isn't. Sorry.'

Tom sighed and looked around at the other occupants of the bus, anywhere but at her.

Dora watched him, convinced she'd put him off her for ever, certain he wouldn't even be her friend now. She felt utterly miserable and bit her lip. She stared out of the window too, so he wouldn't notice if she started crying. It was mostly because she was tired, she told herself.

The bus reached its destination and they filed off, following fellow festival-goers who all seemed to be in the spirit of it already. When they finally were off, they were still not speaking, and by now, Dora didn't know if they just happened not to be talking, or if Tom was seriously sulking. He said, 'Wait here. I'll do some texting.'

Not wanting to ask, or even know, why he wanted to get away from her to do that, she stood by the entrance, watching happy ticket-holders go streaming in.

All humanity – well, almost all – seemed to be passing before Dora. There were dreadlocked hippies wearing tie-dyed drapery; nice girls with blonde plaits, short shorts and tight pink T-shirts. There were groups of Goths, wearing black studded leather, big boots and, in the case of one woman, a surprisingly delicate black net tutu over ripped fishnet tights who reminded Dora of Bib. I wonder if she'll be here, she thought. Lads in jeans carrying ghetto-blasters and cases of lager mingled with a group of jugglers, who juggled as they walked. There were couples with buggies and babies strapped to their bodies who

315

looked as if they led middle-class suburban lives most of the time, and grey-bearded, long-haired, black-garbed men who had probably never had much to do with mainstream society. In vain Dora looked for someone who, like her, felt out of place and anxious.

The sun began to get hotter and she became thirsty. She drained the water in the bottle she had with her and realised that soon she'd have to buy some more. There wasn't a stall selling it outside, but she could see one through the gates.

Had Tom abandoned her? Surely he wouldn't do something like that. But she couldn't help wondering if he found her refusal to gatecrash the festival so irritating that he'd want to.

Time passed. Had she just been waiting, she'd have found plenty to entertain her in the passing crowds, but the tiny shard of fear that she was alone in a foreign country and might have to make her own way back to the bus, the station and eventually the barge on her own niggled like a splinter.

'Hi there.' A tall, blond, tanned man wearing jeans and a T-shirt came up. He looked clean and personable and unthreatening. 'On your own?'

He had a faint accent; what kind, Dora couldn't tell. It could have been from any European country. But he had a nice smile and she gave him a small smile back.

'Only for the moment. I'm waiting for my friend.'

The man grinned. 'Girl or boy?'

'Boy, if it's anything to do with you.' She smiled a bit more this time, so as not to sound rude. She wanted him to think a big strong boyfriend was going to emerge from the crowd at any minute. She wanted to think that herself.

'Well, he shouldn't have left you alone, pretty girl like you.'

316

'He had stuff to organise.'

'Stuff to organise, huh? Want to organise it for yourself?'

Dora would have dearly liked to have organised stuff for herself, but as she didn't know what Tom was up to, she couldn't. She decided she wouldn't wait for Tom indefinitely. In a minute she'd work out how long she'd been waiting and decide how much longer to give him, then she'd make her way back to the barge. 'It depends what you're talking about,' she said.

'Well, is there anything you need?'

By now, Dora's need for a drink had increased considerably. 'Have you got any water?' He had a large canvas bag with him, so it was possible.

'Water?' He looked at her curiously. 'No, I haven't got water. But I have got coke.'

Dora had just worked out what he was saying when Tom appeared from nowhere, took her arm and swept her into the crowd that was going through the entrance.

'I think he was trying to sell me drugs!' she said.

'Too bloody right he was. Sorry I was so long.'

'What were you doing?'

'Getting these.' He produced a pair of tickets just as they reached the man who was checking them.

'Where did you get them from?' Dora whispered as Tom held his wrist out to have a band put round it.

'A tout. Don't worry, there's nothing wrong with them.'

Dora held her hand out and had a plastic bracelet snapped on.

'They must have cost a fortune!' she went on as they walked. 'How did you pay for them?'

'Spent my wages, not that it's anything to do with you.'

The time Dora had spent on her own, worrying, and then being picked up by a drug-dealer, had made her anxious and therefore shrill. 'Of course it's to do with me! If it

317

wasn't for me, you wouldn't have to pay! Here . . .' She fumbled in her wallet, which was in the front pocket of her jeans. 'Have my wages. At least I can pay for my own ticket.'

'Nope. It's my fault you're here. Now put your money away before you get hit on by more people trying to sell you stuff or someone nicks it.'

'No! Tom! That doesn't make sense. If I hadn't been here, you'd have gone over the fence and got in for nothing.'

'If you weren't here neither would I be. Now come on. I want to find the others.'

As Tom wouldn't let her pay, all Dora could do was trot along beside him hoping to goodness 'the others' weren't too terrifying.

But as they walked her anxiety subsided. Most of the people weren't off their heads on drugs, although there was one man staggering along, his eyes rolled back who Tom explained had probably taken ketamine.

There were stalls selling everything, including, in spite of Jo's predictions, useful things, like blankets and soap. There was a stall selling knickers with slogans on them that was doing excellent business and another painting on temporary tattoos and bindis. There were lots of places selling food – no culinary taste was left uncatered for. There was even a stall selling champagne and Pimm's which was a bit of a surprise to Dora, unlike the myriad tents selling what Tom described as Health Burgers.

When Tom finally said, 'There they are! By the Hexagon, like they said,' Dora's growing enjoyment diminished a little. She had quite enough to do getting comfortable with her surroundings without meeting a lot of new people who might well be more scary than her drug-pusher had been.

'Hi! Tom!' A girl about her own age flung her arms round Tom and hugged him. 'It's so great to see you again!

It's been ages. This must be Dora! Hi! I'm Lizzie! I was so pleased when Tom said he had a girl with him.'

Some of Dora's anxiety faded. Not only did Lizzie seem perfectly normal, she and Tom were obviously platonic friends only.

'Hi, I'm Matt,' said a tall boy with short hair and a very wide smile.

'And I'm Dave,' said another, smaller this time, and blond. 'We were at college with Tom. So, Tom!' They hugged. 'How's it going, mate?'

The greetings went on and another girl appeared bearing a carrier bag. 'Look what I've got!' she said when she'd said hello. 'Juggling balls.' To everyone's amazement, she took them out of the bag and instantly began juggling with them.

'I didn't know you could do that!' said Dave.

'I'll teach you. But come and get settled into the tent first. It's massive – or it was when we put it up. It might be a bit of a squash with us all in it.'

Dora didn't know if she was disappointed that she and Tom weren't going to be sharing a two-man tent, or relieved. She tried to decide all the way to the camping area.

'Go to the loo now,' said Lizzie as they passed the toilets. 'It's still quite early and they'll be really disgusting later.'

Dora took her advice.

It seemed to Jo that one minute they were arriving, tying *The Three Sisters* up outside the dry dock the barge was due to enter, and the next it was only she and Marcus, left alone in a space that suddenly seemed far too big for two. And this in spite of the fact that until quite recently, she had lived on *The Three Sisters* all on her own.

'I can't believe they all disappeared so early. It was as if

319

the ship had the plague or something,' she said to Marcus when he found her clearing up in the galley.

'They all had places they wanted to get to in a hurry.'

'I know and I perfectly understand. I just think it would have been nice to go out for a celebratory meal or something.'

'We can still do that.'

Jo mentally kicked herself. She'd more or less invited herself out to dinner with Marcus. How embarrassing! 'It won't be quite the same.'

'It'll be better,' said Marcus.

'What?'

He ignored this. 'The first thing we should do is get you established in the back cabin.' Before she could faint with shock at the thought that he was inviting her into his bed, he went on smoothly, 'I'll move into your cabin.' He was apparently unaware that Jo's perimenopausal symptoms had shot off the scale and back again.

'Um, it's hardly worth it, is it? It's only for about ten days to a fortnight, isn't it?'

'Nothing to do with boats and dry docking is ever set in stone. It could be a month, it could be a week. If you find me some clean bedlinen I'll put it on for you.'

The thought of Marcus wrestling with a duvet cover, stretching across the bunk so he could tuck in the sheet and putting pillow cases on was beyond the limits of her imagination. 'It's all in there, in the cupboard.'

He smiled a little apologetically. 'I'm very domesticated when I have to be, but I think I'll need you to come and find it for me.'

'Of course. I'll strip my bed first.'

'Don't do that, I don't mind your sheets. Just come and find new ones for your bed.'

'It would really be a lot easier if we both just stayed

where we were,' she said. Now she'd got over the shock of being invited into the captain's quarters and the realisation that he wouldn't be in them at the same time, she sounded perfectly rational.

'I insist. I need to be there while we're on passage, but there's no need for it now, until we go back.'

These words pierced a bubble of denial that Jo had kept intact until now. She'd spent so much energy thinking about the journey to the boatyard, Holland and across the sea etc., she hadn't made herself think about the journey back. It was probably just as well. If she'd thought of herself being alone with Marcus, with nothing much to do for over a week, she'd have been chewing her nails with anxiety.

'Ed and Tom are coming back, aren't they? And Dora?' she said feebly.

He laughed softly. 'Don't worry, Joanna, I'm not planning to train you to be my first mate while we're here so we can bring her back alone.'

'Thank God!' she murmured, feeling sick. She knew perfectly well that a first mate did what Ed did, but the terminology was unfortunate just then.

'Ed will certainly be back; Tom, too, possibly; and Michael said he might come down as well. We'll see who's available.'

'Michael should come. All this trouble is for his barge, after all.'

'Was it a lot of trouble?'

Jo blustered. 'Sorry! Did I sound ungrateful? It's just when Michael lent me the barge he never said it would have to go anywhere.'

'Not what you signed on for, you mean?'

'No. And it took a lot of organisation and you had to work really hard.'

'But this is my work. It's what I do, with Ed when necessary.'

She was about to comment that it was funny sort of work when she remembered that gilding cherubs wasn't a run-of-the-mill way to earn a crust either. 'I suppose so,' she said instead, and went down into what had been, until very recently, her bedroom.

It was full of his being: his smell, his things were scattered about, but mostly it was just him. Determinedly, Jo looked in the cupboard for clean sheets and a duvet cover. As she had sneakily taken her own, goose down pillow, when she'd first moved out, she would just swap it back. It would save on washing.

Marcus was not particularly tidy, she realised. Philip, her husband, had been on the verge of being obsessively organised. As Jo was anything but, it had been a point of conflict between them. Until his defection, she had always seen this difference as good – they balanced each other and stopped either becoming extreme. Since then she had wished the Floosie joy of his neat-nik ways.

There was a pile of change on the tiny folding table, and a heap of clothes in the corner. She was just wondering what, if anything, she should do about them, when he came down the steps and appeared behind her, bending his head so he didn't collide with the roof. The space had never been large, now it seemed slightly more cramped than a Wendy house.

'I don't want you to do anything except find the sheets,' he commanded, 'It's a mess.'

'It's OK.' Instantly Jo had to argue. 'It's only some dirty clothes.'

'Yes, but you shouldn't have to deal with them. Go and relax while I change the sheets,' said Marcus, tugging at the duvet.

She and Marcus spent the rest of the morning reading and resting. At least, that was what Jo did. She revelled in the lazy pleasure of just lying around, doing very little. Marcus heated up leftovers for lunch which they ate drinking lager and reading their books. Afterwards, Jo went for a little walk thinking how restful Marcus could be, and how much of a surprise this was to her.

When she got back he said, 'Right, time to get ready.'

'Get ready for what?'

'I'm going to take you out to dinner.'

Frantically she tried to find a reason not to go. 'It's still early!'

He grinned at her. 'We may have to walk a long way to find somewhere nice.'

With the bathroom door locked, Jo looked at herself in the mirror and wished she'd had a chance to see if Carole had left anything useful behind. Some evening primrose would have been something. She didn't expect a girl of Carole's age would have anything really hard core, like red clover, but Jo felt so agitated she would have clutched at any straw – even extract of wheat-grass.

'You're going to a restaurant to have a meal, at the same time, presumably at the same table,' she told herself. 'It is not remotely a date. You'll go halves.' Then a smile appeared. 'Going Dutch is the expression; how appropriate that it should happen while we're actually in Holland!' And then she began the anxiety-inducing experience of getting ready to go out with a man she really, really fancied without a single wild yam for support. The certain knowledge that he couldn't possibly fancy her, given his taste for young things, did not help.

The hard part was not looking as if she'd tried too hard, she decided, wiping off the eyeliner that had got out of hand. Definitely no blusher. That was bound to clash with her first hot flush that would come tonight, sure as eggs were eggs. She had caught the sun a bit, which brought out her freckles – that wasn't necessarily a bad thing, but it had also made her nose a bit red. Could she convert the red into the sun-kissed look she would have preferred?

By the time she had put on and washed off a lot of make-up she looked sort of OK, certainly healthy, and with enough eye make-up to bring attention to what were once her best feature. If they still were, when a fine mesh of laughter lines fanned out from the corners, she couldn't possibly say, but it was the best she could do. Jo couldn't help remembering that the last time Marcus had gone out to dinner with a woman, it had probably been with Carole. Looking over the table at a woman of fifty would be very different from gazing at twenty-something skin and bright, wide-open eyes. It wasn't that she was trying to compete – she couldn't possibly do that – she just didn't want the contrast to put Marcus off his dinner.

'You look wonderful,' he said, when she appeared in the wheelhouse.

Jo clamped down her instinct to say something dismissive and forced a smile. 'Thank you, you're looking pretty cool yourself!'

Now she looked at him she realised that a plain white linen shirt tucked into a pair of navy chinos were indeed rather attractive. They set off his tan and his curly grey hair. She noted this with a disinterest that pleased her. Any woman would have found him attractive just then, not just one suffering from hormone-induced illusions.

Jo had been leaping on and off *The Three Sisters* for months with no problems. Somehow Marcus standing on the dockside holding out his hand to help her made it incredibly difficult. She stumbled, he caught her and didn't let her go. He took her arm and they set off along the quay as one, Jo wishing she didn't keep bumping into him.

'Where are we going?' she asked, when she felt sure she could speak without revealing her swimming senses.

'Into town. There's a nice little restaurant I know there. It's a bit of a step but we can take a taxi back.'

'I wish I'd worn my pedometer,' she said and then felt foolish.

'Your what?'

'You know, it's a thing you wear on your belt, or in my case my knickers . . .' Oh, why had she mentioned her knickers? They were nothing to do with him! 'You're supposed to take ten thousand steps a day, but it's really hard because the pedometer doesn't register every step,' she wittered on. 'It doesn't like going up hills and if you're just moving around the house it doesn't notice at all. Very frustrating.'

'I can imagine.'

Jo decided not to try to make conversation and managed to keep silent up until they reached a street that was full of wonderfully tipsy old houses and antique shops. 'Oh, heaven!' she said. 'Look at the way those houses are leaning out into the street! It's a wonder they don't fall down! And those windows! Do you suppose they have shutters on the inside, or you'd never have kept warm in winter. And look at these shops! Can I cross over?'

She'd had forgotten she was with Scary-Marcus or she would never have suggested zigzagging down the street, running from one shop window to another.

'Is Dora right about them having flea markets in Holland, do you know?' she asked.

'She certainly is.' Marcus sounded amused, as if he was humouring a young child, but Jo found it endearing.

'It's just I've started repairing small decorative items for Miranda's shop—'

'I know.'

'. . . and if I could find some items for myself while I'm over here it wouldn't be such a waste of time.'

'Waste of time?' His eyes crinkled at the corners as he looked down at her.

She smiled up at him, a little rueful. 'Did that sound rude? It wasn't meant to, but you know what I mean.'

'You mean hanging round in Holland with me would be too boring for words.'

She bit her lip to suppress her smile. 'Oh no, I could put it into words, but it wouldn't be polite. After all, you are practically St Marcus of the Barge, fount of all knowledge and skill in that department.'

He chuckled with pleasure and Jo realised that probably not all that many people teased him. The men were all too in awe of his boat-handling skills and the women probably too keen to catch his attention. How wonderful that she was above all that!

But her complacency was short-lived. 'I do assure you that I have other skills.'

His face was perfectly serious; there was no sign that he was teasing her but she knew that he was and couldn't, at that moment, respond. She gazed intently at a perfectly ordinary electric kettle that had found itself in an eclectic collection of old radios and wished for sanity.

A few weeks ago she'd have gone into town and out to dinner with a man she didn't know very well without difficulty. Of course she'd have been a bit shy at first, but she'd have chatted away until she found what his obsessions were and then been a good listener. After all, she was pretty grown up now, her social skills were honed from years of experience of getting people to feel happy and at ease. So it shouldn't be any different with him.

'Where's this restaurant then?' she asked, planning to

ask him all about himself the moment they got there. Then she would only have to nod and murmur for the rest of the evening. It would be a piece of cake.

The restaurant was in the old part of the town in one of the narrow, leaning, half-timbered buildings that Jo had so much admired. Outside was a bench with a mannequin dressed as an old lady seated on it. Its name translated as 'Granny's Kitchen', Marcus told her. They went in.

One of the many joys of Holland was that everyone spoke English, thought Jo, ashamed of her inability to say even the simplest sentence in Dutch. They were ushered into the dining area by a beautiful young woman wearing tight jeans and a tiny apron. A little part of Jo sighed with envy.

They were given menus and looked at them. 'It's rather like Sudoku, isn't it?' said Jo. 'Trying to work out what everything is. Of course that lovely girl will tell us, but it's quite fun trying to see if anything makes sense.'

'I think the puddings are easier than the main courses,' said Marcus after a bit. 'It helps that I happen to know that Dame Blanche is what they call ice cream and hot chocolate sauce here.'

Jo read the description. 'Oh yes, you can work it out, especially if you know what it is already.' She looked up at him, smiling. 'What's *slag*, do you suppose?'

'Whipped cream.'

Jo sighed. 'I know it's awfully bad for you but I love cream with ice cream, the way it hardens as it hits the cold. One of those puddings that people say are better than sex.' Whoops! She'd dropped her guard for a moment and said something silly again. She tried to retreat. 'Mind you, I do hate that expression, don't you? I mean, you might really prefer a chocolate bar or something at four o'clock in the afternoon, but a few hours later – well, I wouldn't want

327

chocolate.' Colour flooded over her like the sea flooding the Netherlands, in an unstoppable wave. If she didn't know perfectly well what had caused it she would have thought it really was a hot flush this time.

'I'm very glad to hear it.'

A sort of croak emerged from Jo and she reached for her water.

'Sorry, I shouldn't have said that. I've embarrassed you,' he said.

She drained the glass.

'It would have helped if you hadn't brought up the subject of sex in the first place, so you do have to take your share of responsibility.'

She swallowed and pulled herself together. 'I didn't, really. I was talking about pudding.'

'Once the word has been tossed into the arena, so to speak, it's quite hard to take it out again.'

She sighed. 'So I've just discovered.'

He raised an eyebrow and then looked down at his menu again without saying anything.

An internal warmth flickered somewhere within Jo's solar plexus. Her radar with regard to men was rusty – she was very dumb when it came to realising when she was being courted but even she felt that there might be something behind his flirtation.

He looked up and stared into her eyes for long seconds before he said, 'What would you like to eat?'

A laugh rippled inside her, revealing itself only slightly. She studied the menu once again.

The proprietress appeared. 'Hi, guys,' the girl said in charmingly accented English. 'Have you decided? Shall I talk you through the menu? Or can I tell you about our special tonight? Fresh Dutch asparagus with ham and eggs. Very traditional.'

'It sounds wonderful,' said Jo, very relieved to have the decision taken out of her hands.

'I'll have the same,' said Marcus, 'and could we have a wine list?'

Alcohol, that was what she needed – Dutch courage, obviously. Her private pun amused her and she relaxed enough to look around her. The room was arranged as a facsimile of an old Dutch kitchen. There was a shelf with cookery books, an old wireless, a coffee grinder and a grater on it. On another wall pictures were painted directly on to it, and everywhere were simple, household objects that were decorative and amusing. Above the stairs to the upper room was a rack of very authentic-looking underwear.

Unexpectedly, Jo didn't feel obliged to make conversation. She just sat, wondering if she'd misread the messages he seemed to be sending. Could he really be trying to get off with her? She hoped the wine would come quickly when it had been ordered.

Marcus produced his reading glasses to examine the list when it arrived. Jo, who had hardly dared even glance at him in the last few minutes, couldn't help observing that she always found men in glasses very attractive. Karen did too, and they had discussed this phenomenon. Her daughter, now that was a good occupation for her brain – Karen could keep her out of trouble even without being there.

The owner came back and Marcus murmured to her. 'I've ordered a nice bottle of Rioja,' he said. 'I think we need something sustaining.'

While most of Jo agreed she definitely needed sustaining, part of her panicked – why did he need sustenance? Just let go, Jo, she ordered herself, just put his foolish words out of your head, you're likely to be misinterpreting them anyway. He was probably just trying to put her at her ease.

Marcus went through the process of trying the wine. Not too pretentiously, Jo was glad to note, considering how snooty he was about her wine. Remembering this old grudge gave her a little backbone and she dared to glance up at him when he raised his glass.

'What shall we drink to?' he asked.

'Oh, to absent friends and to arriving safely – and getting back safely too.' That was an easy one. The wine was soft and delicious. Maybe there was something in all that wine nonsense after all, she thought.

'And to you, for being you.' Marcus didn't take his eyes off her while he drank. Jo wished she dared take off her cardigan but she had never liked her upper arms.

She fitted her glass in among the cutlery and plates on the table with care.

'Joanna,' Marcus sounded serious. 'I think I may have frightened you earlier.'

'Mm. Well, a bit, I suppose,' she mumbled.

'You have no idea of how I feel about you, have you?'

'No! I mean, if you don't just see me as an old friend you've crossed the sea with.'

He took a deep breath. 'I really don't see you as that. Apart from the crossing-the-sea part.'

'So . . .?' She was very tentative.

He swallowed, rearranged his cutlery, scratched his nose and said, 'Actually, I think I fell for you when I first met you, in that pub, all those years ago. You were already with Philip.'

'Oh.' Her mind flew back. Would she have given up Philip for Marcus had he made a move? She couldn't say for sure, but she feared she wouldn't have had the confidence.

330

'Yes. I was too scrupulous to do anything about it. I might have done, eventually, but you got engaged, and so that was it. I went away.'

'Yes,' she said eventually.

'The thing is . . .' He hesitated and then suddenly said, 'Are you still with Philip? Emotionally, I mean. Do you still care about him?'

He was being very direct and she had to respect him for it, but she still found it unnerving. 'No . . . Well, I wish him no harm, I want him to be happy – which is nice of me, considering – but I no longer love him in that way.'

A deep sigh went through him. 'Oh! I can't tell you how relieved I am to hear that.'

'What about you and Carole?' she asked gently.

He smiled. 'I think she'll move happily on to the next man who'll give her a good home. I think I lost interest in Carole the moment I saw you again.'

'Really?'

'Oh yes. Seeing you again reminded me what an attractive woman you are. I realise I had kept you in the back of my mind for years, but sometimes when you meet people again, everything has changed and you can't imagine what you once saw in them. With you, all my feelings came back in a rush.'

'Oh?' It came out as a squeak. Did he really mean it? After all, he was a bit of a womaniser and he might just be looking for a change before returning to a younger woman. She could just be a challenge for him. And then she told herself not to be so cynical.

'Yes,' he went on, smiling warmly at her. 'You're as sexy and as lovely as you ever were, only now you're wise and kind and loving too.'

'Am I?' She sipped her wine, hoping it would help her stop squeaking. He was very seductive.

331

He nodded. 'Oh yes.'

She started to smile, and although she tried to stop it, she just found she wanted to keep smiling at him, very much.

'Golly, I'm hot!'

'Take off your cardigan.' He eased her cardigan down over one shoulder, and the other side fell off in sympathy.

'I hate my arms,' she murmured as she hung it on the back of her chair.

'I love your arms!' said Marcus, surprised, as if hating them was a strange thing. He ran his fingers down the top of one as if he couldn't help himself and then put his hands firmly in his lap. 'So didn't you guess how I felt – feel about you?'

She shook her head. 'How could I?'

'You didn't wonder why I took such trouble to talk you out of your fears, why I was so insistent that you came on the trip, all that?'

'I just thought you were being kind – at least when you stopped me being so frightened.' She frowned. 'Why did you bring Carole, then?'

'Because when she asked me if she could come, I thought you'd bottled out. I was furious – with you – with myself for being such a fool, everything. And I guess I didn't really trust my feelings, if I'm honest,' he added rather ruefully.

'I hope Carole didn't regret coming.' So inviting Carole was slightly out of pique. Well, she couldn't really blame him.

'I shouldn't think so. She'll realise the trip was the catalyst that made her get rid of me, and she'll be glad about that.'

'Would you have got rid of her, if she hadn't dumped you first?'

He hesitated before he answered. 'I can see why you're asking the question and yes, I would have got rid of her, if

I had to. I would have done it in a way that she thought it was her idea.' He suddenly grinned sheepishly. 'It's a technique I've developed over the years.'

She chuckled slightly. 'I'm sure you've developed lots of techniques over the years.'

He nodded, still rueful. 'Tell me about your daughter.'

'Is that one of them? Changing the subject to something safer?'

'Definitely.'

'OK, I'll indulge you.' She let herself get well into one of her favourite subjects for a while and then said, 'Your turn.'

He chuckled softly. 'I haven't got a daughter, or any children, come to that – or not that I know of. I never said I was a saint,' he added, noticing Jo's raised eyebrow. 'You obviously love Karen very much.'

'Oh yes. More than anything or anyone in the world. Even when I still loved Philip, I would have said the same.'

'And you definitely don't love Philip any more?'

Jo nodded, aware she knew it now with more certainty than she had at any time since he'd left her. 'Loving someone is quite hard to stop doing but when he went off a part of me died. My love for him sort of withered away, without its blood supply.' She looked up at him ruefully. 'I'm talking gibberish. Too much wine probably.'

'You haven't had enough wine for that.'

He topped up her glass and she suddenly thought that perhaps he was trying to make her drunk so he could have his evil way with her. Then she realised it would be her evil way too. She took a cautious sip.

'I will never let anything bad happen to you, Joanna. I give you my word,' he said.

Touching as this statement really was, Jo did not receive it with unalloyed joy. She had just begun to look forward to being seduced by this very, very attractive man and he'd gone all noble on her. How typical. He's probably seduced hundreds of women, why should he decide to give it up now? Still, with luck, he wouldn't consider getting her into bed as bad, exactly.

The food arrived just in time to prevent her having to say anything meaningful in return. 'My goodness, there's enough here to feed an army!' said Jo.

'Nearly enough to feed a barge full of hungry boaters,' agreed Marcus.

Jo laughed. She did like being with him. He might say totally unnerving things from time to time, but he didn't dwell on them, or insist on a response. For the first time in a very long while she was enjoying the company of a man who she felt really did want to be with her – at least for this evening.

When at last their plates had been taken away, Marcus inspected the pudding menu. 'Do you want a pudding?'

Jo sighed. 'Sort of. I'm so full I can't move, though.'

'We'll share one, then. Shall we have *slag*?'

'Definitely.' Jo laughed.

'And then we'll have brandy. How often is it that one doesn't have to do anything much in the morning?'

'So they won't want to put her into dry dock at the crack of dawn?'

'I don't think they're planning to put her in dock until about ten, so that's not too bad. This dock is very good about letting families live aboard while there's work going on, but it's better to be out while they're actually working.'

'Does that mean we have to wander the streets until dark?'

'Not at all. We'll hire a car and tour Holland, go to Amsterdam, Delft, all the touristy things, and then some non-tourist ones.'

'Perhaps we might find a flea market?'

'Of course. You can load up with suitable bits of china, restore them and sell them with a huge mark-up.'

'And make my fortune! What more can a girl want?'

'I can think of a couple of things one might want a girl to want.'

She twinkled at him. 'I think ice cream and chocolate sauce might be enough for now.' She was enjoying flirting openly with him.

The sauce came in a separate jug, as did the cream. Even without all the connotations it now had for Jo it would have seemed like a little piece of heaven. Marcus picked up a spoon and loaded it with a combination of ice cream, sauce and cream before carrying it to Jo's mouth. 'Open wide.'

Giggling, she did as she was told. 'That was to die for,' she said.

'But not better than sex?'

'It depends on the sex.' She spoke flippantly, but she did remember that there were times – quite often – when she had occupied her mind with shopping lists and what to do in the garden while Philip had made love to her.

Marcus ate a spoonful himself. 'Wow. That has set quite a high standard.'

Jo sipped the brandy that had appeared at her elbow without her noticing. 'I'm not really comparing like with like. Don't worry.' Then she realised that sometime during the evening she had decided that if the opportunity arose, that if he wanted to, she would put aside her years of conditioning, of being sensible and thinking about the future, and have sex with him, whatever the consequences. It came as a huge shock. Her shock must have showed because he laughed.

'Don't worry, I won't hold you to anything, except perhaps my manly chest.'

Now Jo was really giggly and accepted another spoonful of pudding. 'It's just as well we don't know anyone here. Imagine the scandal, a respectable middle-aged, middle-class woman dining with . . .' she paused for an apposite description.

'A middle-aged, middle-class reprobate?'

'Mm, that's quite accurate.'

'But as we don't know anyone, drink up, it's time we were going home.'

Chapter Twenty-Two

There was no thought of them walking home. A taxi was found and whisked them back to the quay. They held hands in the dark and Jo felt more young and giddy than she ever had done – even when she was officially young and giddy. She realised she was a little drunk when she got out while Marcus was paying the taxi driver and she found herself swaying. 'You're going to regret this in the morning,' she told herself firmly. 'Drink a lot of water or you'll feel awful.' But she knew that drinking water wouldn't stave off a much worse and possibly permanent hangover from her actions. She didn't care – she knew that the promise of the moment was too good to turn her back on, however much she might regret it later.

Marcus joined her and took her arm firmly, walking her the short distance back to the barge with an air of determination that Jo now found irresistibly attractive. He almost lifted her on to the barge and suddenly they were in the dark of the wheelhouse. The moment had come. She had to make her wishes known.

'Marcus?'

'What?'

Jo drew her breath to say she knew not what – something that would give him the hint that she wanted to be seduced, that she wasn't just about to thank him for a lovely evening.

Then he made everything a lot easier by kissing her. The

pressure of his mouth bruised hers. That she hadn't been kissed like that for years and years was her last conscious thought. She swayed in his arms and her head spun, affected as much by his kiss as by the brandy. She twined her fingers into his hair as he crushed her with his passion, and she forgot to breathe. They broke apart reluctantly, panting from lack of oxygen and desire.

'Goodness, you're a good kisser,' she murmured, smiling.

He laughed. 'And my talents don't end there.'

'That's fighting talk! Come down and prove it!' she said.

The thought of undressing in front of a man other than her husband had always terrified her, but now, she didn't even think about it. They pulled at each other's clothes as they got in the way of their searching hands. When at last he had got all her clothes off, he sighed deeply as he held her in the circle of his arms, stroking the curve of her waist. 'I can't tell you how long I've wanted this.'

Jo didn't answer. She felt utterly desired and equally desiring. She wanted him at that moment more than she had ever wanted anything. She dragged his shirt out of his trousers and was at his belt buckle like a tigress on her prey.

'There's something I must say—'

'Not now,' she said huskily and hopped on to the bunk.

It took him less than a moment to join her.

Later he brought them both glasses of water and reality seeped back into Jo's consciousness.

'I've never done anything like that before,' she said.

'I like to think I bring a certain originality to my love-making.'

She giggled. 'You are so smug! I didn't mean that. I

338

meant I haven't ever slept with a man I'm not married to.'

He pulled the duvet away from where it had got tangled between them so now they lay skin to skin. 'What? Not one indiscretion in all the years?'

She considered. 'There was an indiscretion but it didn't get very far.'

'Why not?'

'I was old-fashioned back then, and, as it turned out, stupid, and believed in my marriage vows.'

'Although technically I suppose you are, you don't feel married then?'

'Nope. As I see it, if the marriage vows are broken, they're broken, no matter which of you does it. Why have you never married, Marcus?'

'Ah, well, I've always been a serial philanderer.'

'I'm not sure you can be one of those, unless of course you hop from Cornflakes to Rice Krispies and on to Weetabix in a promiscuous way.'

He squeezed her shoulders and then kissed one of them. 'I didn't realise you could be so flippant.'

'I feel flippant just now. And very – relaxed.'

'I think the word you're searching for is sated.'

'Is it?' She yawned deeply. 'I only know it's very nice, but I'm falling asleep.'

'You go to sleep. We'll carry on this conversation in the morning.'

She opened her mouth to say 'Love you' in the way that she had to her husband for all those deluded, married years. Somehow, she stopped herself. She felt sure she could love Marcus but she retained enough common sense to realise her feelings might be more lust than love, and anyway, it was far too early to tell him. 'Goodnight, sleep tight, don't let the bed-bugs bite,' she said instead.

'Joanna!'

She chuckled and closed her eyes. The trouble was, although she did feel a little flippant she knew perfectly well that in the morning she'd feel anything but.

The double berth in the back cabin of *The Three Sisters* was of traditional size, which meant, Jo was only too aware, small. There was no way they could share it without their limbs entangling, and if Marcus caught a sensitive part of her body as they adjusted their positions, one thing led to another. They didn't get much sleep. At about seven the following morning, Marcus got up to make tea. Jo followed him to have a quick look at herself in the mirror. Daylight could be horribly cruel to the older woman, she thought, and braced herself for the worst.

In fact, she realised, she didn't look too bad. Her left-over make-up had tactfully stayed just under her eyes and not smeared itself all over her face. Her hair was dishevelled but hadn't gone flat, and her skin looked relaxed and positively blooming. As she examined herself she remembered reading that sex was good for the skin, and now she saw what they meant.

She hopped back into bed, bringing the duvet up over her breasts like they did in films. 'Perhaps I should put my designer bra back on?' she wondered. 'Then I'll look like I'm in *Sex and the City*. Except that my bra isn't designer and it looks silly, even when they do it.' She hoped Marcus hadn't heard her talking to herself when he appeared a moment or two later with the tea.

'There was a text,' he said, handing her a mug and getting back into bed. He'd pulled on his trousers to go through the wheelhouse, but didn't take them off now.

'Oh?'

'From Michael.'

'Nothing's wrong?' she asked anxiously. 'He can still

come and help you bring the boat back, can't he?'

'Oh yes, that's not a problem. No, he'd had a message from Karen.' He took a sip of tea.

'What, Karen my daughter?' Jo sat up, immediately alert. 'Is there another Karen in Joanna-land?'

He wouldn't have made this joke if there was a problem, although there seemed to be a wistfulness about him.

'What did she say? She's all right, isn't she?'

'Oh yes, but she's in England. She's got a bit of time off. But she's not sure how long for.'

'Oh my God! And I'm in Holland. Typical.'

He paused and then went on steadily. 'Yes, but there's a train to the airport in a couple of hours. Or you could take a taxi. Perhaps that would be best.'

All the time she was rushing round making preparations for an early departure, she wondered if Marcus was packing her off. Was he relieved that he didn't have to spend the rest of the time in Holland with her? Or even the rest of the day! Perhaps he was grateful for the chance to kick her out of bed in the morning without any recriminations from her?

He didn't seem pleased for her to be going, but on the other hand, he wasn't pleading with her to stay, either. Perhaps she had just been a challenge for him and now he would return to his usual type. But he had seemed so in earnest.

She wondered about this on and off all during the train journey to the airport. She felt addled by all their love-making and attached herself to a couple who were also flying to England, so she wouldn't get confused and lost during the many processes that getting on a plane involved. She was longing to see Karen, but at the same time she longed to stay with Marcus. If he'd given her the choice, what would she have decided? Was she more mother, or lover? The trouble was, even if she was more lover, she couldn't possibly have said to Karen that she couldn't come home because she was all loved up with a man who wasn't her father. If only Karen had had more definite plans, she and Marcus could have discussed things properly.

She fell asleep on the plane, waking from time to time to check their progress. When they were stacked up waiting to land she was grateful because it meant more time to sleep. When they had to taxi a long way once they had landed, she was glad of that too. And when she was finally forced to wake up and get off the plane and retrieve Marcus's grip, which she had borrowed, from the over-head locker, she realised that she had come down to earth in more ways than one.

Marcus may have implied he'd yearned for her for years, but now he'd had her he was almost bound to want to go back to supple, lissom-limbed, Pilates-trained Carole, or her lookalike. He was a very attractive man. He could have any woman he wanted. A night in her arms and between her far too substantial thighs wouldn't bind him to her. She sighed as she shuffled along the passport queue. Never mind, she'd had her grand passion, the most wonderful night of lovemaking anyone could ever imagine, and she'd never let herself regret that.

Dora was lying in the sun on the grass with her eyes closed. Her ankle was entwined in the strap of her rucksack. Tom and most of his male friends were a little way away listening to their favourite band, Eskimo Rolling. They all had their tops off. She was not looking at Tom but she now knew exactly what his naked torso looked like and the knowledge was distracting.

'So, why aren't you and Tom an item?' asked Lizzie. She was sitting up getting her back brown. She had undone her halter-neck top and was holding the front to her. Although there was a group of completely naked people nearby, no one felt the need to join them.

'Because we're friends! It's hard to make the change, don't you think?' The trouble was, Dora realised, because she'd gone out with John for so long, and he'd been her first ever boyfriend, she hadn't had the usual sort of dating and boyfriend experiences that other girls had had.

'But you do fancy him?'

Dora opened an eye and checked Tom's strong, smooth back that tapered into his jeans in a satisfying way. 'I don't know. I suppose so.'

'I so would if he wasn't like a brother! All the girls loved him at college.'

'Er – did he have girlfriends at college?' Dora did feel a bit disloyal talking about Tom like this, but it was a good opportunity to find out things about him, and Lizzie was obviously a good friend of his. She wouldn't say anything nasty.

'Oh yes, loads. He managed to keep them as friends, though, which I think is cool.'

'Good.'

'So, how did you two meet?'

Dora would have quite liked to drift off to sleep. She sensed she wouldn't get much sleep later on, when they were all sharing a four-man tent. Tonight it would be housing not only four men, but two girls as well. 'Through the barge, I suppose. I was going to say through work, but he got me the job.'

They continued to chat, exchanging background details, finding more in common than Dora would have expected. They both had mothers who fussed.

'But Tom's mother's cool,' said Lizzie. 'I remember a whole crowd of us turned up to stay the night one day – we were travelling back from somewhere, can't remember where, and the car broke down. She was great about it. My mother would have gone ballistic. So, where will you go after the festival? Back to work, or back to the barge?'

'Back to the barge, I suppose.' Thinking about the barge and her cabin reminded her that she didn't have a sleeping bag with her. 'I should probably buy a blanket or something,' she went on. 'I didn't bring a sleeping bag because I didn't have one on the barge.'

'I'd love to see it sometime.'

'Well, maybe you could come back with us. Not everyone, though. That might be too much for Jo. Gosh, I wonder how she's getting on?'

'Do you want me to walk up with you to buy a blanket? I really like the Eskies, but I could do with a break.'

Walking through the many stalls felt much less daunting now and Dora realised she'd relaxed into the festival and was no longer the nervous, sheltered girl she had once been.

'So what are you doing now, Lizzie?' asked Dora as they made their way back to the tent.

'Saving up to go travelling.'

'Oh, like Tom!'

Lizzie chuckled ruefully. 'Yes, but he's really going travelling. I'm going to stay with relations in Australia!'

Dora was helping take the tent down when her mobile rang. She hauled it out of her pocket. It was Karen. She screamed and nearly dropped her phone. 'I can't believe it's you! Where are you?'

'At home. My old home. Mum's here, but, Do, you've got to come back as soon as you can. I'm not here for long.'

'How long?'

'I can't really say. I came over with a painting from work. It's got to be repaired. We don't know how long that'll take and I've got to go back immediately it is, so I must see you.'

'Oh my goodness. I'll have to check with Tom. This is so exciting! I can't wait to see you!'

'Nor me. Oh, Mum wants a word.'

'Jo? This is very exciting, Karen being home.'

'I know. It would be lovely if you could see her. Do you think Tom wants to go back to the barge? There's not a lot of point as it'll be in dry dock for a while, and it's not really suitable for living on at the moment.'

'Is Marcus still out there?'

'Oh yes, but one person's not such a problem.'

Dora longed to ask if Marcus had been a problem, and how they had got on, but didn't think now was the moment.

'I'll talk to Tom. The thing is, if I don't go back to the barge, where will I go?'

'Talk to Tom. If all else fails, you could come here. Now Karen's asking me something. Oh, and Philip's here.'

Tom eased his shoulders back after digging out a particularly stubborn tent peg. Dora tried to ignore his chest, which was defined without being over-developed. She relayed Karen's message.

'That's cool, we'll go to my parents.'

'But they don't know me!' Dora protested.

'Tom's parents are really safe,' said Lizzie. 'They'd love to have you. And isn't your mum going away anyway, Tom?'

He nodded. 'Trekking in Peru.'

'But what about your dad? He won't want a guest if your mum's away!' Dora insisted.

'He'll be fine! He'll love you. He's very laid-back. Now, have we got all the tent pegs?'

345

Dora did make Tom ring his parents and ask if she could stay and although it sounded as if he was telling them she was, she decided to stop worrying about it. His parents, Tom assured her, were very pleased to have him home for a bit, 'Although Mum's going off very soon after we arrive'.

They slept for most of the journey home, on the train to the airport, on the plane, and on the train the other end. Having hardly slept while they were at the festival, they found they just couldn't stay awake now. By the time they got into a taxi at the station they had finally caught up and were feeling more human again. Dora had to admit, though, that she had really enjoyed herself.

Tom's father and mother were standing on the doorstep waiting for them. Tom's father looked extremely like Tom, only with grey hair, and his mother appeared to have less sense of vanity than her own mother. She had greying, flyaway hair, very tanned skin and was wearing a hippy skirt and sandals with a polo shirt.

'They'll have heard the taxi,' said Tom. He led the way up the garden path to the pretty, double-fronted 1930s house of the style that Dora had heard disparagingly described as Tudorbethan, but that she had always liked for its little strange-shaped windows and diamond panes.

'Hi, Mum, hi, Dad,' said Tom, dumping his bags down and giving both his parents a hug. 'This is Dora.'

'Welcome, Dora,' said Tom's father, taking her hand.

'Do come in,' said Tom's mother, who kissed her in a rather absent-minded way. 'Would you like the loo? Or shall I show you to your room? Tell you what, I'll show you where the bathroom is and you can join us when you're ready. I always need a good scrub after a journey.'

Dora thanked her, wondering if the fact that she hadn't showered for a few days was so apparent. She didn't want to keep them from their tea or whatever, but she couldn't resist the opportunity to get rid of some of the grime. They wouldn't mind her going downstairs with wet hair, she was sure.

When she came down again she found Tom and his father in the sitting room. The French doors were open and a warm breeze wafted the scent of jasmine into the room.

'So Mum's off tomorrow?' Tom was saying. 'It's a good thing we got back today then, or I'd have missed her.'

'It's only for three weeks,' said Tom's father.

'Oh yes,' said Tom's mother, coming into the room carrying a tray. 'Tea, Dora? I'm Myra by the way. Tom never does introduce us properly. This is Brian.'

'I was going to give her a glass of wine,' said Brian.

'Can I have both?' asked Dora. 'The last decent cup of tea I had seems like a lifetime ago.'

'Of course,' said Myra, setting a mug down on the table next to her.

'It was Dora's first music festival,' explained Tom.

'Oh, did you enjoy yourself?' asked Myra.

Dora was aware that Tom was watching her. 'Yes, once I'd got over the shock of being offered drugs before we even got inside . . .'

'And all the nakedness,' Tom went on.

'It was fine,' finished Dora. 'Tom's friends were very nice.'

'Nice? Not quite how I'd have described them.' Myra took a sip of tea that expressed her feelings perfectly.

'Not my boat friends,' Tom explained. 'These were from college. Lizzie and that lot.'

'Oh, those friends! Yes, they are nice.'

'Are you ready for wine now?' said Brian. 'You seem to have got that tea down you already.'

347

Dora laughed. 'Wine would be lovely. I just had to have a nice cup of tea to feel really human again.'

'Hmm,' said Tom. 'I must remember that.'

Not quite sure what he meant, Dora turned to his mother. 'So you're going trekking? That does sound exciting.'

'Not really, it's an organised tour. My friend wouldn't let us just book flights and take it from there.' She sighed. 'I must finish packing in a moment.'

'How do you know what to take? To Peru?'

'Oh, I've got a kit list from when Tom went to India at school,' she said. 'I've used it ever since.'

'You went to India when you were at school?' Dora was amazed. 'The furthest we ever went to was St Albans.'

'I've added to the list over the years.' Myra went on. 'I never go without gaffer tape. You can mend anything with it. Have you done much travelling, Dora?'

She shook her head. 'I've led rather a sheltered life, I'm afraid.'

'Well, you're young. I didn't get into travel until I was over forty.'

'I'm not waiting till then before I head off,' said Tom. 'Just until I've got enough money.'

Dora felt suddenly bereft at the thought of Tom heading off round the world, leaving her behind.

'That reminds me, I must pack my neck purse. There's something wonderfully freeing about not having a handbag,' said Myra to Dora. 'I just put my credit card and my local currency in my neck purse, a few coins in my pocket, and that's it.' She got up. 'I'll just do that now, and by then supper will be ready.'

'What is it?' asked Tom.

'Lasagne.'

'Vegetarian?' Tom raised an eyebrow at his dad.

348

''Fraid so,' Brian answered.

'The lentil is a much misunderstood vegetable,' called his mother from the kitchen.

'Don't worry, Dora,' said Brian. 'We eat steak and chips a lot when Myra's away.'

Myra came back into the room. 'It's just as well I don't go away very often then. Too much red meat is bad for you. And it's ready. Do bring your glasses.'

Dora decided that Lizzie had been absolutely right about Tom's parents: they were lovely. His father was easygoing and friendly and his mother led an interesting life of her own and so didn't ask awkward questions. Both of them took Dora's presence completely for granted.

After supper Myra finished packing and then they all had another cup of tea before going to bed.

'I'm not sure I'm quite ready to go back to work,' said Dora, yawning, in spite of having slept through most of the journey back from Holland.

'We're not going back to work tomorrow,' said Tom. 'Officially, we're still with the barge in Holland. Tomorrow we're having an adventure.'

'Oh, Tom,' said Dora, guessing he meant another bet. 'I hope you don't mean anything too tiring.'

'Don't worry, sleepyhead, you'll love it.' He got to his feet and, pushing his hand through his hair, asked, 'More tea, anyone?'

Chapter Twenty-Three

❧❧❧

'I can't decide if I'm on holiday or going to work,' said Dora as she and Tom walked to the station together the following day. They had decided to call into the boatyard to tell them about their trip before going on into London.

'You're on holiday,' said Tom firmly. 'And I know they will have been fine without us. They will want a blow-by-blow account, though.'

'Then I'll just ring Karen,' she said. 'She might want to meet us in town or something.'

'You're doing your dare, Dora. You can see Karen another day.'

He sounded stern and a bit parental and she had to check to make sure he was laughing. Seeing his familiar twinkle provoked a sudden rush of fondness for him. She smiled back. 'OK. I'll ring her but I won't arrange anything for today. OK?'

Karen was full of enthusiasm. 'Mum and me are having a great time! Dad's taken the Floosie away so we've got the house to ourselves. It's lovely just catching up. I want to take her shopping and things. She has got a bit old-ladyish since I've been away.'

Dora couldn't help laughing. 'If you could see your mother skipping about a barge you wouldn't say things like that.'

'I'm very proud of her, getting over her fear of boats, but her hair's a mess.'

As Dora couldn't really disagree with this, she laughed.

'Mum's talking of having a barbie on Sunday. Would you and Tom be up for that?'

'Definitely. It would be wonderful!' She told Tom about this when they had disconnected. 'It'll be fun. We'll see Jo and you can meet Karen and' – she shot a glance at him – 'at least you can't arrange anything nasty for me to do on that day.'

'I never arrange anything nasty! You've enjoyed all of the bets so far, admit it!'

Dora inclined her head, indicating that maybe she had, a little. 'I didn't enjoy the loos at the festival.'

'Well, no, who would? But most of it was good, wasn't it?'

'Yes. Actually, it was OK.'

He pushed her playfully and then ran up the steps to the platform.

Everyone at the boatyard was very pleased to see her. Someone made tea and most of the men there crowded into the office so they could hear every detail. Dora was very glad that Tom was there to provide the technical details.

'So you went to Flushing?'

'Yes, Marcus said it was the way he knew best.'

'And is this Marcus as good as everyone says?' asked another man through a mouthful of ginger nut.

'Oh yes,' said Tom. 'No doubt about it.'

'Tom was a bit of a hero too,' said Dora. 'When Ed fell in.'

'Holy sh— sugarlumps! You had a man overboard?'

Dora did a little gentle filing while Tom related every detail. She chimed in only to say, 'We would never have got him back on board if it hadn't been for Tom.'

'Yes you would,' Tom said modestly, but grinning from ear to ear. 'Jo or you would have taken the wheel and Marcus would have come down to help.'

'Not easy to keep a barge in the same place, though,' said Fred.

'And are those continental barges really massive?' someone went on, when every detail of Ed's rescue had been rerun.

'Oh yes. You wouldn't believe it,' said Dora, finishing her filing. 'Some had parking for two cars, let alone one. And one – it made me a bit sad, actually – had a little play area for this little girl. She was swinging away as the barge went down the waterway.'

'Why sad?' said Tom. 'She didn't make me feel like that.'

'I just think that life on those big barges must be quite lonely for a child. I'm an only child but I always had friends.'

Tom looked at his watch. 'Time I took you away from all this, Dora.'

'I'll be back on Monday, I promise,' said Dora to Fred. 'I could stay now—'

'Off you go.' Fred ushered them out of the door. 'We're getting on fine without you to boss us around.'

After quite a bit more banter about Dora's bossy ways and the men's slack attitude to office work, Tom and Dora stepped into the boat and Dora manoeuvred their way back across to the bank.

'You're quite good at this now,' said Tom.

'Mm. I'm getting multi-talented in my old age,' said Dora. 'Get out and make fast, would you?'

'And you speak the language too,' said Tom, taking the line and tying it to a cast-iron ring.

'Almost fluently. Now, what's the torture for today?'

'You're going to eat in a restaurant by yourself.'

Dora sighed. 'That doesn't sound much fun! Surely it would be far nicer to eat together. I really don't want—' She stopped. 'Oh, OK. It's something I should be able to do.

I'm sure you're right. I just hope you haven't chosen anywhere too scary.'

Tom suddenly frowned, staring down at the bottom of Dora's trousers. 'Mm. I don't suppose you feel like buying a pair of kecks, do you?'

'Kecks?'

'Shruggies, slacks, pants . . . trousers?'

At last Dora understood. 'You're telling me it's a problem that I've got muddy? Then why did you let us go to the boatyard? You know it's impossible to get there without getting mud on you!'

'Sorry! Didn't think. Now, what shall we do before your dare?'

'It's lunchtime. Surely—'

He shook his head. 'It's tea.'

'Tea?'

'Mm. A hot brown drink you seem to be quite fond of?'

'I know what tea is. I just didn't—'

'Well, you're going to. But not immediately. What would you like to do first?'

'I can't believe you're asking me what I want to do!'

'Am I so bossy then?'

'Yes,' she said immediately but then realised that although he'd certainly been making her do things, he wasn't bossy in the way that John had been bossy. With John there'd been no discussion, no argument. She'd just said, 'Yes, John,' and, 'No, John,' for the sake of an easy life. And saying 'Yes, John' at the wrong time had nearly precipitated disaster. 'Let's go for a walk through London and look in shop windows and I'll see if I can find any trousers. Is the rest of me OK?'

Tom regarded her quizzically. 'I should think so.'

Dora took this as a no and determined to find a little

jacket if she could. 'Seriously, are you willing to do a bit of shopping?'

'Sure. Especially as it's my fault you have to. I'm not saying I'll sit outside the changing room and comment on every item you try on, I'll buy a paper and read it.'

Dora smiled. 'Cool!' John did not like shopping.

As they got on a bus that Tom assured her would take them to Oxford Street, Dora wondered yet again how he felt about her. There'd definitely been times when she'd thought he was looking at her with something more than the eyes of friendship but he'd never made any move. And there were times when she longed to be more like Carole. Carole would have taken the initiative by now, she was convinced. All that time at the festival and Dora had never even slipped her arm round his waist. On the other hand, an over-subscribed four-man tent was hardly conducive to seduction. She chuckled at the notion and had to look out of the window of the bus so Tom wouldn't see.

'Couldn't we skip the whole thing and just have a jolly time?' she said a little later as they headed down Oxford Street.

'Come on, Dora! Where's the plucky girl who helped me rescue Ed? Eating in a restaurant on your own should be a doddle.'

His praise warmed her for a moment. 'You're just so bossy!'

'No I'm not, I'm being your facilitator.'

She made a face. 'That's just the politically correct word for bossy.'

He shrugged, his head slightly on one side, a grin giving him a dimple at one corner of his mouth. He was far too attractive for his own good, Dora decided, and then wondered if it was her good she was worried about. There

354

was no point in fancying someone who looked on her as a sort of kid sister.

'I do wish you'd told me to buy something smarter,' said Dora indignantly. They were outside a very elegant hotel in Mayfair. 'I can't go in there looking like this!' Especially not on her own, and even if Tom came with her it wouldn't have helped much.

'Yes you can, you look fine. Anyway, it's part of the dare. Just hold your head high and ask for your table. It's booked in my name.'

'I didn't think I'd ever say this again, but I want my mum!'

Tom laughed and it gave her the courage she needed. After all, it wasn't actually dangerous; she wouldn't really die of embarrassment.

'If I'm thrown onto the street, Tom Watkins, I'll do something horrible to you,' she said, and went up the steps and through the door held open by a porter in a very elaborate uniform.

Instantly a beautiful young man swept up to her. 'Can I help you, mademoiselle?' he asked her in a deeply sexy voice.

'Um – there's a table booked – the name is Watkins.'

The young man checked his book. 'Ah yes, follow me, please.' He was wearing a black-tailed coat, striped trousers and a waistcoat. He was, Dora decided, by anyone's standards, completely delicious.

He pulled out Dora's chair, spread her napkin upon her lap and handed her a menu. 'The set tea includes sandwiches, scones with jam and cream and a selection of cakes. Which kind of tea would mademoiselle prefer?' He reeled off a list of teas including several souchongs and oolongs along with the more familiar varieties.

'Earl Grey,' she said eventually.

'Certainly,' He bowed, and left her.

Feeling a lot better about the whole process than she thought she would, Dora took in her surroundings. A piano played tunefully but invisibly from somewhere. There were pillars painted with garlands of flowers and the occasional bird, a theme echoed in the panels which were interspersed with mirrors. She could see herself sitting rather primly on her chair and relaxed her shoulders a little. It was quite crowded, she realised, and wondered if it had been difficult for Tom to get a table. Not everyone was smartly dressed but there were a few examples of what her mother would call 'tea gowns'.

Had she not been on her own, she wouldn't have felt dreadfully out of place in her new but casual trousers and V-neck T-shirt, but she would have definitely bought a skirt had she known where she was headed. And she was slightly surprised that they'd let her in.

Before she had time to get anxious about her scruffiness amidst so much old-fashioned glamour the waiter was back with a cake stand loaded with food.

Dora hadn't had much lunch – Tom had been very firm about them only having a snack, and when she saw the little finger-shaped sandwiches, oozing with smoked salmon and cream cheese, cucumber and ham, she found herself suddenly starving. Now she was worried about how much it was acceptable to eat. She remembered her grandmother going on about 'an ample sufficiency'. She was bound to err on the side of ample.

Her tea arrived before she had reached a conclusion. It was in a china teapot with an echo of the walls and pillars painted on it. A matching jug and sugar bowl were all arranged around the cup and saucer. Dora felt as if she was six again, playing tea parties with Karen, and smiled.

'Mademoiselle, wait two minutes and I will come back and pour for you. But do eat!'

She put a sandwich on to her plate and ate it. It was one mouthful. She took another. They were exquisite – little morsels of perfection. The bread was fresh, the fillings just the right balance and the butter creamy and delicious.

At least the food is lovely, she thought, her private irritation with Tom thawing a little. She was glad he had made them have a horrid hot dog for lunch rather than a sandwich – she wouldn't have been enjoying these ones so much if they had.

The waiter swooped up again. 'Mademoiselle, I will pour your tea. Do you take milk?'

Dora began to wonder why he was singling her out for such attention. She had observed several people pouring their own tea while she was waiting. He placed the cup at her elbow. 'You like the sandwiches, yes?'

'Yes, I do. They're wonderful.'

'I will bring you more if you wish.'

'No – no thank you. There are plenty here.'

'After you must try the scones. I made them myself.' He seemed inclined to linger but was summoned by another table.

Did waiters really make scones? Or did pastry chefs, or whoever did make them, double up as waiters? She ate another sandwich – cucumber and ham this time – while she thought about it.

'Mademoiselle, please, the scones. With the cream and jam.' He was at her elbow, twinkling at her, making her feel pampered and desirable. He took a scone with the tongs and put it on her plate. Then he cut it in half and put a lavish amount on cream on it, then a teaspoonful of jam. 'Please – eat.'

The scone was small but it still filled Dora's mouth so

that she brought her napkin up to her lips to avoid spillage. She chewed, swallowed and smiled.

'Well?' demanded her waiter.

'Delicious, but I think I really prefer the sandwiches.'

'Poof!' he said derisively. 'Try an éclair.'

Partly through embarrassment and partly because of the utter ridiculousness of the situation, Dora began to feel giggly. She struggled to keep herself under control. If this delightful waiter would only go away she'd be able to keep herself in check. Everyone knew about summoning a waiter but she didn't have any personal experience of how to send one away. She put the éclair into her mouth. It was food heaven.

'Well?'

'It was delicious, as I'm sure you know. Now do go and look after some other customers. You'll lose your job.'

'*Pas du tout*. I am in charge today. Do you still prefer the sandwiches?'

'I don't know. Probably not.'

'Try a meringue,' he urged. 'They are tiny.'

Dora only just got it to her mouth intact. Once there it dissolved into creamy sweetness enhanced by the chopped strawberries in the cream. 'That was truly heavenly.'

'I will bring you some more.'

Dora was already feeling slightly sick – any more meringues would make her feel very uncomfortable. She belched discreetly into her napkin and felt a little better. She glanced at the door. Could she – should she make a run for it? She realised she couldn't, even if Tom had paid for it all in advance.

'No, really!' she said as the waiter appeared with five tiny, perfect meringues on a doily-covered plate.

'Mademoiselle . . .' he said reproachfully.

'I really couldn't. They were lovely, but . . .'

'I will pack them in a box for you.'

He had just presented the box to Dora, having curled the gold and pink striped ribbons, when Tom appeared. He did not seem pleased.

'Oh, hello, Tom,' said Dora.

'Could I have the bill please?' he demanded from the waiter.

'Of course.' The waiter raised an eyebrow and then went away to the desk.

'That man!' said Tom, furious. 'He's done nothing but try to pick you up since you got here!'

'No he hasn't, don't be silly!'

'I've been watching. He wasn't like that with the other guests.'

'Spying on me, Tom?' Dora pretended to be indignant, but actually she was rather pleased.

'Just keeping an eye. That greasy, smooth-talking . . .' He paused while he thought of an acceptable word. '. . . man was trying to seduce you with cream cakes.'

'Mm. There are worse ways,' said Dora, feeling very frivolous and lighthearted.

Tom scowled and marched over to the desk. Never had Dora seen Tom being so masterful or, she had to admit, grumpy. While she felt sorry for the waiter and smiled her apologies to him, she couldn't help being a little flattered by Tom's obvious jealousy. Perhaps he didn't see her as just a mate.

He followed the waiter to the desk and got out his wallet. Dora picked up the box of meringues. Tom could eat them in the park.

'Come along,' he said firmly, taking her arm and marching her out of the hotel. Dora barely had time to smile at the waiter in gratitude.

'That wretched man!'

'He was very attentive.' Dora was giggling now.

Tom was marching her along the road like an irate father. 'If I'd known—'

'It was a lovely tea, Tom, and I feel much braver now about going into a restaurant on my own.'

'It's not funny!'

'Yes it is! It's hilarious. Now, stop being grumpy and we can find somewhere for you to eat these meringues. They really are delicious.'

Tom made a growling sound.

Chapter Twenty-Four

❧

Jo had been so excited to see Karen again that she really couldn't think about anything else. Karen had come in the car with her father to pick her up from the airport and flung herself almost into the path of passing traffic so she could run to her mother.

'Mum! You've got a tan. You look amazing.'

Karen had seemed completely different and just the same simultaneously. Mother and daughter hugged for several minutes until Philip guided them on to the pavement where they could hug in safety.

'Darling, I've missed you so much!' said Jo, holding Karen's hand, leaving Philip to carry her luggage.

They had walked, hip to hip, back to the car. Jo ignored Philip, not only because she was so taken up with Karen but because she didn't quite know how to treat him. She felt no animosity but she didn't feel any great warmth either. Especially after her night with Marcus. She would see how she felt when they'd got home. She pushed all thoughts of Marcus aside and concentrated on her daughter.

'I've cooked a meal,' said Karen as they headed out on to the motorway. 'I nearly let Dad pick you up on his own but I couldn't wait to see you. I hope it's all right.'

The two women talked – mostly about what Karen had been getting up to in Toronto – non-stop all the way home while Philip just drove. Eventually he said, 'Here we are,' and they realised they were home.

He opened the boot and got out Jo's luggage, which included what she'd bought while she was waiting for her flight.

'Well, I suppose I'd better go back to the Travelodge,' he said.

'Where's – er – Samantha?' asked Jo, not wanting to hear that she was waiting for Philip in a motel.

'With her parents. She's fine about being at home for a while, being spoilt.' He smiled at Jo in the conspiratorial way of parents.

She smiled back. 'Eventually the roles reverse and now Karen's spoiling me.'

Karen glanced from one to the other. 'Do stay for dinner, Dad. I've made loads.'

He looked at Jo a little diffidently. 'Yes, stay,' she said, her love for her daughter overflowing to her father for a moment, 'I've bought a bottle of malt.'

'I thought you couldn't get duty-free stuff unless you went outside the EU,' said Karen, taking her arm.

'No you can't, but they do have good offers and I've got some wonderful chocolate.'

'You should see what I got you!' said Karen. 'A Touche Éclat for one thing.'

'Darling!'

'Well, I always felt guilty about stealing yours. And I suppose you do need a concealer a bit more than I do.'

Jo laughed and hugged her daughter. 'Cheeky!'

Philip said, 'Let's go in and have a drink.'

'This is quite like old times,' said Karen, putting her fork straight on her plate and screwing her napkin into a ball.

'Yes,' said Jo, who was slightly dizzy through a combination of excitement, alcohol and a lack of sleep. She didn't feel she could add jet-lag to that – the journey was

362

only about an hour – but she did feel it made its contribution to how she felt. She took another sip from her glass which Philip had filled while she hadn't been looking. 'The three of us together.' It was surprisingly easy, although Jo couldn't help wondering briefly what Marcus was doing and if he was thinking about her too.

Philip sighed with satisfaction. 'That was a lovely meal, darling.' He got up and kissed his daughter on the top of her head. 'You've inherited your mother's cooking skills.'

'I'm glad you liked it, Dad.' Karen got up too and returned her father's kiss before gathering the plates. 'Are you staying the night?'

There was a moment of stillness before he said, 'Better not. I'll come and see you again though, if that's all right,' he added to Jo.

'Of course it's all right. This is your home, not mine.'

'It's your home too, Jo,' he said and kissed her cheek. He left the room, leaving the two women still at the table.

'What does he mean, it's my home too?' muttered Jo, tired and confused.

'Oh never mind that,' said Karen dismissively. 'Let's open the chocs you brought and go into the sitting room. I think there's something good on.'

'Yes. This spindly little table is no good for real conversation – there's no room for elbows.'

The following morning Jo remembered what it was like to be taken in hand by her bossy, adored daughter.

'Mum, your hair, it needs a really good cut and colour,' she said as they ate some disgusting breakfast product Karen had found in the cupboard. It seemed to be a combination of pet foods, predominately parrot, but it promised such amazing rejuvenating effects that Jo chewed it stoically. 'You have let yourself go a bit.'

'I'm sure if we planted this, we'd get some interesting hallucinogenic plants.'

'Don't change the subject. Your hair.'

'I'll make an appointment—'

'No, not lovely Joy in the village. I know you adore her but she's been doing your hair in the same way for years. You need a new look.'

Jo sighed, accepting the inevitable. 'Where then?'

'In town. A place Janet told me about.'

'Who's Janet?

'A friend from uni. She's moved to the area and so I got some info from her. You need a leg wax and a St Tropez, I think, although you do have a nice colour. Oh, and definitely some new bras.'

'Darling, are you giving me a make-over?'

'Absolutely!' said Karen, getting up and clearing the table. 'We're going to make you the most glamorous perimenopausal woman on the planet.'

'I didn't know you knew words like that,' said Jo, rather wishing her daughter wasn't so well informed.

A day later Karen and Jo stood outside the shop in Knightsbridge. There was a security guard outside.

'Look,' whispered Jo, 'they check you're posh enough to buy bras here, and I'm not!'

'You look great! You've had your hair done now, and those highlights work really well. No trace of grey any more and your skin is looking fab after that facial.'

Jo had to admit she did feel a lot more human again. She couldn't help wondering if Marcus would like the new, improved, less woolly Joanna.

'Come on, Mum,' Karen chivvied.

'But my underwear—'

'Is fine. After all, you'll take your bra off.'

'Why don't you come too?'

'Way too expensive for me, Mum. I'll meet you here in half an hour. If you come out sooner than that, ring me.'

Bravely, Jo smiled at the security guard and went into the shop. A well-dressed woman in her fifties asked her if she'd ever been before, assuming the answer was no. Admitting this was the case (was this omission so obvious?) she was ushered to the counter where there was a queuing system.

'Please take a number and wait until you're called,' said the woman, who was wearing what appeared to be a designer suit.

'What, like at the cheese counter?' Jo asked before she could stop herself.

The woman smiled – slightly. 'That's right, but as we're not busy this young lady will help you.'

Feeling as if she was going for a dentist's appointment where they would tell her she didn't floss enough, or the doctor's where they'd tell her she was overweight, Jo duly followed.

'In here please, madam.'

Jo couldn't help noticing the signed photograph on the wall. It was of the young Queen with her husband, children and corgis. Prince Philip was looking particularly dashing. Having them gazing down at her did not give her confidence.

'Strip to the waist, madam, and I'll see what size you are. We don't use tape measures here.' The young woman was from some mittel-European country that had possibly been a police state. Jo was wearing a dress and duly stripped, grateful that she'd had the forethought to put on a slip, so her knickers, which, while perfectly respectable and fairly new, would not be on show. There are some embarrassments not even childbirth can prepare you for.

Her upper body was peered at by the young woman. Jo had always felt fairly happy with her breasts, but now she wondered if she was more than averagely lopsided, or if Marcus's fingerprints were somehow visible. She pulled her shoulders back a fraction. At some point she was going to have to tell Karen about Marcus.

'Wait here, I will be back.'

Although she was alone, Jo crossed her arms over her breasts as she stood before the picture of the Queen. It seemed disrespectful to do otherwise. Of course, Karen was grown up now, but Jo sensed she really wanted her parents back together again. What child wouldn't, whatever their age? With Samantha out of the way, and despite the baby on the way, Karen might well be thinking that getting back together was possible. Even without Samantha, Jo wouldn't want that now, she realised. She would just have to make that clearer to Karen as gently as she could.

The woman returned, her arm loaded with bras. 'Which colour would you like?'

Jo tried on a black one. Her pants, under her slip, were black, and she thought it would be good to be matching. It was terribly tight.

'What size is it?' she asked. When told the answer she opened and shut her mouth a few times. 'I haven't worn that size since I was married, and as for the cup – well, I never want to be that far down the celebrity list.'

The young woman, whose English was not really colloquial, ignored this sally. Fitting a bra was not a matter for flippancy. She tugged at the straps and hoiked Jo's breasts a little nearer to the sky.

'Now look.'

Jo looked. 'Wow,' she said, and then, 'Where's my cleavage?' Where she was accustomed to seeing a deep

366

shadow was now a gaping hole, big enough, it seemed, for a small boulder.

'You heff netural cleavage,' said the woman. 'Put your dress back on to see how it looks.'

It looked, Jo was forced to admit, fabulous. 'Oh my goodness, I'll have to have it.'

'Would you like it in another colour? White or cream, perhaps?'

'Oh yes please,' she said getting into the spirit of things. 'Try on another.'

Jo got into it. She tried on bras she could wear under low-cut dresses, bras she could go to the gym in and not bounce and the sexiest black number with velvet straps and little bows. It made her feel like a cross between a courtesan and a painting by Monet. She loved it. She chose three. It was only when she was waiting to pay that she realised that she hadn't asked how much they were. The final amount caused her to reel in shock.

'I'd better go back to being a kept woman,' she muttered as she handed over her credit card, grateful that her expenses had been minimal lately.

Karen was waiting impatiently outside the door.

It was two days after Dora and Tom had been out for tea and Dora was washing up the breakfast things when Karen rang her mobile.

'Hi! Dora! It's me! OK to talk?'

Karen had always assumed the person on the other end of the phone would know who she was, and in Dora's experience they always did. 'Yeah! I'm washing up.'

'Thrilling! I'm dying to see you on Sunday. Are you a couple yet?'

This was a question Dora asked herself quite often recently but she still hadn't worked out the answer. She smiled at her friend's forthrightness. She'd really missed her. 'I don't know, really,' she said honestly.

'You need to find out where you stand, Dora, especially after John.'

'It's not the sort of thing you can ask, is it?'

'Well . . .' Karen paused, possibly thinking better of telling her more timid friend that of course she could ask. 'Anyway, Mum thinks he's the cat's pyjamas and I'm dying to meet him.'

'He's very fond of Jo.'

'Mum's inviting her other barge friends, Bill and Miranda?'

'Oh yes, they're lovely.'

'And some other people, not sure who. It's great – she and Dad are getting on so well. I wonder if they'll come to their senses and get back together?'

Part of Dora went cold. Of course, from Karen's point of view, this was great news, but Dora had heard Jo talk about her ex-husband in terms not of anger, but of boredom. Anger could be worked through, boredom would just stay as boredom. Could Jo go back to a husband who bored her? It was a depressing thought. And now she thought about it again she was sure Jo rather liked Marcus – but then that could just have been the onset of the menopause like she'd said. Life was so confusing at times. 'I thought your dad's girlfriend was pregnant.'

'Oh yes, I suppose she is.' Karen paused. 'But these things can be sorted out.'

Dora didn't speak immediately. She could totally sympathise with Karen's desire for her parents to mend their marriage but she wasn't sure it would be right. 'Maybe,' she said eventually.

'Anyway, Mum and I have had such a good time! She's been in the garden a lot – claiming it back, she said. We've done loads of shopping. I sorted her out with a decent haircut. She's bought all these new bras – an investment, I told her. She's looking amazing – sort of lit up inside. It must be something to do with getting on with Dad, don't you think?'

'Has he moved back in with her?' The thought depressed Dora horribly.

'Oh no, but he's taken time off work because I'm here, and has come round for a few meals, taken us out as a family. Quite like old times.'

'Lovely,' said Dora faintly.

'Anyway, you'll see for yourself on Sunday. I can't wait. And sort it out with Tom.'

'I'll do my best.' Dora laughed.

As if their conversation had conjured him up, Tom appeared in the doorway. 'Dora, you shouldn't have done the washing-up!'

'I'm just doing the frying pan and things. The rest of it's gone in the dishwasher.'

'You're a very good guest.'

She made a face. 'I know. But that was Karen on the phone.'

'Oh yes?'

'She was telling me who's coming to the barbecue. Jo and Philip, her husband – ex-husband – have invited various people. Miranda and Bill are coming, so at least we'll know some of them. Karen says her parents are getting on really well, she thinks—'

'What about Marcus?' Tom interrupted her.

Dora bit her lip. 'What about him?'

'Maybe I'm wrong, but I'm sure he had a thing for Jo. I know you said it's supposed to be women who sense these things, but the way he kept looking at her . . .'

Dora shook her head, biting her lip. 'Karen obviously

thinks there's a chance her parents will get back together.'

'Oh.' He sighed. 'Not much we can do about it, anyway – especially not knowing how Jo feels.'

'No,' Dora agreed, wondering how he felt about her. 'Do you want a cup of coffee or something?'

'Mm. Might as well. Do you want me to make it? I quite fancy real coffee.'

'Then you can definitely make it. I don't know how to work your machine.'

'I'll show you.'

'No need! I'm going into work tomorrow. It'll give me a day to get straight before the weekend. Then it won't be so awful when I go back on Monday. What about you?'

Tom opened the fridge and took out a jar of coffee beans. 'Not sure.'

Dora felt a little deflated. She'd been looking forward to going to work with Tom – it was such a couply thing to do. But then, they weren't a couple, she reminded herself.

'Don't look sad. I'll tell you how to get there.'

Dora thought she pretty much knew how to get there, but she smiled and nodded.

In fact, he did go with her to the boatyard but he disappeared almost immediately. From time to time other people came in to ask her if she knew where he was but she could only shrug and shake her head. He did phone her at lunchtime, though.

'I've had a call from Marcus!'

'Oh?'

'Yes. He was just checking my availability for bringing *The Three Sisters* back.'

'When is it coming back? Will he need me too?' she asked.

'He won't need you, particularly, but you could certainly come. But that's not why I'm ringing.'

'No?'

'I happened to mention the barbecue.'

'Oh?'

'Yes. I think I put my foot in it. I don't think he's invited. He didn't know anything about it and when I said Jo's husband was going to be there – well, he certainly didn't sound pleased.'

'It's just a barbecue.'

She heard Tom sigh. 'I did sort of indicate what you said about Karen, thinking her parents were getting back together.'

'How on earth did you fit that into a conversation about availability?'

'He was on the alert the moment I said "Jo and her husband".'

'Oh.'

'I think he might try and come. It'll be nice to see him if he does. He wants Jo's address, anyway. Can you give it to me?'

Only for a moment did Dora ask herself if this was the right thing to do then she told Tom. After all, Jo probably wouldn't mind if Marcus did turn up and she was used to mass catering. And anyway, Philip knew Marcus too from the old days. Marcus was probably bad on the phone and Tom had misread the situation. After all, he was in Holland. It would be a long way to travel for a burnt lamb chop.

'Cool,' said Tom. And then, 'Will you be all right going home on your own? I've still got quite a lot of things to do.'

'I can't think what, unless you're thinking of actually doing some work. People have been asking for you all morning.'

'Just stuff, OK? But you will be all right?'

'I'll be fine.'

'I just don't want you to—'

'Tom! You've made me do loads of horrible, scary, smelly' – she added, thinking of the festival – 'things. I think I can go a couple of stops on the train by myself. I've got a key.'

'Sweet. I'll see you later, then.'

When he was in no danger of hearing her, Dora indulged in a long sigh.

Tom arrived home that evening just as Dora and his father were pouring a glass of wine.

'It is Friday,' said Brian.

'But we had a glass of wine yesterday,' said Dora.

'That was Thursday. Quite different.'

Dora laughed and then Tom bounced into the kitchen. 'Hey, you crazy kids, what are you up to?'

'Glass of wine, Tom?' asked his father.

'Cool!'

Tom bounced into breakfast with similar brio the following morning. He handed Dora an envelope. 'Hope you didn't have plans for today.'

'No—'

'Well, you have now. It's your final dare. Dad, can I borrow the car?'

'I said yes yesterday. Nothing's changed.'

'Great! I'll be off then,' he said, dashing off, a piece of half-eaten toast still in his hand.

'He's a good boy, really,' said Brian solemnly.

Dora laughed and sighed at the same time and then opened the envelope. Inside was a train ticket and a list of instructions. *Take the 9.45 train, then come out of the station and turn left, past the pub, down the little lane until you come to a jetty. There's a boat tied up there with your first clue. This is a treasure hunt!*

Dora looked at her watch. It was already ten past nine and it took ten minutes to get to the station. She couldn't ask for a lift because Tom had already taken the car.

'I do think he might have given me a lift to the station,' she said, getting up, gathering her plate and mug as she did so.

'Have a nice day, Dora,' said Brian, who, she now realised, must be in on the plot.

'I'll try. As long as I catch the train.'

'You've got plenty of time,' Brian said, returning to his newspaper.

She shook her head. 'I must get my things and I'm one of those people who have to be at the station really early. Bye!'

She ran upstairs, threw all that she thought she might need into the shoulder bag she took to work and then left.

She walked to the station wondering what on earth Tom had in store for her. Perhaps this was what he was up to yesterday, when he wasn't at work. She smiled. She'd miss their bets. Now they were about to end, how would their friendship ever develop further?

Chapter Twenty-Five

❧❦❧

While Dora was waiting for the train, as, inevitably, she had to, she wondered if she was wearing the right clothes. She had put on a light summer skirt and a vest top as it looked like being a lovely day. She had thrown a cardigan into her bag but with Tom, wellington boots might have been a better choice. As she didn't actually have her wellingtons at Tom's house, she forgave herself for not having brought them.

With his instructions in her hand, Dora made her way to the jetty. There, as he had said, was a little boat she recognised as one of the ones used for getting to and from the boatyard. There was a note stuck in the rope attaching the boat to the quay. She pulled it out.

Get in the boat and row a while, until you reach the little isle.

The little isle must be the one opposite her. She hadn't ever been there but she knew people did tie their boats up there. Like the island where Tom moored his boat, it was probably a nature reserve.

Dora overcame her dislike of trespassing, got in the boat and manoeuvred her way across the water. She would quibble with Tom about the use of the word 'row' when she saw him.

The next clue was curling out of the neck of a bottle sticking in the mud.

Go to the left and climb the tree (she squeaked at the

thought of climbing trees in her short tight skirt), *and look inside what there you see.*

Hm, she thought, not great poetry, but she was enjoying herself. She walked along the path to the left and turned a corner. There was a willow lying on the ground, fallen, but supported by the branches at the end. She wouldn't actually have to climb it, but she would have to teeter along the sloping trunk to the crown. She slipped off her sandals and edged her way up the trunk. Sticking out of the branches was a bouquet of flowers. There were some garage-forecourt carnations but also lots of wild grasses and cranesbill. They were very pretty, Dora thought. Tucked in the middle was another clue.

Down the tree and along the bank, you will find a water tank.

Tom! thought Dora, your couplets are getting worse and as for making me climb a tree . . . But she tucked the flowers into her bag when she scrambled back down and set off in what she thought was the right direction. The island was tiny, and yet it seemed to provide lots of opportunities for getting lost. At last she spotted a rusty water tank half submerged in the grass, and as she could also see another clue she knew she was in the right place.

Go left, go right and through the wood and you'll find something that makes you feel good! (I hope) he had added in brackets.

'Well, it's not your rhymes that are making me feel good,' said Dora aloud, suspecting that Tom was some-where, spying on her.

She was aware of feelings of both excitement and anticipation stirring in her. She was trying to feel irritated with Tom for his dreadful rhymes and the general silliness of it all, but she was finding it difficult.

She didn't bother with the left and right bit. She could see the wood in front of her, and as she drew near she heard music. She came upon a clearing, and there was a scene reminiscent of an Impressionist painting. Tom was there, with his back to her. He was placing the stylus on an old 78 record that circled sedately on a wind-up gramophone and then an old Billie Holiday number, poignant and sensual, floated on the summer air.

A tartan rug and several big cushions were spread temptingly about. A wicker picnic hamper was open already. Just at that moment, the sun, which had been partly obscured by cloud, decided to come out, shining through the trees and covering everything with dappled light. Beyond the trees Dora could see water sparkling in the distance. The smell of ferns reached her nose, possibly because she had trodden on some of them. She hovered on the threshold for a few seconds, waiting for Tom to see her. Now that she was closer, she realised that he seemed really nervous. And now he'd set the music playing he began to pace about. She coughed gently, and he looked up.

'Hi!' he said, obviously relieved to see her but not really smiling. 'You got here all right, then?'

Picking up on his anxiety made her feel awkward. 'Yes. It was a lovely idea, doing a treasure hunt. A bit early for lunch, isn't it?' She was aware that things weren't the same between them and it was a struggle to behave in the same chummy way.

'Not all that early. I wasn't sure how long it would take you to get here.'

She smiled. 'The clues were quite easy.'

'Well, sit down. I've got to do some digging.'

'Digging?'

'Mm.' He picked up a spade that was stuck in the ground, went to where the trees were closest together and started sending clods of soil into the air. Eventually he pulled out a bottle of champagne. He brought it over.

'My dad's always going on about old-fashioned picnics where you bury the champagne three days before so it's cold. I only buried it this morning, but it was cold when it went in, so it should be all right.'

Dora sat on the rug, feeling a little shy. Tom produced a couple of stainless steel mugs from the hamper. 'I got these in India, when I went with school. They sold them by weight.'

'What do you mean?'

'Well, I picked them out, and to find out the price they weighed them.'

'Cool. You are lucky, going to India with school.'

'You could go to India, if you wanted. Now, hold the mugs, I'm going to open this.'

'But what are we celebrating?'

'You achieving all your dares, of course. You're now officially a Brave Person.' He smiled at her but his eyes were serious. The champagne flowed into the mugs and he handed her one. 'Here's to you,' he said.

'And to you.' They touched their mugs together and both sipped. Tom's gaze was intense. 'You were going to give me a prize,' she said lightly, setting down her mug, thinking that this was the prize, this lovely picnic.

'I have got a prize for you, but you have to have it after lunch. Hang on, I'll put on another record.'

'How on earth did you get all this stuff here? And I love the gramophone! It's the perfect touch.'

'A ghetto-blaster wouldn't have quite created the atmosphere I'm after.'

'Which is?'

Tom adjusted the way he was sitting. 'Romantic,' he said, without looking at her.

Dora's next mouthful of champagne was gulped rather than sipped.

'Let's have something to eat,' he said when he'd wound up the gramophone again and put on another record. He burrowed in the hamper and brought out a foil-wrapped packet. 'Smoked-salmon sarnies. I made them last night.'

'How did you get all this stuff here on a boat?' She took a sandwich although she wasn't really hungry.

'I cheated. There's a rickety old bridge over there.' He waved towards the trees. 'We can go back in the car.'

'I quite liked arriving by boat.'

'I hoped you would.'

She smiled shyly at him. 'These are really nice. I didn't think I wanted anything really, but now I've started eating . . .'

'Have some crisps. And I've got hot sausage rolls.'

'How did you manage that?'

He produced an old fashioned wide-mouthed thermos flask with a cork for a stopper. 'Try one.'

It was sinfully delicious. 'Golly, I didn't think they made sausage rolls like this these days.'

'I got them in a deli – I think they make them themselves but they've got this really flaky pastry. Have another.'

Dora was about to wipe her greasy hands on her thigh when Tom produced a linen napkin. 'I found them in the airing cupboard. Mum never uses them because she says they're a pain to iron.'

'They are lovely, though.' Dora thought that she had better make sure they were laundered before Tom's mother came home.

'Have some more champagne.' He proffered the bottle.

'I haven't finished this yet.'

'Then hurry up. We've got little éclairs for pudding.'

'You didn't make them?'

'No. But I want to give you your present.'

'Why the hurry?'

'I'm worried that you won't like it.'

'But, Tom, I'm loving all this. The present doesn't matter all that much.'

'Yes it does, but don't worry, it's only small.'

Dora relaxed a little. She drank some more champagne and then ate another sausage roll. 'OK, pudding time, if you're ready. You don't seem to have eaten much.'

'Oh, I'm all right.' He dived into the hamper again and came out with yet another plastic box. 'Éclairs.'

'These are truly yummy,' Dora said after she'd eaten two of the little-finger-sized morsels. 'They're as nice as the ones I had at that hotel.'

'Good. Now, finish your mouthful. It's time for your present.'

Dora wiped her fingers again and sat up straighter. She had picked up on Tom's nervousness. Supposing the present was awful, revealing some unsuspected bad taste in Tom, who she liked so, so much?

It was a fairly flat package, which meant it wasn't a ghastly ornament that Dora would have to have on display somewhere.

'Open it,' he ordered.

Dora didn't feel obliged to save the brown paper wrapping and was inside rapidly. It was a light, khaki-coloured purse on a string. 'Um – it's lovely,' she said cautiously.

'It's a symbol,' explained Tom. 'Don't say it looks like a purse because of course it is. The symbolism is in the sort of purse it is.'

'On a cord?'

'It's for travelling. You keep it under your clothes so it's safe from pickpockets. You keep your credit card, your passport and your money in it.'

Dora moistened her lips. 'Oh, like your mother's, but why have you given it to me?'

379

'I want you to go travelling, with me, when we've saved enough money.'

'Oh Tom!'

'In fact, Dad said he'd give us some money towards it because he says I saved him so much not wanting to be a doctor or anything expensive.'

Dora laughed. 'I love your dad.'

He looked at her earnestly. 'But how do you feel about me? Do you think you could love me too? Enough to go backpacking with?'

A sigh she had been suppressing for a long time welled up in Dora. 'Oh yes, I think I could love you. Enough to go backpacking with, anyway.'

'Yesss!' Tom, who was already on his knees on the rug, tipped towards her so that they both fell on to the cushions together. 'I don't know how I've managed not to kiss you all this time.'

Dora was lying underneath him, laughing up at him. 'You don't have to manage any more, Tom!'

He laughed too and then his mouth came down on hers.

Chapter Twenty-Six

Jo was making salad. She had her big old striped apron on over her new linen skirt. She was wearing a new fitted cardigan over a vest top that she thought was far too low-cut but that Karen had approved of. The skirt was the colour of spilt tea and the cardigan and top were fuchsia. It had taken Karen a few moments to convince Jo that these colours were not too bright, didn't make her look like mutton dressed up as lamb and went perfectly with the handful of chunky jewellery incorporating the same colours that she produced while Jo was standing in front of the shop mirror. Karen had then made her buy some sandals which were so far from the sort of sandals you could walk for miles in that Jo felt they should have a warning label. When Karen escorted her, in the kind but firm way of a female prison officer, to have her nails done, she selected the colour for her toenails herself. 'You can have pale colour on your fingers if you want to, but you must be bolder with your toes.'

Now, as she bent to pick up a fallen lettuce leaf she admired her feet. She didn't like her legs much, although they did look much better now they'd been waxed and tanned, but she did like her feet, especially in her sexy sandals. Quite how long she'd stay in them, she couldn't predict, but she did tell Karen she wouldn't get out last year's Birkenstocks until her feet had had a chance to be admired.

Making salad was soothing. She chopped celery into translucent half-moons, leeks into rings that wouldn't have looked out of place as jewellery, and cucumber into tiny cubes. The carrots and courgettes she grated finely. Lettuce and tomato would only be added as bulk, at the last minute, but she had committed herself to filling the huge old French bowl she used to make bread in, so would need the Little Gems. As she sliced through four cherry tomatoes in one lethal sweep she thought about the salad Carole had made on the barge. It had been good, she acknowledged, but Carole hadn't had the range of fresh herbs to hand, as Jo had now. They would go in later, just before the garlic croutons. Jo loved leftover salad, and part of the reason for the enormousness of the one she was making was to guarantee it wouldn't all be eaten. She stopped chopping and went to hunt for a packet of petits pois in the freezer. Not too many, she decided, but they looked pretty against the cubes of red pepper. No sweetcorn though, Philip's digestion couldn't handle it. She laughed at herself. How easy it was to fall back into wifely ways.

'Hi, Mum! You're looking very – mm – well, sexy, if I may say so.'

Jo smiled at her daughter. 'You may say so.' Jo was glad of Karen's approval and she felt sexy too. It was a good feeling. Her morale had taken such a dive when Philip took up with Sam – Jo was training herself not to refer to her as the Floosie – it was nice to claim a bit back for herself. The fact that she'd had to leave Marcus so soon after their night together had left her full of doubts, convinced that she'd made up a lot of the things she thought he'd said, just because she wanted him to have said them so much.

To save her shoes as much as her feet, Jo slid out of her sandals and found her Birkenstocks; then she found the kitchen scissors, which were in quite the wrong place, and went out to cut herbs.

Philip arrived while she was still finding bug-free sprigs of lemon balm. She had already collected plenty of borage flowers, little blue stars, to go in the Pimm's, but she had wasted quite a lot of time looking at her garden. It looked so much better for a few days' intensive work, she decided.

She watched her husband – ex-husband, she wasn't sure which – walk up the garden path. He had a carrier bag in his hand that she knew was full of the steaks, lamb chops, kebabs and sausages that she had asked him to buy. Karen met him on the doorstep and they hugged. They really loved each other, those two, and Karen had obviously forgiven her father for his amazing lapse in taste. Jo sighed. She was glad that Karen and Philip seemed to have buried their differences and could now hold a civilised conversation together. It made life so much easier. Then she went back to the lemon balm, and found a bit of mint for the new potatoes that she hadn't cooked yet. She could never decide if she should serve them hot or cold. She might have to pop out and buy some French bread. Philip always told her they didn't need it, and admittedly, most of it was always left over, but she didn't feel safe without French bread. She might even make garlic bread. Her parsley patch was thriving so she could.

Miranda was at the door and Jo fell into her arms. 'It's so lovely to see you!' she said.

Miranda hugged her, and she was one of those people who, when she hugged you, made you know for sure you'd been hugged.

'You look fantastic!' said Miranda. 'What's happened to you? Are you in love?'

Jo blushed. 'Karen's taken me in hand. Come in and meet her. Bill, this is so nice. Could you park the car OK?'

Bill kissed her cheek. 'You look wonderful.'

'Come and meet Philip, my . . . husband – Karen's father. They're round the back, with the barbecue.'

Miranda raised an eyebrow at the mention of Philip. 'We brought some bits and pieces,' she said, deciding not to say anything more and burrowing in a bright raffia bag. 'You can never have too much at a barbie, don't you think?'

'Well, Tom and Dora, as well as her parents, are coming so we will need plenty,' said Jo, taking her friend's arm and leading her through the house.

'This house is to die for!' said Miranda. 'Oh, sorry, that probably wasn't tactful, if it isn't yours any more.'

They had reached the French windows by that time, so Jo didn't have to answer.

Jo made the introductions and Philip poured glasses of Pimm's. 'Or there's wine if you'd rather,' said Karen.

'Actually, lovey – gosh don't you look like your mother? – I'd better have wine. I've got to drive home. We tossed for it and I lost.'

'It was definitely your turn, sweetheart,' said Bill.

'Mum! Where are your sandals!' Karen admonished.

'Oh, sorry, I'll go and put them on.'

'Are you still getting ready?' said Miranda. 'I'll come and talk to you in the kitchen. I wanted to tell you how much I sold the little mirror for. You did such a good job on those putti—'

'What on earth are putti?' said Karen.

'All I know is that I'm putty in my wife's hands,' said Bill.

Miranda gave him a playful punch on the shoulder as she passed.

'Oh, that salad looks fantastic! What can I do?' Miranda asked, once they were in the kitchen.

'You can wash and chop the herbs, but check them for bugs first. I was quite careful when I picked them but you'd better give them the once-over.'

'Nothing worse than gritty parsley, although this looks very clean,' said Miranda riffling through it. 'So, how was your trip to Holland? Not too terrifying, I hope.'

'Well, Ed did fall in. Do you know Ed? He's Marcus's mate?'

'I may have met him. That's awful! Was it very difficult getting him back on board?'

'Incredibly difficult. Marcus is going to make sure it couldn't happen again.'

'You can't prevent people falling in entirely, can you?'

'He sort of fell out of the wheelhouse door. I was fairly OK about it at the time but since then I've felt queasy whenever I've thought about it.'

'Oh, are these the sandals?' Miranda was distracted by slender leather straps, iridescent beads and wedged heels.

'Yes – wedgies are definitely more comfortable than straight heels,' said Jo. 'I've learnt such a lot from my daughter in the past few days.' She kicked off her Birkenstocks and wriggled her feet into the sandals.

'Well, you certainly look fantastic.'

'It's the bra – fearfully expensive.'

'But so worth it.'

Jo laughed. It was good to see Miranda again.

'Karen also bought me Touche Éclat and told me how to use it, although' – she lowered her voice – 'I haven't actually bothered today. Too much else on my mind. Do you think we need garlic bread?'

'Not if you've got potatoes, surely.'

'I have, but not that many.'

'Have you got any French sticks?'

'No, I ought to pop out and get some. You need something to put the sausages in.'

'Give Tom and Dora a call and ask them to bring some. And are those two together yet?'

Jo laughed again. Trust Miranda. 'I don't know. I really hope so, they're so well suited.'

'Either way they can bring bread. And then you can have another Pimm's. I love them.'

Jo smiled. 'I remember, at the rally.' She retrieved her phone.

'Don't you keep it in your bra any more?'

'Not these bras – far too expensive.' She scrolled through until she found Dora's number. 'Dora? You couldn't pass a supermarket and get some French bread, could you?'

Jo thought she spotted a change between Dora and Tom the moment they appeared at the gate, but as they didn't make any sort of announcement she resolved to try and get Dora on her own so she could ask what was up. She and Karen went to meet them.

'Let's dump the bread in the kitchen,' said Karen, who obviously had first dibs on her best friend's time, 'and then let's have a drink. Tom?'

Karen's smile was so radiant that Jo felt a pang of confused loyalty – she didn't want her gorgeous daughter taking Tom from Dora and wondered why she felt like that.

Tom smiled back, an equally radiant smile with a hint of mischief but with no more than friendship in it. 'Well, the famous Karen, pleased to meet you.'

'I've heard a lot about you too, Tom, like how you dragged a drowning man into a lifeboat,' said Karen.

'It wasn't quite like that,' said Dora.

Jo got a good look at Dora while she was chatting with

Karen and Tom and she did seem more relaxed, somehow. She took the bread from her. 'I'll take this into the kitchen,' she said, giving Dora an opportunity to follow her if she wanted.

'I didn't realise your garden was so wonderful,' said Dora, not moving, except to make an expansive gesture towards it. 'It was always just Karen's garden, but it's fantastic!'

Concluding that Dora didn't want a heart-to-heart, Jo said, 'I made a lot more of it when you and Karen stopped making dens in it. And I've had a good old go at it over the past few days.'

'It seems bigger than it was when we played here, although I know it's supposed to be the other way round.'

'I did a short garden design course ages ago. It taught all sorts of tricks. You'll have to have a proper tour later.'

Tom had tuned out during the discussion about gardens. 'I probably shouldn't say this, Jo, but you are looking particularly good today,' he said.

'Why shouldn't you say that?' asked Jo, smiling.

'My mother would think it was judging people by appearances or something.'

She laughed. 'Well, I don't mind you saying it one bit.'

'It's the new hair and the bras,' said Karen. 'Costs a fortune but worth every penny, don't you think, Ma?'

'I do. But on the other hand I could have wished that you hadn't announced to the world the private details of my underwear.'

'Oh, pooh. You should get your mother to go there, Tom.'

Tom and Dora exchanged glances at the thought of Tom's mother worrying about a bra that did more than just strap her breasts firmly to her.

'Tom's mother isn't exactly a fashion victim, Karen,' said Dora.

387

'And nor am I!' insisted Jo, laughing.

Dora and Tom exchanged glances again and Dora leant slightly into him. Definitely more than just friends, thought Jo.

'So tell me Dora and Tom,' said Karen, 'Have you two finally got together?'

Jo winced at this second example of her daughter's blush-making frankness but Dora just looked at Tom and smiled.

'Err, well yes,' said Dora shyly. 'Yesterday.'

Tom put his arm proprietorially round Dora's shoulders and grinned. 'We're going to go travelling together when we've saved enough money,' he said.

'Tom arranged a heavenly picnic on an island in the Thames,' said Dora. 'It was very romantic.'

'Oh!' said Jo, nearly dropping the bread in her hurry to hug Dora. 'That's wonderful! I'm so happy.' Then she paused. 'Did I tell you I'd invited your parents?'

Dora bit her lip. 'No, I don't think you did. But I know I didn't tell you—'

'Oh, here they are!' Jo tucked the bread under one arm. 'Cliff! Sukie! Come on in. I'll just dump this!'

Dora saw Jo escaping to the kitchen and knew she had to tell her parents about Tom as soon as possible, before anyone else did. Then she must tell Jo that Marcus might be coming. 'Mum! Dad!' She hugged them both.

Then Karen hugged them too. 'You both look so well! And please don't tell me I've grown, it'll make me think I'm fat!'

'Silly girl, you're as lovely as ever,' said Sukie, who to Dora's relief did seem very relaxed today.

'Mum, you remember Tom, don't you?'

'Oh yes,' said Sukie. She kissed Tom's cheek and while Cliff shook Tom's hand she inspected her daughter.

'Anything you want to tell me?' she asked as they drew aside.

Dora laughed. 'Yes, well, nothing much, but we are now together.'

'An item?'

Dora nodded.

'Oh, I'm so pleased. Your ex future mother-in-law has been driving me mad going on about how happy John is with his new girlfriend.' She turned to Karen. 'Now we'd better go and say hello to your father. I really don't know how to greet him.'

'He and Mum are being very grown up about it. There's no need to be embarrassed,' said Karen.

As always when she was entertaining, Jo liked to spend a lot of time in the kitchen, making sure the food was all that it should be. Today she was also spending a fair amount of time trying to find things. Even though she had spent a few days here, she hadn't liked to pry. She now felt rather like a guest, it really wasn't her home any more and she wasn't quite as saddened by the thought as she had once been. She didn't want to ask Philip where his new young love might have put her favourite china dishes because he probably wouldn't know, and she didn't want to appear territorial.

Finally, the potatoes were cooked and drenched in butter, scattered with chopped parsley and in a bowl that would do, even if it wasn't her favourite Quimper dish that had been a wedding present. She walked through the house carrying the dish. Everyone was staring across the large triangle of garden at the front gate. Jo put the dish down and then looked too. It was a little too far for her to see comfortably and there was a large philadelphus in the way, but the figure who was struggling to open the gate while carrying several bottles of wine appeared to be Marcus.

389

Her first thought was relief that she was wearing one of her new bras and that she'd put her glamorous new sandals back on. Her second thought was that something must be wrong with *The Three Sisters* in Holland, and that he'd come in person to tell her – like policemen do when someone's been killed.

'Um, we sort of invited him,' said Dora quickly and guiltily. 'We hope you don't mind.'

'Erm . . . of course I don't mind,' said Jo, wondering how she did feel. 'Go and help him with the gate.'

But Tom had already leapt over the various borders, fought his way through a stand of ornamental grasses, a patch of white willowherb and a twisted willow, got caught on a climbing rose and was leading Marcus up the path. 'Tom is rather fab, isn't he?' said Karen to Dora.

'Mm,' said Dora, laughing. 'And he's mine!'

Jo realised she had only a few minutes to collect herself while they came through the house. She felt as if she was observing everyone through a camera lens.

Philip was laughing at something Miranda had said and looking particularly handsome, Jo thought. Bill was examining the bottom of his Pimm's glass as if by peering into the cucumber and borage flowers some more alcohol would manifest itself. Irrelevantly, Jo wondered if Miranda had succumbed to the lure of Pimm's in spite of saying she'd just have wine.

Karen was looking stunning – golden skin, blonde hair perfectly cut in a spiky, wayward manner – and Jo felt proud that Marcus would see her daughter looking so good. She conceded that some of her admiration could be put down to the fact that Karen was her daughter but she dismissed it quickly.

Dora, standing next to Karen, was as lovely in a slightly different way. Should those two girls decide to go on the pull together, she thought, they would be lethal.

These and a million other irrelevant thoughts flitted through her mind like moths as her brain barricaded itself against thinking about Marcus. Then he appeared, Tom in his wake.

He came up and kissed her cheek, looking somehow different, yet the same. 'I brought some wine.'

He appeared to want to hand the bottles that Tom hadn't taken from him to her. The part of her brain that was still seeing things from a distance thought he was like a midwife presenting a baby to a new and nervous father. 'Marcus . . .' she said, 'there was no need – how lovely – is everything all right?'

Tom fielded the remaining three bottles and took them to the table.

'I had to come,' muttered Marcus.

The breath left Jo's body suddenly and only long ingrained social skills enabled her to say, 'Marcus, you remember Philip.' She cleared her throat to stop it sounding so husky.

Philip came forward. He looked wary and had stopped smiling, as if he sensed something. 'Of course, Marcus old chap, long time no see. This is a bit of a bolt from the blue, isn't it?'

They shook hands, rather as boxers shake hands before a match, because convention required it.

'This is my daughter, Karen,' Jo said, but Karen didn't take his hand. She obviously sensed something too.

'And you know Miranda and Bill, don't you?' Jo said quickly.

'Of course.' Miranda came forward and kissed Marcus.

Bill raised his hand. 'Looking forward to hearing about your latest trip—'

'No we're not!' said Miranda. 'I mean – not everyone

391

here is interested in boats,' she finished lamely, picking up on the tension.

'And this is Sukie and Cliff, Dora's parents. This is Marcus, who took the barge to Holland with us all on it.'

'Not all of us,' said Philip, bristling.

'No, we weren't invited, either,' said Bill.

'Come and have a drink,' said Jo in hostess mode. If she concentrated on doing her duty she might be able to resist the urge to run screaming into the house. 'There's Pimm's, but if you'd prefer wine . . .' She remembered how he had always appeared to despise her supermarket bargains and added, 'It's quite drinkable, Philip bought it.'

'We've run out of Pimm's, Mum,' said Karen, looking curiously at Marcus. 'Shall I make some more?'

'We've run out of Pimm's, the bottle,' said Philip. 'We'll have to go on to wine.'

'Bill will rustle you something up if you've got some sweet vermouth and gin,' said Miranda helpfully.

'I think we have . . .' began Jo, suddenly aware that she had no idea what alcohol lived in the cupboard any more. Maybe it didn't even have drinks in it now. The situation was hideously awkward, she just hoped Marcus wouldn't stay long.

'I'll have some wine,' said Marcus.

'I'll go and see what we've got to drink, anyway,' said Karen, and she, Dora and Tom disappeared into the house.

'Well, Marcus,' said Philip, handing him a glass. 'What have you been up to in the past twenty years or so?'

'He's a barge skipper,' said Miranda. 'The best there is.'

'Well, thank you for that vote of confidence, Miranda,' said Marcus with a smile.

Jo realised that she'd never seen Marcus with Miranda and Bill before and felt a pang of something she couldn't identify.

'So this "barge skippering",' said Philip, 'is it a lucrative profession?'

Jo winced. Philip sounded so pompous.

'Philip!' said Jo. 'You can't ask things like that!'

Both men ignored her. 'Oh yes,' said Marcus. 'Well, lucrative enough, anyway.'

'People pay a lot of money to have their expensive vessels moved about the place,' said Bill. 'Speaking as one who has.'

Cliff decided to enter the conversation. 'I always thought you could describe sailing as standing under a cold shower tearing up fifty-pound notes.'

Marcus and Bill both looked at Cliff. 'Barges aren't quite like that.'

'No,' Miranda agreed. 'It's a hot shower. In other words, much more comfortable. But the fifty-pound note bit is the same.'

'Good God!' said Philip. 'I had no idea.'

Jo looked about her, wondering if she could flee back to the kitchen, ostensibly to help with the Pimm's preparation. Then she decided she couldn't.

'Philip, darling,' she said, 'how's the barbecue? Is it about ready to cook on yet?'

'Oh yes,' he said, moving to where a large chimenea doubled as a barbecue. 'Those coals are nice and grey now.'

'I'm always too impatient with barbecues,' said Miranda. 'The neighbours practically got up a petition to ask me to stop having them. I didn't actually poison anybody, but the food was always disgusting.'

Jo laughed, hoping she didn't sound hysterical. 'I'll go and get the meat then.' But before she could move she saw Karen and Dora, both bearing trays of prepared meat. Tom had the bowl of salad in both hands.

'I'll get the bread,' said Jo, itching to leave the prickly

atmosphere of the sunny summer Sunday for the safety of her kitchen.

'No you don't, Mum, you've been working all morning, you relax and have a drink with your friends. We'll do this bit.' Karen was insistent.

Philip went over to where the meat had been placed on top of the low wall that surrounded the paved area. 'How many people are you expecting, darling? Any more surprise guests?' He shot a glance at Marcus. 'Jo always over-caters desperately, don't you?'

'Possibly,' said Jo, unrepentant, 'but I'm going to put the rest of the meat back in the cool. It won't do any good sitting in the sun. And you will cook the chicken thoroughly, won't you? You can't be too careful.'

'We'll do it, Mum.' Karen obviously wasn't going to let her mother escape. She picked up one of the trays of meat. 'Why don't I get a cool bag? This could go in if it was sideways?'

Jo wasn't sure if this sentence made sense but the idea was sound. 'I'll come and—'

'No!'

Dora came up behind her friend. 'No,' she said, more gently, but just as firmly.

'Well, you don't know where anything is any more than we do,' said Karen, logically.

Jo sipped her Pimm's. It was now mainly water from the melted ice.

'Jo,' said Bill, 'can I pour you a glass of wine if there's no more Pimm's? Philip's busy.'

'Thank you,' she whispered, and cleared her throat. She mustn't sound as nervous as she felt, it was undignified in a woman of her age, and with her new bra, possibly unnecessary.

'Can I see your garden?' asked Marcus suddenly.

'Of course!' said Jo, delighted at the thought of being relieved of his disturbing presence for a few minutes. She waved an expansive hand. 'Help yourself!'

'No,' he said firmly, 'I want you to show it to me.'

'We'll keep an eye on things here,' said Miranda cheerfully.

'Don't you want to come too?' she asked.

'Oh no, gardens are wasted on me. I'll keep an eye on Philip's barbecue skills and make sure Bill keeps the glasses topped up.' Miranda smiled encouragingly – to Jo's fevered mind, like a chaperone giving her charge permission to dance with a much-approved-of partner.

There was nothing for it, she would have to show Marcus round her garden and be on her own with him for the first time virtually since they'd got out of the same bed. It would have been easier if she hadn't always felt gardens to be particularly sensual places. It was the fragrance, the velvety textures, the gentle rustlings – they all combined to make Jo feel gooey, even when she wasn't with a man she'd recently had a life changing sexual experience with. She shivered despite the warmth of the day.

Chapter Twenty-Seven

She led him down the path, wishing, for the first time, that she hadn't designed it to lead all round the garden the longest way possible, ending with a bench in a secluded corner. A rose which should have been tied back hung over it creating dappled, scented shade. She dreaded reaching it – her emotions might explode. She knew she felt the same about him but she still wondered if he'd meant what he'd said that evening. She had convinced herself that it had just been a one-night stand, and he hadn't even texted her. But he was here now, clearly upset about something.

She stopped several times on the way, hoping to bore him into going back to the others. She didn't trust herself to be alone with him. 'I used to grow vegetables there – just a few things, sugar snap peas, runner beans, things like that. My parsley patch has survived though. And I'm very fond of my golden hop although it does need a bit of training . . .'

His blatant lack of interest stopped her. He took her by the arm and Jo regretted insisting to the lad who created them for her that the paths should be wide enough for two people to walk abreast. 'I don't want to talk about herbaceous borders, I want to talk about us.'

Jo caught her breath. 'Is there an "us"?' She had assumed, in the moments when she forced herself to have a reality check (something she did as little as possible), that she and Marcus weren't meant to be. Why should he want to stick with a woman of fifty when he could so easily get one so much younger?

'I don't know. You and Philip seemed to be very cosy. You called him "darling".'

She turned to him. 'Oh, that's just habit!'

'Is it? You really don't want to go back to him?'

'I told you before, no, and anyway, I couldn't. His girlfriend is pregnant. All this is hers now.' And then she did what she most wanted not to do and burst into tears.

His arms went round her automatically and she found herself sobbing on his chest, feeling the hard muscle beneath her cheek. 'Listen, Joanna, I only want you to be happy. If this is what you want, this house, this garden and . . . Philip, I'll back off. But . . .'

Why oh why did he stop speaking just when he seemed about to say something wonderful. 'But what?' She looked up at him, aware that a tear-stained face was not attractive after the age of about eighteen.

He lowered his head and kissed her cheek. 'You silly woman. I want you for myself.'

Jo sniffed and wiped her nose on the back of her hand and then wiped her hand on her new linen skirt. 'Come on, let's go down here where we can sit and I can compose myself. We mustn't be long though, people will talk.'

'As long as we talk first, I don't care.' He took her hand and led her to the rose-shaded area by the bench.

'I think this rose is called Lady Hillingdon, but I can't remember.'

'I don't care a flying-f— fish what it's called.' Then he pulled her into his arms and kissed her properly.

For the first few moments Jo worried about being seen from the house and then she forgot there was a house and just let herself be kissed until she began to kiss him back. She was clinging onto him to stop her knees buckling and then she guided them both to the bench so they could sit down. At last they broke apart.

'I hadn't made that part up then,' said Marcus.

'What do you mean?' She was breathless and still not quite in the present.

'We do have the most amazing sexual chemistry.'

Her reply was a shuddering sigh.

'Joanna, if you want a house and a garden like this, I can give you one. You don't have to live on *Hildegarde*, which I admit is hardly perfect – or any barge.'

'It's a bit early – I mean, this has come as a bit of a shock.'

'Has it? Surely you knew how I felt about you?'

'I thought it was just lust,' she muttered, blushing profusely.

'Lust is a much underrated emotion,' said Marcus, and turned her chin with his finger so he could kiss her again.

Foolishly, Jo opened her mouth to protest and was lost to his onslaught.

'What the hell do you think you're doing?' said a rather red-faced Philip. 'Take your hands off my wife.'

'Sorry, I couldn't stop him coming,' said Miranda from behind Philip. 'And I can see you obviously don't need me now,' and then she tiptoed away.

'I think you relinquished your claims to Joanna when you took up with another woman,' said Marcus, getting to his feet.

Jo inched back into the corner of the bench. If she got up too, the rose would take someone's eye out.

'That's not the point! How dare you come to my house and make love to my wife?' Philip went on, his voice rising in anger.

'Philip,' said Jo sternly. 'Marcus is right. I'm not your wife any more. You left me for another woman.' She didn't press the point about how much younger Samantha was or the fact that she was pregnant.

Philip looked at her with a mixture of bewilderment and pleading. 'Jo, if you want to come back here, I'll work things out with Sam . . . Seeing you here, in your proper home, made me realise . . .'

Jo got to her feet, ready to explode with indignation, but before she could, Karen arrived, closely followed by Tom and Dora. Jo removed the eye-threatening spray of Lady Hillingdon and took a deep breath.

'This is really neither the time nor the place for this conversation,' she began, faintly surprised to hear this old cliché coming from her own lips. 'We have guests. Come along, back to the barbecue, everyone.'

Rather to her surprise, they all followed her meekly down the path. Even through her distress she couldn't help thinking how like a bad television drama the whole situation was, involving as it did a lot of designer shoes, short skirts and St Tropez fake tan.

Bill was happily turning over steaks and chicken breasts, oblivious to the drama going on at the end of the garden path.

'Have another drink, everyone,' said Miranda, greeting the party as it arrived back on the patio, correctly assuming that Philip's hosting skills would have deserted him. 'Sukie and I were just saying how lovely your garden is, Jo. And there's food ready.'

'Thank you.' Jo's gratitude wasn't just for this information but also for Miranda taking over the social bit for her. She struggled to become the hostess again. 'I think we should all get eating. Sukie, Cliff, help yourselves to some garlic bread.' She looked at the bread and realised she had absolutely no recollection of making it. Was this early-onset Alzheimer's or had Marcus's kisses wiped her memory?

There was a moment's hiatus where Jo prayed that everyone would go on pretending that there had been no scene at the end of the garden. Plates were passed, knives and forks distributed, bottles clinked against glasses.

'What's going on?' demanded Karen, just when Jo had started to relax a little.

'Darling, I don't think—' Jo began.

Marcus interrupted her. 'I was having a private conversation with your mother, and your father . . .'

Philip exhaled loudly and indignantly.

'I do wish everyone would just get eating,' said Jo, clinging desperately to her duties as hostess.

'Yes, come along.' Miranda came to her rescue. 'Tom, Dora, Cliff, Sukie, everyone, fill your plates. I would just hate to see all this lovely food wasted.'

Thankfully, everyone did as they were told and settled themselves on seats, or the wall, depending on age and need for comfort, and began eating. Then Dora noticed that Jo hadn't got anything. She leapt up and put a bit of salad and a lamb chop on a plate and brought it to her. 'There you are, eat that.'

'Can I have a fork, do you think?' said Jo.

'Oh goodness, here.'

There was a moment's reprieve from the ghastly scene that was about to erupt while everyone except Jo chewed and murmured about how nice it all was. Jo couldn't have eaten if she'd been paid ten pounds a mouthful.

Marcus had taken a plate as far away as he could and still be on the patio. Philip shot him sidelong glances of resentment and dislike from time to time. Jo almost expected little snarls to emerge from him, as from a jealous dog.

Jo got up. Staying seated made her feel trapped. She

handed things round, noting cynically that although Philip and Marcus were treating her like an old bone, she couldn't help feeling they may not have shown any interest in her at all if the other hadn't been present.

Bill, Sukie and Cliff were all looking a little startled but politely chose to ignore the air of tension and kept up a discussion about barges with admirable valour. Miranda seemed to be having a one-sided conversation with Philip about antiques and Tom and Dora were telling Karen all about the festival. Marcus was just sitting there, watching everyone in silence.

Jo could bear it no longer and, mumbling something about more bread, she headed resolutely towards the kitchen. Once inside, she rested her head on the cool surface of the worktop and sighed.

'Jo?' She heard Marcus say quietly behind her.

She lifted her head and turned towards him. There was a gentle but resolute air about him.

'Jo?' he said again. 'I've never been with a woman I wanted to spend the rest of my life with – until now.'

His words made her heart contract. She looked up at him and saw how much he meant them in his eyes, but she just couldn't speak.

'I'm staying at the White Swan,' he said. 'I know you can't leave your guests just now, much as I yearn to carry you away, it wouldn't be fair. I want you to come because you want to be there as much as I want you to be there. No pressure.' Then he was gone.

Almost, Jo could have laughed at his words. Pressure from something, it could have been love, was building up in her diaphragm until it threatened to burst out of her, in the form of either tears or laughter.

She stood still for a few minutes, her mind in turmoil. Her guests were outside wondering what was going on but

401

were thankfully too British to demand an explanation. And as for Karen and Philip . . .

'Mum, there's something going on between you and Marcus, isn't there?' Karen said as she and Philip materialised in the kitchen behind her.

Karen looked so vulnerable and yet so defiant, Jo knew she had to tell them the truth. 'Yes,' she said quietly.

'And you think you can trust him?' Philip said. 'He's never had much of track record . . .'

Jo bristled, her resolve strengthening. 'If you don't mind me pointing this out,' she said, more calmly than she felt, 'your own staying power seems a bit lacking of late.'

Philip harrumphed. 'I may have made a mistake.'

'I'm sure you have,' said Jo, suddenly feeling very tired, 'but it's too late to undo it.'

'Would you go back to Dad if you could?' asked Karen.

Jo looked at her daughter and shook her head. 'No. I'm sorry, darling, but I couldn't. Not now.'

'Jo, I can sort things out, really I can—' Philip insisted.

'I don't want you to,' said Jo firmly. 'You leaving me was possibly the biggest favour you could have done me. I wouldn't go back to you even if Sam wasn't pregnant. And deep down I think you wouldn't want that either.'

'But, Mum, if Dad says . . .'

'Sorry, Karen. I realise it's probably quite upsetting for you, but I really can't go back to your father.'

'But why not?' Karen insisted, a little petulant.

'Because I love Marcus.'

'Do you?' Philip said, although she could tell he knew she meant it. He sighed and smiled at her sadly and Jo caught a brief glimpse of the Philip she had known and once loved. 'If that's what you want, I wish you every happiness.' And he walked back out into the garden.

'Mum?' Karen said.

Jo turned to her daughter and took her in her arms, stroking her hair as she had done when she was a child.

Karen sighed and then pulled away. She smiled at her mother and then grinned. 'I'm not sure I like the idea of a stepfather, at my age, but at least he's good-looking.'

Jo laughed and linking arms with her daughter they went outside.

As Jo and Karen walked slowly back to their guests, Jo's emotions were all over the place, but she felt certain of one thing: Marcus did love her and she loved him. Karen was disappointed, of course, but she was an adult now and she seemed to have taken it very well, considering. Philip too.

There was a moment's silence as they rejoined the others and then everyone resumed their conversations.

'We found the trifle,' said Karen, winking at Jo.

Chapter Twenty-Eight

Jo parked her car feeling rather guilty and yet elated. After hugs and kisses and see you soons and a promise of a 'proper' catch-up from Dora and Tom, Jo had crept away early from her own party. Now, as she pulled Marcus's grip out of the car she decided the guilt added a certain frisson to her pleasure. She was a married woman – well, technically she was still married – going to join her lover in a fabulous hotel. It was so unlike her, she couldn't help giving a little skip. If someone had told her a year ago that she'd have turned into the sort of woman who did things like that, she would have believed she'd fly to the moon first.

She went into Reception, blushing and laughing to herself. 'Can you tell me which room Mr Rippon is in? I've arranged to meet him.'

'Oh yes, Madam, he told us to expect you.' As the man behind Reception gave her directions, she realised she hadn't given her name. Had Marcus given a detailed description of her too?

He met her in the corridor and she realised they must have phoned from the desk to say she was on her way. And then his arms were round her, hugging her so hard she thought she'd suffocate.

'You came,' he whispered into her hair.

'I can't breathe,' she squeaked.

'Sorry. It's just that I let you slip through my fingers once, I'm not going to let you go again.'

'But perhaps we could just go to the bedroom, couldn't we?'

He gave her another squeeze and then laughed. 'You can go anywhere you like. The world is your oyster. You are the pearl.'

'Oh for God's sake, Marcus!'

He had propped the bedroom door open and now he edged them both into the room without letting go of Jo. Then he kicked the door shut and released her.

'Are you sure this is what you want? A life with a roving vagabond instead of a safe middle-class, middle-England life with Philip?'

'My life with Philip wasn't safe, was it? I might as well try my luck with the roving vagabond.'

He put his arms round her and kissed her again and then murmured into her hair. 'You're going to make a lovely vagabond's moll.'

And middle-class, middle-England Jo sighed in satisfaction.

Back at the house, the older members of the party were carrying on as if nothing unusual had happened, all except Philip, who had driven off, presumably to see Samantha.

Dora, Tom and Karen had taken a bottle of wine to a little table in the garden and were sitting round discussing the situation.

'I do think you should have told me, Do,' said Karen, still a bit indignant that Dora hadn't forewarned her about her mother and Marcus. 'I mean, you must have realised there was something going on between them.'

'I didn't, not really,' said Dora, defending herself.

'I told you I thought he fancied her,' said Tom. 'He looked at her a lot, when she wasn't looking at him.'

Karen regarded Tom. 'Boys aren't supposed to notice stuff like that,' she said.

'I don't see why not. Do you two want more trifle, or shall I just help myself?'

'Help yourself,' Dora and Karen said in unison.

'Well, at least I don't need to worry about you and him, Do,' said Karen.

Dora laughed. 'You don't need to worry about your mother, either. Marcus is a really good guy. He may have had a bit of a bad rep with women before, but I suspect he's always wanted her and will settle down for ever.'

'I just don't like the thought of my mother having hot sex, that's all.'

Dora giggled. 'Don't think about it then! But I think they're a great couple.'

Karen leaned forward and patted her friend's hand. 'I think you and Tom are a great couple too. I knew I was right to make you go and live with Mum.' She raised her hands in a triumphant gesture. 'Even from across the Atlantic I can make things work out for the best.'

'Karen!'

'It's all right, no need to thank me. Now, do you know of any other gorgeous men that I might like? I quite fancy Going Dutch myself.'

Wedding Season

Sarah Stratford is a wedding planner hiding a rather inconvenient truth – she doesn't believe in love. Or not for herself, anyway. But as the confetti flutters away on the June breeze of yet another successful wedding, she somehow finds herself agreeing to organise two more – on the same day and only two months away. And whilst her celebrity bride is all sweetness and light, her own sister soon starts driving her mad with her high expectations but very limited budget.

Luckily Sarah has two tried and tested friends on hand to help her. Elsa, an accomplished dress designer, but who likes to keep a very low profile, and Bron, a multi-talented hairdresser who lives with her unreconstructed boyfriend and who'd like to go solo in more ways than one. They may be very good at their work but romance doesn't feature very highly in any of their lives.

As the big day draws near all three women find that patience is definitely a virtue in the marriage game. And as all their working hours are spent preparing for the wedding of the year – plus one – they certainly haven't got any time to even think about love . . . or have they?

Read on for an extract . . .

Chapter One

Sarah stood by the lych-gate and surveyed the perfection of the summer morning. It was June and the sun was shining with the promise of a perfect day. The church was an early English gem, surrounded by closely mown, dew-spangled grass, ancient lichen-covered gravestones and clipped yews. She'd already seen Sukie, the florist, who'd been there since dawn, and now some of her anxiety left her. Two years of work had come to fruition. It was all going to be all right.

Then she screamed as someone appeared from behind a tombstone. 'Agh! Hugo! You brute! You gave me such a fright!' As her beating heart caught up with her brain and she realised she wasn't being attacked, by a stranger at least, she went on: 'You had me thinking it was Halloween for a moment there.'

Hugo, tall, blond and rumpled, always gave Sarah the impression that he'd just got out of bed – and not his own.

'Sarah, you're so sweet, I should give you up for Lent,' he drawled in reply.

Sarah smiled. Hugo was one of the best photographers she dealt with and they always exchanged sallies and insults, but she had deliberately never got to know him as a friend – she felt it was more sensible to keep the relationship strictly professional. 'We both seem to have got our seasons mixed up.'

'As long as we've got the day right. Perfect for it, huh?'

Sarah nodded. 'And you'll love the bride. She's really beautiful.'

'Bridesmaids?'

'Darling. Two little sweeties – we won't call them angels until we know how they behave – and one big one to keep them in order. Heavenly dresses.'

'Second families to worry about? Bride and groom's parents still married to each other and pitching up?'

'Yup. Marriage does work for some people, apparently.' She smiled again slightly, pretending she was joking.

Hugo rumbled his amusement. 'Don't you believe in "happy ever after" then?'

'Not very often. Which is why I think it's important that the wedding is as wonderful as it can possibly be.' She gestured to the scene of perfection before them. 'It might be the only happy memory.'

Hugo inspected the dew that had gathered on his perfect shiny shoe. 'Honestly, Sarah, if the people who pay you to organise all this knew how you feel . . .'

'They don't need to know about my feelings, only about my ability to find the perfect venue and a personable photographer who makes everyone look fabulous.'

He chuckled again, taking the hint that she needed to get on, along with the compliment. 'So, anything I need to know?'

Sarah considered. 'I don't think you should have any trouble. The bride's mother has put an awful lot of energy into this and is very anxious that nothing happens to spoil that, but she's got a great hat. I'm sure she'll succumb to your ready charm.'

Sarah could never understand why she was the only one who realised Hugo's ready charm was part of his stock-in-trade as a photographer, but she admitted that, for a wedding planner, she did have more than the usual amount of cynicism. And for good reason: she hadn't been in the business more than a couple of years and already two of the perfect weddings she had organised had broken up, one barely eight months after the happy pair drove off in a cloud of dried delphinium petals. Five of the six girls from her school who had got married the moment they hit twenty-five had since separated. There was also her sister's debacle of a marriage, not to mention (and Sarah never did) her own heartbreak, recovered from but not forgotten. No, in Sarah's eyes, happy-ever-after was the rare exception that proved the rule.

'Well, I'll just prowl around a bit more,' said Hugo, unaware of Sarah's thoughts. 'Find somewhere really picturesque to take the less formal shots.'

'Try to avoid grass stains on the dresses, if you can. Please! I always get complaints.'

He tipped his head and closed his already heavy-lidded eyes, indicating that while he heard her request, he wasn't necessarily going to concede to it.

'It's all right for you, no one ever moans to you!'

'Because I'm the best,' he said simply.

And because he was, and they both knew it, she just said, 'I'd better get back to the hotel to make sure everyone's there who should be, and not too many people who shouldn't.' She frowned. 'I'm still not convinced it wouldn't have been better to have the reception at the bride's home – it's fabulous, but they decided it was less upheaval to have it at a hotel. It is a very good hotel, of course. But the money!' She raised her hands in a gesture of amazement. 'Now, I must get on.'

She turned away, aware of his sleepy gaze on her back. She hoped he wouldn't get the bridesmaids to lean against lichen-covered gravestones and thus ruin their dresses for ever, but accepted that for him getting the right shot was

411

vital and nothing much else came into consideration. She was good at managing people and she usually got what she wanted out of them, but she was never convinced that Hugo took any notice of her at all.

As she walked back to her car she wondered if Ashlyn was the sort of bride who would encourage people to open the champagne before the wedding and turn what should be a morning of solid preparation into an extension of the hen party. But her mother would probably put a stop to anything like that. A glass for everyone during the final hair and make-up session was fine, but only one!

She arrived at the hotel to a diorama of potential tragedy. Everyone was more or less static when they should have been calmly getting on with dressing the bride.

Instead, Ashlyn was sitting at the dressing table in a chemise, stockings and French knickers, with her mobile phone in her hand, tears of rage adding the wrong sort of sparkle to her eyes. Elsa, the dressmaker, waiting to help her into the dress now hanging on the back of the door, stood awkwardly inspecting her nails and picking bits of fluff off her black trousers.

Bron, in charge of hair and make-up, had also stepped back. Ashlyn's long and slippery tresses were half up, half down, and her frantic texting had threatened her French manicure. The perfect make-up already needed reapplying.

'What's happened?' demanded Sarah, instantly aware she was witnessing an unfolding calamity.

There was a moment's tense silence and then the bride answered: 'My fucking bridesmaid has decided not to come!'

Shock settled round the room like dust after an explosion. Sarah had never heard Ashlyn use language like that before. A moment's reflection made her feel it was justified.

'Oh no,' said Sarah, her eyes shut, wondering how on earth two enchanting three-year-olds could possibly manage without an accompanying adult bridesmaid.

'Oh yes.' Ashlyn bit out the words between her newly whitened teeth. 'She's decided that a weekend away with her new boyfriend would be more fun than attending her best friend's wedding!'

'That's so out of order,' murmured Bron, wondering when she could carry on doing the bride's hair.

'And to think I paid for that bitch's weekend at Barnstable Spa, which is not exactly cheap!' Ashlyn went on. 'And Mummy paid for her dress – another small fortune.' Elsa, who'd also made the bridesmaid's outfit, winced. 'Well, at least I can change her disgusting wedding present for something decent!'

Sensing that the bride was beginning to move on from this disaster, Bron stepped forward with her comb and pins, preparing to carry on defying gravity with Ashlyn's water-smooth hair. Elsa's shoulders relaxed and Sarah said, 'We can manage perfectly well without her. Poppy should be able to take your bouquet from you and we can ask your sister-in-law to take it from her. Don't worry.'

Ashlyn gave a huge sigh. 'I should have known not to trust her. She sat on my guinea pig when we were little and I've never forgiven her.'

There was a tiny pause, showing respect for the dead guinea pig, and then Bron said bravely, 'OK, if I can just get back to doing your hair. We haven't got all day.'

As Bron laughed, a little awkwardly, Sarah wondered if there was a bit of puffiness around her eyes this morning, or if she'd imagined it. She didn't know Bron very well, perhaps she always looked like that.

Elsa stopped picking at her trousers and seemed calm, waiting for the moment when her dressmaking skills might be needed. Ashlyn's mother had insisted that she attended, principally so she could make final adjustments to the chief bridesmaid's dress, as she'd missed her final fitting. Most probably she would only be required to hook up Ashlyn's dress at the back and break it to the bride that the dress would look better if it wasn't worn over the French knickers she'd had such fun buying, but over nothing at all. She had a thong in her bag if Ashlyn preferred that option.

Then the door opened and the bride's mother walked in. 'Everything all right, darling?'

There was a moment's silence. No one wanted to be the messenger that turned the bride's mother's big day into a disaster. Then Ashlyn bit the bullet. 'Fulvia's backed out. She's going to Paris with her boyfriend instead.'

Mrs Lennox-Featherstone screamed, not loudly, but loud enough to alarm her husband who called anxiously through the door.

'Is everything all right in there?'

'No it is not!' hissed his wife. 'That – trollop – whom we've taken with us skiing, for God's sake, has backed out!'

Sarah realised this was probably the moment when she really earned her money as a wedding planner and co-ordinator. 'It's all right, Mrs Lennox-Featherstone, we can manage perfectly well without her.'

'I've paid for that dress,' said her client's mother. 'Over two thousand pounds – and it's not spending the wedding in a plastic bag!'

Elsa jumped. It was not her fault the dress was not going to be worn or that the enormous amount of hand-beading had taken her so long to do – it was time-consuming. But she couldn't throw off her feelings of guilt.

'That's all right,' said Ashlyn, calm now her mother was having conniptions, 'Elsa can wear it. She and Fulvia are the same size and, unlike Fulvia, she's been a real friend.'

Elsa gasped loudly. 'Ashlyn, I—'

'Yes you have,' persisted Ashlyn, as if it was their friendship that Elsa had been about to deny. 'You sorted me out when Bobby and I had that huge row and we've had such fun together! That lovely day looking at fabric. And you haven't forgotten that time at—'

'Stand up and let me look at you,' snapped Mrs Lennox-Featherstone, obviously feeling there wasn't time for reminiscencing just now. 'Why do you persist in wearing black? It's absolutely the wrong colour for you. Drains you. Well, put on the dress and let's see what you look like. It's all right, Donald,' she called through the door. 'You can go away now. It's all going to be fine.'

'Um, I can't wear the dress,' said Elsa.

'Why not? We know it fits,' said Ashlyn's mother.

'Because I'd feel a fraud, not being Ashlyn's real bridesmaid,' said Elsa, sending Sarah a look that told her she needed help.

'It might be a bit awkward with – er – Fulvia's parents coming to the wedding.' Sarah had already wondered if she could leave them seated so near the top table and decided that she had to.

'I don't suppose they know about their little tart's defection,' snapped Mrs Lennox-Featherstone. 'Although they should have guessed, sending her to that awful school. None of the pupils leaves without an A level in bitchiness.'

'OK,' said Sarah, taking charge. 'It is a shame that Fulvia has backed out but, as I say, we don't really need her.'

'Oh yes we do,' said Ashlyn and her mother simultaneously.

'Not only did the dress cost a fortune,' went on Mrs Lennox-Featherstone, 'but the photographs will be unbalanced without a big bridesmaid.'

'Hugo is an excellent photographer,' said Sarah. 'I can assure you that—'

'I want Elsa,' said Ashlyn, like a child on the verge of a tantrum. 'I like her a lot more than fu—' She glanced at her mother and went on to use her ex-best-friend's name without the alliterative expletive. 'Fulvia.'

'So you simply must be her bridesmaid, dear,' said Mrs Lennox-Featherstone. 'What the bride wants, she must have.' She gave a tight smile and glanced at her daughter.

'I can't!' persisted Elsa, feeling more and more uncomfortable.

'You don't want to spoil Ashlyn's big day by being selfish, do you?'

'Of course not,' said Elsa. 'But being a bridesmaid is a really big thing. It should be someone who's known Ashlyn all her life not someone she's only met—'

'I've known you nearly two years,' said Ashlyn. 'I like you – *and* you haven't killed any of my pets!'

Elsa tried to laugh at this attempt at lightheartedness. 'No, but . . .'

'Please!' said Ashlyn. 'I really want you to.'

'I can't,' said Elsa, finding some determination at last.

'Why not?' demanded Ashlyn's mother, who wouldn't take no for an answer without a very good explanation.

'Seriously, I can't!'

'But why not?' demanded Ashlyn, who took after her mother and was curious as well as demanding.

'My armpits!' she said rather desperately and with all the firmness she could muster – given the word she was being firm with.

'What about your armpits?' said Ashlyn, a frown disturbing her perfectly shaped eyebrows.

'I haven't shaved them. At least, not for a few days . . .' Elsa faltered, anxiously regarding the women who were al

416

looking back at her, appearing to condemn her for slovenly, unhygienic habits.

'Not a problem,' said Bron smoothly, having kept out of the fraught discussion until now. 'I have disposable razors in my kit.'

Mrs Lennox-Featherstone, who, like the others, had perched on the edge of the double bed, stood up and came across to Elsa. 'I realise that as a family we're asking an awful lot of you, but this is Ashlyn's special day; we've been preparing for over two years. Please help us out.'

Elsa regarded her client. She knew as well as anyone how long this wedding had been in preparation as she had been thinking about, designing and eventually making the dresses for it. It had been her first really big contract and she'd put into it not only the expected blood, sweat and tears, but a good chunk of her soul too.

'We would all be so grateful.' The older woman put her hand on Elsa's shoulder, and Elsa realised she'd never seen her vulnerable before. Bullying, Elsa might have stood up to, but not this heartfelt plea.

'OK,' she said, really wishing she could find it in herself to refuse, but conceding that she was finally beaten. 'On the condition that Ashlyn doesn't wear those knickers,' she added. That was something she wouldn't budge on.

'What's wrong with my knickers?' said Ashlyn indignantly. 'They're silk chiffon and Bobby's going to love them!'

'I'm sure he is, but they'll show through your dress where it glides over your thighs. It'll spoil the line. I've got a thong if you don't want to go knickerless.'

Distracted from Elsa for a moment, Ashlyn's mother turned to her daughter. 'Darling, I really do think you'd better wear something. You can't go to church without pants on.'

417

'Whatever,' said Ashlyn, 'as long as Elsa agrees to be my bridesmaid.'

Sarah, aware the room seemed very crowded all of a sudden, took charge once more. 'Elsa, you go to the bathroom and have a shower and a shave – sorry, that sounds a bit weird! Mrs Lennox-Featherstone, you go to your room and get dressed. Bron will want to do your hair soon. And Ashlyn, you sit still so Bron can finish yours and then she'll touch up your make-up.'

'Let's open a bottle of champagne,' said Ashlyn when her mother had left the room and Elsa had been sent to the bathroom with a razor and an exfoliating scrub. 'I put a couple of bottles in the mini-bar fridge.'

Sarah really wanted to say no. She knew it was fatal for people to start losing control at this stage but she was weakened by events. She wouldn't have any herself but she really appreciated how welcome it would be to the others. 'OK then, if you must.'

'Can you open it for us then, Sarah?' The bride fluttered her eyelashes just a little and Sarah sighed.

'Get the glasses Bron, there's a dear,' she said.

Everyone had a glass, and Sarah realised it had been a good idea after all. Just seeing the champagne pour creamily into the flutes had a calming effect.

Practically Perfect

Katie Fforde

Will Anna's grand designs prove just a pipe dream?

Anna, a newly qualified interior designer, has risked everything on buying a tiny but adorable cottage so she can renovate it, sell it on and prove to her family that she can earn her own living.

Outside, the chocolate-box cottage is perfect, but inside all is chaos: with a ladder for a staircase, no downstairs flooring, candles the only form of lighting, Anna's soon wondering whether she's bitten off more than she can chew.

Her neighbour Chloe comes to the rescue, providing tea, wine and sympathy – and a recently rescued greyhound, Caroline. But just as Anna's starting to believe she's found the perfect idyll, the good-looking yet impossible Rob Hunter arrives on the scene, putting up more obstacles than the Grand National. Can Anna get over all of life's hurdles?

'A witty and generous romance – Jilly Cooper for the grown-ups'
Indepedent

'Can be scoffed at one sitting – tasty!'
Cosmopolitan

arrow books

Flora's Lot

Katie Fforde

Bidding for love can be a costly business . . .

Flora Stanza has sub-let her London life in a bid to join the family antiques business. Her knowledge extends only to the information she has crammed from daytime TV, but what she lacks in experience she makes up for in blind enthusiasm. So she is more than a little put out when she doesn't receive the warm country welcome she expected. Her curt cousin Charles and his fiancée Annabelle are determiend to send Flora packing, and their offer to buy her out is tempting . . . until a strange warning makes her think twice.

Stuck with a cat about to burst with kittens, Flora has little choice but to accept the offer to stay in an abandoned holiday cottage miles from any neighbours, let alone a trendy wine bar. And between fighting off dinner invitations from the devastatingly handsome Henry, and hiding her secret eco-friendly lodger William, Flora soon discovers country life is far from dull as she sets about rebuilding the crumbling business . . .

'A fairytale-like, gently witty read . . . Heartwarming –
made for sunny days in the park'
Cosmopolitan

'A sweet and breezy read – the ideal accompaniment
to a long summer's evening'
Daily Mail

arrow books

Restoring Grace

Katie Fforde

Nothing is ever picture perfect . . .

Ellie Summers' life is unravelling. Finding herself pregnant – and her sexy but idle boyfriend Rick less than enthusiastic about parenthood – she needs a plan. Fast.

Grace Soudley's life is also coming apart at the seams – her only security is the beautiful yet crumbling old house she was left by her godmother. But unless she can find a fortune, Luckenham House will disintegrate around her.

When Ellie and Grace meet, the two very different women find they can help each other out. Ellie needs a place to stay; Grace needs a lodger. Both of them need a friend. But then the disconcertingly engaging Flynn Cormack arrives on the scene, apparently determined to help. And when Grace discovers some beautiful painted panels hidden behind the tattered dining-room curtains, the whole business of restoration starts to get serious . . .

'A heart-warming tale of female friendship, fizzing with Fforde's distinctive brand of humour'
Sunday Express

a r r o w b o o k s

ALSO AVAILABLE IN ARROW

Paradise Fields

Katie Fforde

Just when Nel's found her Eden, there's trouble in paradise . . .

It's not as if Nel hadn't enough on her plate already: organising a
farmers' market in the picturesque Paradise Fields and keeping
track of her unnervingly beautiful teenage daughter – plus sorting
out a houseful of animals – are quire enough to keep her busy. The
last thing she needs is yet another complication in her life, but when
her old friend Sir Gerald dies and his son, Pierce – accompanied by
his glamorous American wife – takes possession of The
Big House, it seems that preserving the Fields is not on his list of
priorities.

Nel takes up arms, determined to fight for the meadow and the
market she loves. But whom can she trust? She's pretty sure her
friends Sacha and Vivian are on her side, but her sensible boyfriend
Simon, an estate agent, is less encouraging. And then there's Jake,
the infuriating yet attractive stranger who kissed her under the
mistletoe. Maybe she's been a celibate widow for a little too
long . . .

'A romantic rural romp' *Daily Mirror*

'Delicious' *Sunday Times*

arrow books